<u>**An Unlawful Death**</u>

By

Lynn F. Weston

For Tim

Chapter 1

Prologue

*The peace and solitude of the chambers, as yet devoid
of the everyday activity of a barrister's trade, welcome
her as she makes her way to her corner of the shared
room. With head held high and a confident step, she
revels in the empowering sensation of being head
honcho, the number one, the only authority, in the
hallowed offices of Weymouth House Chambers,
deserted at this unholy hour of the morning. Even the
cleaner has not arrived yet and yesterday's wastepaper
bins are still overflowing with discarded briefing notes,
empty envelopes, sandwich cartons and scrunched-up
chocolate wrappers.*

*She pauses to gaze for a moment at the gently
swirling dust motes, caught in a beam of watery
sunlight that peeps through a gap in the closed window
blind, and breathes in the day-old fusty air. The faint
leathery essence of the opulently quilted sofa and club
chairs overrides the staleness however, and underlines
her sense of awe at this physical incarnation of the
tough, well-established profession she has entered. She
basks in the silence which is broken only by the distant,
barely audible rumble of early morning London traffic.
She feels watched only by the hundreds of familiar
green, red and gold leather-bound legal volumes, all
safely ensconced in their ranks of floor-to-ceiling
shelves.*

*As the newest and youngest lawyer in their
team of three, she is determined to get ahead and make*

her mark by putting in these early hours to keep up and excel in her career. She means to assuage the doubts about her work that her colleagues are so poor at disguising and show them she means business in her goal of becoming a successful barrister – she knows she can do the job as well as if not better than them. First things first though, and after switching on her desk lamp and laptop, she lets the latter warm up while she enters the tiny coffee corner, artfully concealed behind a stunning bronze-gilded tri-fold screen. This is tall enough with its scrolled top and attractive enough with its Florentine pastoral design to detract visitors from its real purpose of hiding the everyday clutter of coffee machine, mugs, sugar and milk capsules. Here, lost in thought, she goes through the motions of making the day's first strong, black, brew – steaming hot and bitter. She is oblivious to the faint click of the office door opening and the subtle alteration in the still air of the chambers. She is shocked when a heavy warm arm grips her upper body in a tight vice-like hold and feels the firm body of her attacker pressed against her back. She struggles to turn, gasping; but, too late, a searing pain crosses her throat and the metallic taste of her own blood rises into her mouth.

'Sweet dreams, bitch.'

These are the last words she hears along with the gurgling of her lifeblood as it drains out of her body. She senses herself being released and falls forward and down. And the world goes black.

Chapter 2

Corpus Delicti (the body of a person who has been killed unlawfully)

Pausing at the top of the small flight of stone steps leading up to the glossy black door, Sam White, cleaner, lit up his third cigarette of the morning, turned and surveyed the almost silent mews with its tiny park bordered by rhododendron bushes. He had arrived earlier than usual at his first job that Tuesday as his wife had dropped him off about half a mile away on Waterloo Bridge on her way to a headteachers' conference held in a west London hotel. Normally Sam took an early overground train from Sydenham into central London and then walked briskly – as part of his daily exercise routine – along the almost deserted Embankment pathway for at least two miles. There were always a few homeless souls huddled under filthy blankets. Despite this, Sam took pleasure in the river's silent dankness interspersed by the pungent scent of spring foliage along his route which gradually morphed into the dusty concrete pavements and lofty buildings of the Temple district. Checking his watch, he noted it was six fifty-two precisely; good – the half-mile walk had taken him a mere seven minutes.

'Hello, Tabs!'

Sam greeted the small calico cat that rubbed itself up against him and tossed the remainder of his cigarette towards the bushes where old Ben, a vagrant and street sleeper, would almost certainly be lurking. Trying to keep himself awake, Sam barely noticed the

Chubb locks failing to respond as he turned the keys. The door opened with a light click as soon as he turned the Yale, and he stepped into Weymouth House Chambers. The cat darted in ahead of him and Sam glanced at the highly sensitive alarm as a matter of course, momentarily forgetting that it would not go off; the building had of course already been unlocked save for the Yale. He was accustomed to the young barrister, Belinda Radford, coming in early of a morning to catch up on her work. Sam crossed the marble-floored vestibule flanked by the clients' waiting room on the left and the lavatories on the right, and made for the small cleaning room-cum-kitchenette behind the stairwell. In what he considered to be his sanctuary, Sam first played a quick game of mah-jong on his mobile, before opening the small door which led from the back of the room out into a quiet rear courtyard.

'Out you go, Tabs! I'll get you some milk later.'

Sam followed his feline companion outside and had one more cigarette before collecting the vacuum cleaner, cleaning sprays and cloths. Glancing at the open door of the ground-floor clients' waiting room, he paused for a nanosecond as a somewhat peculiar scent entered his nostrils. He shrugged and continued to carry all the tools of his trade with ease – being well-muscled and strong – up the thick-piled carpeted flights of stairs with their gleaming oak banisters, to the second floor. He passed by the closed individual consultation cubicles, WC and archive room on the first floor as it was his habit to start from the top of the building and work his way down. He used his small finger to press down the handle and his shoulder to push open the barristers' main office door. The main light had not been switched on and nor had the uplighters beneath the few oil paintings in the room. The window blind had not yet been opened but the glow from Belinda's laptop and her Anglepoise lamp lit up the room in subdued hues of blue and green. The three mahogany desks and swivel chairs, large leather settee and armchairs were, however, empty, and the bookcases devoid of any earnest researchers scanning the titles on the shelves. The gentle purring of the laptop and the acrid aroma of coffee were the only signs of life. Sam's glance fell on the lacquered tri-fold screen that had toppled backwards and he decided to right it, before his first task of emptying the waste bins. Depositing his cleaning equipment on the floor, he moved towards the screen.

'Holy shit!'

Protruding from the base of the screen was a slim, stockinged foot, its toes splayed awkwardly. A high-heeled court shoe stood nearby, upright and half filled with blood, like a goblet of partly drunk claret. As Sam lifted the panelled screen, he came face to face with Belinda's lifeless brown eyes.

'Sorry, Madam, you can't come in here yet. Could you wait downstairs with the others until we call you?' Detective Inspector Lydia Carlisle let the annoyance sound in her voice, as she blocked the entrance to the chambers, her tiny frame at odds with her imperious tone. It was eight o'clock and she had only been at

8

Weymouth House Chambers for half an hour, but she could feel her nerves already beginning to fray slightly.

'But … what's happened to Belinda?' demanded the plump woman of indeterminate middle age standing before her. Taking in her dyed yellow-blonde hair, her too-tight blue blouse and navy pinstripe trousers and breathing in the slight musty mothbally smell which emanated from her, Lydia disliked the woman on sight.

'I can't release any details yet. Who are you?' Hoping to distract this pushy person away from the crime scene, Lydia opened her tablet and tapped on her page of notes. She looked up expectantly.

'Sharon Hardy. Clerk to the barristers – been here longer than any of them, though! Can I go into my office?' The woman gestured to a half-glassed door next to the main office.

At that moment, Sergeant Terry Glover, Lydia's uniformed colleague, appeared panting and wheezing at the top of the stairs.

'Sorry, Detective. She shoved right past us. Excuse me, Madam, please could you accompany me back down to the waiting room? No one's supposed to be up here yet.'

'Of course. But – poor Belinda. I can't believe it. And what about the appointment diary? We've got clients coming in today – would you like me to cancel them?'

Lydia observed how Sharon snapped into office mode; while it was a perfectly professional and sensible suggestion, it grated on the detective. She should have thought of that herself, but in the heat of the call-out and making sure the correct scene-of-crime protocols were followed, she had overlooked this aspect of a busy workday in a barristers' chambers.

'Fine,' no way was Lydia going to thank this irritatingly helpful woman, 'do it in your office but leave the door open. Sergeant – call Sergeant Davis and tell him to come up here. You go back down to the lobby and try not to let anyone else past you. Think you can do that?'

Lydia's sarcastic tone was not wasted on either Terry or Sharon Hardy who smirked as she smoothly unlocked her office door, switched on the light and sat down at her desk in one well-practised movement.

Lydia was left alone on the landing, knowing she had been testy and sharp, and resolved to be more pleasant to others – for the umpteenth time. She attributed the acerbic side of her nature to her father, but that did not mean that it was OK. She caught a glimpse of herself in a huge, gilt-framed mirror at the top of the stairs. Staring back at her was a tiny yet wiry and toned figure in a beige, figure-hugging jumper dress and brown pixie boots. Her white-blonde hair was cut in a spiky elfin style and she had large blue eyes that frequently tricked people into thinking she was an innocent pushover. This often proved to be an advantage though and Lydia had risen quickly within the Met's criminal investigation department. She knew that she had become infamous for solving crimes due to her tenacious and uncompromising nature.

Sergeant Clive Davis, her second uniformed officer, lithe and energetic, took the stairs two at a time and in a few seconds was at Lydia's side.

'Stand outside that office door and don't let her go anywhere,' she whispered to him and gestured towards the office of the barristers' clerk. Taking a deep breath, Lydia turned and re-entered the room where the body lay.

'So, Nick, what do we know about Belinda Radford?' Lydia addressed her partner, Assistant Detective Inspector Nicholas Fairman, who had perched on one of the office chairs, his laptop balanced precariously on his knees.

'Twenty-eight years old, Caucasian, brown eyes. Lives – sorry, lived – alone in a flat in Chalk Farm—' he began.

'OK, Nick.' Lydia held up a hand to stop him. 'Could you jot down a few notes for me about her background, training, qualifications, how long she's been working here, et cetera, and email it over to me? That would be great.'

Nick nodded, well used to Lydia's curt interruptions and watched her as she stood still and surveyed the chambers carefully. The forensic team of three, Norman Combe, Beth Monkton and Max Burgh, were working steadfastly since being called in at half past seven that morning; the dusting for fingerprints was well underway and the scene-of-crime photographer was already uploading her first pictures. Elsewhere in the building, uniformed offices were combing every nook and cranny for a possible murder weapon. Lydia approached Julie Morris.

'May I have a look, please?' Lydia took care to be a little more courteous than usual as Julie could be as spiky as herself.

'Sure', replied the photographer, turning her laptop to face Lydia. The first few snaps were wide-angled shots of the room, taking in the paintings, tall bookcases, empty desks, and window with a half-open taupe blind. Gradually, the photos zoomed in on the fallen tri-fold screen and finally on the carnage behind it. Belinda Radford lay awkwardly; her head twisted to one side, and her body and legs bent in a parody of the classic cobra pose that Lydia practised in her yoga classes. Belinda's cream-coloured suit reminded the detective of raspberry ripple ice-cream – so much blood. Lydia wondered if she would ever really get used to the sight of it.

'So it looks like she was taken unawares from behind and her throat was cut before she could do anything to defend herself. Any traces of a weapon?' asked Lydia.

'Nope, nothing,' replied Julie. 'They'll be taking her away for the post-mortem in a bit, thank goodness. Christ, the smell in here makes me feel sick.'

Lydia's mobile phone beeped at that moment and she began skimming over the notes that Nick had just emailed to her:

'Belinda Radford. Twenty-eight years of age, Caucasian with brown eyes. Unmarried, lived alone in Chalk Farm apartment. One brother, grew up in

Lymington where parents still live. Studied Law then Professional Training at Curtis Hall Legal Services. Weymouth House Chambers is her first tenancy. Other two barristers in the practice – '

'Excuse me.' A familiar and courteous yet somehow gratingly persistent voice intruded into Lydia's space and she looked up in vexation. Sharon Hardy stood in the doorway to the chambers; behind her in the corridor stood Clive, grinning sheepishly. What is wrong with these policemen? All it takes is a gutsy woman and they are anybody's, thought Lydia.

'I've managed to reach most of our clients today and the others I've left voicemails for.'

'OK, Ms Hardy. Go down to the waiting room now,' said Lydia in what she hoped was a dismissive tone.

'Er, well, I was just wondering if you would all like me to make some tea? I've got a tea and coffee machine in my office … and some biscuits,' came Sharon's response.
Before Lydia could say "no", Max, the most junior of the forensics officers called out,

'Yes, please! We're parched. White no sugar.' It would have been churlish of Lydia to contradict her colleague, and admittedly they had all come straight in somewhat early in the morning; it was probably time for a break.

'All right. But not in here – we mustn't disturb the evidence,' she replied testily.

'There's an archive room down on the first floor,' said Sharon helpfully. 'You could use that as a base and I'll put the tea in there for you.'

'Fine.' Lydia turned away and looked back down at her phone.

'Oh, Ms Hardy, before you go, are the other two employees here yet?'

'Yes – though we call them tenants, Detective! QC Sir William Bond and Attorney Anthony Greenwood are waiting downstairs. I took the liberty of calling them in early – they don't normally get in much before nine, you know!'

Nodding at Terry, who was still standing on guard on the ground floor, Lydia strode into the clients' waiting room as assertively as she could. The three males sitting on black leather tub chairs looked at her apprehensively.

'Who's who, then?' she demanded. No time for niceties, she thought.

'William Bond QC. I'm the Senior Tenant here.' The older of the men appeared to be in his fifties; he had thinning grey hair, was average in height and was somewhat overweight. He wore his expensively tailored suit well though, and came across to Lydia as regal yet personable. He indicated to his right.

'And this is my colleague, Anthony Greenwood.'

Lydia locked eyes with those of a tallish, dark-haired tanned young man in his thirties and immediately felt a thrill of attraction. Anthony had brilliant white teeth and bright blue eyes that really seemed to look at her. Quite the charismatic barrister in court no doubt, was the cynical thought which ran through her mind. She turned to the third person in the room.

'So you must be Samuel White.'

'Yes, officer. I found the body,' replied a fit-looking forty-something man, wearing jeans and a t-shirt.

'It was effing awful. She was—'

'Stop right there. I'll be taking all of your statements in due course.' Lydia continued,

'Wait here until you're called.'

She turned and left the three men, suspects, as she now considered them and made her way up to the archive room for a well-deserved cup of tea; it was, after all, still only half past eight and it would be a long day ahead.

Chapter 3

Prima Facie (on the face of it)

By seven o'clock that evening Lydia had had enough. The hundreds of legal files and folders in the low-ceilinged archive room seemed to be closing in on her and the table she and Nick had used for the four preliminary interviews was covered in a snowdrift of paper. The Weymouth House staff had been interviewed and agreed to being fingerprinted. Belinda's body had been transported to the hospital awaiting the post-mortem and Lydia had been informed that the dead woman's parents had come to London and officially identified their daughter. Forensics reports were awaited; there was, however, no sign of a potential murder weapon.

'Right, Nick, let's call it a day. Have you saved all the recordings OK?'

'Of course, Boss. Fancy a bite to eat somewhere?' replied Nick; Lydia suspected he was secretly hoping for an expenses-paid dinner.

'No, sorry – you and Sergeant Glover can go home. I just want to take another look around the chambers – Sergeant Davis can stay on guard downstairs then he and I'll call it a day as well. Let's meet at the station first thing in the morning.' Lydia wanted time alone to mull over the day and marshal her impressions.

The barristers' chamber and scene of crime, focus of so much activity over the preceding twelve hours, was silent. With the main light switched off, the room was tinged only by the orange-hued rays of the setting sun reaching through the window and caressing the spines of the legal volumes in their tall bookcases. The hilltops and monasteries on the now upright ornate tri-fold screen were also highlighted as if the sun was going down in Tuscany as well. Lydia enjoyed the sensation of sinking down onto a soft leather sofa and allowing her thoughts free rein. She replayed in her mind the questioning of the individuals they had met that day allowing her initial impressions to unfold before she would listen to the tapes more thoroughly in the office over the next few days.

'Hello, Mr White. May I call you Sam?' she had asked of their first interviewee prior to Nick recording the formal caution. Lydia often liked to lull her suspects into a false sense of security by creating a mood of first-name familiarity.

'Yep, no worries.' Sam nodded, his muscular arms folded in front of him revealing a tattoo of a skull peeking from his left t-shirt sleeve. She smelt a slight whiff of cigarettes as Sam settled himself in the chair opposite.

'You were first on the scene and found Belinda, is that right? What time was that? Talk us through it,' continued Lydia as soon as the caution had been read.

'Yeah, normally I get in at around seven fifteen but today my wife was driving into the city for a conference so she gave me a lift. She dropped me off at Waterloo Bridge at quarter to seven and it was just after ten to seven by the time I arrived here, so I had a bit of time to spare.' Sam appeared very relaxed, Lydia thought.

'Did you go straight up to the chambers, Sam?'

'Er, no, smoked a fag first out on the front step and then went into the back room to get my cleaning stuff. Then I let Tabs out the back …'

'Tabs?' interjected Lydia.

'Oh, just a street moggy that comes in sometimes. She ran in ahead of me when I unlocked the front door. She always does that! Wants her milk.' Sam smiled fondly.

'So by the time I let her out and had another ciggy in the back yard, it was probably just before seven when I got up to the top office and found the body lying there – it was awful—'

Sam's face registered the shock as he revisited the scene in his mind; for a moment Lydia thought he might actually cry.

She broke in quickly not wanting the flow of valuable facts to be interrupted by tears.

'Did you close the back door again when you came in after your cigarette?' she asked.

'Yep, definitely did. Always do.' A man of routine, thought Lydia.

'The strange thing is,' she continued, 'I was told by the scene-of-crime officer that the back door out to the yard was ajar. After you called the police at just after seven o'clock – from the Weymouth House landline, according to our records – did you go back down to the cleaning room?'

'Nope. Just waited on the top landing until your lot arrived at about ten past seven and then went straight down to the waiting room on the ground floor as I was told to. The lawyer guys showed up around eight and then we spoke to you.' Sam began to fidget and look around the room. Interesting, mused Lydia; one minute he seems assured and confident, the next he is virtually sobbing and now he's jumpy and nervous. Or maybe he just needs another cigarette?

'Just a couple more questions, Sam, and then you can go – I expect you've got another job to go to today?' Lydia decided to turn the conversation round to what was probably a more interesting topic for Sam – himself.

'Yeah, I do a morning clean at a gym after I've finished here at the law office. The gym's a good gig cos I'm allowed to use the weights after I've finished my shift,' Sam brightened up a bit. 'I'm a bit of a fitness freak. Apart from the blimmin' smoking!'

'How well did you know Belinda?' Lydia's final question was intended to be a curveball and she wasn't disappointed with Sam's hesitant response.

'Er, not very well really. Nice lady ... always said hello to me. Unlike those other jerks that work here. She used to sneak down to have a puff with me in the back yard sometimes. Once she told me she wanted to be a better lawyer than them, show them what she was capable of ...' Sam tailed off.

'OK, thank you Sam. We'll be in touch for further questioning in the next few days.'

Lydia waited until the cleaner had left the room and then turned to Nick.

'If Sam's not the murderer then whoever did it might still have been in the building at the time he discovered Belinda's body at just before seven. Perhaps they didn't expect him to be here earlier than he normally is. Maybe they heard him coming up the stairs and hid in the first or second floor WCs or the ground floor waiting room while Sam was phoning the police up in the chambers – at one minute past seven exactly, according to the police log. Then they skedaddled down the stairs and out of the back door – leaving it open in their hurry to escape.'

'I think you may be right, Boss. Pity we can't ask that cat to be a witness!' replied Nick.

Sharon Hardy had marched straight to the chair opposite Lydia and slumped down heavily. Her blouse gaped slightly at the buttons and biscuit crumbs appeared to be sprinkled over her front like iced powder on cupcakes. Bet she'd already eaten half a dozen of those biscuits she so generously supplied us with, thought Lydia.

'I know who did it!' Sharon began without waiting to be cautioned. 'What happened was …'

'Wait, Madam. We have to read you your rights before recording this interview,' interjected Nick.

Once this was done, Lydia opened her mouth to ask the first question. Too late; once more Sharon took the lead and an outpouring ensued.

'That cleaner – he's useless. Always late – always leaves the back door to the yard unlocked after he's had his smoke. Thinks I don't notice the smell of fags on him – says he's trying to give up – that's a joke! Can't stand him. Well, as I always said to

Belinda – bless her soul – anyone off the street could just slip into that yard through the gap between the buildings, open the door from the outside and Bob's your uncle. Then wouldn't it be just easy enough to grab a knife and—? '

'Stop. Ms Hardy. Let me ask the questions.' The sharpness in Lydia's voice succeeded in stopping the woman in mid-sentence.

'What time did you arrive at work this morning?'

'Quarter to eight, like always. Came in to find your nice chatty policeman – Terry isn't it? – in the hall downstairs. He told me that Belinda was hurt and I went straight up to chambers to find out what was going on. Met you yourself there, as you know … and I phoned Sir William and Attorney Anthony. Anyway, as I was saying, my money's on one of those homeless guys – you know, the ones that sleep in doorways covered in cardboard. Always on the lookout for a fix. There's usually a dog.'

Sharon's stream-of-consciousness style of speech was beginning to give Lydia a headache. She attempted to gain control of the interview:

'OK. Interesting. Tell me about yourself, Ms Hardy. Barristers' clerk aren't you? How long have you worked here?'

Shifting her weight on her chair, Sharon took the change in tack in her stride.

'Well, I'm the boss here really you know! Started here fifteen years ago with old Sir Richard Weymouth – such a dear he was, if a bit of a stick-in-the-mud! Dead now. Mind you, the new QC, Sir

William – he's wonderful, too. Attorney Anthony looks like a stayer – I hope so anyway—'.

'What's with the "Attorney"? Isn't that an American term?'

'Yes! Exactly! We call him that because he looks like a film star in an American courtroom drama! The pearly-white teeth, the eyes—'

'I see,' interrupted Lydia, thinking that she really did see. 'So it's a nickname of sorts. OK ... do continue.'

'Where was I? Oh yes, Belinda. She's the first female barrister we've ever offered a tenancy to, believe it or not – hurray for emancipation, yeah? She—'

Once again Lydia had the feeling the interview was getting away from her and she decided to bring it to an end – for now.

'Thank you, Ms Hardy. That'll be all for today. We'll invite you down to the station for a more detailed statement in due course.'

Sharon stood up, 'Yes, fine. I'm not leaving town! Now, I've got a chambers to run.' Clomping heavily towards the door, she turned once more.

'More coffee? Tea?'

'No,' Lydia was determined to have the last word.

The door closed, leaving a waft of stale body odour and a blessed silence.

'What a nightmare!' said Nick covering his face with his hands.

A true gentleman. That was how Sir William Bond, QC, had come across, reflected Lydia as she thought back to their meeting. Expensive suit and a mere essence of Clubman after-shave cologne. A bit tubby – bet Sharon feeds him pastries galore.

'Terrible business, this. Poor young Belinda – her first tenancy, too.' The QC spoke in an educated rapid-fire voice that would strike fear in the guilty party in a courtroom, thought Lydia.

'Did you offer her the tenancy yourself, Sir William?' she asked.

'Just William will do fine. Yes. Our previous tenant – John Flint – left just before Christmas and Belinda was his replacement. We're quite a small chambers but we could offer Belinda access to our facilities, an office base and admin support … that would be the superb Sharon, of course. Poor, poor Belinda … I'm absolutely devastated. Such a pretty girl, too.'

Old-school chauvinist thought Lydia. I wonder what he thinks of my looks – not.

'How was Belinda doing workwise?' continued Lydia.

The QC hesitated before replying.

'Well, she was very hardworking – committed to the job, of course. I thought she was overdoing it actually especially when Sharon told me that Belinda was getting in at about six in the morning sometimes.'

Lydia decided to push the point a little.

'Do you think Belinda needed to put in those extra hours?

'Oh no, not at all,' William seemed adamant. 'Belinda was a dedicated lawyer. But I feel she suffered from a lack of confidence, possibly as she was the only female in chambers. Really though, she didn't realise how good she was! Of course, I always tried to encourage her and she always deferred to me when she wasn't sure about a particular point of law, but on the whole, she wanted to prove herself on her own – so I guess she was trying to go over and above what was expected of her.'

'Thank you. How well did you know her on a personal level?'

'Not well at all, Detective. Just on a work colleague basis you know. And she hadn't been with us very long.'

'On another note, I was wondering why there are no CCTV cameras installed here at the premises … isn't that the norm?' asked Lydia.

'Ah yes – on my to-do list. Sir Richard Weymouth, whom I replaced, definitely had a foot in the last century; it wouldn't have occurred to him to update the security. Any more than it would have occurred to him to allow a female lawyer to set up base here!'

'OK. And finally, why do you think someone would murder Belinda? Any ideas, William?'

A slight pause before replying. Well-practised for courtroom effect, thought Lydia.

'I have no idea. In my long experience of dealing with criminal cases, such things tend to happen spontaneously so I imagine that the perpetrator was a chancer, perhaps a burglar looking for things to steal.

We have a few valuable items in chambers – books, paintings and so on. Maybe they didn't expect to find anyone in so early ... it's all so awful.' William broke off, his voice quavering at last.

The QC's eyes looked distinctly tearful but despite her desire to delve deeper, Lydia wrapped up the interview, promising to contact him again for a further appointment.

That left "Attorney" Anthony Greenwood. Once again, Lydia felt a jolt of electricity at the direct look he gave her with his clear blue eyes. Very handsome, she thought. And he knows it. Charm offensive incoming.

'Thank you for waiting, Mr Greenwood. I know you must have plenty of work to be doing.'

'Oh, no worries. Anything to help. Poor Belinda.' Anthony looked suitably grave.

'Tell us about yourself,' Lydia decided to cut to the chase. She was looking forward to finding out about Anthony.

'Not much to say, really,' said Anthony, rather modestly. 'I'm thirty-five years old, married, two children and live in Hampstead.'

'Nice part of London. You barristers must be earning well?' Lydia cut in, eying Anthony's blatantly expensive and sharp suit that flattered his slim build and breathing in a whiff of his pine-scented after-shave that he had obviously just re-applied.

Anthony flashed her his whiter-than-white smile.

'Not doing too badly. My wife doesn't need to work! She looks after the kids and paints – modern art, you know?'

'So, how did you get along with Belinda?' Lydia drew him back on track.

'Oh, fine. I get on with most people really. Belinda was fun – a bit naughty – and good with her clients, I think.'

'What do you mean by "naughty"?' asked Lydia, a guileless expression on her face.
Anthony had the grace to redden slightly – much to Lydia's secret satisfaction – and answered,

'Well, you know, we used to poke fun at some of the clients after they'd left the chambers – behind Sir William's back. And sometimes we would imitate Sharon's boring voice – that kind of thing.'

'And?' Lydia just knew there was more.

'Erm, we'd pop out for a drink now and then … usually to our local such as LEWB –that stands for Legal Eagles' Wine Bar – about five minutes away from here.' Anthony made this sound like the most natural thing in the world. 'When things got a bit stressful in chambers.'

'I see,' said Lydia. 'Did you get on well with Belinda professionally as well?'
Anthony baulked at the detective's sarcasm but chose not to rise to the bait.

'Well, Belinda was only a junior so to speak, being quite newly qualified, and I've had a lot more experience than her. My own cases tend to be fairly complicated, but I tried to help her where I could, plus Sir William wanted me to keep an eye on Belinda …

professionally, of course, Detective,' he replied. Smooth, thought Lydia. She went on,

'And did she appreciate your "help"?'

'Oh yes, she was very pleased to have an experienced and successful man on hand to show her the ropes and advise her,' came Anthony's response with not a trace of humility, to Lydia's private amusement; she made a mental note that this was a not-so-young chauvinist in the making.

Lydia had closed the interview at that point, anticipating probing Anthony's patronising nature at a later date.

Yes, it was the end of a sad yet intriguing day, thought Lydia. She had found out quite a lot about the main players involved except for Belinda herself, and Lydia was keen to delve further into the deceased woman's background. Time to leave these stultifying chambers now so gloomy and full of shadows. Time to get out of London, this crowded, dusty metropolis and head to Lymington, Belinda's home town, to learn more about this enigmatic young barrister who had lost her life so violently. Yes, a day in the New Forest – complete with its restorative sense of fresh air and wooded solitude – would be the perfect next step in Lydia's investigation.

Chapter 4

Uberrimei Fidei (of the utmost good faith)

April was the perfect month to be in this part of the
world mused Lydia as she drove along fresh country
lanes lined by spiky gorse and soft-fronded bracken.
The morning sun poked its fingertips through the
overhanging branches of trees creating a dappled effect
on the road ahead. Very different indeed from the
choked streets of London that she had left behind her,
the abject horror of Belinda's murder and the thorny
meeting with Nick at the station early that Wednesday
morning. She had tersely ordered him to transcribe all
the interview recordings of the day before and to email
them over to her by no later than the end of the day.
Moreover, she had instructed him to schedule in a staff
meeting as well as draft a press statement for her
perusal. She knew Nick assumed she would be
enjoying a day out of the office but Lydia considered
the trip to be vital to the investigation. She had
received an email from Belinda's father replying to her
enquiry as to when he and Mrs Radford had last seen
Belinda; it transpired that she had been to the New
Forest only a few days earlier to visit her parents.
Lydia also wanted to be alone that day to allow her
thoughts free rein to focus on the impressions she
would be sure to gather on meeting Belinda's family on
their own territory. Chief Inspector Geoff Cordell,
Lydia's superior, had granted her permission to travel
to the New Forest solo, trusting in Lydia's

professionalism and tried-and-tested instincts and determination.

A short distance outside the Georgian market town of Lymington, the Radford family home lay embedded in forest and surrounding parkland. At least that was what Lydia assumed until on pulling up outside the large medieval building with its imposing wooden front door, it dawned on her that the perfectly tended park was actually the front garden. Nice for some.

The woman who had opened the door and was now standing before her looked ten years older than her age of fifty-three according to Lydia's notes. Red-rimmed eyes, straggly uncombed dark blonde hair and a shapeless grey tracksuit combined to give a picture of utter misery. Hardly surprising, Lydia thought to herself. She has just lost her daughter after all.

'Good morning. I'm Detective Inspector Carlisle. And you must be Mrs Radford?' Lydia kept her voice low and reverential despite the clichéd words. 'I'm so sorry for your loss.'

'Call me Felicity. Come in.'

Barefoot, Belinda's mother led the way through the house and into a sunny conservatory with exquisite views of the immaculate lawn, broken only by an oak tree and what Lydia thought were probably heather and gladioli.

'Take a seat, Detective. Hell, it's all so awful. We'd only seen Belinda at the weekend and—'

Seeing that Felicity was about to crumble, Lydia interrupted.

'Is your husband here?'

'He's out with the horses – we run a livery you see. I'll call him on his mobile – would you like a drink?'

Lydia nodded, reflecting that manners and hospitality among such people would always prevail even in the worst of times. Interesting also that it warranted a telephone call to summon her husband; it must indeed be a massive estate. About ten minutes later, Felicity returned bearing a tray of coffee and biscuits, and accompanied by two men, who both shook hands with Lydia.

'Hello. I'm Gordon. And this is our son, Julian – Belinda's brother.'

'Morning. Thank you for your email and for being willing for me to visit you here at home … and I'm so sorry for your loss,' replied Lydia, feeling that although she had already expressed her condolences to Felicity, it was a matter of respect to extend them to Belinda's father and brother as well.

Lydia could see the family resemblance between the Radfords; they all had the same brown eyes and tall, slender build. She knew that Julian was two years younger than his sister, and that he was in banking. Intriguing to note that neither child had followed their parents into a clearly comfortable and privileged country life.

'So do you run this place by yourselves?' asked Lydia, addressing Gordon Radford who seemed to be bearing up slightly better than his wife. Wearing a Harris Tweed suit minus the waistcoat, and with the top button of his white shirt undone, he looked quite the country gentleman.

'Well, we have staff to help with the animals – trainers, grooms and so on – but I like to keep an eye on everything.' His deep voice with only a hint of a Hampshire accent radiated class and status. Gordon went on, 'Felicity does the accounts. Julian likes to come down for the auctions, and Belinda ...' Gordon's voice broke and he struggled to continue.

'... Belinda adored the newborn foals. I inherited this business from my parents – it's been in the family for a couple of hundred years. We breed pedigree Beaulieu ponies, you know.' Gordon was clearly trying to hold it together despite the look of anguish on his face.

Nodding, Lydia turned to Julian who was a carbon copy of his father albeit slightly shorter and with a trendier haircut. She asked,

'You live in London don't you, Julian? When did you get down here?'

'Yes – I live in Blackheath but I work at Spitalfields. I met up with Mum and Dad yesterday evening after they'd been to identify my sister's body and we travelled down here together last night.'

Of all of them, Julian appeared to be in best control of his emotions. Almost too sure of himself, suspected Lydia.

'I'm staying here for a day or two and then I've got to get back to London – important bank seminar coming up,' he explained.

'When did you last see or speak to your sister?' Lydia decided to cut to the chase.

'A few months ago I think. We don't – sorry, didn't – socialise much together. Never have done ...'

Julian was interrupted by the ringing of his mobile phone. 'Sorry, I have to take this … it's work.'

He disappeared swiftly out of the room.

The ensuing silence was broken by the sound of heartbroken sobbing from Felicity who was slumped on a wicker sofa.

'I can't stand it. My poor Belinda – why did this have to happen to her? What monster did this?' Felicity's desperate pleas for answers were rhetorical questions, reflected Lydia. For now anyway. She caught Gordon Radford's eye.

'Would it be possible for you to show me around your property, Gordon? Helps me to form a picture …'

'Of course. Come this way, Detective.'

The land surrounding the Radfords' house reached as far as the eye could see. Pausing on the patio outside the conservatory, Lydia was just wondering how much of it belonged to the family when Gordon answered her unspoken question.

'The Heathers Livery and Equestrian Centre consists of the paddocks and landscaped forest areas from the end of the garden right up to those beech trees in the distance. Beyond that the New Forest tends to be heathland and woods – full of wildlife … badgers, deer … and I've even seen polecats.'

He was obviously extremely knowledgeable about his part of the world and proud to occupy such an enviable position in it.

'It's beautiful,' murmured Lydia.

'This is wild gladiolus native to the forest,' Gordon indicated the scarlet spikes of flowers piercing the lawn. He went on, 'and that's—'

'Heather?' interjected Lydia.

'Yes that's right, Detective. Hence the name of the estate, The Heathers. It grows everywhere.'

As they made their way across the sunny garden, Lydia admired the heather in its various shades of pink and pale purple growing – almost floating – in what looked like shimmering pools of amethyst set in the emerald-green grass. Enough of the poetics she told herself. Let's get down to business.

'Gordon – about your daughter. I know it's very soon but I'm as keen as you and your wife are to find the person who murdered Belinda.'

'Of course. Sorry to blather on about plants and polecats! Helps take my mind off things you know.' Gordon met Lydia's glance; tears were forming in his eyes.

'We're both absolutely devastated of course. But I'm trying not to show it too much in front of my wife … she's fragile enough as it is and this has absolutely crushed her.'

Indicating the land with a sweep of his arm he continued, 'All this would have been Belinda's. And Julian's of course. Though neither of them were all that interested in running it when they grew up. Just wanted to leave the forest and go up to London as soon as they could.'

An edge of bitterness crept into his voice. Lydia reflected that she too had wanted to escape the confines of her upbringing and could well understand the

Radford youngsters for wanting to make their own way in life despite what their parents wished for them.

They had arrived at one of the paddocks adjoined by a manège, a word Lydia remembered from her girlhood pony lessons. Here, a chestnut coloured pony was trotting around the perimeter on a lunge line held by a grey-haired horseman, clearly experienced as evinced by the confident way he handled the animal.

'That's Jim. In his seventies now. Grumpy old sod but brilliant with horses – commands utter respect from them. He used to have his own farm but sold it a few years ago and lives in one of our cottages now.' Gordon waved over to the man who nodded in curt reply. 'We own several properties on the estate – we let the staff lodge in them as part of the package.'

'So how many employees do you have, Gordon?'

'Twelve in all. Two estate managers, plus grooms, a couple of trainers like Jim and some stable hands – running a livery is quite involved. Beaulieu ponies are known all over the world – we get a lot of interest at auction.'

Watching the chestnut being put through its paces, Lydia appreciated its natural grace and solid hardiness. Again though, Gordon was veering away from the issue that had brought her here. Time to rein him in.

'You mentioned that Julian likes to help you at auctions?'

Gordon showed no surprise at Lydia's sudden turn in the conversation; he merely sighed.

'"Help" is putting it a bit strongly. He's only interested in the money the horses bring in. Dollar signs in his eyes – always has had.'

'Is that why he went into banking?' asked Lydia.

'Well, he didn't do too well at school, struggled a little with his handwriting – being left-handed didn't help – and only ended up with one A Level. So instead of going to uni like Belinda, he got his first job as a bank clerk at eighteen and worked his way up. Seemed to take to it. Left home and went up to London as soon as he could.' Gordon rolled his eyes. 'We don't see much of him really. Got his own circle of friends up there now, of course … he's been even more distant lately, now that I think about it.'

Lydia changed tack and led Gordon back to the painful subject of his dead daughter.

'Did Belinda have many friends?'

'Well, as a child I suppose she was a bit isolated. Into animals and flowers – she could identify butterwort at sixty paces and liked to observe the bats at night. She recorded thirteen species of bat in her little notebook and wrote down exactly when and where she saw them in her diary … we've still got all her old diaries …' Gordon smiled at the memory and went on,

'She went to an excellent private school in Lymington. They both did actually but Belinda was more academic than Julian. Sometimes she brought friends home to look at the ponies but I don't think she had a best friend or anything. Although Felicity might know more than me on that front.'

They skirted several more paddocks containing grazing mares and foals of varying colours and markings and passed through stable yards where yet more ponies were being tended to. Gordon nodded to his staff; they in turn lowered their heads in respect. The news of the murder had clearly spread and Lydia felt true sympathy radiating from Gordon Radford's staff.

'Belinda and Julian were never very close, Detective. I think Julian felt in her shadow as she was very high achieving. Quite sporty – that was down to the school of course – but mainly studious you know. She got it into her head to become a barrister even though I told her she had a tailor-made job helping to run the business here – she would have been able to assist Felicity with the admin.'

I bet Belinda would have baulked at that, guessed Lydia. Most probably wanted to escape the idyllic yet outmoded lifestyle mapped out for her – just as Lydia's own father had tried to keep her from being a modern, independent woman.

'When she got into UCL to do Law, she was over the moon. She loved it there, and I know she made some good friends there. She got a first, you know ...we were so very proud of her too of course—'

Gordon's voice broke and Lydia knew that the eggshell veneer holding him together was on the verge of cracking.

'Let's go back to the house,' she suggested.

Lydia learnt little more from the Radfords on returning to the family home. Felicity had already retired to her bed and Julian was nowhere to be seen. Gordon did however describe Belinda's visit the previous weekend, which was of course a key reason for Lydia's visit to The Heathers.

'It was the last time we saw her. She came down to look at the spring foals – she loved them as I told you earlier. We went out for dinner to our favourite restaurant – Albon's – in Lymington on Saturday night and she went back up to London on Sunday late afternoon.'

'How did she seem?' asked Lydia.

'Fine. A bit worried about keeping up with her colleagues in the barristers' chambers I think, but on the whole she was happy enough. I didn't pick up on anything at all.'

'OK. Well, if you think of anything, please don't hesitate to call me; let's swap numbers,' said Lydia. 'And could you give me Julian's mobile number as well?'

'Sure, no problem.'

Finally, after exchanging contact details with Gordon, it was time for Lydia to leave.

'Gordon – rest assured, I'm going to do everything in my power to find Belinda's killer and bring them to justice. Take care, and we'll be in contact as soon as we know anything.'

'Thank you, Detective. I appreciate your coming down to us; drive safely now.'

Before starting her car, Lydia's phone bleeped – it was Nick emailing her the interview transcripts and draft press release. Bedtime reading she thought.

'Good night New Forest,' she said aloud as she drove through the gloomy woods back to London. The sun was going down, and the shapes and silhouettes of the trees on either side of the road took on completely different and rather sinister identities in the darkening twilight.

Chapter 5

Culpa (blameworthiness or a fault)

Staring out of her fourth-floor office at New Scotland Yard, Lydia relished the view of the slowly moving river on its meandering way to the sea. As much as the countryside had its attractions, there was also nothing quite like the incongruous sense of contrast within London. While she loved the calmness of the boats and ferries floating past the London Eye, she also cherished the teeming pavements and inviting shopfronts of the inner city, and delighted in the edginess and excitement of the urban nightlife. A day's respite in the New Forest had been quite enough to rejuvenate her and she was happy to be back enjoying the diversity and buzz of the capital.

'Morning, Boss. Enjoy the trees?' asked Nick who had knocked and then entered her office without waiting for an answer. Lydia could tell he was still smarting from her abruptly delivered command of the previous day. All credit to him, though; he had drafted the press statement and got all the interviews transcribed and over to her on time as requested. He had also come prepared with printed-out notes.

'Hi Nick. Yes – lovely neck of the woods down there. The Radfords are pretty well-heeled – they've got a huge estate. The parents are still in shock, of course. The brother's a bit blasé, I thought—'

Lydia decided that now was the moment to melt the icy atmosphere Nick had brought in with him.

'By the way, thank you for the transcripts. Nick. I had a read through of them last night when I got back and I've got a few questions. Would you like a coffee and a doughnut?'

Moving over to her coffee maker, Lydia indicated the carton of fresh sugared doughnuts and smoothly poured out two cups of frothy latte – Nick's favourite.

'Sit down and let's go over what we've got so far and discuss next steps,' she continued.

Somewhat appeased, Nick settled himself into one of the blue easy chairs next to the picture window overlooking the Thames and Embankment gardens.

'Sure. Are you happy with the press statement, Boss?'

'Yes … though I've deleted the part about the missing murder weapon, Nick – no need to let the world know we haven't found it yet! So it now reads:

"On Tuesday 5th April this week, barrister Belinda Radford, 28, originally of Lymington, Hampshire, was found dead having suffered a vicious attack at her place of work, Weymouth House Chambers, Temple, London. The perpetrator or perpetrators may still be at large and the public are warned to take care. Police enquiries are ongoing."
Happy with that?'

Nick nodded agreement, adding,

'Yep … short and sweet. Or maybe not so sweet. I'll get it sent out today. And by the way, I'm in the process of setting up the staff meeting as requested.'

'Good, thank you, Nick. Right, so the preliminary forensic report should be coming through any moment now. Who was the last person to see her alive – apart from the murderer obviously?' asked Lydia.

'Well, I did a bit of digging around and the guy at the Chalk Farm ticket office remembers seeing her early on Tuesday morning at the tube station – she was one of the first ones through the barrier apparently.'

'Great, Nick. What time was that?'

Lydia noted that her praise seemed to smooth Nick's ruffled feathers a little. Getting there, she thought. She made yet another mental note to be less spiky towards her colleagues. Why did she have to have inherited the acerbic gene from her father? Why not more of her mother's empathy?

'Just before six. The ticket office guy says he sees her quite often at around that time. Nobody else seems to have noticed her on the way to work, and then Sam White, the cleaner, found her at just before seven as we know.'

'What about the night before? Was Belinda with anyone on Monday evening?' asked Lydia. 'I think it's important to know where she was and who she was with the night before … the same for the other suspects, incidentally. Any detail might have some bearing on who killed her.'

'Agreed. I was just coming to that! Let me just check my notes. Right, so Belinda was at work all day and left the chambers at around five thirty p.m. – not particularly late for a lawyer, I guess, and not as late as us sometimes! – and then Sharon Hardy locked up at about six p.m. The arrangement seemed to have been that the two women took it in turns or agreed in advance who was going to secure the building at the end of the day,' replied Nick.

'Because of Belinda's late nights at the chambers I suppose,' said Lydia thoughtfully.

'Yep, exactly. Anyway, as far as I can make out, she spent the Monday evening at home – alone. I sent Sergeants Terry Glover and Clive Davis to seal off her flat and they did a quick search around. They found some Indian takeaway cartons in the bin and had the presence of mind to root around until they found a menu in there as well – probably thrown away by Belinda.'

Lydia could tell Nick was warming up to his theme; he waited a couple of seconds and then continued,

'Terry texted me the Indian takeaway restaurant's number and I phoned them up. The Bombay Raj confirmed that they had delivered a meal for one to 39 Haverstock Hill at about eight p.m.'

Lydia had to ask the question,

'How did they know it was for only one person then?

'Ha! She only ordered one poppadom,' replied Nick smugly. 'If there'd been two people eating – even just one portion of curry and rice – I'm sure they'd have asked for two poppadoms!'

'Hmm. Well, maybe. Good work, Nick.' Lydia sipped her coffee thoughtfully. 'What about phone records? Did she call anyone on her landline or mobile at all?'

'Nothing on her mobile on Monday evening. The last calls from her landline were to the Indian restaurant on the Monday night and to her parents in Lymington on the Sunday evening – lasted about five minutes,' replied Nick.

'Probably to let her parents know she'd got back to London safely.' Lydia remembered Gordon telling her that Belinda left the Radford home late on Sunday afternoon. 'What about during the day on Monday?'

'Just business calls on the chambers' phones. And it looks as though she didn't make any private mobile calls or texts during work time.' Nick smirked and went on, 'Unlike some of our own colleagues … '

Lydia raised her eyebrows in mock surprise, though she knew that Nick was referring to Sergeant Terry Glover who had been caught calling his girlfriend on his mobile phone while on field duty a few months earlier. Loose lips sink ships and all that. A severe reprimand from his superior had made sure it would never happen again. Hopefully.

'So our Belinda's a good girl then. Gets in early, nose to the grindstone, works hard all day, goes home. What's not to like about her?' Lydia wondered aloud.

'Well, someone obviously didn't,' replied Nick. 'I'll have a look at her mobile records going back a few weeks and get back to you if there's anything of note. Did you say you had some questions about the transcripts?'

'Yes, I've made a note of a few details to follow up. Right – Sam White, the cleaner. Says he went straight up to the top floor to start cleaning there first. Why? Is that normal? Then he called the police immediately after he found the body. Was it "immediately" though? Maybe he gave himself time to get rid of the murder weapon first. Plus I've come across killers who call in the murder they've committed – they think it'll deflect suspicion from themselves. And I want to go over that back door being open after he said he closed it. Did the cat get back in again?'

'There was definitely no cat when we got there, Boss. I'll arrange for Sam to come in to see you for further questioning. Anything else strike you?'

'Sharon Hardy. Arrived at chambers forty-five minutes after Sam found the body. Does she always start work so early? I mean I know she's Ms Bossy Boots but surely she's got her job down to a T by now? Also, she must know that building like the back of her hand having worked there so long, so if she wanted to hide a murder weapon – a "knife" maybe, as she so helpfully suggests – it would be easy for her to get rid of it. And why is she so quick to blame others? Thinks she can sidetrack us perhaps? Get her in to see me as well, please.'

'No problem,' said Nick. 'What about William Bond and Anthony Greenwood?'

'Yes, I need them in, too. Bond makes out that Belinda was dedicated and worked hard but he didn't advise her against coming in early to work even though he thought she was overdoing it. What kind of

"senior" tenant is that? He's a QC for goodness sake –
he must have some brains. But then I reckon Sharon
Hardy has him wrapped around her little finger, too!
He says he only knew Belinda on a work basis, but I'm
wondering if he would have liked to get to know her
better. Maybe he even tried, seeing as he thinks she is
so "pretty". Know what I mean, Nick?'

Nick nodded and Lydia continued, 'And as for
Greenwood. A definite charmer with the ladies – so I
imagine. Just how "naughty" was Belinda? And just
how did he "help" her? And when was the last time
they went out for a drink, and where did they go? He
doesn't make any assumptions about a murderer, like a
burglar or whatever like Bond does, so I'd like to pump
him a bit more.'

'OK, Boss, leave it with me. I'll try to make
appointments as soon as poss for them to see you.'

'Great. Thanks, Nick. Could you also do a bit
of digging into their personal lives as well – Sam's and
Greenwood's wives, Bond's and Sharon's families, et
cetera. Have a look at the previous barrister whom
Belinda replaced – John Flint his name is. He might
have an axe to grind for all we know. See if you can
arrange for a list of Weymouth House Chambers'
current client names for all three barristers, and get
uniform to check out the rough sleepers in the area as
well as any recent burglaries. Please.'

'Yep, will do,' Nick replied. Lydia suspected
he was especially relishing the idea of presiding over
those colleagues "in uniform" who were junior in rank
to him. Ambitious guy – wants a speedy promotion no
doubt, guessed Lydia.

Nick topped up their coffees. 'So, Boss – tell me all about the New Forest.'

Lydia gazed reflectively out of the window at the familiar skyline of the South Bank buildings across the river.

'OK. Well, Felicity Radford is a wreck. I think she was probably closer to Belinda than the father – Gordon, his name is. It seems to have been a typical nuclear family – two kids with Belinda and her younger brother, Julian ...'

Nick broke in, 'You mentioned he seemed a bit offhand?'

'Yes, definitely on the, shall we say, "unconcerned" side. More interested in his phone and getting back to London than discussing his own sister's murder, I thought. Gordon Radford did mention though that Julian and Belinda were never close as siblings growing up.'

'Strange,' said Nick. 'You'd have thought having the run of a large estate in the country would have made them quite attached to each other.'

'Yes, it is fairly isolated where they are. But it seems they were completely different as kids. Belinda was the studious sort while Julian wasn't ...' Lydia paused, thinking back to Gordon's words. '... academic. Neither of them wanted to stay and run the horse business though, and both gravitated to the big lights of London.'

'Did they socialise much up here?' asked Nick.

'Apparently not with each other, but I think it's worth a bit of digging around to find out what Julian gets up to in his spare time.'

'Was it huge then, this place of theirs in the New Forest?'

'Nick, it went on as far as the eye could see! Fields, stables, cottages; masses of horses – well, pedigree Beaulieu ponies, actually, as I was informed – and quite a few employees who live on the estate.'

'Did you see any of them?'

'Yes, they all seemed very sorry about what's happened to Belinda; I expect some of them knew her as a child, especially one or two of the older ones that have been around for a while.'

'So the Radfords are not short of a bob or two,' said Nick, a tad enviously.

'I doubt it. Might be an idea to look into their financials, though. Julian is rather attracted to money according to his father.'

Several coffees later, Lydia wound their meeting up. She and Nick agreed that Julian needed a closer look, and she also asked him to arrange for her to visit Belinda's Chalk Farm flat as soon as possible. Nick had gone off with a lighter tread than he had entered her office with at the beginning of the day. Phew, thought Lydia. A few sugary doughnuts and playing to his strengths was what it had taken to get Nick back on track. Cracking the whip was quicker though. She sent a quick summary of proceedings so far to her boss, Chief Inspector Geoff Cordell and glanced through her emails. The preliminary forensic report on Belinda's death was ready. Lydia decided to grab a sandwich from the canteen and go and sit outside on the Embankment overlooking the river to read the report in the warm sunshine. Not strictly legit, she knew – she was risking a reprimand by perusing such sensitive information in public. But it was only on her phone and Lydia needed some fresh air away from the office to clear her head. Bending the rules a little to catch her prey was how Lydia justified it to herself.

Silly cow. She got what was coming to her alright. That was the last straw – how dare she speak to me like that? Who did she think she was? She always was above herself but that was a step too far even for her. Dear Belinda always thought she was better than anyone else with all her grand talk of being a great barrister one day and 'proving' herself. Best female lawyer of the decade, I don't think. Well, all that swotting and studying, early mornings and late nights came to nothing, didn't it? Brains aren't always better than brawn, are they? One neat slash was all it took – all that promise and high hopes bled away for ever. She would never have made it anyway in a man's world as Father always used to say ... I tried to tell her, but no, she wanted to 'succeed' without the help of any man, wanted to do it all on her own, make her own money. Didn't think much of women who depended on men, though in a way I agree with that. Darling Belinda never wanted my help except when it suited her; then it was all acting friendly and could you do this, could you do that, want a coffee, shall we 'do' lunch, fancy a drink and let's have a laugh? Then when she got what she wanted, and took all my advice, it would be a kick in the teeth, all cool and distant again and not even a thank you – she never really

*appreciated me. Always swanning around in her suits
and heels – power dressing she called it. I must join a
gym she said. I must lose weight she said. Really?
Looked down on fatties and on anyone not remotely as
slim as her, didn't she? Looked down on most people in
my honest opinion. I put a stop to that though, didn't I?
No more of that condescension, thank you very much.
As Father used to say, appreciate what you're given.
The world's your oyster but nothing comes of nothing.
Stick before carrot. A clip round the earhole and be
grateful for what you've got.*

Chapter 6

Feme Sole (a woman who is not married)

Death by single cut across the throat from left to right, from behind. Jugular vein severed, causing massive bleeding out with death following shortly after. The head had been pulled back causing the carotid artery and jugular vein to be tightened and moved further back in the neck. The implement used for the killing was then pushed into the neck just in front of the spine and moved sideways, then efficiently withdrawn. The preliminary forensic report comprised a toxicology report that revealed nothing of significance; there was evidence of the victim's Indian meal of the previous evening and black coffee. Also included was an autopsy report which was straightforward and contained no real surprises except for an estimate of the killer's height suggested by the angle of the fatal slash. It seemed that the murderer had been shorter than the victim; however, Belinda Radford had been relatively tall, at five foot ten and a half. There had been no skin under Belinda's fingernails; she obviously had had no time to put up any kind of fight, supposed Lydia. The report concluded that a perpetrator skilled at using a knife would have been able to cut the victim's throat in such a way as to avoid getting blood spatter on themselves by slashing rapidly and then pushing the body forwards and away from their own person. Forensics matched the blood taken from the floor of the barristers' chambers to that of the victim; fingerprints and hair samples lifted from the furniture and fittings were still being processed. The time of death was estimated to be between six a.m. and seven a.m. on the day of the murder.

A further report on fingerprints found at Belinda's flat and the contents of her personal laptop would follow once the forensic search of the murdered woman's home had been carried out. It was Thursday – only two days after the body had been and discovered and suspects were still being evaluated – but Lydia was impatient to move the investigation forward.

Gazing at a restored Thames barge as it glided elegantly by, Lydia sank back into the park bench in the Embankment gardens, a stone's throw from the New Scotland Yard office block. She'd devoured her alfresco lunch without really tasting it, her thoughts ebbing and flowing like the tide on the river, as she tried to imagine Belinda's final, terrible moments. She pictured the unsuspecting barrister preparing her eagerly awaited morning coffee and the stealthy manner in which the murderer must have sneaked up behind her and confidently slashed Belinda's throat in one clean movement. Lydia's musings finally turned towards the dead woman's parents whom she had met the day before at their New Forest estate near Lymington; she could relate to how they must be feeling when she thought of her own family.

In a way, her upbringing had been quite similar to Belinda's, except that Lydia had not had the luxury of a brother, which meant she was the sole focus of her parents' hopes and ambitions when it came to carrying on the family name. Like Belinda, she too had a father who would have preferred her to aspire merely to a low-level career and leave the hard stuff in life to men. Similar to the murdered barrister, Lydia also had a mother who had done just that – sat back and settled for a risk-free but unadventurous life. Yes, there were definitely some similarities between Lydia's mother and father, Patrick and Christine Carlisle, and the Radford parents when it came to their outlook on life. Given the fact that Lydia and Belinda were in the same age bracket, and their parents were of the same generation, this was probably to be expected. Lydia guessed that Belinda too had suffered from the bigotry that their fathers brought to bear on them to a greater or lesser extent, and also recognised Belinda's determination to pay homage to the still only one-hundred- year-old process of female emancipation and equality. Lydia knew too that her own character flaws, which sometimes impeded her police work but also made her determined to forge ahead, were inherited from Patrick Carlisle.

She thought back to the last time she had visited her parents; in fact, like Belinda going to the New Forest, Lydia had also gone "home" the weekend just gone by – a couple of days before Belinda's murder. She remembered the resentment that had simmered away under the surface just like the gammon joint that was slow cooking in its pot on her mother's range.

    'God, Cambridge has changed so much! It's so busy and it's almost impossible to get parked and—'

    'Well, Lydia, if you came home more often, you would know what the traffic's like here.' Her father frowned and went on, 'And anyway, it can't be as bad as London with all that pollution … caused by those filthy car fumes, no doubt.'

'I think the congestion charges have helped with that, dear,' said Christine. 'Anyway, let's not spoil the day. How's work going, Lyddie? Actually, rather than tell us now, why don't you and I have a quick wander down to the river? We've got about an hour before lunch is ready – we'll take Betsy with us.'

Lydia jumped at the chance to have some time alone with her mother and to soak up the atmosphere of Cambridge in all its early spring glory. She also adored her parents' border collie, Betsy; not being able to have a dog in London was the worst thing. Her parents had retired and now lived in a handsome Georgian terraced house in Tennyson Close, a stone's throw from the old market square and entrance to King's College, jewel in the crown of the University of Cambridge, and as residents they were entitled – free of charge – to stroll through the stunning manicured college gardens that stretched alongside the River Cam. Fortunately for Betsy, dogs were allowed during the winter months until the end of April. It was a calm and gentle environment compared to Lydia's childhood background which comprised a forces' military lifestyle with its officers' married quarters and a stark adherence to command and order. This had characterised the Carlisles' existence until the day that Patrick could finally draw his pension from the RAF. It also meant that Lydia could now visit and spend time with them more frequently than before by means of the plethora of high-speed trains and fast motorway links between London and Cambridge, as opposed to enduring slow rail links and B-roads to the somewhat remote RAF base her parents had resided in previously.

With a warm sun on their faces, Lydia and Christine walked swiftly through Clare College and expertly led by Betsy navigated their way through the hordes of tourists that insisted on stopping to take photos and blocking the paths like so many herds of mountain goats on a sun-steeped Mediterranean island. They entered Trinity Hall, Lydia's favourite college; she always felt a sense of peace in its walled garden with its spectacular borders of crimson hollyhocks and azure lupins that lined the paths down to the river. They sat down on a bench, and, with Betsy settled down beside them, gazed at the narrow river with its punts gliding by, laden with day-trippers.

'Why on earth is Dad still so crabby, Mum? Surely he must have got over me not doing the right "female" thing by now? It's the twenty-first century for goodness sake.' Lydia glowered, her feeling of serenity on hold. She knew she was reverting back to childhood mode, begging for her parents' approval as opposed to being the modern independent professional she was with a promising career in the Met. How was she going to resolve this once and for all?

'Don't frown, Lyddie! You look just like him, darling,' smiled Christine. 'You'll always be his little girl, and he means well really.'

'I'm twenty-eight years old!' Lydia pouted, uncomfortably aware that she actually sounded like an eight-year-old now. 'He's the only one in the whole world that doesn't get what I do. *He* had a brilliant career in the RAF, so why can't *I* make a success of being in the police?'

'It's exactly that – he had responsibility and command, and earned respect in his thirty years' service but now he's retired and it's all gone. He's having to adjust. He's probably a bit bored too if I'm honest. Maybe I should get him to do more of the chores round the house. Stop him brooding so much.'

'I somehow can't see him vacuuming or dusting, Mum. Even though he makes most of the mess himself and he's the untidiest person I know! But anyway – what's that got to do with me? He's always been a bit harsh. To both of us actually.'

'That's just his way. Being squadron leader in the forces meant he had to be strict with those under his command, and that spilled over into his home life, I think. He's proud of you, Lyddie, but he just doesn't know how to express it.'

Lydia was not convinced. Lovely though her mother was, her empathetic nature seemed misplaced when it came to her father. She agreed unconditionally with everything Patrick said and did – or so it appeared to Lydia.

'What about you, Mum? What do you really think about my job? I've been with the Met for five years now … '

Christine cocked her head to one side, looking for all the world like Betsy the dog, and considered Lydia's question.

'Well, I think it's great that you've chosen a job that is … *worthy* – I think that's the right word. But—'

'But what, Mum? You think I should have got married to a nice safe man who could support me while I have his children after I left uni? And by the way, my Psychology degree actually comes in very useful at times … understanding the criminal mind and all that.' Lydia was fuming again.

'Lyddie. I'm sure it does and of course I'm pleased that you're so ambitious career-wise. In fact, if I could have my time again … well, what I really wanted to do was be a vet.'

'You never told me that, Mum! So why didn't you?'

'It was harder for women in those days. And anyway, I was useless at the right subjects for veterinary medicine – like Chemistry and so on. As you know, I did end up doing a degree – in History, and worked in a reference library for a few years.'

'And then you met Dad and had me.' Lydia knew the rest of the story. It seemed a waste of a life to her, and she was fairly certain her mother thought so too though she would never admit it. Cleaning up after a man and keeping a spotless house was not what Lydia aspired to; she wanted a career that would make a difference and make the world a better and safer place.

'OK, Mum. You think I do, what was it … a *worthy* job? So what was the "but" actually going to be about?'

'I just worry about you, Lyddie. All those murderers and criminals you have to deal with. I don't know what I'd do if anything happened to you – and you are our only one. Please take care.'

'Of course, Mum,' replied Lydia, placated now by a mother's obvious fear for her daughter's safety. 'I can look after myself, you know.'

'I hope so. Changing the subject, any boyfriend on the scene? It's been a while since Alex, hasn't it?'

Lydia shook her head. 'Far too busy for all that, Mum.'

'OK … Come on then, Lyddie. Let's get back – lunch will be ready.'

Christine and Lydia rose from the bench and together with Betsy wended their way back through the charming old university town. There was just enough time to browse the arts and crafts market stands in the town centre before entering Tennyson Close once more.

Throughout lunch – delicious as always – Lydia tried hard to sidestep her father's caustic remarks about the police and how it was not a "proper" force. Not like the RAF. Or the Army or Navy, for that matter. It was, though – as ever – the stereotypical gender ignorance that pressed Lydia's buttons.

'So, Lydia, are the other policemen in your department pulling their weight in the Radford case?' asked Patrick.

'Dad, not all police officers are "men", you know.'

'I know that. Lots of very fine policewomen have died in the line of duty. I hope you're being careful down there in London, Lydia?'

'Well, I have a bulletproof blouse, Dad. Colour co-ordinated to match my handbag.'

'No need to be sarky, my girl. I hope you don't speak to your superior officer like that.' Patrick slammed his glass of wine down on the table, spilling most of it as he did so.

The barbed comment hit its mark and Lydia flinched inwardly. She was indeed fully capable of being sarcastic to her boss, Chief Inspector Geoff Cordell, who had pulled her up on it on several occasions. Not only that, but her sharp tongue often run away with her when it came to her colleagues, as Nick for instance very well knew.

'Well, at least I know where I get it from, Dad. Maybe we should go into therapy together.' Lydia stared defiantly into her father's large blue eyes, so very like her own.

'Coffee anyone?' asked Christine.

Back on the Thames park bench, Lydia thought back to her mother's concern for her wellbeing and her prescient remark about murderers; she wondered if Felicity Radford had expressed similar worries to her daughter Belinda about living and working in a large cosmopolitan city. No doubt Christine would react in the same devastated manner as Felicity if anything happened to Lydia. Lydia's father's stubbornness and uncompromising nature inherited by his daughter, contributed – ironically – to the key attributes Lydia needed for catching Belinda's murderer and solving the case, as she was very well aware. She was just about to get up and go back to her office, when her mobile phone rang.

'Hi, Boss. Enjoy your lunch? Where are you, anyway?' The sound of Nick's voice brought Lydia back to the present with a jolt.

'Yes, thank you. Just on my way back to the office … I've read the preliminary forensic report – riveting reading, Nick – but there's nothing much in it that we haven't already figured out for ourselves really.'

'Indeed. Just to say I've arranged your meeting with Belinda's brother, Julian Radford, at his bank first thing tomorrow morning. Plus, I have the key to Belinda Radford's Chalk Farm flat on Haverstock Hill; we ought to go straightaway. Forensics are on the way; they've been itching to get in for the last day or two, but obviously have had to wait until your return from the New Forest. They need you to be there.'

'OK … meet me in the lobby of the Yard in about five minutes, Nick? Please.'

'Sure. On my way.'

Entering the dead woman's apartment, Lydia felt a keen sense of déjà vu. Like Lydia's own flat in Battersea, Belinda's home was tidy with a few soft touches such as reed diffusers and fluffy cushions. However, here at Chalk Farm, the sense of calm and order began to change once the forensics team of three, Norman Combe, Beth Monkton and Max Burgh, arrived, spread out and began their work.

'Very tidy, wasn't she, Boss?'

'Well, no man to mess things up!' teased Lydia.

'I don't know what you mean,' answered Nick, pretending to be offended. 'My girlfriend thinks I'm a whiz round the house, you know.'

'For a start, there are no man-shoes or battered trainers chucked down any old how in the hallway,' said Lydia, as they moved from the front door and into the open-plan lounge and kitchenette.

'No male jackets or anoraks decorating the backs of chairs or piles of man-things on the coffee table,' she continued, trusting that Nick would recognise she was being ironic.

'Man-things? Such as?' asked Nick innocently.

'Oh, you know – coins, lighters, bits of string ...'

'Ah, you mean useful things – the stuff we keep in our pockets that have to be emptied out and checked every day,' said Nick, playing along.

'Exactly. And look – all the washing up's been done,' continued Lydia as they took in the tiny yet immaculate kitchen with its built-in cream-coloured units including a slim-line dishwasher.

'I do all the cooking at home, Boss.'

'Sure. But I bet you use every pot and pan, and your girlfriend's the one that loads and unloads the dishwasher, eh, Nick?'

Nick nodded sheepishly. Moving around Max Burgh who was now dusting for fingerprints on the light work surfaces and dark furniture, and Norman Combe, the lead forensics expert, who was now carefully going through the contents of Belinda's desk drawers, Nick led the way to the tall dark wooden bookshelves on either side of a picture window that looked out onto a charming little courtyard garden, replete with colourful hanging baskets and trailing plants, to the rear of the flat.

'Lawbooks, lawbooks and yet more lawbooks. No chick lit or a detective novel to be seen,' noted Nick, running his eye along the shelves.

'Dedicated woman. Serious reader. The CD and DVD collections are more escapist though, Nick. Look – Miles Davis, Santana … "Twelve Angry Men", "To Kill a Mockingbird", "The Winslow Boy" …'

'Still, there's a definite courtroom theme going on here when it comes to films, Boss! Is your flat like this? Full of police handbooks and law movies?'

'Funny you should say that … yes – but I keep fact and fiction in separate rooms – so the police manuals and training DVDs are all in my office, and my fun reading and film collection are in my sitting room,' replied Lydia.

'Yes, Belinda doesn't seem to have had much of a boundary between work and pleasure, really.'

'Good point, Nick. Probably accounts for the early mornings and late evenings in the chambers. Totally devoted to her profession, which may have been her downfall in this case, of course. Being alone in the office with no one to call for help.'

Belinda's laptop was being wrapped and boxed by Beth Monkton, the number two in the forensics team, and a digital specialist. Underneath where the laptop had been lying, Lydia spotted some charity circulars almost obscuring a few pages of yellow paper containing print-outs that appeared, at first glance, to be blog entries and so she asked Beth to bag them up for examination later as well. Having finished downstairs, Lydia and Nick climbed the white-painted metallic spiral staircase that led up to a first floor consisting of two bedrooms and a spacious bathroom.

'This one's obviously Belinda's room,' said Lydia. 'Everything in its place ...'

'... no boxer shorts lying on the floor. Yes, I get the picture, Boss.' Nick reciprocated somewhat drily.

'Joking aside, this room must be the spare room. I wonder why she needed one, Nick? I mean it's completely neat and tidy – not full of old junk, like mine. Even though Belinda was obviously self-disciplined and organised, it just looks as though it's ready for someone to stay – even the bed's made up. Who would that be for, I wonder? And who were her friends?'

After a glance into the spotless bathroom where Belinda's makeup, tubs of face cream and a selection of expensive French perfumes were placed neatly in height order, Lydia and Nick descended the stairs once more, and let themselves out through the French doors into the tiny garden. It was a peaceful spot, shielded from the traffic noise of Haverstock Hill by brick walls covered in vines and creepers, themselves interplanted with hanging baskets full of flowers in vibrant hues of scarlet, orange and purple. Even the noise from The Limestone, a busy pub next door, did not penetrate this calm haven. There was a small mosaic-topped table with a clean metal ashtray on it, and two chairs positioned neatly on the stone slabs covering the entire garden.

'Hmm, well, the flat doesn't really tell us much more about Belinda's murder though it gives us a more of a picture of the person,' said Lydia, once they'd returned indoors. 'As far as we know, she didn't have a cleaner, so Belinda was tidy – almost obsessively so. Organised and efficient on the home front and at work – nothing was going to get in the way of her career.'

'Totally committed to the job,' agreed Nick. 'Hardworking and ambitious, too.'

And all that without the need of a man, thought Lydia. Do you see, Dad?

After bidding farewell to Norman, Beth and Max, Lydia and Nick parted ways outside the flat, as they were using different tube lines to get home.

'So, Nick – it's nearly Friday! I'm looking forward to putting Julian Radford through the wringer in the morning – and I'm taking Sergeant Davis with me.' Lydia added as she recognised Nick's eager look of anticipation. 'Thanks for coming with me today, though.'

'No problem. I'll check my emails when I get home later; see if anything else's come in while we've been out of the office.'

'Now who's the dedicated one? Working overtime, Nick?' Lydia teased.

'Well, I like to impress the boss, you know! Bye.'

As Lydia made her way home through the rush hour that was just beginning to reach its peak, she reflected further on the parallels between herself and Belinda. She knew that she too was as committed and ambitious as the murdered barrister. She also had a calm oasis of a home, unsullied by untidiness. I'm sure as hell not *quite* as tidy as Belinda though, she thought. Must have inherited that from Dad.

Chapter 7

Ad Valorem (in proportion to the value)

'Doing OK for yourself, then, Julian?' Lydia looked round the opulent, marble-floored foyer of the European Karienhaus Bank situated opposite Liverpool Street Station. Sergeant Clive Davis stood tall and silent behind her, notebook in hand; he had been instructed to quietly observe and take careful notes of Lydia's interview with Julian Radford who'd been happy to be addressed by his first name, as confirmed by Lydia's first meeting with him in Lymington two days earlier. Recording interviews electronically was more reliable in some ways but Lydia considered that she often had more leverage if she could dig deep with her questioning, safe in the knowledge that her acerbic tone would not be preserved for all eternity.

'Thank you. Not bad, actually,' replied Belinda's brother, looking rather smug and not at all in a state of bereavement, mused Lydia. Julian's expensively-cut pinstriped suit flattered his slim figure, but one too many business lunches would soon put paid to that, she thought.

'We could stay here, Detective, or go over to Spitalfields Market for coffee or tea, if you like?'

Lydia liked to interview her suspects on their own home ground or workplace, as it told her so much more about them, but then considered that the re-gentrified Spitalfields probably counted as Julian's territory – at least in his eyes. After all, he came from a background of vastly landed gentry in the New Forest.

'Sure. Do you know a quiet café with good coffee?' she replied.

Lydia glanced longingly at the stalls laden with colourful jewellery, imaginative artwork, exotically printed fabrics – all the things she loved to linger over – as Julian led the way through Spitalfields Market to a French-style coffee bar on a less crowded upper floor. Clive Davis trailed behind; he hated shops and markets and was looking forward to a big fat milky coffee to get himself in gear for the Friday morning ahead.

Seated, and with a glass of the bar's signature sweet *café bombón* in front of her, Lydia went in for the kill.

'So you didn't stay very long in Lymington this week, then? Don't your parents need you, Julian?'

Julian ran his hand through his immaculately-coiffed brown hair and took a sip of his black espresso. Lydia remembered from the search of the barristers' chamber and from the forensics report that Belinda had also had a taste for bitter coffee with no milk.

'As I told you on Wednesday, Detective, I had an important seminar to get back to. It's this afternoon, in fact, so I got back to London last night. I did actually stay in the New Forest for two whole days, you know.'

'Not long really, considering your sister's been murdered?'

'Well, there's nothing I can do, is there? And I can't afford to mess up with work.'

Lydia considered Julian's guileless expression and the lack of emotion in his dark brown eyes and thought that as he apparently hadn't been particularly close to Belinda, it was hardly surprising he wasn't more distraught about her death.

'What about your father? And your mother? They're so devastated.'

Julian had the grace to look slightly rueful and continued,

'I've been speaking to my mother on the phone every day actually … and I do feel sorry for her.'

'Nice. And your father, Julian?'

'He can cope – and he's got to keep the estate running. And anyway, real men don't cry, do they? That goes for me as well.'

Lydia sensed a crack in Julian's nonchalant façade, and decided to dig deeper. She loved to understand the motives and psychology behind human behaviour; "A Criminological Perspective" had been her favourite module while studying for her degree. It was one of the reasons she chose to pursue a career in the police force; not only could she bring wrongdoers to justice, but she could also learn more about why people acted the way they did. She would also be learning more about herself at the same time of course.

'Really? Has it been hard to keep up a front given that Belinda has been brutally killed – slaughtered, actually?'

Next to her, Clive Davis shifted uncomfortably in his seat. He was familiar with Lydia's killer instinct which belied her sympathetic tone of voice, and a small part of him felt secretly sorry for Julian Radford who had had no idea of the mauling that was on the cards.

'Ermm, well, yes. It's just that I've been a bit preoccupied recently—'

'Overtime at the bank? Counting the dollars?' Lydia snapped. Hardly pausing for breath, she continued, 'Where were you on Monday evening, Julian?'

Julian seemed confused by the sudden turn in questioning.

'The night before Belinda's murder. A whole three days ago. Remember? Don't play the busy man-about-town card with me. Where were you, Julian?'

'At home, I think.'

'You think? Come on now – don't waste my time. Were you at home or not?'

'Yes, at my house in Blackheath, Detective.'

'Did you go straight there from work or did you make a detour to Chalk Farm?'

Julian looked genuinely surprised, thought Lydia. Duly noted.

'Oh, you mean did I go to Bel's flat? No, I've only ever been there once and that was for a New Year's Eve do that she had – sort of a combined flat warming party and New Year's celebration. She insisted that I went – wanted to show off her successful baby brother to her friends I imagine, not to mention showing the world her trendy flat – incense … ugh! That was the last time I saw her, come to think of it.'

'What was it like? The party I mean,' Lydia asked.

'I remember the posh canapés – curried pakora, chicken tikka kebabs … that kind of thing. We never had anything exotic like that at home in the New Forest as kids, so I guess Bel went to town a bit. And I remember it was snowing.'

'Who was there?'

'Um, mostly work colleagues ... quite a boring lot, really. Just talked about court cases most of the time. Yawn. There was an older barrister, William Bond I think he's called, with a clerk woman who stuck to him like glue and a young smarmy one ... "Attorney" Anthony they called him – ha! His wife, who's an artist I believe, was quite fun though. The cleaner was there – his wife, Joanna, I think her name was – she was alright too. And there was a quiet guy – tallish, who I vaguely know from somewhere – helping to serve drinks and who I didn't speak to all evening.'

Julian rolled his eyes, obviously reliving an evening during which he was not able to impress many people with his sparkling career in banking, suspected Lydia.

'Going back to Monday, what time did you get home to Blackheath that evening, Julian?'

'Oh, er ... just after eight o'clock probably. That's usually about right on a weekday. And I stayed in all evening,' continued Julian, anticipating Lydia's next question.

'Can anyone corroborate that? Flatmates, maybe?'

'I live alone ... in my own house – not a flat,' Julian said, pride at his success in life emanating from his very pores, thought Lydia.

'So no one can vouch for you? What did you do all evening, Julian?'

Julian smirked and continued,

'I didn't say I was on my own, Detective. Just that I live alone. I was with someone actually … who can also vouch for me the next morning as well.'

Lydia glanced at Clive Davis, to make sure he was noting all this down.

'Name and contact details of the "someone", please,' she said.

'Is this confidential?' Julian enquired.

'That depends on what you tell us,' answered Lydia curtly.

'Well, I don't want details of my private life getting back to my parents. They wouldn't approve, especially not my father.'

This is when he tells us he's gay, thought Lydia. She replied,

'We don't divulge information to members of the public or to those who are connected to an investigation. So, no, we won't be telling your parents anything you tell us today.'

'OK. Precious …' began Julian.

Clive Davis's head shot up in surprise, and he paused, pen hovering over his notepad.

'Go on, Julian,' said Lydia.

'… Temishe. 49 London Road, Crystal Palace. I'm not sure of the exact postcode. SE something or other.'

Clive Davis interjected,

'So, is the name *Precious Temishe*? Just want to get my facts straight.'

'Yes, that's right. Precious is a junior doctor at Guy's Hospital. She's originally from Nigeria, but is training here in the UK. She's a practising trainee – very ambitious and works incredibly long hours …' Julian said with a hint of pride. 'She came to Belinda's New Year's Eve party with me.'

'And how long have you been seeing Ms Temishe?' Lydia asked.

'About a year now. She's doing so well, but my father would go berserk if he knew I was dating a … person of colour.'

'Really?' Lydia replied. 'Your father came across as a reasonable man to me, Julian. Surely he'd be fine with a mixed race relationship even if he does live in deepest darkest Hampshire?'

'Well, I don't want to take any chances with my inheritance, so I want to keep it quiet for now.'

Lydia thought that Julian's mercenary nature beggared belief. Gordon Radford's comment made during her visit to the New Forest estate that his son was only interested in money now made absolute sense.

'So you've been so preoccupied with Ms Temishe that you haven't given much thought to your own sister's murder?'

'I guess it does look a bit like that,' admitted Julian. 'But I want to be supportive to Precious; I want the relationship to work out. She's a great girl. We message each other all the time, and—'

'So who do you think killed Belinda?' Lydia pressed on in an attempt to steer Julian away from the fascinating topic of his girlfriend to the clearly less interesting one of his sister.

'Erm … don't know. Maybe a lowlife off the street? I do know that my sister liked to work lonely hours with nobody else around … a bit dangerous if you ask me. At least Precious is always surrounded by other doctors and nurses at Guy's.'

'OK. Julian. We'll be checking your alibi – please give Ms Temishe's telephone number to Sergeant Davis. We'll most likely be in touch again, so don't leave town without letting us know, please. Just another couple of questions. When did Belinda first meet your girlfriend?'

'At the party I told you about. She got on really well with my sister actually – but then Precious gets on well with everyone. And before you ask, yes, I did warn Bel to keep quiet about my relationship – she wasn't to tell our parents about it under any circumstances. Did you have another question? I need to get back to work.'

'Yes. Have you ever been to Belinda's place of work?'

'Ermm … no. We didn't see much of each other as I said.'

Lydia went to settle the bill, and after bidding Julian goodbye, she and Clive made their way back to New Scotland Yard.

'Would his parents really be that bothered about Precious Temishe?' Clive asked.

'Maybe before Belinda's death, but I don't think so any more – he's the only child now. And even if they are concerned, perhaps it will give them a bit of a shake-up. I mean, it's not exactly the Dark Ages even in the depths of the New Forest! Anyway, check Precious out and let me know as soon as you can.'

'Yes, Guv,' replied Clive. 'I'll type up the report on this morning's interview and get it over to you asap.'

On her way back to her office, Lydia looked in on Nick, who, like her, was based on the fourth floor of New Scotland Yard albeit with a view of open-plan offices with dying plants in their windows unlike Lydia's stunning panoramic outlook over the Thames.

'Hi Nick, how's it going?'

'Good thanks, Boss. Beth Monkton, the digital specialist from forensics, has already got back to us with her preliminary report on Belinda's laptop. Nothing out of the ordinary, so far. Just letters and emails pertaining to the Chalk Farm flat purchase last year, budget spreadsheets with tax and NI contributions, and some folders containing law documents and general information such as legal terminology in Latin – all available from the public domain. Nothing directly related to her work.'

'What about social media?'

'As far as Beth can see, Belinda wasn't on Facebook. But she was on LinkedIn – Beth's going through the contacts on there and will get back to us on that. How did the interview with the suave-but-cool Julian go?'

'OK. He's still a cold fish in my opinion. Appears to be more concerned about hiding his relationship with his girlfriend from his parents than about his sister's death.'

'Really? How come?'

'She's Nigerian and Julian thinks he might be cut out of his parents' wills if they knew. Ha! That would be comeuppance.' Lydia could not help but smirk a little at the thought of Julian's reaction if there was ever a serious chance of him not inheriting the family fortune. She continued,

'Apparently, Ms Precious Temishe will most probably be providing Julian with an alibi so he might be off the hook – for now, anyway. I tried pumping him as to whether he'd seen Belinda on the Monday evening – I was thinking along the lines that maybe they'd had an argument as a precursor to him killing her the next morning – but it seems not.'

'But is he still a suspect?' Nick asked.

'Oh yes. Belinda might have threatened to tell their parents about Precious for instance; if not on the Monday night, then maybe at some earlier point. That could have been motive enough for him to plan to do away with his own sister at a later date. Money means a lot to Julian … now of course he inherits everything.'

'Hmm. OK, let's keep it in mind. Boss, we've got Ben James, a rough sleeper coming in for a "chat" in about an hour. Sergeant Terry Glover just messaged me and he's bringing him in.'

'Good. Come and get me when he's here.'

Lydia barely had time to go to her office, check her computer for emails and knock back a coffee before Nick called her just after midday. On entering the interview room, her nostrils were assailed by a strong stench of urine, whisky, cigarette smoke and vomit. Great, she thought. It's like being round the back of a pub at throwing-out time. The smell emanated from what appeared to be a ragged scarecrow slouched at a table alongside Sergeant Terry Glover. Nick was sitting opposite and motioned Lydia towards the chair next to him.

'Afternoon everyone,' she said, sitting down.

'Detective Inspector Carlisle, this is Benjamin James of no fixed address,' said Nick.

Ben James was thin with long, straggly dark hair, streaked with grey and white. His face was long and furrowed with dirty wrinkles that covered every inch of his skin. His eyes when they met Lydia's were dark and empty.

'May I call you Ben?'

A slight nod encouraged Lydia to continue.

'How old are you, Ben?'

'Fifty – give or take a year or three,' came the muttered, gravelly-throated response.

'Why do you think Sergeant Glover has brought you in for questioning?'

'He picked on me! Just cos of the cat!'

Lydia looked inquiringly at Terry Glover, who said,

'Yes, I found Ben asleep this morning behind some bushes just opposite Weymouth House Chambers. Nice little den he's got there – sleeping bag surrounded by ciggy ends and a cat all cosied up to him. I remembered talk about that moggy on the day of the murder.'

'That's Mr Mews to you, if you don't mind,' interjected Ben, cackling hoarsely. 'Cos he sleeps in the mews, like me, geddit?'

'Thank you, Ben,' Lydia managed the slightest of smiles at Ben's attempt at humour and went on, 'do you remember anything about last Tuesday morning? That's three days ago,' prompted Lydia.

'It mighta been three days ago. It was the day I got a-woken up by doors opening and closing, footsteps running, someone falling over …'

'Falling over? What did you hear exactly?' Nick asked, looking up from his notes.

'In the side passage next to that law building. Someone came running along it, tripped over, dropped summat clangy – made one helluva noise.'

'Did you see anything?' asked Lydia.

'Nope. Kept me eyes shut and tried to get some more kip. And then the footsteps ran off.'

'What do you think the "clangy" thing was that was dropped?' Nick interjected.

'Dunno. Summat metal maybe. Like a … knife? I heard all about that lawyer lady that got done in – word on the street is that she got stabbed or slashed or summat. Once the cops started showing up, I vamoosed away from there. Just had time to pick up a fag end dropped by that guy what does the cleaning and went to hook up with me mates under Waterloo Bridge. Just got back to the mews last night – it's a good patch and it's all me own.' Ben yawned, clearly wanting to go back to sleep.

'OK, Ben. Thanks – you've been really helpful,' said Lydia. 'We might need to question you again so please stay in the vicinity.

'No worries, dearie. I ain't leavin' on a jet plane!'

Chapter 8

Per Pro (on behalf of)

The weekend had passed in a flash. In no time at all, Lydia was back at her desk at eight o'clock on Monday morning, going through the full forensic report on Belinda Radford's Chalk Farm flat, provided by Norman Combe. Fascinating though it was, Lydia found her mind wandering back to a conversation she had had on Saturday morning over coffee with her friend, Marie, after their fortnightly yoga class at the Oval Community Centre.

'You're very pensive, today, Lydia! Don't tell me the "prana" is finally working?'

'You know I don't really get all that life force meditation stuff, Marie! I do yoga just for fitness and to build up my core strength. No, I'm just thinking about a case I'm working on … I'm at a bit of a standstill.'

Lydia paused, pensively sipping her green tea.

'Is that the female barrister who was murdered last week? I read about it in the papers,' said Marie.

'Yes – Belinda Radford, poor thing. Four days in and we haven't really made much headway as to who the killer might be. Quite a lot of suspects all of whom are candidates in my opinion but no real leads yet. I'm not really supposed to talk about it but it's stressing me out a bit to be honest.'

'I know you can't discuss the details, Lydia, and I can assure you it won't go any further,' said Marie in a low voice despite them being the only ones in the café. 'But one thing I could suggest is that maybe you could retrace Belinda's steps exactly a week later to the day; you know, arrive at the barristers' chambers, have breaks when she had breaks, speak to her colleagues, and so on. It might give you a feeling, an insight, you know?'

'Marie, that's a great idea – no wonder you're a psychologist by trade! I do think I need to get into Belinda's mindset to try and get a handle on what might have triggered the attack on her. You know, come to think of it, Hercule Poirot always said that to catch a killer you had to understand the victim. Merci, mademoiselle.'

'Well, you can thank me when you catch the bastard. And when you get your next promotion – drinks on you!'

'Well, here's hoping. If not, I'll be changing careers.'

At eight thirty, Lydia picked up her notes and headed for Chief Inspector Geoff Cordell's office.

'Morning, Sir,' she began. 'Good weekend?'

Geoff Cordell was a fifty-something individual, fit and with a full head of dark blonde hair that made him rather handsome for his age in Lydia's opinion.

'Morning, Lydia. Fine, thank you.' Looking away from his computer, he continued, 'Thanks for sending the reports over on the Radford case – I'm fairly well up to speed so far. I've read your transcripts of the interviews with the parents from last Wednesday, and the brother on Friday. What are your feelings on them?'

'Well, Sir – I think the parents can be discounted. They weren't even in London at the time of the murder – their staff down in the New Forest have attested to that. Plus I can't imagine their devastation about Belinda's death is faked. Julian Radford though … he's a cool character – not to mention money-grabbing. I'm keeping an open mind on him even if his alibi does check out.'

Geoff nodded. 'Quite right. So, what's next?'

'Well, on Friday afternoon, we interviewed Ben James, a rough sleeper – I'll get the transcripts over to you as soon as possible. The work colleagues at the chambers are next. We're collecting full statements this week but first I'm going over to Weymouth House Chambers this morning to relive a day in the life of Belinda Radford. I mean, retracing her steps at work on the Monday before she was murdered on the Tuesday morning. See what I can pick up.'

'Excellent – good idea. I've got full faith in you, Lydia. Let me know if there's anything you need, resource-wise and so on. Delegate your other cases for the moment and focus on Belinda Radford. And keep me in the loop, please.'

'Of course. Thank you, Sir.'

Lydia left her superior's office with mixed feelings. She was grateful that she had more or less free rein in the investigation but at the same time the pressure to solve the murder was mounting.

Arriving at Weymouth House Chambers, Lydia hesitated before entering. She turned and observed how quiet the mews was even though it was mid-morning on a Monday. It would have been quieter still at six thirty on the mornings when Belinda chose to come in to work early. The only noise was the gentle snoring that sounded from behind the glorious rhododendron bush on the opposite side of the road. Ben, she thought.

'Come on in, Detective,' instructed the tinny voice from the intercom, and the black front door clicked open. The clerk to the barristers, Sharon Hardy, stood there and the musty odour Lydia had noticed the week before wafted gently towards her.

'Good morning, Ms Hardy,' Lydia began.

'Morning! Let's go straight up, I'll make you a cup of tea. Or would you prefer coffee? And I have some lovely fresh croissants, and—'

'Stop,' said Lydia who actually found herself holding up her hand as if to stem the tide of words streaming from Sharon Hardy. 'White coffee would be fine. But I'd like a quick look around down here on the ground floor first.'

Sharon looked slightly abashed, but not for long.

'No problem! I'll show you around. Here's the waiting room, those are the WCs and over there—'

'Yes, I know my way round. I'm here to retrace Belinda's possible movements a week ago to get an idea of her routine before we conduct the follow-up interviews with you all. Slight change of plan.'

'Oh, what a good idea,' gushed Sharon. 'Do you have any leads yet? Poor Belinda. My money's on that old tramp outside. Or maybe he's got an accomplice, or …'

At that moment, the front door bell rang and Sharon hurried to open it. Lydia took the opportunity to head for the cleaning room behind the ground floor stair well. Sam White, the cleaner, was there, packing away a vacuum cleaner; he was clearly ready to leave. His packet of cigarettes and lighter were on the draining board and he already had his leather jacket on.

'Hello – how are you? Is it still OK to call you Sam?'

'Oh, morning, Detective. Yeah, Sam's fine. Getting over poor Belinda's murder ... you know how it is ...' Sam did not appear particularly surprised to see Lydia and judging by his less than chipper demeanour, was still deeply affected by his discovery of Belinda Radford's dead body six days earlier. He continued, 'I'm just on my way out.'

'You told us that Belinda used to join you for a cigarette out in the courtyard sometimes. Can you cast your mind back and think whether she did that a week ago today? Last Monday morning?' Lydia refrained from adding that she was trying to figure out if anything had happened that day that might pertain to finding Belinda's killer; after all, Sam was still officially a suspect.

Sam looked thoughtful for a second or two.

'Yeah, I'm pretty sure she did. It would have been around eight o'clock and I was half way through my shift. I remember now – she was dreading the day ahead and needed a fag to calm her nerves. Something about a feedback meeting with Sir William. Wanted to fit in well, she said. But still wanted to be the best female barrister around! I told her I thought she probably was already and that she'd be fine.'

'Hmm. Did she seem nervous, Sam?'

'More wound up, if you know what I mean. Excited, kind of.'

'How long did Belinda stay down here with you?'

'Oh, about a quarter of an hour or so. She spent a couple of minutes stroking Tabs – that's—'

'Yes, I know who Tabs is. Otherwise known as Mr Mews,' interrupted Lydia.

Sam looked a little puzzled so Lydia enlightened him.

'The homeless gentleman who sleeps out in the mews has a different name for Tabs.'

'Ah, you mean Ben.'

'Yes. Incidentally, was Ben out there last Monday morning?'

'To be honest, Detective, I don't remember seeing or hearing him. But that doesn't mean he wasn't there, I guess.'

'Indeed,' replied Lydia, making her way to the open back door that led out to the small courtyard behind the building. She stood on the gravelled ground and tried to imagine Belinda and Sam enjoying a smoke and each other's company. After she had re-entered a few moments later, Sam locked the back door from the inside and they walked back out into the vestibule together.

'Do you always leave and enter by the main front door, Sam?'

'Yeah. The back door is only unlocked when I'm actually in the cleaning room. Plus there's the microwave and fridge in here – can't be too careful these days …'

'Sure. We'll be in touch again soon. Would it be alright for us to visit you and your wife at home later this week? Say, Thursday morning?'

'Yeah, no problem at all. Let me know roughly when and we'll sort it out timewise with work.'

'Much obliged, Sam. See you then.'

Lydia bade the cleaner farewell and turned to leave; as she did so, she caught sight of a photo attached to the fridge by a magnet. It was of nine people all facing the camera, smiling and raising glasses of bubbly. Behind them, through the window, it was clearly snowing. Must have been Belinda's New Year's Eve party, she thought. I wonder who took the photo?

Popping her head round the door of the ground-floor clients' waiting room, Lydia greeted the well-dressed couple in their thirties sitting quietly together on a black leather settee. Before she could introduce herself, however, a familiar strident voice called out from behind her, making her jump.

'Detective! Do come on up – kettle's on!'

Lydia smiled at the clients apologetically, and followed Sharon up the stairs to the first floor, averting her eyes from the unwelcome sight of the clerk's too tight beige trousers which revealed her untoned behind and podgy ankles. Lydia was led to the room where she and Nick had conducted their preliminary interviews the day of the murder; the first-floor archive room, she remembered.

'Thank you, Ms Hardy. Would Belinda have come in here last Monday at this time?'

'Possibly! To look something up maybe. Usually, though, she just went straight up to her desk in the chambers.'

'Well, the chambers is where I want to go then. Did I say that I was retracing Belinda's steps today?'

'Of course you did, Detective. No problem, let's carry on up then!'

Sharon took the lead once more, and panting slightly, paused for breath as they reached the top floor. Lydia could not help but notice their reflection in the large gilt-framed mirror she'd noticed before that was positioned opposite the top step; her tiny sparrow-like frame contrasted with Sharon's stocky figure to an almost comical extent. Little and Large, thought Lydia.

'By the way, Ms Hardy, who were those people down in the waiting room?'

'Mr and Mrs Faith. Steven and Amanda. Esteemed clients … Sir William's case,' replied Sharon, once she'd got her breath back. 'Only today, he's asked Attorney Anthony to go over it with them.'

'Oh? Why's that?'

'Sir William's sister's been taken ill, and he's got to go down to Kent to help. He's all she's got – neither of them are married, and—'

'Has he already left?'

'No, you should just be able to catch him. He's come in to check his emails, collect some documents and so on. And always time for a cuppa! And a pastry, of course!' Sharon grinned affectionately at the thought of her boss enjoying her generous offerings before turning and clomping off down the stairs.

'Of course,' echoed Lydia, addressing Sharon's back. God, this over-helpful woman was getting on her nerves.

The barristers' chambers looked very different from the previous week's scene of crime, thought Lydia. No longer crawling with fingerprint experts, forensics personnel and police photographers, the room felt calm and professional. Only the tall shelves of lawbooks seemed to be on the alert – watching every move that Lydia and the two men in the room made. Anthony Greenwood was standing behind his desk, gathering files and documents. His expensively-cut suit accentuated his slim lean build as ever.

'Morning, Mr Greenwood.'

'Good morning, Detective,' replied the lawyer smoothly. 'We meet again.'

Lydia felt the same jolt of chemistry as she had the previous week, as her eyes met his bright blue ones with their intensive gaze.

'Mr Greenwood,' she began.

'Do call me Anthony. Any news on Belinda? I'm afraid I have to see some clients right now; is there another time we could meet?'

Was that a double-entendre, or was he just being polite, wondered Lydia.

'We'll contact you to come to the station this week for a formal interview … Anthony.'

Anthony nodded, and armed with his paperwork, strode out of the room. Lydia turned to the other man, seated at his desk and glued to his computer screen.

'Sir William – nice to see you again. I understand you've been called away?'

'Hello, Detective Carlisle. And remember – just William's fine,' came the clipped reply from QC Sir William Bond. In contrast to Anthony Greenwood, he was rather more stodgy in build, and his pinstriped suit, though obviously rather costly, did not flatter his large frame. He went on, 'Yes, I do apologise – I'm leaving now. My elder sister's very unwell – she's got Alzheimer's and has had a fall. I'm catching a train down to Whitstable in an hour. Have you found out anything about poor young Belinda's murder yet?'

'I'm here to get a feel for Belinda's last full day at the chambers a week ago today, and we're conducting formal interviews with all her work colleagues later this week at the station. I really wanted to start with you as you're the senior tenant here … I was just wondering if it would be convenient if I and DI Fairman came down to Whitstable tomorrow and met you there to take a fuller statement? I really don't want to waste any time, and as you're not going to be here in London—'

Showing no surprise at all at what might have seemed an unorthodox approach, Sir William replied,

'That would be absolutely fine. Anything to help. I've got an office in the Whitstable house – I often work on my cases there. Eleven o'clock?'

'Great, thank you.' Lydia took down the address, and the lawyer switched off his computer, nodded to Lydia, picked up his briefcase and left.

Alone in the chambers, Lydia wandered over to the tri-fold screen and admired its stunning pastoral landscape. The screen concealed the coffee corner in which Belinda had been standing when her throat was cut from behind. It was where the detective had had her first glimpse of the murdered woman, and she tried once more to imagine what went through Belinda's mind in those final fatal seconds. Not much, Lydia hoped.

'Ah, there you are, Detective!' Sharon's loud voice suddenly burst into the calm of the room like a gunshot on a silent moor. 'Your coffee's ready!'

Lydia spent the rest of the day sitting at Belinda's desk or wandering around the building, soaking up the atmosphere of a working day at Weymouth House Chambers. This mainly consisted of a slow trickle of clients coming in to see Anthony Greenwood, the efforts of a young temp who had been drafted in to help Sharon with admin, and a deluge of beverages thrust upon her every half an hour by the omnipresent clerk to the barristers.

For bleeding hell's sake. Belinda, Belinda, Belinda – that's all they talk about. Stupid bitch is dead but she won't lie down. I got rid of her, didn't I? Glad to see the back of her, I am. No more strutting around thinking she's better than all the men in the whole wide world; no more top barrister in London for her now. Just goes to show being "academic" and "intellectual" doesn't always pay, does it? I did enjoy that coup de grass or grace or whatever it's called – a mercy killing for dear Belinda. Just as Father showed me. Brilliant at the one clean slash, he was. No messing around chopping and hacking, no squealing and screaming from my darling Porky-Worky, was there? That was a relief, though, really. Belinda didn't squeal either – no time! That's how good I was to her ... not that she would have thanked me. Only interested in herself and being "independent" – duh! How hard is that actually? Enjoyed showing off though, didn't she – like that stupid party thing she had on New Year's Eve: oh, welcome to my fancy new flat! Have a cauliflower bhajee, won't you? Pretending to be all friendly as if she actually meant it – any other time, cool as a cucumber, wanting everyone to look up to her. Never appreciated my help and advice, ever. Looked me up and down and paid me compliments but I knew she was really thinking I could lose a pound or two. Still, no more of that nonsense! Mind you, that detective needs to watch her step round me as well. Skinny cow – and those big blue eyes! Reminds me of Nanny, before her head got chopped off. That was a bit sad – and I was surprised that there wasn't more blood really. But as Father said, man up, waste not want not, and enjoy your Sunday roast leg of goat. Appreciate what you're given. Not like stupid Belinda – never grateful for anything. Still, the funeral should be a laugh. I can't wait.

Chapter 9

Ex Parte (done by one side only)

Enjoying the warm breeze, Nick looked less pallid than usual – that's London for you, thought Lydia.

'Enjoying the sea air, Nick?'

'It's great, Boss. Reminds me of when I was a kid; we often used to come down here to Whitstable or one of the next towns along – Herne Bay or Margate.'

Lydia was pleased she had asked Nick to accompany her to interview Sir William Bond at his home on the Kent coast.

'Good of you to come, Nick, and thank you for driving us. Sorry about the short notice.'

'No problem. How did you get CI Cordell to agree to this little jaunt?'

'Well, he trusts my innate wisdom and judgement of course, Nick! No, really he sanctioned it due to it being a high-profile murder case with no time to lose. He even offered to do the press briefing in my stead today.'

'Cool. So what did you learn by reliving Belinda's last day yesterday?'

'Well, it mainly reaffirmed what we felt when we visited her flat – she was a very organised person, efficient and routine-oriented. Not spontaneous really, especially in her working life. It would therefore be easy for anyone who knew her even a little to work out where and when she would be at any given time.'

'Tragic to think that by being so dedicated meant that her routine was predictable enough to get her murdered. On another note, I've arranged for Sharon Hardy to come into New Scotland Yard tomorrow morning, and Anthony Greenwood in the afternoon. Thursday morning I've agreed for Sam White to be interviewed in Sydenham as he's working locally there, so it's worked out well that we see head man, William Bond, first off today. And I do like a day out of the office as you know!'

The view from their waterside café was idyllic. Fishing boats bobbed around in the enclosed harbour, and pleasure cruisers offered daytrips out to view the wind farm and the imposing sea forts guarding the Thames estuary, or to go seal watching. The sun was shining and the sea was a sparkling blue colour. A perfect spring day despite the light wind. Lydia glanced thoughtfully through her notes on the table in front of her.

'I'm hoping we'll get a breakthrough by the end of this week. It's now exactly one week to the day since the murder last Tuesday. The final forensics reports should be in soon and we may have more of a picture then.'

'Indeed,' answered Nick. 'I wonder what William Bond's set-up is?'

Lydia was also keen to see the QC on his own territory; it was so very much more enlightening to understand a person in surroundings that were familiar to them. You never knew what they might inadvertently give away about themselves – another crossover between Lydia's interest in psychology and her police work. Thank goodness Geoff Cordell endorsed this particular aspect of her policing style.

'OK. Let's get going, Nick. If we're lucky, we might even have time to have some oysters for lunch afterwards.'

Shortly before eleven o'clock, having parked on the neatly tended gravel drive of a handsome sixties property in Whitstable's Joy Lane, Lydia and Nick stood before an imposing white front door. Before Lydia could even ring the bell, the door opened and a young blonde woman in a nurse's uniform smilingly welcomed them and ushered them in.

'Good morning, Detectives. I'm Olive Westbrook, Jennifer Bond's carer.'

'Hello, Ms Westbrook. Is that a South African accent I detect?' Lydia asked as they were led through a dark hallway guarded by an enormous, almost brooding, grandfather clock, to an altogether much brighter living room with a stunning panorama of the coast through the large picture window.

'Yes, that's right. I took this job to experience life in the UK ... the pay is good – at least compared to Johannesburg,' replied the nurse. 'Do take a seat. Tea? Coffee? Or a cold drink – we've got some lovely fresh elderflower lemonade? And I'll go and inform Sir William that you're here.'

Lydia and Nick both accepted the offer of cool elderflower lemonade, and sat back to enjoy the sea view. A few minutes later, William Bond entered, followed by Olive bearing their drinks and a plate of homemade cookies. Crikey, thought Lydia. What with Sharon in London and Olive in Whitstable, William certainly has his sweet tooth catered for all right. His portly physique was less evident today though, as he had ditched his expensive London suit for more casual and loosely-fitting shirt and trousers.

'Hello again, Detective Carlisle. Long time, no see.'

'Indeed,' replied Lydia, smiling at the QC's attempt at humour, and noting again his clipped and educated manner of speaking. 'William, I think you know my colleague, DI Nicholas Fairman.'

'Lovely place you've got here,' said Nick pleasantly. 'Been here long?'

'Thank you. Well, I bought this house about twenty years ago. It's been a boon now that Jennifer is so unwell, as there's space for the live-in carer whom you've just met, and I can bring work home from time to time.'

'Are you from the area originally?' asked Lydia.

'Yes – from Dunkirk.' William added, noting the detectives' puzzled looks, 'not the one in France. The one here is a small village between Canterbury and Faversham, and is also called Dunkirk.'

'Did you grow up in … Dunkirk?' enquired Nick.

'Yes. My parents had a smallholding – some grazing land for sheep and a couple of goats. We also kept rabbits, and there were dogs and cats galore.'

'That must have been fun for you and your sister,' remarked Lydia.

'It was. Jennifer still remembers parts of our childhood – in her more lucid moments, naturally. She sometimes asks for a pram. As a child, she used to wheel one around with her pet hen in it, like a mother with her baby.'

'And you? Did you enjoy life surrounded by animals, too?' Nick managed to sound suitably interested, thought Lydia.

'I did, yes, though not as much as my sister. After I'd gone to university to study Law, Jennifer stayed on and helped our parents on the farmstead – until they died, actually. Eventually, we sold the old place and moved here – much easier to run, and the sea air is wonderful. I've kept a few items that belonged to the old folks – like the grandfather clock and a few pieces of furniture – a comfort to poor Jennifer, you know.'

'Did either of you ever marry?' Lydia hoped she had hit a conversational tone, rather than a probing one. However, William continued quite chattily,

'No, sadly. No children either. But my sister and I have always been close – I come down here a couple of times a month from my flat in Covent Garden. More often than before now, as Jennifer's prone to falling these days. That's why I came down yesterday, as you know.'

Noticing that Lydia and Nick had finished their drinks, he said,

'Shall we go through to my office, Detectives? I know you'll be wanting to take my statement and it's more conducive there. No views of the sea to distract us.'

Sir William's office was indeed a serene and orderly space, dominated by a large antique walnut desk; it was here that Nick set up his recording equipment before formally cautioning the QC.

'Thank you for agreeing to see us today, William,' began Lydia. Glancing at her notes, she continued, 'I've got several questions … firstly, please could you summarise who is attached to, or works at Weymouth House Chambers?'

'Of course. As you are aware, I'm the Senior Tenant – I've been at Weymouth House Chambers for two – no, nearly three – years now. I offered Anthony Greenwood a tenancy about a year ago and Belinda joined in December. Then there's Sharon Hardy, our clerk, who's employed at the chambers – as opposed to us self-employed barristers – she's been there for years; we inherited her! She keeps us all toeing the line, thank goodness! Plus there are sometimes temporary admin staff to help out at busy times and Samuel White the cleaner who comes in most mornings … he started around six months ago.'

'So, apart from Ms Hardy, you're quite a new group really,' observed Lydia. 'This leads me to my second question. Who preceded you and why did they leave?'

'My predecessor was Sir Richard Weymouth, who originally set up the chambers – he retired and I bought them from him. He's passed away now, sadly. Anthony replaced a young man who ultimately decided that the legal profession was not for him … his name was James Chapman. There was also another tenant originally – John Flint. Belinda was his replacement—'

'Could you tell me why he left?' Lydia decided not to mention that she'd already requested a background report on John Flint; it would be interesting to see what Sir William would say.

'Well, to be honest, he didn't really fit in ... we tenants have to get along, you know, especially when there are so few of us in one office!' William continued, 'it caused a bit of bad blood at the time, but eventually about six months ago John decided to move on to pastures new.'

'Did he resent Belinda taking his place?' asked Lydia.

'I don't think so, really. He only met her once or twice – and even handed over some of the cases he was dealing with to her ... I believe he's got his sights set on moving to Australia actually.'

'OK. My next question ... were there any other contenders for the role apart from Belinda?' asked Lydia.

'Yes, there were quite a few actually – Anthony, Sharon and I debated hard and fast! Before you ask, I admit it's rare for a barristers' clerk to be so involved in the "recruitment" process, but Anthony and I were fairly new and she was more than happy to help, seeing as she was familiar with the way things are run at Weymouth House. She knows everything about everything.'

Of course she does, thought Lydia, who went on,

'So how did you come to choose Belinda?'

'Well, Anthony and Sharon would have preferred a man, I think – but I felt Belinda stood out from the crowd. Fresh, enthusiastic – a little self-deprecating ...'

'In what way?' interjected Lydia.

'Oh, she mentioned how she was a simple girl at heart, up from the country and so on. But I saw through all that and felt that she'd be a sincere and dedicated associate. Smartly dressed as well, and good looking.'

'Is that a prerequisite for the job?' The words were out before Lydia could stop them. She remembered William's comments the previous week about Belinda's prettiness and could not resist the urge to fish around a little.

'Er, no, of course not. But it helps. Good for the clients, you know?'

'No, I don't, actually. But anyway, you took Belinda on, and you mentioned last week that she was getting on quite well professionally?'

'Very well, in my opinion. She was assiduous and committed herself to leaving no stone unturned for her clients. Great in court, and wonderful to get along with in chambers. As I mentioned before, I did feel she was overdoing it on the work front – no need for all those late nights and early mornings, really. I told her so at her feedback meeting –'

'Ah, yes, the feedback meeting. That was last Monday, wasn't it?' asked Lydia.

'Yes ... the day before she ...' William choked up a little, and continued somewhat tearily, '... I knew she was nervous, but it was only an informal meeting to check how she felt about Weymouth House and us, of course! From my perspective, I told her, she'd adjusted well and I especially praised her for the high-profile cases she had dealt with. She was delighted and told me that she loved the sense of camaraderie, even if we do sometimes represent opposing clients! She also said that her extra hours had obviously paid off. I doubt whether she would have stopped coming in early and staying late, though – Belinda really wanted to be more than successful. Dear girl.'

Despite William's old-school chauvinism, Lydia felt that he had been genuinely fond of Belinda. She decided to change the line of questioning.

'Just a couple more questions. Where were you on the evening *before* Belinda's body was found?' she asked.

William did not appear unnerved by the sudden turn in questioning; probably used to it in the courtroom, guessed Lydia.

'Oh, you mean last Monday night? I was at the ballet … at The Royal Opera House in Covent Garden. One of the reasons I chose to buy a flat in Covent—'

'What did you see?' interrupted Nick; it was clear from his tone of voice that he would be checking on William's story.

'"Mayerling". It was a brilliant performance – do you know it, Detective?'

Nick shook his head.

'I would highly recommend it – full of intrigue and connivance. And before you ask, no, I wasn't with anyone. The usherettes will remember me though – I go so often to see operas and ballets that they know me very well there.'

'So you didn't go to Belinda's flat at all on the Monday evening?' asked Lydia, the idea of a late-night contretemps leading to a violent crime the following morning floating around in her mind.

William really did look surprised this time.

'No! I've only ever been there once – she invited the whole chambers to a New Year's Eve do at her flat ...' William flushed slightly, and Lydia went in for the kill.

'Yes, we know about the New Year's Eve party. How long did you stay?'

'Well, I was one of the last ones to leave – having such a good time, you see.'

'And how good a time was that, William?'

'Oh – it wasn't what you think, Detective. I gave her a peck on the cheek at the end of the evening … I'd had a little too much to drink, I dare say, and I wasn't driving due to the snow. But Belinda made it clear that that was as far as it would go … very diplomatic she was. She had her young man there, you see … I'd momentarily forgotten and got carried away! Rather embarrassing, in fact. But work comes first, and when we started back at the chambers in the New Year, we both acted as if nothing had happened.'

'I see,' said Lydia. 'And were there any other "personal" moments between you and Belinda from New Year's Eve up until her murder last week?'

'No, Detective, none at all. She'd made her feelings known and I respected her for that, naturally.'

'And my final question. Moving on to last Tuesday morning. What time did you arrive at Weymouth House?'

'Just after eight. I was met by the police and shown into the clients' waiting room – I met your own good self there shortly afterwards, if you remember?'

'Yes, I do. Is that the time you usually get into work?'

'No! It's more likely to be nine or nine thirty. Very, very occasionally I get in earlier if there's something particular going on … I always let Sharon know when I do that – she gets coffee and cakes or biscuits ready so that breaks me in gently to the day! But I particularly recall that on that morning I had in fact got up and dressed especially early to interview my new cleaner at my Covent Garden flat. She arrived at the ungodly hour of seven a.m. – something to do with her children – and I hired her on the spot. I showed her round the flat and we chatted a little. Then I got the call from Sharon to go straight to chambers as something had happened to Belinda. We both left the flat at about five to eight.'

'Can she verify that, William?' asked Lydia.

'I should think so; I went through a housekeeping agency, so they'll have all the details. Her name is Anastasiya something or other … Ukrainian.' Sir William took out a visiting card from "A Clean Sweep" housekeeping agency and handed it to Lydia.

'Are you still of the opinion that an intruder killed Belinda?' interjected Nick; he had obviously re-read the preliminary interview notes, thought Lydia approvingly.

'Yes. Collateral damage, no doubt. Perhaps a tramp or burglar broke in to see what they could steal and were surprised to find Belinda there so early, and … committed the atrocity.'

'OK, thank you, William. That will be all for now.' Lydia nodded to Nick to stop recording. As if on cue, the door opened, and Olive popped her head into the room.

'Sir William, Jennifer wants to see you – would that be alright?'

'Of course. Bring her in, please.'

A couple of moments later, Olive reappeared, holding the hand of William's sister. Jennifer was obviously rather older than her brother – probably in her mid-sixties – though similar in appearance, thought Lydia. She had fine grey hair and was somewhat stocky in build; her voice, however, had no trace of the rather intimidating courtroom tone of William.

'Willemmy …' Jennifer said tremulously. 'I can't find Honeybun. Where is she, Willemmy?'

'Now, now, Jen. You know Honeybun's in Heaven with Ma and Father. She's quite alright. Now, say hello to the nice detectives, and then Olive will give you some toast and golden syrup.'

Jennifer obliged by dipping a curtsey to Lydia and Nick, giggled, and then scuttled out of the office, pulling Olive by the hand after her. William looked fondly at her retreating back, and then rather apologetically at the detectives.

'Poor thing. She can't help herself, you know.'

After the goodbyes, Lydia and Nick sat in their car for a couple of moments, before turning and making their way back down William's drive.

'So what do you make of it all, Boss?'

'Well, I think William is kind-hearted and a gentleman, really, even if he is a bit old school when it comes to being PC. "Dear girl!" "Usherettes!" He needs a lesson in the twenty-first century.' Like my own father, thought Lydia.

Nick nodded and went on,

'I don't see much of a motive for killing Belinda. Unless you consider his mortification at Belinda rebuffing his tender advances after the New Year's Eve party.'

'Indeed. He glossed over it a bit in my opinion but it might actually have been terribly humiliating for William deep down,' said Lydia reflectively. 'And for all we know, he might still have been trying it on with Belinda ever since. Perhaps she resisted him once too often.'

'Well, we'll check out his alibi about the opera house and the cleaner, and I suggest we keep him on our radar for now. So, Boss, what about those oysters you promised me?'

'Agreed. And yes to oysters. And we could treat ourselves to some special Whitstable ale as well. I wonder if there's an alcohol-free version?'

Chapter 10

Alibi (elsewhere)

Lydia was not looking forward to the formal interview with Sharon Hardy, first thing Wednesday morning. Just thinking about how to steer the conversation away from the clerk to the barrister's free-association style of talking gave her a headache.

'Morning, Ms Hardy,' she began. 'DI Fairman – I see you have the recorder set up. Please could you read the caution and then we'll begin.'

Nick obliged and Lydia opened her mouth to ask the first question. Too late; Sharon Hardy hijacked Lydia's carefully planned script of questions.

'Funny to be here at New Scotland Yard and see you both at work in your natural habitat so to speak! It was only two days ago that you were at the chambers, Detective, and I was making you coffee! How's Sir William? And dear Jennifer? Any news about poor Belinda? I think—'

'Wait, Ms Hardy. I'm asking the questions,' said Lydia in most imperious voice she could muster, wondering how Sharon knew about their visit to Whitstable the day before; she certainly hadn't mentioned it to her. Oh yes, she thought – Sharon knows everything, of course; she must be in constant touch with Sir William.

Sharon Hardy sat back in her chair which seemed to be rather too small for her bulk and folded her arms across her not insubstantial bosom.

'Thank you, Ms Hardy. Now, let's start again. So, I'd like to ask you about Monday last week – the day before Belinda was murdered. How did she seem to you?'

'Ooh, now let me think. Well, she was a bit nervy first thing because she had a feedback session with Sir William that day. But I put her right – everyone comes to me for a bit of sympathy, you know. Sir William himself—'

'OK. And later, after the feedback session – how was Belinda then?' enquired Lydia.

'Oh, cheered up completely. It all went well – just as I told her it would! So I went out and bought some cream cakes to celebrate! I hold those chambers together you know – nothing like tea and a pat on the back. Been there longest of them all, I have—'

'Yes, so you told us,' interrupted Lydia. 'Where were you on the Monday evening before the murder?'

'At home, alone – not with Belinda, if that's what you're thinking, Detective! Yes, by myself all evening. Except for Ruskin of course and when I took him out for his walk in the cemetery.'

Nick raised an eyebrow, and Sharon continued cheerfully,

'I live in Nunhead right opposite the south entrance to Nunhead Cemetery. It's not just graves, you know! Brilliant place for walking a dog and there's a wildlife pond, and you can go blackberry picking in the autumn and—'

'Can anyone vouch for you?' put in Lydia.

'Oh yes! Lots of other dog walkers out and about at the same time – usually between seven and eight in the evening. And I walk Ruskin the mornings, too! All our dogs are friends! It's a social thing for them. Like I said—'

'Thank you. Moving on to the Tuesday morning, I understand you arrived at the chambers at seven forty-five. Is that the time you usually get into work?'

'Yes, that's right. Nice and early! Like to get the place set up and ready for the day. Sir William and Attorney Anthony appreciate that, you know. They don't normally get in until later and it gives me time to prep their coffee and biscuits! Sometimes I stay on a little in the evenings as well – top and tail the day, I do!'

'And what about Belinda? She also liked to work early sometimes and stay late, didn't she?' interjected Nick.

'Yes – she would run it by me so that I knew what was going on and we made sure we arranged between us who was going to lock up at night. Mornings weren't such a problem as the cleaner starts quite early and often unlocks the front door and turns off the alarm. Talking of that awful Sam White …'

Tiring of forever interrupting Sharon's flow of words, Lydia nodded to indicate that the clerk could continue on the fascinating topic of Sam.

'… I don't trust that cleaner, Detectives! Always smoking, and leading poor Belinda down that path as well! And not just nicotine either …'

Sharon's voice had dropped to a whisper, so that Lydia and Nick were obliged to lean in more closely to hear her. Loves an audience, thought Lydia, resisting the urge to wrinkle her nose at Sharon's whiffy body odour.

'I've smelt that marijuana stuff sometimes. At least I think that's what it is, not ever having smoked it myself of course! Sort of like cheesy socks?'

'Do any of your other colleagues – apart from Belinda – smoke as far as you know, Ms Hardy … nicotine or otherwise?' asked Nick.

'No! Sir William and Attorney Anthony just wouldn't do such a thing …'

'What about any clients?' Nick was not going to let Sharon Hardy off the hook, noted Lydia.

'Well, occasionally, if they're a bit nervous or something, they might ask if they can light up … then we send them out to the back courtyard. And just normal ciggies of course – can't have them smoking out the front in the mews! Wouldn't look good for Weymouth House, would it?'

Just for once, Sharon actually ended a sentence with a question, and Lydia quickly jumped in.

'Indeed not, Ms Hardy. You mentioned before that you thought the murderer might have been someone from outside having entered the building – a homeless person, or a—'

'Yes! Definitely a vagrant. Maybe that one that sleeps under the rhodo bush out front or … or … one of his tramp buddies. Easy enough to sneak in through the courtyard seeing as that dopy cleaner always leaves the back door unlocked – to let that moggy in he says! I'm a dog person myself, you know. And—'

'You suggested the use of a knife before', said Lydia, glancing down at her notes. 'How did you come upon that idea?'

'Oh! That nice policeman told me when I came in on the morning of the murder. Terry, was it?'

Damn and blast him, thought Lydia employing some of her father's favourite expletives. Note to self; words with Terry about his loose tongue.

'Tell me about the cases being handled in the chambers,' Lydia said, hoping that the change in questioning direction might throw Sharon off her track. However, to her chagrin, Sharon, undaunted, took it in her stride.

'Well, we have a good number at the moment ... but, Detectives, what about client confidentiality?'

'It's a murder investigation, Madam,' interjected Nick.

'Oh, yes, of course! Well, that's alright then, isn't it? Let me see ... there are several litigation cases and lawsuits ongoing – well, for example, there's the Wall sisters ... that's one of Sir William's cases; the Grace family is Attorney Anthony's ... just about to go to court on that one, he is; Belinda was working on the Allan v. Broughton case, and one with Misses Bigbury and Warriner. And as you know, the Faiths with Sir William—'

'Ah, yes, I briefly met them,' said Lydia. 'Could you give me more details about their case?'

For the first time during the interview, Sharon Hardy seemed to hesitate, thought Lydia. Well, well, well.

'Ermm … well, it's a civil suit to do with the company they work for. Sir William is dealing with it – Steven and Amanda Faith knew him from way back when he used to live in Kent and asked their solicitor to hire Sir William to represent them in court.'

'Do the barristers work together on cases at all? Sir William seems to be a busy man being senior tenant *and* having to manage his sister's care,' remarked Lydia.

'It doesn't really work like that, Detective! They're all essentially self-employed and just work on their own individual cases. Having said that, Sir William liked to help Belinda build up her knowledge, so he had her look up the finer points of things like intentional tort law sub-clauses for him; he'd make out he'd forgotten a detail, but really it was to boost her confidence and give her some background experience – kind soul that he is! So thoughtful, you know, and—'

Here we go again, thought Lydia. She asked, 'What's tort law?'

'Oh, it's all to do with suffering harm or losses due to a so-called civil wrong which could lead to legal liability,' came the confident reply. Sharon went on, 'like a wet floor in a factory could cause someone to slip and break their leg and the factory would then be liable if the person suffered pain or loss of earnings, and—'

'Do the Faiths work in a factory?' Lydia interrupted.

'No! They're employed by Tanleigh Auto Dealers UK, you know, the car company … they're both based in the Bromley showroom. Steven Faith is a salesman, and Amanda is too – but she also does the publicity side of the business.'

'So what's the "civil wrong" they're bringing?' Lydia tried her best to keep up with the legal jargon.

'Something to do with Amanda being knocked down by a car while it was being reversed into the showroom. I don't think she was badly hurt!' Sharon added, when she saw the look of concern on Lydia's face. 'Probably broke her stilettos!'

'OK. So what's "intentional" tort law?' Nick intervened.

Sharon looked slightly shifty at this, but explained,

'Oh, er … well, that's when a person might "accidently-on-purpose" suffer an accident in order to sue or make a claim, you see.'

'So is that what's going on with the Faiths?' asked Lydia.

'Ermm … yes, Detective. And before you ask, I have to admit that I don't think Belinda was very happy about it … Sir William probably had to help her to understand the legalities. What she didn't realise is that intentional tort happens all the time. I had to put her right on that! "Sir William knows what he's doing, dear," I told her more than once. I know all about these things, and—'

'I see. Just one more question; did you go to Belinda's New Year's Eve party?' asked Lydia, knowing she had, but curious to observe Sharon's reaction.

'Of course! She would never have *not* invited me – very close we were!'

'OK, that will be all for now, Ms Hardy. If I need to ask you any more questions, I'll visit you in Nunhead, if I may?'

'Yes, of course! I guess you detectives want to see us on our home territory! I'll bake some flapjacks! And you can meet Ruskin!'

Sharon Hardy heaved herself from her seat, and tromped out of the interview room, leaving behind a waft of her peculiar bodily scent, which Lydia now realised contained accents of stale dog.

After lunch, it was the turn of Anthony Greenwood.

'Good morning, Detectives.' The lawyer's voice was velvety smooth and his clear blue eyes met those of Lydia who was ready for the charm offensive this time. She smiled engagingly back at Anthony before instructing Nick to read the official caution and to start recording.

'Hello, is it still alright to call you Anthony?' Lydia began.

'Of course. No problem.' Anthony gave her a flash of his brilliant white teeth. Veneers no doubt, guessed Lydia. He can afford them.

'So, I'd like to begin by asking you about the Monday before Belinda was murdered. Were you in chambers that day, Anthony?'

'Actually, no, I wasn't. I was in court all day advocating in a legal hearing. Alibis galore, of course.'

'Thank you – we'll be checking. What about the Monday evening? asked Lydia, adding, 'We're trying to establish who Belinda might have seen or been with that night. Where were you?'

'At home in Hampstead with my family – again, they can all vouch for me.'

'Ah, yes. Hampstead. Not far from Chalk Farm is it?'

'Well, it's on the same tube line, if that's what you mean, Detective,' came the slick response.

'Did you use to travel into work with Belinda?' Lydia was warming to her theme.

'No, never. She tended to leave home in the mornings much earlier than me – I usually get into chambers between nine and half nine, if I'm not in court – on those days I go straight to the law courts, of course.'

'I see. You said in your preliminary statement that you sometimes went out for a drink with Belinda. How often was that?'

The barrister looked a little wary.

'Oh, now and then. Every few weeks, or so.'

'Where did you use to go?' asked Nick.

'Sometimes to a bar or pub near here. Maybe here at Temple or on the Strand. The Hobgoblin or Legal Eagles or somewhere. Straight after work normally, especially on a busy day.'

'Your suggestion or Belinda's usually?' Lydia was intrigued to know who called the shots though she was pretty sure who.

'Well, mine, really, I suppose. Belinda often seemed a little lost and confused and I was willing and able to help her out.'

I bet you were, thought Lydia, who continued,

'Did you explain "intentional tort law" to her by any chance?'

Anthony looked somewhat surprised at a mere police officer using such terminology, thought Lydia rather smugly.

'Yes, it was one of the areas of law we talked about on occasion. She was new to working in chambers and no doubt appreciated an experienced man giving her a few pointers. Tort law was one of her weaknesses but is one of my specialisms.'

'Was law all you discussed?' asked Lydia.

'Oh no! We had a laugh as well as I think I mentioned to you before. We used to talk about how badly some of the clients would lie or have a bet on how long Sharon could talk for without drawing breath – things like that. Belinda could be quite mischievous.'

'When and where was the last time you went for a drink with Belinda?' interjected Nick.

Anthony reddened, much to Lydia's secret amusement.

'Er, well it was the week before she … er … died, actually. The Thursday evening. There'd been a full-on day with some tricky litigation issues about some warring cousins, and I could see the poor woman was totally stressed out so I proposed a drink at Legal Eagles – that's a bar near here – to wind down. But that wasn't the first time we went out for a *proper* drink to be honest.'

'What do you mean by "proper"? And yes, be honest.' Lydia was quick off the mark.

'Ermm … well, more than just a drink, Detective.'

'Oh, was there a meal as well?' asked Lydia, keeping a poker face.

'And where did you go?' pressed Nick.

'Yes, we did have a bite to eat. And it was The Limestone at—'

'Chalk Farm. Yes, we know it. Right next door to Belinda's flat,' said Nick. Lydia silently gave him a high five.

'Well, Detectives, it seemed like a good idea – being on the way home for both of us. And it was Valentine's Day and she was on her own. I felt a bit sorry for her.'

'And did you by any chance go to Belinda's flat after your drink?' asked Lydia.

'Er, yes. She invited me in for a coffee. It was a freezing cold evening … and it would've been rude not to accept …'

'Was that the first time you'd been there?'

'No. The second time actually. I'd been there on New Year's Eve at a party she invited us all to – with my wife.'

'Yes, we've heard about the party. So – going back to the second occasion – when you went to her flat for coffee after eating at The Limestone, did you discuss finer points of law with Belinda then?' Lydia met Anthony's gaze unflinchingly. 'In the bedroom, maybe?'

'Look, Detective, it was only the once – a one-night-stand kind of thing – and Belinda needed some attention. It's very hard for a man in my position, you know. Successful barrister. Experienced. Women tend to throw themselves at me and—'

'You couldn't possibly be expected to be able to resist, Anthony. I understand completely.' Lydia wondered whether Anthony would pick up on her sarcasm but apparently not.

'Good, thank you for your understanding, Detective.'

'What about your wife? Does she know about the "advice" you so kindly gave to Belinda?' added Lydia.

'No! Of course not. She mustn't know. And I know this statement is confidential so I trust you will keep it so, Detectives.' Anthony injected some courtroom bravado into his voice; too little, too late, mused Lydia.

'Indeed, Anthony. Did Belinda know to keep your liaison secret as well?'

'I made it clear to her that it was a one-off and was to remain between the two of us.'

'And what did she say to that?' asked Lydia.

'"See you in court!" she said. She was joking of course – wicked sense of humour she had. Detectives, is there going to be much more? Only I have a client appointment this afternoon, and Sir William has also asked me to have dinner with him this evening.'

'If we have any more questions, we'd like to visit you and your wife at home in Hampstead, please,' said Lydia. 'We'll be discreet about your illicit encounters, don't worry.'

Anthony nodded his assent, rather doubtfully thought Lydia, and got up to leave, smoothing out his finely-cut trousers.

'Just one more question, Anthony,' Lydia waved him back to his seat. 'Who do you think killed Belinda?'

'Well, erm – I don't really buy the idea of a burglar or a rough sleeper, like William and Sharon. I think it was probably more of a planned assault than a botched burglary. I actually consider it quite likely to be a disgruntled client – someone that Belinda had upset or annoyed. She was, as I said, rather inexperienced in the legal world, and I feel she might have rubbed someone up the wrong way.'

An interesting angle, considered Lydia, who responded,

'Any client in particular?'

'There are several who would fit the bill. The old East London gangland families are the worst – they can outwit the strong arm of the law, you know.'

'Not if I can help it,' said Lydia. 'Goodbye for now, Anthony.'

After the barrister had left the room, Lydia turned to Nick. 'He certainly needs to bone up on #MeToo, don't you think? "Women throw themselves at me", my foot!'

Chapter 11

Caveat (a warning)

Sitting on the overground train headed for Sydenham mid-morning on Thursday, Lydia reflected on what they knew about Sam White, cleaner at Weymouth House Chambers.

'So Sergeant,' Lydia addressed her colleague, Sergeant Terry Glover, who was accompanying her and who was detailed to take notes. 'Sam was the one who discovered Belinda's body last Tuesday morning, having arrived slightly earlier than usual to work, and called it in to the police at seven oh one.'

Terry nodded and looked at the briefing notes Lydia had supplied him with.

'Yes, Guv. He says he let the cat out and definitely locked the back door before making his way up to the top floor even though we found it open when we arrived on the scene at ten past seven.'

'OK. I'm going to ask him about that door again, about why he went straight up to the chambers in the first place, and I'll pump him for anything else he might remember once he'd called the police. Oh and Sergeant – don't say anything unless I ask you to.'

Terry nodded and Lydia hoped he would refrain from blurting out any holdback evidence this time.

The Whites lived in a Victorian terraced townhouse in Challen Close, just off the busy Sydenham Road, and not far from the railway station. Sam opened the door, unlit cigarette in hand, and ushered Lydia and Terry in.

'This is Joanna, my wife,' said Sam. Joanna White stepped forward and shook hands with both police officers.

'Morning. Welcome.'

'Thank you both very much for seeing us today to help us with our enquiries,' began Lydia.

'No problem. Thanks for coming down here to Sydenham ... it's helped as I had an early-morning clean at a restaurant in Forest Hill, and Jo's arranged to go into work a bit later this morning.'

'Great,' replied Lydia, thinking that the Whites had been very amenable considering her penchant for studying her suspects in their own environment; not all suspects were so accommodating in her experience. 'May we sit somewhere with a table so that my colleague can take notes, please?'

'Sure,' answered Sam. 'Let's go through to the conservatory. I'm allowed to smoke in there!'

The conservatory adjoining the kitchen-diner was bright and airy. Joanna set about making some coffee and everyone settled themselves round the large pinewood table. Watching Joanna, Lydia was struck by the contrast between her and her husband. While Sam was fidgety, well-muscled and dressed in ripped jeans, Joanna was composed, slimly built and wore a neat navy-blue trouser suit. Sam's shaved head was also at odds with his wife's luxuriant dark tresses.

'I understand you're a teacher, Joanna?' Lydia began conversationally. 'Where do you work?'

'Yes, I'm headteacher at Forest Hill Primary – just down the road from here.' Joanna's voice was clear and polished.

Terry interrupted, much to Lydia's annoyance,

'Quite a contrast to being a cleaner, isn't it Sam?'

'Yes – opposites attract, I reckon!' Sam did not appear to take offence, thought Lydia with relief. Terry hadn't seemed to have put his foot in it – yet. Sam went on,

'Joanna's the brains in this house! Chalk and cheese we are – everyone says so. Though I *am* doing a Computing course at the moment. And Joanna and I do have keeping fit in common.'

'Yes,' continued Joanna. 'We're both members of the same gym and go running together a lot. Having different professions gives us more to talk about in the evenings as well.'

Reasonable, considered Lydia privately.

'OK. Let's go back to last Tuesday morning … sorry, Sam,' she added, noting his distraught expression, and continued in a more gentle tone,

'So you stated that you arrived at Weymouth House at just after quarter to seven?'

'Yes, that's right. Six fifty-two to be precise. Jo dropped me off, didn't you, love?'

Joanna nodded and added,

'Yes, I let him out of the car on Waterloo Bridge at exactly six forty-five; I remember looking at the car clock because I didn't want to stop too long on a double yellow line!'

'Thank you. Sam, are you sure you locked the back door before you went up to the top of the building?'

Sam nodded. 'Yeah, definitely. Cos I always do that once I've let Tabs out, as I said before.'

Lydia went on, 'Thank you. I was also wondering why you thought to go up to the second-floor barristers' office straightaway?'

'Oh – that's because I always start at the top of a building and work my way down. Most cleaners do that – means you know you've done everything before getting back down to base with all your cleaning stuff – hoover and all that.'

'I see. Now, do you remember anything else at all, before or after you called the police? Any noises or anything else strange?' Lydia asked.

Sam thought for a moment.

'Nope, not really. Except ...' he paused. '... I noticed as I was going upstairs that the door to the clients' waiting room on the ground floor was open. Normally it's closed ... but I didn't think much of it at the time.'

'OK. Moving on to Belinda herself. You told us that she occasionally joined you for a cigarette outside in the courtyard, didn't you?'

Sam nodded.

'Was it always a cigarette or something stronger, Sam?'

'That bloody woman! Can't keep her effing mouth shut, can she?' Sam's sudden fury was palpable to all; even Joanna looked shocked, mused Lydia. Curious.

'Who, Belinda?' Lydia asked innocently.

'No – that old cow, Sharon. Always did have it in for me. The one time I had a little spliff and she sniffed it out.'

'What about Belinda? Did she sniff it out as well?' Terry interjected. Good one, Terry – for a change, thought Lydia.

'Well, yeah, she did actually, but she was fine about it. "I disapprove of drugs, even for recreational use" she said to me. "But I won't say anything if you never do it again on our premises." Respect.' Sam started patting his pockets, clearly looking for his lighter. Time for another cigarette, thought Lydia. Nerves?

'Hmm. Alright – now, could you tell me if you've ever been to Belinda's flat at Chalk Farm?'

Sam calmed down as quickly as he had flared up, his lighter and unlit cigarette ready to hand.

'Yeah, just once. We were both invited to her New Year's Eve do.'

Joanna nodded assent, and added,

'It was a nice evening. The flat looked lovely … Christmas decorations still up, candles lit, nice and warm though it was snowing outside! Lots of Indian nibbles, and Belinda was lovely. It was interesting to meet the chambers' staff – Sam's told me so much about them! Belinda's brothers were there; one of them brought his girlfriend – very pleasant Nigerian doctor. I liked Miranda, too – the younger barrister's wife.'

Lydia was impressed by Joanna's diplomatic style, especially as she was probably simmering beneath her calm exterior; there would be a major row later between the Whites, she reckoned. Reason: Sam's smoking habit. And not of nicotine.

'Just a couple more questions, Sam,' Lydia said. 'Where were you the evening before the murder … the Monday night?'

Sam looked perplexed for a moment as if he couldn't imagine why a detective would be asking such a pertinent question, mused Lydia, and then replied,

'At the gym, right, Jo?'

'Yes, that's correct. Monday's our cardio night at "Fit for Life" at Penge. We were there all evening – they'll be able to vouch for us.'

'Thank you. And finally … who do you think murdered Belinda, Sam?'

Sam hesitated, before saying,

'I know it sounds a bit off … but I wouldn't put it past one of those lawyer twats she worked with at the firm.'

'Oh? And why's that?' Lydia asked.

'Well, they're always so friggin' condescending. Look right through me as if I'm not there and I'm the one that cleans their khazis! Except for Belinda, of course. Lovely lady – always very nice to me. Very ambitious she was – wanted to do well in a man's world, so she told me.'

'And you think she might have posed a threat on that front for the other barristers at Weymouth House?' Lydia was intrigued to hear what would come next.

'Yeah! She was definitely better than all of them. Especially that smarmy jerk – the youngish one. Always looking her up and down he was.'

'You mean Anthony Greenwood?' Terry interjected.

'Yeah – that one. Though I don't like pointing the finger at anyone, I'd lay odds it was him.'

'Hmmm,' said Lydia, thoughtfully. 'But if he was looking her up and down, doesn't that imply he found her attractive? Why would he want to hurt her?'

'Um … yes, you're right, I guess—'

'And did you ever witness him actually threatening Belinda?' continued Lydia.

'Erm … no, now that I think about it. It was just a thought – probably been watching too many cop shows!'

'OK, well, if you do think of anything that might help us with our enquiries, please do contact us. Thank you Sam and Joanna. We'll be in touch if we have any more questions as well.'

After an exchange of mobile phone numbers, Lydia and Terry said goodbye to the Whites and walked the short distance back to Sydenham station in silence. Once on the train, Lydia asked,

'Thanks for coming today, Sergeant. Did you get everything down OK?'

'Yes, Guv. I'll type it up and email it over to you by the end of the afternoon. I bet there's a juicy domestic going on at the Whites! She didn't know about his little weed habit, did she?'

'Apparently not. And I think I can guess who really wears the trousers in that house.'

Back at New Scotland Yard after a hastily snatched sandwich from the canteen, Lydia brought Nick up to speed with the events of the morning.

'Interesting,' said Nick. 'So, Boss – what do you make of Sam White?'

'Well, he could have a motive, I suppose. If Belinda found him smoking a joint and he felt she wouldn't keep her promise to stay quiet about it. He might have been afraid of losing his job,' Lydia said thoughtfully. She added,

'They all have motive, actually. Anthony Greenwood didn't want his wife to know about his extracurricular activity with Belinda – who might have threatened to spill the beans, especially if she was really taken with Anthony and wanted to take it further.'

'Yes, sure. And what about the lovely Sharon?' Nick asked.

'Well, she *is* very protective over Sir William. Almost motherly, what with all the cakes and so on. Maybe she felt that once Belinda found out about the Faiths' not-so-kosher "intentional tort", she wanted to make sure William didn't get into trouble, be disbarred or whatever they call it. That could be motive for murder.'

'Sir William also has a motive, Boss, as we know. Belinda's rebuffing of his advances might have gone deep – pushed him over the edge. Plus with Belinda not being entirely on board concerning the Faiths, perhaps he was also worried about the financial side of things. He's probably earning a fair whack from that case.'

'Good point, Nick. Money is often a motivation for crime, as we very well know in our line of work. Julian Radford is a case in point. Keeping Precious a secret from his parents meant he felt he was protecting his substantial inheritance.'

'What about Ben James? Is he a serious suspect?'

'They're all serious suspects until further notice, Nick! Ben or one of his cronies might well have seen an opportunity for burglary, and Belinda might have been collateral damage. Arrange for Ben's "mates" at Waterloo Bridge to be checked out, would you?'

'Sure thing, Boss. What do you think about Anthony's idea about the clients? East End gangster families and all that?'

'Let's look into it. Especially the Faiths – definitely some dodgy dealings there, I reckon.'

'Shall I get Mr Mews checked out, as well, Boss?'

Lydia looked at Nick in surprise until she understood his joke.

'Yes, Nick. Everyone's a suspect, remember?'

Then it was Friday evening once more. Lydia let herself into her bijou Battersea ground floor flat, unzipped her trademark boots – these with kitten heels – and went through to her home office to turn on her laptop. She padded through to her neat and tidy kitchenette to pour herself a large glass of very welcome cool Chardonnay, checked that the back door and rear windows were locked, and moved through to her calm and cosy sitting room with its shelves of easy reading and her prized film collection. Putting on a soothing Lana Del Rey CD and lighting a candle, she flopped down onto her comfy sofa. It was times like these, she thought, that she needed a dog – an adoring companion who would listen attentively to every word she said and not offer a single opinion or contradict her in any way.

'Oh, Belinda,' she said aloud to an empty room and took a sip of her wine. 'I feel I know you a bit better now – but who did this to you? What can I tell your parents?'

Lydia felt as though she had the corner pieces and most of the side pieces of a large jigsaw puzzle, but no illustration to guide her. She wondered if she had missed something … she had motives – of sorts – to consider; but she knew she had to dig more deeply into opportunity. She did not trust a single one of the suspects or their stories, and hoped that visiting both Sharon and Anthony at their respective homes the following week would shine some more light on the mystery. There was also Belinda's funeral to be attended. She knew that being methodical and careful was the right way to move forward in this case; but boy did she need a breakthrough. Lydia knew that she had to maintain her reputation for intuitive "brilliance" to solve the case before it became lukewarm or even cold.

A "ping" sounding from her computer alerted her to the arrival of an email. Mum, probably, she thought. Settling herself down at her desk, she opened the email, not recognising the sender.

Hello, Miss Snoopy Detective. You won't be able to track this email so don't even try. It's encrypted, you see. Think you're so bloody clever, don't you? Just like that Belinda slut – she couldn't keep her snout out of anything, either. Going to bring us down, wasn't she? She can't nose around any more though, can she? And neither should you if you know what's good for you. What is it about all you modern women? Hate men, don't you? Consider yourselves above everyone else? It was so easy to track down your private email address. Father taught me to follow the scent and not to stop until I caught my prey. Then – a quick slash with a sharp knife and it would all be over. Then – rabbit pie for tea, and enjoy it, he would say. Now, Lydia Skinny Carlisle – why don't you just step down, call off your hounds, sorry – officers – or you'll be sorry. Just bugger off and leave things to be run as they should be – by those who know what's what in the world.
With warmest regards from a well-wisher.

Lydia sat back in her chair, contemplating the modern-day equivalent of a message made up of letters cut out of a newspaper or magazine.

'Well, well, well,' she murmured to herself. 'More pieces of the puzzle. Thank God.'

It was a turning point, Lydia felt. She had been handed a break on a plate and intended to follow it through to the end. She had no doubt that she was meant to feel intimidated by the sinister message, but what the killer did not know was that for her, Lydia Carlisle, it had the opposite effect, and that she would rise to the challenge of the threat.

'Bring it on,' said Lydia out loud, raising her glass.

Chapter 12

Ad Hoc (for a particular purpose)

'Morning, Sir,' said Lydia the moment Chief Inspector Geoff Cordell answered his mobile. 'Apologies for phoning so early and on a Saturday, but I've been threatened.'

'No problem – you know you can always call. Go ahead – what's happened?'

Lydia went on to describe the contents of the sinister email, relieved as ever that her superior officer was so very understanding; even so, eight o'clock in the morning at the weekend was the earliest she dared phone him.

'OK, Lydia. This is serious. Forward the email over to me and I'll get the techies onto it, despite the perp bragging about encryption and what have you. First thing Monday we'll call an emergency conference at the Yard with everyone involved in the case; I'll get my secretary to liaise with DI Fairman – I know he's already in the process of setting up a staff meeting. Are you alright, Lydia?'

'I'm fine, thank you,' answered Lydia. 'Don't worry – I'm not going to answer my door to any strangers.'

'I'll send a car down to Battersea to keep an eye— '

'No need, Sir. I can look after myself,' said Lydia, feeling as though she was talking to her father.

'Overruled, DI Carlisle. And it's not just because you're a woman; I'd be pulling out the stops to protect any of my officers. This is a vicious murderer whose behaviour's clearly beginning to escalate and I'm not taking any chances.'

'Thanks, Sir – I appreciate it really.'

'No worries. Oh and Lydia – make sure you're sitting down when you read the papers today … there's been a massive response to the press release. The press must be a little short on news this weekend!'

Lydia groaned. 'Oh God. OK … and I'll be in touch.'

'Bye, Lydia. Take care, and keep me posted on any developments.'

Lydia spent a good part of the morning reading the media responses and theories regarding Belinda's death. These ranged from gruesome retellings of past lawyers who had been murdered at work; a conspiracy theory involving a secret plot to bring down the British legal system; and a surprisingly in-depth account of pony branding techniques used in the New Forest.

A phone call to her mobile from Gordon Radford late on Saturday afternoon was the only further event that Lydia felt was significant enough to inform her senior officer of – Belinda's father was clearly trying hard to keep it together and make the necessary arrangements for her funeral, while suffering immense grief at the devastating loss of his daughter.

'Good afternoon, Detective Inspector; I hope it's alright to call you at the weekend,' Gordon had begun.

'No problem at all,' replied Lydia, aware that she was echoing her own boss's words from earlier that day. 'That's why I gave you my number. How are you and your wife coping?'

'Well … you know. Felicity is still in pieces and I'm run ragged running the estate. It's times like these when Julian's help would be useful, of course.'

Fat chance of that, thought Lydia.

'Indeed, Gordon. What can I do for you?'

'I was just phoning to ask if there is any news? After all, it's been ten days now as the press are keen to point out. And to let you know when the funeral is.'

'We're working round the clock to catch your daughter's murderer, Gordon. We've just had a bit of a breakthrough that I'm hoping will lead to an arrest—'

'Really? Are you allowed to tell me what that "breakthrough" is?'

'Not as such. Let's just say that the perpetrator has made contact, and we're pulling out all the stops—'

'Made contact? Gosh, isn't that a little *psychopathic*, Detective?'

'I think so. Not to mention dangerous. Look, I don't like to talk about this on the phone, but you're welcome to come up to New Scotland Yard, and we can fill you in further.'

'Thank you. I'll come up next week; probably Thursday or Friday, if that's alright with you. Now, about Belinda's funeral. It's going to be on Tuesday week – that will be three weeks to the day that she was … taken from us. It will be at Bournemouth crematorium at eleven-thirty in the morning.'

'Quite a way from where you are,' commented Lydia.

130

'I know, but there aren't any crematoriums in the New Forest. We'll be scattering her ashes here on the estate, though. So, at least she'll be home then.'

Lydia could hear Gordon's voice cracking up, so she continued as sympathetically as she could,

'Of course. I'll be coming to the funeral too, of course. I'll be bringing my colleague, DI Fairman, if that's OK? I know it's hard, but I really do hope you and your wife can support each other through all this. And as you know, you can always call me.'

After the goodbyes, Lydia spent some time emailing Geoff and Nick informing them of the funeral details; while she was on her laptop, she heard the sound of a car pull to a stop outside her flat. Peeking through her window blinds, she saw a police car parked in front of her sitting room window.

'Thanks, Sir,' she murmured.

By the time Lydia entered the conference room at New Scotland Yard at ten o'clock on Monday morning, the team was already assembled. Geoff Cordell and Nick were standing in front of the video conference screen, deep in conversation, while Sergeants Clive Davis and Terry Glover were at the coffee station chatting quietly and washing down biscuits with large cups of tea. Julie Morris, the police photographer, was in a huddle with the forensics team comprising Norman Combe, Beth Monkton and Max Burgh. Ruth Simons, Geoff's PA, was setting up a laptop and projector; she would also be taking the meeting minutes. Lydia made her way over to help herself to a coffee, before sitting down and laying out her papers. She looked up as Geoff cleared his throat and began speaking.

'Thank you all so much for coming and at such short notice,' he said. 'And apologies for interrupting your schedules but the situation with Belinda Radford's murder has taken a serious turn.'

He signalled to Ruth to flash up the threatening email Lydia had received onto the screen. There was a hush for a minute or two while the poisonous words sank in, then Geoff nodded to Lydia who began to speak.

'Morning everyone, and thank you from me as well for being here. Thanks too for all your hard work so far. First of all, though, I really don't want you to worry too much about me ...' she said, looking pointedly at Geoff. '... I'm being well protected. And Tech is working on the identity of the email account user or registrant as we speak.' Taking a sip of her coffee, she went on, 'We're two weeks in since Belinda Radford was killed and the press is on our backs as you are all no doubt aware. Not to mention the agony the parents are going through. I'd like us to pool our resources – cross-reference what we know – and make a clear plan of action.'

There was a general nodding of heads around the room, so Lydia continued,

'Julie, let's start with you.'

'Sure. Well, as you know, I took the original scene-of-crime photos on the day of the murder ... here they are,' answered Julie, nodding at Ruth, who inserted a USB drive and opened up the pictures of Belinda's body exactly as it had been found nearly two weeks earlier. There was silence as the disturbing images were scrolled through; the team was well used to gory and violent scenes, though Lydia noticed that Beth, the forensics number two, averted her eyes when it came to a close-up of the deep, bloodied gash to Belinda's throat. She understood how Beth felt only too well.

'So what do these pictures actually tell us … I mean apart from the facts listed in the autopsy report that we've all had a copy of … about Belinda's being dealt a death slash from behind and having no time to fight back?' asked Lydia.

'Well, it was probably a large knife that was used – we haven't found the murder weapon yet – and the cut was most probably delivered from left to right. The autopsy report also suggests that the assailant was probably shorter than the victim, judging by the angle of the weapon,' said Nick.

'Would that be left to right from the victim's perspective?' asked Terry Glover.

'Good point, Sergeant Glover,' answered Lydia. 'Yes, from Belinda's left to right, making the murderer most likely right-handed. Action Point One: Sergeant, could you ascertain who amongst the suspects identified so far is right-handed or left-handed?'

'Yes, Guv. And I'll put together a list of all their heights, as well' said Terry.

'Great, thank you. Anyone else think of anything?' asked Lydia.

Norman Combe, the lead forensics expert, looked up from his notes.

'Well, clearly the attacker must have been very quiet for Belinda not to have heard anyone creeping up behind her. That might suggest the perp knew the building well ... or was a seasoned criminal.'

'Indeed. We haven't yet established how the perp got in, but we're fairly sure they *left* by the rear entrance, leaving the door open in their haste to get away. Is there anything more relating to forensic evidence, Norman?'

'The preliminary report that you've read pretty much says everything: the blood spatter is identified as the victim's, and hairs and fingerprints found on the furnishings in the law chambers mostly belong to the people who work there, who agreed to their prints being taken on the day of the murder. There are also some unknown prints that are probably the clients'; we've yet to identify them. The findings from the Chalk Farm flat... ' Norman paused to pass around copies of the completed report on the case. '... show some interesting features. Obviously, there are fingerprints from the victim in both the flat and the chambers; then, firstly, there is one identical and as yet unknown set of prints in both the victim's flat and the chambers. Secondly, there are four unknown sets in the flat but not in the chambers. Thirdly, there are only one set of prints in the spare room – the victim's own, and finally, there are fingerprints from work colleagues all over the living room area, kitchen and bathroom of the flat, though the prints are slightly deteriorated.'

'Probably from the infamous New Year's Eve party,' remarked Nick.

'And …' continued Norman, 'some prints found in Belinda's bedroom match those of—'

'Anthony Greenwood,' Nick interrupted. 'Sorry to spoil the surprise, Norm! We know about Anthony's little escapade.'

Max Burgh, the third member of the forensics team, piped up,

'Hate to rain on your parade, Nick, but actually Greenwood's aren't the only prints found in the bedroom apart from Belinda's of course. There's another set of unidentified fingerprints both there and in the bathroom.'

'Hmm. Action Point Two: find out who they belong to – Norman and Max, could you head that one up? I'm also wondering about the "young man" Sir William alluded to who was also at the New Year's Eve party. And let us have a further update on the unknown fingerprints in the law chambers asap,' interjected Lydia. Looking at Beth, she continued, 'Beth, we've seen your report about Belinda's personal laptop; anything else to add?'

'Yes, I've got the updated report right here … copies for you all,' answered the forensic team's digital specialist. The LinkedIn contacts all seem pretty bona fide. Mostly law associates and work colleagues; nothing suspicious. What is more interesting are Belinda's blogs – the ones she printed out on yellow paper – that we found in her flat and you asked me to examine. I found the original entries on her laptop … she'd decided to go digital, but kept it private. Nothing on-line.'

'So what was in these blogs?' asked Lydia, feeling a familiar sense of excitement creeping up inside. Another breakthrough, possibly?

'Well, nothing exactly *incriminating* about anyone else as far as I can see ... it's more the style of writing that's unusual. In this day and age, most youngish people use electronic media such as their mobile phones for everything – appointments, dates, notes and so on. And they use the modern type of shorthand, like "gr8". But Belinda's blogs are incredibly detailed ... there are times, dates and full conversations – almost verbatim. Properly punctuated although she does use a few abbreviations like "tbh" and "imho". That's "to be honest" and "in my honest opinion" to the uninitiated! All fascinating reading, if a little tedious. The blogs begin on 1st January this year – incidentally, we also found a box of handwritten diaries in a cupboard in the spare room. They cover the time she started at university until last Christmas.'

'Thanks Beth,' said Lydia, thinking that the spare room of the flat was obviously exclusive to Belinda and her private belongings, and kept very tidy with the bed made up ... just because that was the way Belinda was. She went on,

'Action Point Three for me – comb through said diaries, and go through the blogs as soon as I can. Can you email them over to me today, please, as well as send over the box of diaries?' asked Lydia. This was another breakthrough in the making; she felt sure of it.

After a welcome sip of her coffee, Lydia continued,

'I remember Belinda's father telling me that she wrote diaries as a child. Sergeant Davis, could you contact Gordon Radford and ask him to bring them up this week when he comes to see us this week. He told me they still have all her childhood diaries down at the New Forest estate.'

Clive nodded, and Lydia turned to Nick.

'Nick, could you bring everyone up to speed with the interview statements and alibi checks?'

'Sure, Boss. Ruth – please could you show us the initial transcriptions? Right, so we've been looking at where the suspects were on the Monday evening before the murder ... the idea being there might have been some kind of set-to with Belinda leading to her being brutally killed the next morning. Plus we're trying to establish where the key players were between six and seven a.m. which is the time frame for Belinda's murder given in the autopsy report. OK, starting with the work colleagues. Sir William's night-at-the-opera alibi checks out for the Monday evening; the staff there remember him – he's a regular there and always makes a point of greeting them all very politely. However, we're still waiting for the cleaner to come back to us to verify his story for the Tuesday morning; apparently he was at his Covent Garden flat prior to being called into chambers at just before eight a.m. The "A Clean Sweep" housekeeping agency are having difficulties contacting Anastasiya Shcherbyna; apparently she's had to return to Kiev as her mother has had a stroke. They're going to keep on trying, though.'

Nick paused for breath and went on,

'I'd like to know more about the work he conducts down in Whitstable; a bit irregular if you ask me. Anthony Greenwood does seem to have been at home on Monday evening as well, according to my telephone call with his wife. We still need to delve into how he managed to get into chambers so quickly after the barristers' clerk called him in just after phoning Sir William, at a few minutes before eight a.m. I think that merits a visit to Hampstead, though – if nothing else, it will be fun to see him squirm.'

'Don't minute that, Ruth!' said Geoff.

Nick went on,

'Sharon Hardy's alibi for Monday evening appears to be dogs. And their owners. We've had an invitation for tea and cake in Nunhead, haven't we, Boss?'

Lydia pulled a face, muttering, 'Can't wait. Go on, Nick.'

'Sam White is still a person of interest, especially as he was the one who "found" Belinda's body, and appears to have a motive of sorts – his fondness for smoking a certain dodgy substance which Belinda may have disapproved of more than he's letting on. It's been confirmed by the gym he attends in Penge that he was there all Monday evening with his wife. Moving on to the family, the brother, Julian Radford, has a huge motive for wanting his sister dead. Money. His girlfriend has provided him with an alibi for the Monday night, but we're still bringing her in this week to dig deeper, plus we need to check out his whereabouts on the Tuesday morning. With regard to the rough sleepers …' Nick turned to Terry. 'Sergeant, could you fill us in here? Your report hasn't reached me yet.'

'Yep. Clive and I spent a lovely afternoon down on the South Bank interviewing Ben James' mates. They weren't all there, though. Couldn't get much sense out of most of the ones that were there; they were either drunk or stoned out of their brains. They "vaguely" remembered Ben showing up under Waterloo Bridge on the morning of the murder, going on about a murder, footsteps, something about a knife, a cat ...'

Nick rolled his eyes at the mention of the cat.

'OK, I get the picture. Anything else of interest?'

'One thing that's just struck me,' said Clive Davis. 'Was that if it wasn't Ben who broke in and killed Belinda Radford, then maybe he at least picked up the knife – the "clangy" thing he went on about – and put it or hid it on his person. Maybe he still had it went he went to join his cronies at Waterloo Bridge?'

'But why? And what would he have done with it?' asked Lydia.

'Who knows? Those blokes are a law unto themselves, aren't they, Terry?' answered Clive.

'Yep, certainly are. Maybe he decided to keep it for his own protection ... or more likely, thought he could sell it to fund his drinking habit ... shall we go back and question Ben – put him under a bit more pressure?' continued Terry.

'OK, Sergeant, but don't be too harsh. And make sure you send the report over to me sharpish,' said Nick.

'Thanks, Nick. Another lead that I'd like to follow up is the Faiths,' said Lydia. Aware of the looks of surprise on her colleagues' faces, she explained,

'Steven and Amanda Faith are some of Sir William's clients who may have something fishy to hide or cover up. And see if there's anything in Anthony Greenwood's theory about clients with East End gangland family connections. So … Action Point 4: I'm going to their car showroom in Bromley this afternoon; see what I can find out. Nick, you can come with me.'

'Thank you all so much again for coming this morning,' said Geoff. 'Ruth, please get the minutes out by tomorrow. Lydia, let's touch base at the end of the week. And now, Action Point 5: lunch on me. Don't get too excited – just the canteen, I'm afraid!'

Chapter 13

Mens Rea (intention or knowledge of criminal wrongdoing)

Lydia's ankle boots squeaked on the rubberised floor as she and Nick wended their way between the brand-new Honda cars artfully placed in the showroom of Tanleigh Auto Dealers UK. The Bromley branch was a large outlet, second only to the main dealership located in Manchester. There were several potential buyers admiring the sleek new cars, accompanied by eager sales staff – keen to earn their commission no doubt, thought Lydia wryly.

'Can I help you, Sir?' asked the high-heeled, immaculately-dressed and made-up female sales assistant, addressing Nick. Before he could answer, Lydia broke in,

'Morning. We're not here to buy a car, though.'

'Apologies, Madam. Do I know you? You seem familiar ...'

'DI Lydia Carlisle,' said Lydia, showing her card. 'And this is my assistant, DI Nicholas Fairman. We have indeed met, Mrs Faith – albeit very briefly – at Weymouth House Chambers, a week ago today in fact.'

Recognition dawned on Amanda Faith's face.

'Of course. You're investigating the death of Sir William's young barrister, aren't you?' Without waiting for an answer, she went on in her cut-glass accent, 'Well, follow me; I think it would be better if we go to the private customer suite.'

Lydia and Nick followed Amanda to what could only be described as a glass box, jutting out into the showroom. Inside, there were several tartan-patterned sofas, a couple of coffee tables and a tall hot drinks machine.

'Can I offer you coffee or tea?'

Once Amanda had placed their paper cups of tea on a table, she continued,

'Do help yourselves to sugar and milk. I'm just going to fetch my husband; we'll be right back.'

Alone in the soundproof – at least, hopefully, thought Lydia – glass pod, Nick turned to Lydia,

'How on earth can she manage on those heels? Must be at least four inches high.'

'Hmm. Not surprised she got knocked over,' answered Lydia. 'OK – Nick, I'll do the questioning, and if you could take notes, that'd be great. But do butt in if you think of anything relevant to ask them.'

Five minutes later, Amanda returned accompanied by Steven Faith, whom Lydia also remembered from a week earlier. She took in their smart appearance; Amanda, in a tight-fitting leopard-print dress which together with her mane of highlighted blonde hair made Lydia think of a predatory wild cat on an African plain, and Steven, in a leather jacket and cowboy boots that ratcheted up his height to an inch or so taller than his wife. The lion and its tamer, thought Lydia.

'Morning all,' began Steven, with a strong hint of cockney in his accent. 'What can we do for you?'

'Well, Mr Faith, we'd like to ask you and your wife a few questions about Weymouth House Chambers – as you are, I'm sure, aware – that barrister Belinda Radford was murdered on the premises there almost two weeks ago.'

'Yes, we were so very sorry to hear about that. We knew Miss Radford,' said Amanda. 'But what does it have to do with us?'

'How long have you been Sir William Bond's clients and how well do you know him?' answered Lydia.

'We've known Sir William for years,' said Steven. 'At least fifteen, would you Adam and Eve it – right, Mand?' Amanda nodded assent, and added,

'Yes. Longer, I think. Back before he became a barrister, Sir William was lawyer to my family down in Blean – just outside Whitstable. When he moved away, my family then started using Melvin Solicitors Canterbury on his recommendation – and when Steve and I got together and started out in business, we carried on using them for legal matters, too.'

'We'll return to the *legal matters* in a while,' interjected Lydia, noting with inner satisfaction the worried glances exchanged between the Faiths. 'Go on.'

'It turns out that if a case is to go to court, Melvin Solicitors often hands it over to Sir William at Weymouth House – much to our delight, needless to say.'

'Hmm, OK. What about the others barristers – Anthony Greenwood and Belinda Radford – how well do … or *did* in the case of Ms Radford … you know them?'

'We've only got to know Mr Greenwood fairly recently so he's not what I'd call me china,' said Steven. 'He does deal with some of our case at times when Sir William can't for various reasons. We had some dealings with Miss Radford so we knew her a bit better – she used to join in our meetings with Sir William sometimes. Bit of a cold fish, she was … not that I'm happy she's brown bread of course,' he added hurriedly.

'She was just … inexperienced,' put in Amanda. 'Not very good at reading between the lines, if you know what I mean?'

'What sort of "lines" do you mean?' asked Lydia. 'Would that be related to tort law by any chance?'

'Er, what law?' interjected Steven. Not very convincing, thought Lydia.

'Tort or indeed *intentional* tort law comes in when people make an accident happen on purpose to make a claim …'

'Hang on, what are you suggesting, Detective?' Steven's faced turned red and his voice rose in pitch. 'Some berk drives one of our cars backwards into the showroom without looking and knocks me wife down. She cracked a rib and suffered severe shock, you know. It was NOT her fault! Of course we're going to sue—'

'Steve, calm down,' said Amanda, laying a hand on his arm. 'Let me explain. What happened was that one of the new salesmen was bringing in a new car. He didn't check his rear-view mirror and didn't notice me until it was too late. I was injured and shocked, and our solicitor thought advised us to bring a civil suit against the owners of Tanleigh Auto Dealers UK as it was a workplace accident. We went to see Sir William a few times as he'd been preparing for the trial.'

'I see. So did you deliberately stand behind the car that was being reversed, Mrs Faith?' interjected Nick. Good one, thought Lydia.

'That's exactly what Miss Radford asked us,' replied Amanda without batting an eyelid. 'Very disapproving she was, too. Sir William and Sharon – you know, the barristers' clerk – tried to explain to her that whether or not an accident is intentional, the law still calls it a civil wrong and the injured party has the right to sue.'

'So it's a kind of loophole, is it?' asked Lydia, noting that Amanda hadn't *actually* answered Nick's question.

'Yep. And with any luck, we should get a lot of bees out of it,' continued Steven. 'That's bees and honey. Money,' he explained on seeing the puzzled looks on the detectives' faces. 'Sorry. It's me East End upbringing!'

'Did Miss Radford try to dissuade you from bringing the suit?' enquired Lydia.

'Oh yes. She implied that it was unethical – and said she didn't want to paint Weymouth House in a bad light,' answered Amanda. 'But Sir William assured us that it was all above board, and Sharon – bless her heart – said she would talk to Miss Radford about it later.'

'Ah yes. Ms Hardy. Very helpful, isn't she?' put in Nick.

'Yeah! Makes a good cup of Rosie, she does. Doesn't half rabbit though,' said Steven.

'You speak very … *colourfully*, Mr Faith! Tell us more about your Cockney roots,' Lydia smiled encouragingly.

'Well, I grew up in Wapping; me family were part of the Brindle clan. A few of them are still around Aldgate and Limehouse – though it's all getting so re-gentrified now, I hardly recognise the old haunts any more. And the price of 'ouses there! But me family does try to keep up the old ways, like the rhyming slang and the old knees-ups. Me old grandpa and grandma were pearly king and queen for a while, and—'

'Weren't the Brindles involved in some kind of money-laundering scandal recently?' interrupted Nick.

Steven looked slightly embarrassed, but not for long.

'Ermm, they might have been, I think. A bit of gang stuff … nothing to do with me though. Me mum and dad didn't want any Barney Rubble. They wanted me and my brother to do better in life.'

'That's why you married me, wasn't it darling?' said Amanda sweetly, winking at her husband. She ran a hand over her immaculately coiffed tresses, and continued,

'Steve and I met at a friend's wedding in Rochester – and the rest, as they say, is history.'

'Yeah, love at first sight. Even though we're like chalk and cheese – everyone says so!' added Steve. Rather like Sam and Joanna White, mused Lydia.

'Returning to Ms Radford. Were you ever afraid that your case might have been threatened by her at all?' Lydia could almost feel the metaphorical kick under the table that Amanda gave her husband.

'Not at all, Detective,' came her smooth reply. 'We had, and still do have, every faith in Sir William.'

'Yes, every "faith", excuse the pun!' added Steven Faith, chortling at his own joke.

Lydia pressed on,

'Did you feel she might have at least taken what she saw as a slightly unethical approach any further? Reported the case to the Law Society or something like that?' asked Lydia. Again, she noted the shifty look that passed between the Faiths.

'To be honest,' replied Amanda, 'I did think it crossed her mind … but then of course, she was killed … terrible shame.' Managing to look suitably downcast, she continued, 'poor Miss Radford.'

'Are you completely recovered from your accident now, Mrs Faith?' asked Lydia, not trying very hard to inject any sympathy into her voice.

'Oh yes, thank you. It happened about eight months ago – last August – I'm fine now …'

'So when did you first visit Weymouth House?'

'Not long after our solicitor passed the case over Sir William … in September, I think it was,' put in Steven. 'Sir William put us on fast-track, seeing as he knew us, and he had it all in hand. And we've been going in every few weeks or so. We're fairly close to winding it all up now, thank the Lord.'

'Moving on, any ideas as to who the murderer might be?' asked Lydia.

'Ain't got a Scooby,' replied Steven.

'Where were you both on the morning of the murder two weeks ago tomorrow?'

If Lydia expected the Faiths to be indignant, she was disappointed,

'We were both right here,' answered Amanda firmly. 'As always, seven o'clock on the dot. That's when we have our morning briefing with the team and they can verify that – no problem.' Steven nodded his agreement.

At that moment, the door to the glass pod opened, and a smartly-attired young assistant poked his head in.

'Sorry to interrupt, Steve. Your client's just arrived – I think they want to wrap up that Jaguar deal.'

'Thanks Bob. I'll be right there. Case in point … young Robert Bridges there – he can vouch for us! Detectives, if there's nothing else? Steven continued, not bothering to hide his pride, 'This is an important sale – local business wants a whole fleet of jams … sorry, that's jam jars. Cars.'

'That's all for now,' answered Lydia. 'Thank you both; we'll be following up on your alibis and will be in touch if there's anything else.'

Lydia and Nick were shown out of the showroom, and made their way back to Bromley station a few minutes' walk away, their voices low.

'So, what do you think, Boss? Are they involved?'

'They could be. They obviously stand to gain quite a bit from the civil suit, and wouldn't want anything getting in the way of that,' Lydia continued, 'Amanda Faith is the brains behind those two, and I can imagine her being quite capable of getting Steven to do her dirty work, But would they actually really go so far as to murder Belinda?'

'Yes, I agree that Amanda is a hard nut ... she didn't like the way our questioning was going and was careful about what she said. But they were surprisingly upfront about Belinda potentially putting the kybosh on their case. Or just confident that it would all work out well for them?'

'Hmm. What about the whole gangland thing, Nick? Any mileage in that?'

'Possibly. I'll look into the Brindles; see if there's anything going on and if Steven Faith is connected. Though he came across to me as being relieved at not being part of the gang world any more.'

'They're definitely *relieved* now that Belinda's dead ... "poor Miss Radford" indeed,' said Lydia. 'Could you ask Sergeant Glover to verify whether the Faiths were indeed both there at the morning meeting in the car showroom on the day of the murder? And get more information on this tort lawsuit. Please.'

'Consider it Adam and Son!' Nick added with a smirk, 'done. I'm sure Sir William will be happy to oblige, Boss.'

149

Back at New Scotland Yard, Lydia had time to catch up on her emails before the end of the working day. Ruth, CI Geoff Cordell's PA, had already completed and distributed the minutes of that morning's meeting; Lydia skimmed through them before bringing up the pages of Belinda's blogs that had been emailed over to her by Beth Monkton.

'Thank you, Beth,' murmured Lydia, and settled down hoping to immerse herself in – at least one – slice of Belinda Radford's life.

1st January

Happy New Year, dear Diary!

Goodbye to writing, hello to typing! So welcome to Belinda's Blog Number One! I may as well move into the twenty-first century, but knowing me I'll probably print it all out anyway. Anyway, here I am, a little hungover, but am v. pleased that last night went off so well. The flat looked fabulous and the food must have gone down well – not much left over anyway!! Indian canapés were an inspired choice, imho. Cheers, Bombay Raj. Everyone who was invited came: Sir W., Anthony and his wife – Miranda, Sharon, the Whites, and even Julian put in an appearance with his new girlfriend, Precious. They'd all come by taxi or public transport ... ostensibly so that they didn't have to drive in the snow, but really so that they could drink to their hearts' content – and they did! Am so pleased that Tom could make it too – he made it his business to keep the wine flowing and the music playing. I can always rely on him for that. Even if Shostakovich did dominate! Everyone was here by half past eight and most people seemed to get along OK, thank Goodness.

Julian was a bit of a show-off as usual about all the commission he makes and his banking connections, but Precious stole the limelight!! She's so lovely – training to be a doctor at Guy's, although she didn't know Martha and Skye (pity they couldn't make it btw). And her dress – wonderful colours. Quite what she sees in Julian is beyond me, though – he can be such a prat at times tbh. Anyway, they talked quite a lot with Sam White and his wife, Joanna – she's very nice as well. So happy that Sharon could make it – I know she was worried about leaving her dog.

'Ruskin's at a sleepover!'
She does make me laugh sometimes. She stuck quite close to Sir W. last night, but they were both friendly enough with everyone, really. Anthony and Miranda mingled, and talked quite a bit to Tom who regaled them with his knowledge of Soviet Russia!! Miranda was rather arty, quite tall with lots of curly red hair, positively oozed patchouli, and was wearing an orange and green flowing kind of outfit; quite a contrast to her more, shall we say ... "urbane" husband ...
The only downside was when Julian cornered me in the kitchen.

'Bel,' (the only time he calls me that is when he wants something) 'what do you think of Precious?'

'Very nice,' I said. 'I hope you're going to treat her well.'

'Of course! Why wouldn't I?' I was just about to remind him of the shoddy way he dumped Sue, his girlfriend of three years – on WhatsApp no less – when he went on,

'Don't mention her to the parents, will you?'

'You're not implying they're racist, are you, Julian?'

'No! It's just ... I don't want to jinx this relationship. I'm keeping it under wraps for the moment – to see if it works out or not. You know how Father always goes on about me finding a suitable wife to take over the estate. Maybe I'm being over-cautious, but I'm not sure they would find her "suitable" ...'

'I'm sure Mother would love her,' I said.

'Don't say a word to either of them,' he practically snarled at me. Then he stalked off, back to being the golden boy of the ball. I wouldn't be at all surprised if he's afraid he might be cut out of Mother's and Father's wills. As if!! Mind you, I agree with staying schtum about a new relationship ... until it's got legs, as they say. Tom never tends to show much affection to me in public anyway, so not everyone realised we're an item ... Anyway, everyone stayed after midnight – it was a special moment when we all linked arms and sang Auld Lang Syne, and raised a toast to the New Year – and to my new flat!! Sir W. lingered a bit – he even tried a clumsy kind of kiss – but had no choice but to tactfully leave, seeing as Tom was still there. And still is here, actually ... I'll take him up a special cup of New Year's Day tea and then we can cuddle up under the duvet ... or maybe go for a nice walk on Hampstead Heath which I'm sure looks glorious with all the snow.. After all this time, still chemistry between us, I think – the only problem is he's shorter than me. But, hey, what's a couple of inches between old friends, my dear Diary?

Tom? Lydia stopped reading and thought back.
She knew she'd missed something vital and in a
moment or two it came back to her. Jo White had
mentioned there being "brothers" at the New Year's
Eve party as opposed to the more accurate "a brother";
she must have assumed the unattached male was
another Radford sibling. And there was the "young
man" alluded to by Sir William as well as the "tallish"
guy Julian had mentioned. This would also probably
account for the set of unidentified fingerprints found in
Belinda's flat that matched the same ones in the
chambers, and now they had a first name to go on.
Tom – he must also be the mystery person who'd taken
the photo attached to the chambers' fridge … the one
person NOT in the picture! However, before Lydia
could process this information further, her phone rang
– it was Nick.

'Boss! The knife's been found. Looks like it's
the one used to murder Belinda.'

Chapter 14

Res Ipsa Loquitur (the fact speaks for itself)

Sharon Hardy had plodded along the uneven pavement, eyes straight ahead, and turned into the mews. Her bulky physique seemed even larger than usual due to the bottle green woollen cape she habitually wore; it sat on her like a changing robe covering a shy matron on a crowded beach. It was just after four o'clock and she had popped out to buy some "dainties" for Sir William and Attorney Anthony; iced buns to go with their afternoon cup of tea. The black front door of Weymouth House Chambers was straight ahead. She glanced around the quiet mews as she walked; the park was empty as it was near the end of the working day, but between the rhododendron bushes Sharon could just make out the blue and white sleeping bag that she knew belonged to Ben, the rough sleeper, or that down-and-out drifter, as she liked to think of him. Detouring over to Ben's den, she called out,

'It's your lucky day, Ben! I've got you a doughnut. Are you awake?'

Approaching the sleeping bag, she could make out a lump in it. She pulled open the sleeping bag, wrinkling her nose as she peered in, and jerked back as a small furry cat yowled at her.

'Hello, you smelly old moggy. Oh hell's bells!'

'So, Boss that, by and large, is what Sharon Hardy reported to us – the knife was in the sleeping bag next to the cat. She called it in straightaway and

154

I've just sent uniform over to retrieve the knife from the sleeping bag,' said Nick.

'Right. Get it to forensics immediately; they'll be happy to work overnight on it. I'll go over to Weymouth House first thing in the morning – could you check that Sharon Hardy will be in? Arrange for Sergeants Davis and Glover to bring Ben James in. And Nick … we need to find out who a certain "Tom" is – Belinda mentions him in her blog … it seems he was also at her New Year's Eve do, and he might very well be the source of the other set of unidentified fingerprints in her bedroom at Chalk Farm that matched up with a set in the chambers. Could be a "person of interest".'

The following Tuesday morning – two weeks to the day that Belinda had been killed – was a maelstrom of activity for Lydia and Nick. Nine o'clock found Lydia once more at Weymouth House Chambers, and again on the receiving end of Sharon Hardy's torrent of words as soon as she stepped into the lobby.

'I knew it! That tramp did it – killed our Belinda, he did! The knife was right there hidden in his sleeping bag! I bet he thought the police wouldn't look in there. Plain sight and all that!'

'Calm down, Ms Hardy. It does look suspicious, but we'll know more when forensics have had a chance to examine it. See if there are any fingerprints, test for blood, and so on. '

'Good morning, Detective,' came the smooth voice of Anthony Greenwood. He had just descended the stairs, closely followed by Sir William, who went on,

'Let's just pop into the waiting room, shall we? Sharon, any chance of some coffee, please?'

Sharon nodded eagerly and lumbered off as fast as she could manage. Lydia and the two men settled themselves on the tub chairs.

'I think we all know – especially in our line of work – that despite Sharon's excitement, this does not necessarily mean the murderer has been identified,' began Anthony.

'Indeed not.' replied Lydia. 'The evidence needs to be scrutinised, the owner of the sleeping bag – Ben Jones presumably – questioned and we still have other leads to consider.'

Sir William raised his eyebrows at Lydia's last comment and asked,

'So how can we help you, Detective?'

'Please could you tell me exactly what happened yesterday?' Lydia took out her ipad in order to make notes.

'Well, Sharon came rushing in, all of a tizzy talking about a knife and a cat, and about Belinda …' began Sir William.

'… about four-ish, I'd say.' Anthony continued, 'And personally I'd call it "bellowing". We sat her down and told her to phone the police immediately.'

'She was very agitated,' said Sir William.

'Indeed I was!' came Sharon's loud voice as she re-entered the room bearing mugs and a plate of biscuits. 'Right under our very noses that knife was!'

'Did you touch the knife at all, Ms Hardy?'
asked Lydia, taking a sip of her coffee.

'No! Of course not – I'm not that stupid!'

'Did you see anyone in the vicinity?' Lydia
continued.

'No! That derelict person wasn't there, nor any
of his cronies. Just the moggy! I'm a dog person
myself as you know and—'

At that moment, Lydia's mobile rang. Seeing it
was Nick, she picked up the call.

'Nick. You OK?'

'Hi, Boss. We've got Ben James in; we need
you asap.'

'Sure, I'm on my way.'

After finishing the call, Lydia announced to the
Weymouth House staff,

'I'm going to have to go back to the Yard. Ms
Hardy, I'd like to hear more from you – would it be
OK if we come to see you in Nunhead tomorrow – you
agreed to us visiting you at home, remember? That's if
Sir William and Anthony can do without you?'

'Sharon. Take the day off tomorrow – you've
had a nasty shock. We'll manage without you.' said
William.

'Well, if you're sure … thank you, Sir William.
See you tomorrow, Detective,' replied Sharon
gratefully. 'I'm at thirty-nine Limesford Road, right
opposite the south cemetery entrance.'

'We'll contact you to confirm the exact time,
but it's likely to be around ten o'clock, Ms Hardy,' said
Lydia.

'Wonderful! Gives me plenty of time to do some baking!'

Having returned to New Scotland Yard, Lydia resisted the temptation to wrinkle her nose at the pungent odour that preceded her as she entered the interview room. There was Ben, slouched at a table, as dapper as ever, thought Lydia, safe in the knowledge that her ironic musings were confined to her own mind, as she eyed his unkempt hair, and filthy hoodie and jogging bottoms.

'Morning, Ben. Morning Sergeant Glover. DI Fairman.' Nodding towards Nick, she continued, 'please read Ben his rights and start recording.'

While Nick spent a few minutes following this instruction, Lydia studied Ben's demeanour carefully. Shifty, yes, but a murderer? Hmm, well, we'll see.

'Do you know why you're here, Ben?' she began.

'Nope, dearie, I don't. I told ya everythin' last time. Being picked on again, aren't I?' came the rasping reply.

'A knife, possibly the one used to murder Belinda Radford – that's the barrister that was murdered exactly two weeks ago today – was yesterday found in your sleeping bag outside Weymouth House Chambers. How do you explain that, Ben?

Ben's empty eyes fixed on Lydia's face and after a few seconds of mucus-rich coughing, he answered,

'What ya accusing me of, lady?' Ben seemed genuinely indignant, thought Lydia, as Ben went on, 'I dunno what ya talkin' about … I didn't put no knife in me sleepin' bag!'

'Who do you think did then, if it wasn't you? Who'd touch your things?' asked Lydia, wondering if Ben would register her sarcasm.

'Dunno. Hardly go there now. Lawyer lady got slashed, coppers everywhere and I figure it's best not to be around there too much – even though it's a good gaff. Waterloo Bridge with me mates is safer, methinks.'

'What about Mr Mews?' asked Lydia. 'Who's looking after the cat?'

A grin, showing more gaps than teeth, appeared on Ben's lined face.

'Good one, Ma'am. Glad you remember me little buddy. Yeah, well, you got me there. I can't just leave him, can I? I goes back every day wiv a bit of fish or summat.'

'So you've got no idea how the knife got into your sleeping bag? Isn't that where Mr Mews sleeps?'

'Yeah – he loves it even if I'm not there … and if I've been out 'n about, he always comes out of me bag to greet me when I call 'im. Purring and that. But … NO! … I dunno how that knife got in there.' Ben was showing signs of agitation, so Lydia changed tack slightly.

'Last time we spoke, you said you heard doors slamming, running footsteps and a clanging noise possibly being made by a dropped knife on the morning of Ms Radford's murder. Did you pick up the knife? Was it the same knife that was found in your sleeping bag, Ben?'

Ben looked truly confused, thought Lydia, as he continued, clearly rattled.

'I told you, lady. I ain't got no idea if it's the same knife! All I know is it mighta been a knife I heard falling on the floor. I DIDNA pick it up! I stayed in me bag, turned over and got some more kip until you lot turned up. Like I said, I ain't been back there much since then.'

'OK, thank you. Sergeant Glover, please accompany Ben out.'

Alone in the room with Nick with the recorder switched off, Lydia said,

'So do we really think Ben's original story was a lie, Nick? That he wasn't drink-addled and has clear-mindedly spun us a yarn? That he didn't hear doors, the sound of footsteps and a knife being dropped? That in actual fact, he crept into Weymouth House, slunk up to the second floor, viciously killed Belinda, hid somewhere in the building when he heard the cleaner, crept out again, and then stashed the murder weapon in his own sleeping bag?'

'Unlikely. Although his sleeping bag wasn't searched at the time owing to Ben being asleep in it. Bit of a slip on our part, if I may say so.'

Lydia nodded. 'You're right. Sergeant Davis probably couldn't stand the smell. But Sergeant Glover's report that finally came through this morning says that the other rough sleepers at Waterloo Bridge corroborated Ben's story of him turning up in there on the day of the murder – apparently he was waffling on about a knife, but none of them actually saw him with one. Glover and Davis are meant to be going back to pump Ben's cronies again – I sincerely hope they didn't harass them too much; after all, it's not a crime to be homeless.'

'Hmm,' said Nick. 'Boss, I don't think Ben any more picked up that knife and put it in his sleeping bag than Mr Mews did.'

After yet another hurried lunch at the canteen, Lydia and Nick repaired to Lydia's office to spend an afternoon combing through the evidence and reports they had received since the previous day's team briefing.

'OK, Boss, so we've had a memo from Sergeant Davis saying that Gordon Radford has agreed to bring in Belinda's childhood diaries this week – he's coming in on Thursday.'

'Great. And a nice table from Sergeant Glover has come up with a preliminary list of who's right or left handed, and the heights of those connected to this case. It's rather interesting I think, Nick,' said Lydia picking up a print out:

Suspects in alphabetical order	Right-handed	Left-handed	Height
Sir William Bond	Yes		5 ft. 9
Amanda Faith		Yes	5 ft. 7

Steven Faith	Yes		5 ft. 8
Anthony Greenwood	Yes		5 ft. 10
Sharon Hardy		Yes	5 ft. 4
Benjamin ("Ben") James	Yes		5 ft. 6
Julian Radford		Yes	6 ft.
Samuel ("Sam") White	Yes		5 ft. 9
NB: Victim			
Belinda Radford	*Yes*		*5ft 10.5*

'Yes, Terry's getting his teeth into this one alright!' answered Nick.

'We'll probably have to add in this "Tom"', said Lydia. 'We know he must be about five foot eight according to Lydia's blog.'

'Sure thing, Boss. Now – fingerprints. So, Norman Combe and Max Burgh's report is divided into the law chambers and the Chalk Farm flat. Obviously, the prints from the people who work at Weymouth House are all over the building, and there are loads of unknown fingerprints as well. Interestingly, the Faiths are not in the system, so they haven't shown up … although that doesn't mean they haven't been to the chambers – indeed, they told they have. However, some prints *have* cross-referenced to names in the database. We have a Martha Bigbury and a Skye Warriner … we're finding out who they are as we speak.'

'They're clients – I remember Sharon Hardy mentioning them,' said Lydia, who picked up the thread. 'It's a similar story at Belinda's flat. Old prints belonging to the Weymouth House staff have been identified in the lounge, kitchen and bathroom – most probably from the New Year's Eve party – as well as some unknown fingerprints. I guess these might be from the partners of the guests: Anthony Greenwood's and Sam's White's wives, and Julian's girlfriend. Of more interest, are the two sets of fingerprints upstairs in the bedroom and bathroom. One set belongs to Greenwood as we know, and the other set I'm guessing are those of this mysterious Tom.'

'On it, Boss. We'll find him,' said Nick. 'Regarding the email account user of whoever sent you that threatening message, I'm afraid that Tech has come up against a brick wall. The perp knew how to hide their tracks.'

'Great – not,' replied Lydia.

At that moment, both Lydia's and Nick's phones beeped, signalling the arrival of an email.

'Ah. Forensics have come back on the knife, Nick. Let's have a look.'

Summary of forensic findings on alleged murder weapon used in homicide of Belinda Radford, female, twenty-eight years of age

a. The alleged murder weapon appears to be a kitchen knife of a type commonly used in approximately 30% of homicides committed in the UK (see figure 1 in full report = photograph of whole knife).

b. Length of alleged murder weapon: 32cm from handle to tip (handle = 12cm/blade = 20cm).

c. Trace evidence shows that 20mm (or 2 cm) of the tip of the alleged murder weapon pierced the deceased's carotid artery and jugular vein. Relatively low force would have been necessary to penetrate the thin skin covering this area of the body and to cause lethal rupturing due to the sharpness of the knife's tip (see figure 2 in full report = photograph of tip of knife).

d. No fingerprints were identified, due to the alleged murder weapon having been wiped.

e. While no trace evidence visible to the naked eye was present, minute traces of DNA were recovered on the alleged murder weapon, using forensic means of identification. The tip primarily presents direct trace DNA transferred via blood that matches that of the deceased, Belinda Radford, female, twenty-eight years of age. The remainder of the blade and the handle display indirect trace DNA in the form of cellular material *(i.e. skin and hair/fur) belonging to two separate human transferors and one feline transferor.*

f. *Due to the alleged murder weapon having been wiped, hence the DNA trace being minute, it is impossible to ascertain whether the indirect human transferors are male or female. The feline transferor is almost certainly a short-haired cat.*

g. *The empirical data outlined above including photographs is available in full detail by clicking* **here** *and downloading the comprehensive report.*

'Hmm,' began Lydia meditatively. 'Apart from confirmation that it's the murder weapon, there's not a lot to go on really, though it looks at least as if the perp knew how to wield a knife effectively.'

'Yes, and was canny enough to wipe it down. No doubt one of the "human transferors" was Ben; I guess some of the trace DNA came from inside his sleeping bag. And we know who the feline donor is! So, who is the *other* human transferor that's left a tiny clue for us, Boss?'

'Short of getting DNA samples from everyone known to Belinda which is not actually legal until we've made an arrest, we're still very much in the dark. Still, I feel as if we're getting closer. Now, people I still want to see are: Miranda Greenwood and Precious Temishe.'

'Precious is coming in on Thursday to make a statement, and we have a day out in Hampstead on

165

Monday to visit the Greenwoods. Not to mention Nunhead tomorrow!'

'Thanks for reminding me, Nick,' said Lydia, not bothering to hide the sarcasm from her voice.

Chapter 15

Sui Generis (belongs in a particular category)

'Cheers for driving again, Nick.'

'No problem, Boss – it's hardly very far from the office, is it?'

Lydia and Nick had arrived half an hour ahead of their meeting time with Sharon Hardy in Nunhead, and, having parked their car further along Limesford Road, around the bend from number thirty-nine, decided to take a quick stroll around the famous cemetery as it was such a gorgeous, sunny day.

'I've heard it referred to as the Highgate Cemetery of south London,' remarked Lydia, 'a bit more unkempt, though.'

'Yes, definitely not what they call "manicured",' said Nick, as they glanced around the lopsided tombstones, moss-covered plinths topped by broken statues, and ivy-covered fallen branches in the undergrowth.

'I like the daffodils,' Lydia went on. 'It's quite dark in here, isn't it – the yellow brightens the place up.'

Stopping at a grimy, glass-encased noticeboard, they read all about the various events held in the cemetery: guided tours, evening bat walks, an open day … a talk about the many angels depicted or carved on stone or marble. A newspaper article told of the recent discovery of the grave of Jack the Ripper suspect, Thomas Cutbush.

'Good name! Nunhead's answer to Karl Marx, maybe,' said Nick. 'Hey, look – there's a puppy party at the weekend! Do you think Sharon Hardy will bring … Ruskin, is it?'

'Yes, I bet she'll bake some dog biscuits for the occasion,' responded Lydia. 'Definitely a good place to walk a dog. My parents' Betsy would love it here …'

'You could have one, couldn't you, Boss? Your back garden opens right onto Battersea Park – perfect walking ground!'

'Well, I'd feel bad about leaving a dog alone all day in the flat. And you know what it's like sometimes in our line of work, Nick – late nights, interrupted weekends … '

'Sure. I guess Sharon Hardy has fairly regular hours, so it's not such an issue for her dog.'

They stood to one side to let a woman with three Westies pass, then took a footpath through a group of fragrant-leaved linden trees in danger of being strangled by the omnipresent verdant ivy.

'Ah, here's the pond,' said Lydia. 'And blackberry bushes. Sharon mentioned them, didn't she?'

'All the better for making blackberry crumble, I expect, Boss,' replied Nick. 'Right, how are we going to tackle Ms Hardy?'

'Apart from trying to get a word in edgeways, I only really want to skim over the morning of the murder and her discovering the knife – we might squeeze a little bit more out of her on those two points. I'd like to see what she knows about this "Tom" and whether she was aware of the Belinda and Anthony

Greenwood scenario, and of course … find out more about the delightful Sharon herself.' She grimaced. 'I'll do the talking and you take notes … but don't hold back if you think of anything.' Lydia sensed that Nick would not have been satisfied merely remaining silent; he was eager to dig down further in this case, and his interrogation technique was both subtle and perceptive. He nodded in response.

After a few moments gazing at the blue-sheened dragonflies hovering over the pond's surface and listening to the tapping of an earnest woodpecker, they continued walking. In a matter of minutes, they arrived back at the south entrance to the cemetery.

'OK, here goes, Boss. Ready?'

'Indeed. I could do with a cuppa now.'

A high-pitched yapping greeted Lydia and Nick as they rang the bell of Sharon Hardy's small Victorian terrace house, with its bright yellow front door and hanging basket full of colourful red and pink trailing geraniums that dominated the pocket-handkerchief sized front garden of thirty-nine Limesford Road.

'Hello, Detectives! So glad you could make it – kettle's on, and I've baked some flapjacks just like I promised, and some rocky road as a special treat! Shh, Ruskin! Be nice to our visitors! Do come in, both of you!' Lydia doubted whether Sharon had even drawn breath in that first outpouring of words.

'Thank you, Ms Hardy, and good morning to you, too,' she replied.

Nick also nodded in acknowledgement, and they both stepped into the house. Lydia's first impression was of an olfactory nature; that peculiar musty smell that she had noticed the very first time she had had the pleasure of meeting Sharon Hardy two weeks earlier. Definitely dog, damp clothes, and something else she could not quite put her finger on. Nor wanted to.

'Through here! We'll sit in the sitting room – I keep it for best, you know!' said Sharon, leading the way into a front room directly to the left of the front door. The room was small, stuffy and dark despite its average-sized window, and seemed cramped, probably due to the pair of tall old-fashioned brown corduroy armchairs, several occasional tables, a tea-trolley and a glass-fronted tallboy full of knickknacks. Lydia immediately felt claustrophobic and made for the chair nearest the window. Just like my grandmother's old place, she thought.

'Lovely! Now, Ruskin will keep you company while I bring everything through. Tea or coffee?'

After Lydia and Nick had politely opted for coffee, Sharon bustled off towards the back of the house. Nick bent down to stroke the rather rotund, brindle-coloured Cairn terrier that sat to attention at his feet.

'Cute dog,' he remarked. Ruskin gazed up at him adoringly, completely ignoring Lydia.

'Hmm. Looks as though he has a fine line of ancestors,' remarked Lydia, indicating the wall of framed photos of Cairn terriers of varying colours, proudly displaying prize rosettes. 'Got your notebook ready, Nick?'

The clinking of tea cups heralded Sharon's return, and there followed some fussing while three small tables were pulled out of the shadows and placed in front of each of them. Today the clerk to the barristers was clearly in dressed-down mode; sheepskin slippers, a navy blue fleece that only served to emphasise her bulk, and beige slacks. Definitely not leggings, thought Lydia. Not with the stirrups.

'Ooh, I think Ruskin likes you, Sir! Likes a man's hand, he does! Cairns work hard but need to be kept at it otherwise they get bored, you know. We always had them in our family – pure breeds, of course— '

'Of course,' interrupted Lydia. 'Ms Hardy, just to summarise what we know so far: you've worked at Weymouth House for fifteen years and started there well before the current incumbents, Sir William Bond and Anthony Greenwood, and the deceased, Belinda Radford.'

'Yes, I—'

Before Sharon could break her flow of thought, Lydia went on,

'You always got on well with Belinda, calming her nerves on the day of her feedback session with Sir William, and talking through some of the finer, more unorthodox points of law with her, am I right?'

Sharon nodded, and Lydia continued,

'On the morning of Belinda's murder, you arrived at work at seven forty-five, only to be met by the police. You've a strong inkling that Ben James, the tramp who occupies the rhododendron bush in the mews outside Weymouth House Chambers, is implicated, especially as you were the one who came across the alleged murder weapon in his sleeping bag. Have you anything more to add?'

'All correct, Detective. I walked Ruskin in the cemetery as usual at between six and seven in the morning – loads of my fellow dog walkers can corroborate that – and got into the chambers to be confronted by the most devastating experience I've ever encountered in my whole life. Darling, darling Belinda …' Sharon's voice broke, but she rallied. 'More coffee?'

'Thank you,' replied Lydia, nodding politely. 'The flapjack is delicious by the way. Do continue.'

'Well, about the knife. As you know, I decided to take that old tramp a doughnut – have to be charitable now, don't we? I'd popped out to get some buns anyway for Sir William and Attorney Anthony seeing as they're finding the whole business so awful. No reply from Ben when I called over to him but I could see a lump or a bump there in the sleeping bag and I was worried in case he'd died or something! But it was that scraggy little cat … cuddled right up to a knife! Any news on that, by the way?'

'We've had a forensic report on it, but I'm afraid it's confidential for now,' replied Lydia, adding, 'I have a couple more questions that have emerged during the course of our investigation. Firstly, going back to Belinda's New Year's Eve party that you said you went to?' asked Lydia.

'Oh yes, very clear in my mind that is. Remember it as if it was yesterday … I've got somewhat of a good memory, you know, always have had …'

'Apart from Sir William, Mr and Mrs Greenwood and Sam White—' Lydia noticed the scowl that appeared on Sharon's face at the mention of the cleaner's name. '– and his wife, who else was there at the party?'

'Belinda's brother and his girlfriend – very nice lady, I thought. And …, oh yes – Belinda's young man! Not that she'd admit it though. Acted all coy at work when I asked her about him! "Just a friend!" she said. But I knew better, of course. I can always sense when someone's keeping something back you know and—'

'What was this "friend" like and do you remember his name?'

'Er … Ted. Or Tim. No, it was Tom, I think. Yes, that's it. Not particularly tall, dark-haired, stout rather than skinny … didn't really stand out. He was going around topping up people's drinks and changing the music the rest of the time! Not very lovey-dovey towards Belinda really. He—'

'Did he say where he worked?' put in Nick.

'No, just made polite conversation. Talked to that cleaner's wife quite a bit, though. Maybe he's a teacher like her? Looked the academic type. The haircut, you know. I think—'

Lydia was slowly wearying of constantly pulling Sharon back on track.

'May I use the facilities, please, Ms Hardy?'

'Yes, of course – I'll show you where!'

Lydia found herself following Sharon's large rear end up some stairs once more – just as at Weymouth House. Great, she thought. She was guided to an upstairs bathroom, and locked herself in with a sigh of relief at the moment's respite from the oppressive sitting room and its overbearing owner. After a few minutes, she flushed the lavatory and splashed some cool water on her face from the washbasin. The clanging and banging of the plumbing system that had clearly seen better days provided the perfect cover for her to have a snoop around upstairs.

There were three doors leading from the upper landing, two of which were firmly closed; however, the door to the room at the back of the house was ever so slightly ajar. Lydia listened for the sound of voices from downstairs; well done, Nick, she thought. Keep her talking. She pushed open the door and poked her head into a musty-smelling room, made darker than it should be with its heavy net curtains. It was obviously Sharon's bedroom; a large, old-fashioned wooden double bed dominated the room and a tall darkwood wardrobe stood to the right of the room, its doors open, revealing an untidy assortment of blouses, trousers, jackets and coats, and exuding a whiff of mothballs. Lydia caught sight of three pale faces looking at her and realised with a jolt that it was herself, reflected in the three dusty mirrors of an old winged dressing table facing into the room. Talk about Miss Havisham's lair, she thought.

She withdrew her head and started down the stairs in the nick of time; Sharon had quietly appeared on the bottom step.

'Everything all right, Detective? Sorry about the pipes up there! Takes a while sometimes.'

'Yes, fine. I was just admiring your photos here on the wall,' replied Lydia, pausing half way down the stairs and peering at the old black and white framed pictures of various animals, mainly dogs and ponies.

'Oh yes, I've always loved my animals – they were my friends growing up, you know!'

'So where did you grow up, Sharon?'

'Near Fordingbridge – down south. Never liked it much though! In the middle of nowhere, everything shut on a Sunday. Boring! Still, that's when I learnt to cook and bake I suppose. And I always had my furry pals of course – used to breed and show my Cairns at the local county show!'

'When did you move to London?'

'As soon as I could! Left school and came straight up here – started off as a washer-upper in a pub, nearly twenty years ago now, would you believe! Then I put myself through night school, got some A levels, did a secretarial course and started doing temp work in law offices. Loved it so much that I even did a part-time law familiarisation course! I was thrilled to get the Bar Clerk job at Weymouth House, of course. Mainly down to my organisational and people skills as the IBC – that's the Institute of Barristers' Clerks, in case you didn't know! – advises. Plus I— '

At that moment, a yapping noise heralded the escape of Ruskin from the sitting room, closely followed by Nick.

'Oh sorry! He was scrabbling at the door,' said Nick. 'I think he wants to go out.'

'Come on, Ruskin! Detectives, do go and sit back down.' Sharon disappeared through to the back of the house and the sound of the back door being unlocked echoed through the house.

'So did you find out anything, Nick?' asked Lydia in a low voice once they were again ensconced in the dingy sitting room.

'Nothing much we don't already know, Boss. It was mostly singing the praises of Sir William.'

'OK. Let's see what she makes of Anthony Greenwood and his dangerous liaisons.'

Sharon returned and Lydia went straight to the point, not wanting to stay a minute longer than necessary in this depressing house.

'How close were Belinda and Anthony Greenwood, would you say, Sharon?'

Sounding genuinely surprised, Sharon replied,

'Oh! Well, he used to help her a lot, what with her being new and so on. And he is a very experienced …'

'… man. Indeed.' Lydia could not resist finishing the sentence for Sharon. 'Do you know how far his "extra-curricular" help went?'

'I don't know what you mean! Integrity is Anthony's middle name! And anyway, he's married!' Sharon's voice rose in indignation.

'Well, he has admitted to going out for after-work drinks with Belinda. I'm surprised she didn't mention that to you, Sharon?'

176

'As I said before, she did use to keep things back sometimes – often had a little secret smile on her face! I assumed she was thinking about Tom – the young man from the party. Attorney Anthony, though … well, I'd never have thought it—'

Lydia felt absurdly smug that they knew something that Sharon did not, but also disappointed that this line of enquiry was going nowhere.

'OK. Well, if you think of anything else that might help us find Belinda's murderer, do get in touch.' Lydia and Nick stood up to go.

'Detective Fairman! Would you like some rocky road to take with you?'

'So, she won you over then, did she, Nick?' remarked Lydia drily, once they had turned the corner of Limesford Road and were standing by their car.

'Erm … 'fraid so!' answered Nick, his mouth full of cake.

'That house, though – like stepping into the past. All darkness and old brown furniture; upstairs was just the same, as far as I could see,' continued Lydia.

'Pictures of animals,' went on Nick. 'But not a single photo of family or people.'

'Yes, I noticed that, too. OK, so we know more about Sharon Hardy now. And she's confirmed a sighting of the mysterious "Tom". Interesting that she hadn't picked up on Belinda and Anthony, though … considering she thinks she knows everything that's going on,' said Lydia. 'Could you get one of the sergeants to interview some of the dog walkers who use the cemetery? See if they remember seeing her the morning of the murder. I'm sure Terry or Clive will enjoy getting up early and taking a nice morning walk among the gravestones.

'Ha. Anyway, let's get back to the Yard, Boss. It's nearly lunchtime.'

'Don't tell me you're hungry again, Nick?!'

Chapter 16

Ab Initio (from the start of something)

After a snatched lunch, Lydia and Nick reconvened in Lydia's office to share updates and reports on the case.

'Remember those fingerprints in the chambers belonging to a Martha Bigbury and a Skye Warriner, Boss? Well, we've tracked them down due to their being in the fingerprint database, and they're coming in this afternoon – in about twenty minutes or so.'

'Great. Do we know anything about them?'

'Turns out they're nurses at Guy's Hospital, and involved in some sort of medical litigation case being handled by Weymouth House.'

'OK, Nick. Doesn't Julian's girlfriend work at Guy's?'

'Yes, Precious Temishe. It would be too much to hope for a connection though – they've got about sixteen thousand employees, you know, Boss!'

Martha Bigbury and Skye Warriner were waiting in the interview room as Lydia and Nick entered. Both appeared to be in their late twenties, well dressed in smart skinny jeans and chic tops, and were immaculately made up. They sat close together and wore expressions of deep sadness

'Good afternoon. Thank you so much for coming in,' began Lydia. 'As you know, we're investigating the murder of Belinda Radford, whom I believe you're both acquainted with. Ms Bigbury, can I start with you?'

'Oh, do call me Martha,' said the blonde, blue-eyed long-haired beauty. Lydia wondered how nurses had time to be so well turned out. Martha continued,

'We're so shocked about Belinda. We're – were – very close to her. We've been away travelling in the Far East and have only recently got back. We've only just heard about her death. It's so awful.'

'Yes,' said Skye Warriner, dark blonde, big green-grey eyes and cheekbones to die for. 'The internet was very unreliable where we were. To think that poor Belinda might not be dead if she'd only come with us …'

'What do you mean, Skye? Is it OK to call you that?' asked Lydia. Skye nodded and explained,

'The three of us had been discussing going on a long haul holiday for years – ever since uni – and we'd finally decided to do it. But then Belinda got the position at Weymouth House and decided not to come with us. "Next time!" she said. "I need to make my mark – it's a golden opportunity for me to show the world what women can do!" We're a little bit feminist you see …'

'So you were uni friends?' put in Nick, who'd been entering notes on his ipad.

'Sort of. We were in the same hall of residence – an intercollegiate one. Connaught Hall in Tavistock Square … we had rooms on the same corridor. Belinda was studying law at UCL, but Martha and I were at King's, doing nursing – the Florence Nightingale faculty down at Waterloo.'

'We hit it off straightaway,' said Martha. 'We used to go down to the dining hall for meals together, went out on the town together and stayed in touch even after we all graduated and started working.'

'Yes,' continued Skye. 'We've been meeting up at least three or four times a year for the last six or seven years.'

'When did you last see Belinda?' asked Lydia.

'It was before we went away ... so towards the end of February, wasn't it, Martha? We had a meeting with Belinda at Weymouth House. She was dealing with a legal case for us, you see.'

'Could you tell us about the case?' asked Lydia. 'I know it's probably confidential, but ...'

'Of course. Anything to help find the brute who did this to poor Belinda.' said Skye. 'It's basically a medical negligence claim brought against the NHS, or rather, against Martha and me. We were both working for children's services and there was a three-month year old baby boy who was admitted with infant pneumonia. Anyway, we monitored his respiratory and heart rates by the book, and didn't notice anything out of the ordinary at first, did we Martha?'

Martha continued,

'No. But after a week or so, we – independently of each other – noticed some drastic falls in his heart rate and breathing levels, and on each occasion summoned a doctor. However, the doctors didn't do much except wait for the rates to stabilise again. Then, one night, the child had a seizure, and it turned out he was suffering from cerebral atrophy. While he is not completely brain damaged, he will need significant care for the rest of his life – which the parents can't really afford ...'

'So the parents are suing the hospital, and the powers-that-be are trying to blame you two?' guessed Lydia.

'Yes. The hospital is saying that we failed in our duty of care as nurses, but, in our opinion, it's completely disregarding the role of the doctors – who didn't react appropriately when we informed them,' said Martha.'

'Luckily, we kept records of all our reports, emails and correspondence from when it all went pear-shaped at the hospital, and we decided we would not be scapegoats. Our solicitor, Gupta Legal Services, agreed to take on the case and use Belinda as barrister, as we believed she would absolutely do her best for us in court. So we met with Belinda who said that she'd have to get special permission from her boss in case it was perceived as a conflict of interest seeing as we knew each other, but that she was sure Sir William would be fine with it. It was her first medical litigation case and I think she leapt at the chance to gain more experience and recognition,' said Skye.

Martha continued,

'Not that she'd've admitted that to us! We knew she'd do her utmost and she believed us one hundred percent. We want our names cleared of course, but also want the hospital to recognise that the negligence lies with the doctors, so that the parents can get some sort of compensation to help with the upbringing of the child. Poor little thing.'

What's the betting most of those doctors are arrogant males, mused Lydia privately. Trying to blame the female nurses to cover up their own inadequacies. Hopefully, they've got another think coming. She asked,

'When you met Belinda at Weymouth House, did you stay long?

'A couple of hours,' answered Martha. 'We had coffee, and we went through all the documentation. As we were about to go on our trip, we left it with Belinda to process and arranged to meet up again when we came back ...'

'We're guessing you tracked us down due to our fingerprints in Belinda's office – although we were about to contact the police anyway, once we heard about poor Belinda,' said Skye. 'As Martha said, we've only just got back from travelling in Vietnam and Cambodia. Our prints are in the system – it's mandatory for all nurses these days.'

'I see. Thank you for clarifying that point. We've been trying to contact you for a while now, but it makes sense that you've been away and didn't get our messages. On another note, do you by any chance know a doctor at Guy's named "Precious Temishe"?' asked Lydia.

Skye shook her head, but Martha replied after a couple of moments,

'Not personally, but I recognise the name – it stands out, doesn't it? Yes – I remember now! Belinda mentioned that her brother was dating a trainee doctor from Guy's.'

'Oh yes, I remember now,' continued Skye. 'She said that Julian had brought his new girlfriend called Precious to her New Year's Eve party. She thought that lovely though Precious was, she must be wearing rose-tinted glasses when it came to her brother … Belinda didn't get on very well with him. We met him once or twice at uni, I think, but no more than that.'

'So were you two invited to Belinda's party?' interjected Nick.

'Yes,' replied Martha. 'But we both had family commitments out of town and couldn't make it, unfortunately,'

'Now, I've got another question for you. Did Belinda mention a "Tom" to you at all?' asked Lydia.

'Oh yes! We know Tom. Tom Lovell,' said Skye. 'He was in halls as well. He studied History and Politics at King's – on the main Strand campus. He was in our group of mates … we used to go out drinking and clubbing quite a bit. We're still in contact. A little.'

'So were he and Belinda an item?' asked Lydia, glancing over at Nick to make sure he'd made a note of where to find the elusive owner of the hitherto unknown set of fingerprints in Belinda's bedroom.

'Sort of … on and off. They hooked up a couple of times as students, but then went their separate ways after we all graduated. They've always kept in touch, though. Tom's a lecturer at Goldsmiths College, New Cross,' continued Skye.

'Did you know he was going to be at the New Year's Eve party?' asked Lydia.

'Yes,' said Martha. 'They were back on – though I always had the impression that Belinda was far keener on him than the other way round. A few weeks into January, and he called it off yet again. A bit of a dark horse, he is.'

'Was she upset?' asked Lydia.

'More resigned, than anything,' replied Martha. 'We took her out for a consolation drink. "It's never going to work out between me and Tom, is it, girls?" she said. Sadly, we agreed with her. We like Tom, but he's the non-committal type, if you know what I mean. "He's a good stopgap though until someone better comes along!" I said to her ...'

'And did she ever mention anyone "better" after that?' put in Nick,

'No ... but then we didn't see much of her after the end of January and we were away during March,' Skye said. 'Anything could have happened in that time, of course ...'

'Who's going to take over your litigation' asked Lydia. 'I take it you've going to continue with it?'

'Of course,' answered Martha. 'We're not taking the fall for a bunch of snotty doctors! I believe that Belinda's colleague, Anthony Greenwood, is handling our case now. Quite eye-catching, isn't he? I'm glad – we didn't really take to the older barrister, William Bond. Bit of an old-school "ladies' man" ... he came on to Belinda, so she told us.'

'Yes, she said she had to tactfully cold-shoulder him,' continued Skye. 'Without risking her position at chambers.'

'Going back to the "eye-catching" Anthony Greenwood,' said Lydia, 'were you aware of any relationship between him and Belinda?'

'No, but it wouldn't surprise me,' answered Skye. Martha nodded in agreement and went on,

'After it fell through with Tom, Belinda might have wanted to cheer herself up, and Anthony Greenwood is rather ... "fetching", shall we say! I'm sure she would have told us all about it once we were back. It's all so terrible; we've got presents for her from Vietnam and Cambodia and everything ...'

Both nurses were quiet for a moment, and Lydia noticed that their eyes were filling with tears.

'You've both been so helpful. Thank you very much indeed,' she said. 'We'll be in touch if there's anything else we need; or indeed, do please contact us if you think of anything that might help solve Belinda's murder. And no doubt you'll be going to the funeral'.

Martha and Skye nodded and stood up to leave.

'Nail the bastard who killed our dear friend, won't you, Detective?' said Martha.

'You can count on that,' replied Lydia grimly.

'Get this Tom Lovell in, Nick.'

'Already on it, Boss. I've just arranged to have him brought in tomorrow – right after we see Precious Temishe. She's coming in first thing to give her statement.'

'Good. Thank God we've tracked down this Tom at last. But why on earth hasn't he come forward before now?' Lydia was fuming. 'It's not as though he's been conveniently out of the country like Martha and Skye.'

'According to Sergeant Davis's email, Mr Lovell was rather reluctant to come in, refused to say anything and was generally quite evasive.'

'Hmm … definitely the evasive type if the nurses are to be believed,' put in Lydia. Typical non-committal male indeed, she thought.

'Talking of the nurses – what did you think of their story, Boss?'

'All reasonably bona fide, and they've filled in a few gaps in the investigation. But I'm not convinced about them saying they've been incommunicado for the last few weeks; it's my experience that people of our age will do anything to get a WiFi connection.'

'Maybe not where they were; it could well have been a bit unreliable. Or perhaps they wanted to "switch off" from the rest of the world?'

'I don't think they're the "switching off" kind, Nick. But granted – they might not have followed the UK news headlines. Could you get the techies to check if they were posting on social media at all? Look into flight records and also check with the Foreign Office as to whether they happened to make any contact with local consulates while they were out in the Far East. Interesting what they made of Sir William. It must have been quite tricky for Belinda to snub him diplomatically … I bet he didn't like being rejected by a "pretty" young girl.'

'Probably not, Boss. Takes us back to the idea that he might have been more rattled than he makes out. It's a wonder that Sharon Hardy hasn't picked up on the Sir William/Belinda "connection", for want of a better word.'

'From what we've seen of Sharon, she thinks he can do no wrong. Probably wishes he'd pay *her* more of that kind of attention! As for Anthony Greenwood, she was way off the mark about him and Belinda,' said Lydia pensively. 'I'm inclined to agree with Martha Bigbury about the one-night stand with Anthony being a way for Belinda to comfort herself after the failure of her sort-of-relationship with Tom.'

'Possibly. A bit naughty though; she must have known about Mrs Greenwood,' said Nick, a trifle sanctimoniously, mused Lydia.

'Not a crime, Nick! Anyway, I'm sure Anthony would have obliged to help a damsel in distress despite his being married.'

'Good point. I wonder what his wife's like! Going back to Sharon Hardy, she was quite on the button about Tom being a teacher – a university lecturer is quite close.'

'I'm going to put him through his paces tomorrow alright, Nick.'

'Knowing you, Boss, I'm sure you will.'

What a day, thought Lydia that evening once she had kicked off her shoes, changed into some leggings and a t-shirt, and settled down on her sofa with a glass of Shiraz. Sharon Hardy on her own territory, not to mention the revelations of the two nurses, played on her mind. Her musings were interspersed with thoughts of the Radford family, Belinda's friends, colleagues and clients, and even Ben James and his cat.

'What am I missing?' she wondered out loud. It was coming together, but all too slowly – even though it was only two weeks and a day since Belinda had been killed. Her thoughts drifted to the elusive Tom and his lack of commitment; what is it with men? They want to control you to prove their maleness like her and Belinda's fathers; or they can't keep it in their pants – like Anthony Greenwood; or else they slip away once they realise you're a strong, modern woman who wants an equal partnership.

'Cheers,' said Lydia, raising her glass to an empty room.

Chapter 17

Caveat Emptor (buyer beware)

Precious Temishe was sitting waiting in the interview room, cup of coffee in front of her, as Lydia and Nick entered. Sergeant Davis was standing by the window and could hardly keep his eyes off the petite, sweet-faced young woman – dressed in an elegant magenta-coloured shirtdress – that he was supposed to be chaperoning, noted Lydia.

'Morning, Dr Temishe,' began Lydia. 'I'm DI Carlisle and this is my colleague, DI Fairman. Thank you very much for coming in today to assist with our enquiries.'

'No problem at all, Detectives. And do call me Precious. I'm not completely qualified as a doctor yet anyway.'

'How much longer do you have in training?' asked Lydia, while Nick set up the recording equipment.

'Another two years as a junior and then after a whole lot of exams and so on, I hope to finally become a fully-fledged doctor.'

'Will you stay on at Guy's then?'

'Possibly, though I'd quite like to move to the US eventually. I think I'll have had enough of London after so many years here. Though I do get back to Abuja a couple of times a year to see my family, of course.'

'So how would relocating to America affect your relationship with Julian Radford?'

Precious paused before replying,

'Well, he can come with me if he likes ... if not, I'd still go!'

That's my girl, thought Lydia. She went on,

'Returning to the reason we have invited you here, would you answer a few questions regarding the evening before Belinda Radford was murdered?'

'Of course. And may I say how dreadfully sorry and shocked I am about Julian's sister. I very much liked her the one time I met her back on New Year's Eve'.

Nick read the caution, and Lydia dove in.

'Where were you on the Monday evening?'

'I was with Julian the whole evening at his house in Blackheath. I got there about eight thirty, we cooked dinner together and then watched some TV – a couple of episodes of "Orange is the New Black" ... on Netflix to be precise.'

'We'll be verifying that through their streaming records, of course,' put in Nick.

'Did you stay the night, Precious?' asked Lydia.

'No ... I often do though. But we both had early starts the next day; I had to be in at Guy's for an eight o'clock briefing, and Julian said he needed to be at work by eight for an international video conference, I think it was. So I left around eleven that evening – Julian walked me to the station and I was home by about eleven forty-five. I live in Crystal Palace – not that far away and I was lucky with the train connections.'

'So although you can vouch for Julian on the Monday evening, you don't know where he actually was all through the night and early Tuesday morning?'

For the first time during the interview, Precious looked slightly less sure of herself.

'Ermm, well I can only assume he went back home that night and left the house around six thirty or seven the next morning to get to Spitalfields for eight o'clock. He sent me a few texts ... he always does ... in fact, he messaged me later that morning from work to inform me about Belinda's being found dead ...'

'Did he seem very upset at that point?' asked Lydia disingenuously, remembering how cool Julian had seemed when she had quizzed him about his murdered sister.

'As much as one can be in a mobile phone text, I suppose, Detective. I know they weren't that close but I'm sure he's devastated ... he's been very down these last couple of weeks. He's also been supporting his parents a lot recently ... he's very concerned about them so he tells me.'

I bet he is, thought Lydia. There's that inheritance to think of, after all. She went on,

'Have you met Mr Radford senior and his wife yet?'

'No ... it's unfortunate that the first time we meet will be at poor Belinda's funeral,' replied Precious. 'It's going to be so very sad.'

'Do you by any chance know a Martha Bigbury and a Skye Warriner? They're friends of Belinda's and are at Guy's as well – nurses.'

'No, can't say I do,' said Precious after a moment's thought. 'But there are thousands of staff employed there, you know.'

'Yes, I do know … well, it looks as though you'll be meeting them at the funeral too,' replied Lydia.

After wrapping up the interview and directing Sergeant Davis to accompany Precious out of the building, a task he was very eager to take on, Lydia and Nick compared impressions.

'Well, Boss, she seems pretty straight up. I don't think she herself is involved or is covering up for Julian in any way.'

'Yes, nice lady. What she sees in that cold fish Julian is anyone's guess, Nick.'

'Opposites attracting again, Boss! Or maybe he's on his best behaviour around Precious.'

'Hmm … though she can't provide him with an alibi for the crucial time of between six and seven on the Tuesday morning as yet. Julian could easily have made a detour to Weymouth House, got in, murdered Belinda, and then got to his bank by eight o'clock,' replied Lydia.

'How would he have got in, Boss?'

'Well that goes for any of the suspects, doesn't it? The perp's either got keys to Weymouth House or they slipped in somehow,' replied Lydia, who went on thoughtfully, 'Or in the case of Julian, maybe Belinda let him in? Perhaps he wanted to talk to her again about not telling the parents about Precious and she agreed to meet him? And if she then refused to play ball, he might have lost his rag, sneaked up behind her while she was making coffee and done the deed?'

'But would he have come armed with a knife just in case Belinda declined to keep quiet about his girlfriend?'

'Hmm, maybe he grabbed one from somewhere in the building on the spur of the moment? A fingertip search of the premises was done by uniform the morning of the murder; they didn't find anything as we know. But remember, they didn't know exactly what weapon they were searching for at that point.'

'Sure,' replied Nick, who continued, 'And they were looking for something that was there as opposed to something that *wasn't* there.'

'Good thinking, Nick. Get one of the sergeants over to Weymouth House to do an inventory of the cleaning room Nick – I'm wondering if any cutlery and so on is kept there. And they could ask the staff if there's anything missing. I'm sure the charming Sharon would be happy to oblige.'

At that moment, Sergeant Terry Glover poked his head round the door.

'Tom Lovell's here, Guv. Shall I bring him in?'

'Yes. Oh and could you arrange for some coffee, Sergeant? Please.' added Lydia.

After Nick had read him his rights, Lydia wasted no time in introducing themselves and interrogating Tom Lovell.

'Hello. I'm DI Carlisle and this is my assistant, DI Fairman. So, Mr Lovell, could you please tell us why you haven't come forward before now? You must have heard about Belinda Radford's death.'

Tom, a not very tall but muscular man with longish dark hair and a hint of body odour, glared at Lydia, his anger barely hidden.

'Is it a legal requirement to go to the police just because one of my friends has been murdered?'

'Well, no … what do you mean by "one of my friends"? Have any more of your friends died, Mr Lovell?' interjected Nick.

A surly response from Tom met this question head on.

'Not pertinent to this questioning, Detective Fairman.'

'OK. Let's cut to the chase,' said Lydia. 'A set of unidentified fingerprints has been found in Belinda's bedroom and, interestingly, the same set has been found at her place of work. If we were to take your fingerprints, would they match, Mr Lovell?'

'I'm afraid you're not going to get the answer to that question. You know as well as I do that you can't take my fingerprints unless I'm under arrest, Detective Carlisle.'

'If we suspect you've committed an offence, then we're legally allowed to, though, Mr Lovell.'

'So what offence are you alleging I might have committed?' answered Tom. 'You don't seriously think I killed Belinda, do you?'

'Why do you think we've brought you in?' Lydia was beginning to lose her patience. 'Now tell us how long you knew her, what your relationship status was and where you were on the night before and on the morning of Belinda's murder – that's two weeks and two days ago.'

'I know when she was killed, thank you,' replied Tom somewhat testily. 'I've known Belinda for about ten years, ever since we were at university. We were in the same hall of residence and hung out together with the same crowd.'

'Including Martha Bigbury and Skye Warriner. Yes, we've already spoken to them,' interrupted Nick.

'So that's how you tracked me down,' said Tom. 'Christ, those two can't keep their mouths shut.'

'Nice way to talk about your friends,' remarked Lydia. 'We would have found you eventually though, seeing as quite a few of Belinda's work colleagues met you at her New Year's Eve party, and she mentions you quite a lot in her blog …'

For the first time, Tom looked slightly worried rather than sullen. Good, thought Lydia. Let's shake his tree a little more and see what else falls out.

'Now please answer my second question and describe your relationship with Belinda.'

'Just casual really. We hooked up for sex now and then; we always had a thing for each other, even back at uni. But nothing serious,' replied Tom. 'At least not from my point of view.'

'And what about from Belinda's point of view? Did she have more feelings for you than you for her, Mr Lovell?'

Tom smirked a little.

'Goes with the territory of being a free-minded, liberal thinking socialist, Detective Carlisle. Fair-minded ... I like to give all my admirers a level chance. I even have to fight my students off, you know.'

'Oh you mean at the college where you work?'

'Yes, Goldsmiths, down at New Cross. Where I'm missing giving an important lecture on Bolshevism versus the Tsarist regime, I'll have you know.'

'Sorry to inconvenience you, Mr Lovell, but this is a murder investigation. And surely you'd like to know who killed Belinda?'

Tom shrugged. Bastard, thought Lydia, who continued,

'So you're awash with females who are attracted by your intellectual mind, and Belinda was just one more, is that it?'

'Yes. Can't I have my cake and eat it too?' Tom asked smugly.

'Of course. But what about Belinda? Was she OK with that? Or did she want something more?'

'It was fine for years – friends with benefits kind of thing – and we got together again over Christmas and New Year. As you obviously know, I was at her little party and met all her new lawyer friends. I must say, Belinda seemed to change a bit once she got the position at Weymouth House; hinting about settling down, her body clock and all that.'

'So you did a runner?' interjected Nick. Bang on, thought Lydia.

'Not straightaway, Detective Fairman. I let her down gently – a couple more dates and that was that.'

'Did you ever go to the chambers?' asked Lydia.

'Ermm, yes. She invited me for a coffee once … that was when she told me our dalliances had to stop once and for all. More's the pity,' Tom's face had the hint of a leer.

'So Belinda knocked it on the head when she finally figured out you weren't going to commit?'

'Yes, well – plenty more fish in the sea for me,' answered Tom.

'Where were you on the Monday evening before Belinda's murder?'

'In bed. Mostly. Why is that relevant, Detective?'

Lydia sighed inwardly at the unhelpfulness of the man before replying,

'To establish if there'd been any contact between Belinda and her murderer that might have led to a revenge or rage killing the next morning. So where were you on the morning of Belinda's murder, specifically between six and seven a.m.?'

'In bed. I don't start work till after lunch on Tuesdays.'

'Were you alone … in bed?' asked Lydia, hardly able to keep her disgust at bay.

'That's for me to know and for you to find out, Detective Carlisle,' Tom replied smarmily, and went on, 'and anyway I don't have to give you any further information without a lawyer present. I do know my rights, you know.'

'No worries,' answered Nick. 'We'll just interview every one of your students and see if they can vouch for you, Mr Lovell.'

'Knock yourselves out, Detectives.'

'What an arsehole!' Lydia was fuming after they had wrapped up the interview and Tom had been escorted out of Scotland Yard.

'We do seem to have our fair share of dickheads in this investigation, that's for sure, replied Nick.

'Could he have murdered Belinda?' asked Lydia.

'If there's no alibi, then he'd certainly have had opportunity, seeing as he knew his way to Weymouth House Chambers, and Belinda might have let him in,' said Nick.

'Yes, I guess it could have been a response to Belinda irrevocably finishing their "convenient" relationship. Perhaps he didn't like letting her off the hook; saw her as his property,' replied Lydia thoughtfully. 'And if she told him about her fling with Anthony Greenwood, he might have reacted with anger or jealousy.'

'A murder of passion, as they say, eh Boss?'

'Indeed. Could you arrange for his students to be questioned regarding whether any of them were with him the Monday evening and early on the Tuesday?'

'Sure, Boss.'

'And if they were, you could ask what the hell they see in him. Just joking. God knows what Belinda found so attractive about him, but at least she found the strength to cut him adrift … it would be terrible to think that it might have led to her death, though.'

199

*For crap's sake. I warned that detective bitch to keep her beak out of my life. Thinks she's so bloody clever doesn't she? Sniffing around in my business and getting those nincompoop sergeants running about like headless chickens. That reminds me of the time Father beheaded Henny-Penny and her body went on running around the yard before we plucked her and ate her for dinner. Belinda didn't go running around after I slashed her neck though, did she? I expect Father would have belted me for not giving him a laugh, mind you. He liked to give me a good walloping ... especially when he'd had a few too many ... I didn't dare blubber like a girl though – he could be strict like that. He'd definitely approve of me offing that dumb cow – 'Ms' Barrister of the Year, my arse. Women are meant to lie down and think of England, not run the country – leave that to us men, Father used to say. I completely agree ... why can't these skirts just do what they're meant to do – stay in the kitchen and cook a nice lamb stew for their man? A little job's OK for some pin money I can see that, but why not let the man of the house bring in the dosh or wait for the parents to snuff it? Meanwhile, the little woman can get nice and plump, and then open her legs on demand. That's what the female of the species is for, isn't it? Dear Belinda never saw that point of view of course though, did she? Well, you work hard, she would say, so why can't I? All very well, but why did she always try so hard to be **better** than me? Smarter, slimmer, cleverer ... and she knew it. Still, she's well and truly gone now and can't taunt me any more. Washed away like muck off a stable floor.*

Chapter 18

Terra (land)

'Thank you for bringing these in, Gordon,' said Lydia, relieving him of the box of Belinda's old diaries the next morning. 'How are you and Felicity holding up?'

'It's very hard. Felicity is in absolute pieces; she can't even think about the funeral, so that's all been left to me to organise,' replied Gordon Radford.

'I'm so sorry. Is there anything we can do?'

'No, Detective, it's all right. The family is rallying around and at least Julian thinks to phone us every day or so now.'

'Would you like a coffee or tea?' asked Lydia politely.

'No, thank you; it's already past eleven and I'm supposed to be meeting Julian for lunch over at Spitalfields; we've got to discuss the final details for the funeral plus he says he's got something to tell me … wonder what that could be?'

Lydia had a fair idea; Julian was going to unveil his "secret": his girlfriend, Precious Temishe, no doubt. After all, he wouldn't want to shock his parents too much at the funeral, would he?

'OK, well, see you Tuesday at Bournemouth Crematorium, Gordon. I'll look after Belinda's diaries, don't worry.'

Lydia had a quick look through the box of Belinda's childhood diaries; there were ten in all, handwritten, one for each year from the age of eight up till she'd left home for university at eighteen. She placed the box next to the one containing the ten diaries covering the years from age eighteen to twenty eight that Beth had had sent over. Planning to make a start on reading them after lunch, Lydia made her way to Chief Inspector Geoff Cordell's office to bring him up to date on the Radford case.

'Morning Sir,' she began. 'I've got quite a lot to catch you up on.'

'I expect so,' replied Geoff. 'Help yourself to a coffee – Ruth's just made a fresh pot.

Lydia obliged, and after sorting through her notes, began by describing the visit to the Faiths' car showroom on Monday afternoon.

'Interesting stuff, Lydia. So is there anything in the East End gang theory?'

'To be honest, I don't think so really,' replied Lydia. 'Steven Faith comes from the Brindle family but as far as Nick has been able to ascertain Steven hasn't had any connection with them for years; here's a copy of his report. The gang involvement idea – brought up by one of the barristers, Anthony Greenwood, is a red herring in my opinion. Maybe even one he invented himself!'

'I'm inclined to agree, Lydia. The intentional tort angle seems to be a much more likely avenue for investigation; money is always a powerful motive for murder in my experience.'

'Indeed, Sir. Definitely a few more cages to rattle on that front.'

'OK. Now tell me about this knife business.'

'Well, it was found by Sharon Hardy, the clerk to the barristers, inside the sleeping bag belonging to Ben James – the vagrant who hangs around outside Weymouth Chambers. Forensics have more or less confirmed it as being the knife used to murder Belinda Radford and there is trace evidence on the blade. They're hedging their bets by saying "alleged" murder weapon, but it seems fairly obvious it's the one. Whether Ben James was capable of using the knife to commit such a cunning murder, or indeed, sober enough, I'm not so sure, Sir.'

'Yes, he'd have to have planned it all quite carefully, and from what I know of him, having read your previous report, Lydia, he just doesn't have it in him.'

'I'm waiting on an inventory report of potential items, cutlery and so on, at Weymouth House, plus any information as to what might actually be missing … I'm guessing the knife might have been "in-house" as it were, maybe easily accessible for *either* a deliberately thought-out murder *or* a spontaneous attack,' said Lydia. 'There are quite a lot of contenders that fit either category, in fact; there are the work colleagues – including the cleaner – who all have opportunity and potentially, motive, and there are several other people who have clearer motives but might have found it more difficult to enter the building, though not impossible. And needless to say, there are probably a few more suspects who might arrive on our doorstep.'

'OK, so talk me through the colleagues and the latest on them, please.' said Geoff.

'Well, there's Sam White the cleaner, and Sir William Bond QC; but nothing new on them at the moment. We're still investigating Sir William's legal work outside of the chambers and we're still waiting for "A Clean Sweep" to locate Anastasiya Shcherbyna, Sir William's cleaner in London – she's supposed to vouch for him the morning of the murder. I'll update you when I have more information, Sir.'

'Good, thank you. Go on.'

'Nick and I went to visit Sharon Hardy at home in Nunhead; it was like going back into the past with all the old furniture and net curtains! She's definitely a maverick … the best motive we've come up with is potentially protecting Sir William from being accused of any dirty dealings to do with the Faiths' legal case that Belinda might have uncovered or disapproved of. However, Sharon was also the one who discovered the murder weapon. She maintains she was walking her dog in Nunhead Cemetery at the time of the murder and I've asked Sergeants Davis and Glover to ask around for potential witnesses.'

'Hmm. OK, and what about the other barrister?'

'Anthony Greenwood is definitely on our radar. His wife doesn't know about his dalliance with Belinda hence he might have killed her to shut her up. We're off to Hampstead on Monday to discuss the alibi she gave her husband.'

'I'd like to be a fly on the wall on that one, Lydia! So the work colleagues – barring their alibis – all had opportunity to kill Belinda as they all have access to the building, i.e. keys. What about the suspects with stronger motives … like the brother and the dodgy boyfriend you emailed me about?'

'Ah yes, the charming Julian Radford. Well, the money motive is quite high on the list; Julian was apparently scared that his parents would cut him out of their wills if they knew he was involved with a black person. He'd forbidden Belinda to tell them about Precious Temishe and so he could possibly have murdered Belinda to stop her spilling the beans; after all, there's a fortune at stake. He's got no alibi for the time of the murder and one possibility is that Belinda might have let him in to the chambers and that it was an argument that escalated into an anger killing.'

'Hold on, Lydia … didn't you say at the meeting on Monday that the death cut was delivered left to right from the victim's point of view, making the perpetrator most likely right-handed? So …'

'Ah, yes. Let me find Sergeant Glover's table … oh bugger,' exclaimed Lydia, checking her ipad. 'Julian is left-handed. I remember now his father telling me that as well.'

'Don't rule Julian out just yet. Now what about the mystery boyfriend?'

'Tom Lovell … right-handed, ha!' said Lydia. 'Now he's a piece of work, Sir. Very unforthcoming about his whereabouts at the time of the murder. Thinks it's amusing to have us using our resources to question all his "conquests".'

'Sounds as though he's fairly certain one of them will provide him with an alibi … what's his motive?'

'Potentially a case of possessiveness and even jealousy once Belinda gave him to understand that she wasn't going to do the friends-with-benefits thing anymore; she might even have given him some kind of ultimatum. He's admitted that he'd been to the chambers on occasion, so knew his way around.'

'If he's got so many willing bed-partners, why would he be that bothered about Belinda cutting him adrift, though, Lydia?'

'Maybe the playboy façade is just that – a persona. I'll speak to the friends again, the nurses Martha Bigbury and Skye Warriner – see if they can throw more light on his character.'

'Are those two suspects?'

'No, I think we can rule them out. Tech came back; said there are a few Facebook posts from both of them in Vietnam and Cambodia, though not many, and the airline confirmed their flight details. Plus the Foreign Office had a record of Skye Warriner reporting a stolen ipad to the British consulate in Ho Chi Minh City during the dates in question – so they were definitely out of the country at the time of Belinda's murder. Also, I can't really think of what motive they'd have had, after all Belinda was helping them with their medical litigation case.'

'OK, Lydia. Anything else?'

'I think that's about it for the moment, Sir. There's Belinda's funeral on Tuesday down in Bournemouth which Nick and I are going to – by the way, I do appreciate your allowing us to go, Sir.'

'No problem. I've diverted our resources budget to cover it seeing as it's such a high-profile case, and you might pick up on something relevant to the investigation, Lydia.'

'Thank you. I've also got twenty of Belinda's childhood diaries to go through; I'm hoping they might offer some clues as well.'

'Good, thank you for bringing me up to date; have a good – and safe – weekend. By the way, I've arranged for a car to watch your flat again. And the officer has been instructed to radio in any suspicious passers-by.' said Geoff.

'Thank you, Sir. No real need, I'm sure, but I do appreciate your concern,' said Lydia. 'See you next week.'

On returning to her office, and checking her emails, Lydia found a message from Sergeant Glover with an inventory of kitchen implements found at Weymouth House. Not, as expected, in the cleaning room which doubled up as a small kitchen, but in a small cupboard next to the ground floor clients' waiting room. The items consisted primarily of plates, cups and saucers, plus a container of cutlery and a rack of knives ranging from small and pointed, serrated and carving. No knife missing from the rack, but the barristers' clerk had confirmed to Terry that a largish, sharp knife used by staff to cut birthday cakes et cetera was unaccounted for.

'What a surprise,' muttered Lydia, before arranging for fingerprints to be taken from around the cupboard area.

Eight-year-old Belinda's diaries were essentially lists, thought Lydia, reflecting on the ten dog-eared, hand-decorated notebooks before her that she'd finally got round to ploughing through. Lists of creatures Belinda had seen in the woods and fields of her childhood home; lists of names of people she knew; lists of likes and dislikes. All painstakingly recorded in her neat yet childish handwriting with its sometimes imperfect spelling, and occasionally accompanied by childlike drawings of the various flora, fauna and people that made up her world, such as:

Animals, Birds and Insects I saw today. 24th of April.
Dog – spanyel. At home in the kitchen. Eight o'clock in the morning.
Cats – ginger one and white one. Sleeping in the conservatry. Nine o'clock in the morning.
Pony – brown. At the stables. Ten o'clock in the morning.
Butterfly – tortuseshell. In upper field. Lunchtime.
Squirel – grey. In woods. Two o'clock in the afternoon.
Or:
Peeple I know. 29th of June.
Muther.
Father.
Julian – stupidest person ever. Yuk.
Bryan the gardner.
Tracey the cleaner.
Jim the trainer.
Pammy the stable girl – my favritest person in the whole wide world.
And:

My favrite things. 19ᵗʰ October.
Foals. Specially my one.
Buttercups.
Bats (but I hate snakes!!)
Spagetti.
The colour pink.
Sticker books.
  Lydia ran her eye over these and dozens more
similar lists and sighed. Just another nineteen years or
so of diaries to get through, she thought.

By 5pm that Friday afternoon, and after working her
way through ten handwritten diaries, Lydia felt she had
quite a good idea of who Belinda was – at least as a
child and teenager between the ages of eight and
eighteen. After much of the same type of entries for
four years, Belinda's diaries, while still showing her
fondness for lists, evolved into more introspective
writing as she reached adolescence and started
secondary school – Talbot Forest, just outside
Lymington. While her spelling had improved,
Belinda's punctuation needed some work, mused
Lydia, as she perused one of the thirteen-year-old's
entries:
Wednesday 27th of September
Goodness Julian is such an idiot Today he and his
stupid friends just had to gatecrash my break time with
Annie and Helena creeping up on us and scaring us
with those stupid masks Trick or treat ha ha! He thinks
hes so funny being the grand old age of eleven! Annie
said to ignore him and Helena reckons hell grow out of
it as soon as he gets interested in girls I wish!

209

The fifteen-year-old Belinda's writing style was a little better; at least Lydia could just about follow the now properly demarcated sentences:

Friday 19th October
This years hockey trials started yesterday but I dont really want to play hockey any more. It was fun for a couple of years and I know Im good at it but am so over it now what with GCSEs coming up. I think I want to focus on those really. How am I going to tell Miss Vernon though?!

My GCSEs: English Language.
English Literature.
Maths.
Triple Science.
Geography.
Latin.
French (ugh!).
Art.

Monday 4th May
Sarah and Rachel have ganged up against me now. So vile after all the times theyve been to The Heathers and had free pony rides. I so need a best friend, Annie and Helena are besties and theyre nice to me but Im the odd one out. I cant talk to Mother or Father, theyre always so busy and Julian is such a dick at times. I think Ill go and cry into Posys mane. For the millionth time I wish that Pam our lovely stable girl hadnt left. Life can be so unfair – I think thats why I want to be a lawyer and make things fair in the name of justice! Miss Burgess says Ive got to work really hard to go into Law so thats what Im going to do. Important tests

are coming up and Ill just get stuck in. Julian laughs at me and calls me a nerdy swot but I dont care!

By the time Belinda had reached seventeen, she'd actually heard of apostrophes, thought Lydia meanly:

Tuesday 3ʳᵈ June

For Christ's sake Father doesn't agree with my A Level choices ... he wants me to do soft subjects like Art so that I can have something to do when I'm helping with the admin here! But I still want to be a lawyer and for that I need Sociology and maybe Politics. I suppose I could do English, that should keep him happy! And Economics. I know he wants one of us to help run The Heathers but not me. I love the foals but I'm not really into all the husbandry side of things and making money. Julian would be more suited but I guess he hasn't got the brains! But he's a male so that's OK then.

By the time Belinda had left school at the age of eighteen, and was about to start university, her writing had improved dramatically; almost perfect grammar and sophisticated vocabulary, considered Lydia. The dead girl had also developed a definite penchant for addressing her diary as a confidante and reproducing word-for-word conversations, as in:

Thursday, 12th August

My dear Diary,

I'm so delighted – three A*s and an A! The parents were highly thrilled, too.

'Congratulations, my dear, bright girl!' said Father. Mother maintained that she "always knew" I had it in me! I'm off to UCL to read Law and I can't

wait. I'll doubtless be a little sad to leave the New Forest and Mother will be distressed, naturally ... I've had to sugar-coat it all a little:

'I'll phone every weekend, I promise. And I'll definitely be back for Christmas and I'm not missing foaling season, Father.'

'Good – I need you around for that, Belinda. The folks on the estate are going to miss you too, you know.'

'Well, you've still got Julian!' I said. Ha ha. As if he's any help at all.

'You will be careful up there, won't you, darling?' said Mother; I could tell she was holding back the tears ...

I'm very much looking forward to life in London; it'll be an adventure – shops galore, a myriad of museums and galleries and, hopefully, a plethora of new friends. No more nuisance of a little brother, and I'll have you to confide in, dearest Diary!

Lydia had stopped reading at that point; it was a natural break after all. Once Belinda had left The Heathers and went off to university, that left ten years of her life for Lydia to follow through on. As much as she felt sympathy for the murdered woman, there were limits as to how many of Belinda's diary entries she could read literatim all in one go. She resolved to pick up where she left off as soon as she could.

After Saturday's yoga class, Marie asked,

'So Lydia, how's the case going? Did you do the "day in the life of" your poor victim?'

'Well, we're two and a half weeks in now … I have some leads – highly confidential still – but nothing definite yet. Yes – I did spend some time following in Belinda's footsteps – genius idea, Marie! I do feel as if I know her a whole lot better now. What a dedicated and hardworking woman she was. Poor thing; she tried so hard to escape the life that was preordained for her by her parents, which was to play the little female at home while the men ran the family business. I've been reading her girlhood diaries and I can see why she worked so hard to get away from the country, move up to London and dedicate herself to her career in law. I've got another ten years' worth of diaries to get through …' Lydia groaned.

'Stick with it. There are bound to be some clues as to why someone wanted her dead, and I'd bet my bottom dollar it's something to do with the type of person she was or became. And – I know it's a psychologist's cliché – but the answer will often lie in one's childhood.' said Marie.

'Thank you, Sigmund Freud!'

'You're welcome. But I prefer Mary Wollstonecraft if you don't mind. Brilliant philosopher and so ahead of her time when it came to women's rights and equality.'

'Indeed, Marie. There are a few males I can think of that would do well to read up on Ms Wollstonecraft.'

Chapter 19

De Jure (rightfully)

Anthony Greenwood paced nervously round his large, well-appointed kitchen complete with Aga and a massive American-style fridge, waiting for Detective Inspector Lydia Carlisle and Assistant Detective Inspector Nicholas Fairman to arrive; they were following up on their promise – or was it a threat? – to interview him and his wife at home in Hampstead. Sir William had given him the Monday morning off and Anthony was dressed down; in his case, this meant shiny brown brogues, slim-fitting dark blue trousers and a pale green tailored cotton shirt that accentuated his trim build. The children were at school – an independent preparatory school in Belsize Park – and his wife, Miranda, was pottering around in her studio. Staring out of the large picture window overlooking the outdoor swimming pool and well-tended garden, so quiet despite being only minutes from Hampstead's bustling high street, he wondered whether she would stand by the alibi she gave him for the Monday evening the night before Belinda was murdered; three weeks ago now.

'Shall I put the kettle on, Tone?' Anthony started; he hadn't heard Miranda enter, so deep in thought he'd been.

'I can do it, darling. They're due here any minute now. Will you be … er … alright with vouching for me again?'

Miranda settled her somewhat bulky body hidden under one of her habitual multi-coloured kaftans onto a kitchen chair, and fixed her green eyes on her husband as he filled the kettle and placed it on the hob.

'Of course, Tone. You *were* here all evening anyway, weren't you? I won't mention the part about when you popped out for a drink with a friend – I was in the studio then anyway, so I wouldn't have noticed whether you were in or out, of course.'

'Thank you, darling,' Anthony replied. 'I appreciate it, really I do. And I think it's probably best if we don't mention to the detectives that we travelled into central London *together* early on the morning Belinda was killed. Remember?'

'Ah, yes,' answered Miranda. 'The kids were at Lily's birthday sleepover the night before and her mum very kindly took them into school the next day. It was so nice to be able to get out and treat ourselves to a slap-up breakfast in the city, wasn't it Tone?'

Anthony nodded and went on,

'I know we've been having a few problems lately, but I do love you, you know.'

'Likewise,' said Miranda, playing with a strand of her bright auburn hair that had escaped from her red and orange bandanna. 'We're so lucky with what we have, the children, the house ... I'd hate to lose it all.'

Anthony looked thoughtfully at his wife.

'Well, you're not going to lose anything, darling, don't worry. And when this is all over and they've caught poor Belinda's killer, we can go on a nice holiday; how about Guadeloupe?'

'That would be wonderful, Tone. Talking of poor Belinda, I feel so sorry for her … and I expect you miss her terribly too, don't you? And it's so awful for her family. The parents must be devastated; the brother maybe not so much – I remember him as a bit of an unemotional type, you know – when we met him at her New Year Eve's party?'

'Oh yes, that party. Anyway, you'll be seeing most of the people that were there at the funeral tomorrow.'

'That reminds me! I must sort out lifts for Hugo and Saskia into school, and double-check if Tricia can take them in the evening. Actually, I might see if she can take them tonight if it's an early start. What time are we leaving in the morning?'

'I think about seven should be OK to get down to Bournemouth; the funeral's at eleven thirty so that should be plenty of time.'

Miranda trundled out of the kitchen, and as Anthony removed the kettle from the range, the intercom connecting to the electric gate bleeped, announcing the arrival of the police detectives.

'So, how long have you both lived here?' asked Lydia, while Nick busied himself with setting up the recording system. Anthony seemed to be avoiding looking at her – pity, thought Lydia who was rather looking forward to his blue-eyed gaze, and it was Mrs Greenwood who answered.

'Nine years now – we've been married for ten, and the children came along eight and six years ago.' replied Miranda, who had settled down on the plush sofa next to her husband. Jack Sprat and his wife, thought Lydia.

'It's a beautiful home,' she continued, looking around at the sumptuous furnishings and stunning, if unconventional, art works. 'Are these your pictures?'

'Yes. So Tone – that's what I call Anthony – told you I'm an artist then? I paint for myself mainly, but sell a fair few as well … usually to friends and family.'

'Rather unusual subject matter – reminds me of Damien Hirst, and my old school biology text book, if you don't mind my saying so,' put in Nick.

'Everyone says that! Well, I was always fascinated by anatomy at school, and at college I just went a step further and peeled back the skin, to see what really lies beneath the human exterior. Gore and guts, you call it, don't you, Tone?' Miranda looked fondly at Anthony, who had been staring absently into thin air; he now jumped to attention, saying,

'It's still art, though, darling! Anyway, Detectives, can we get on with this; I need to get back to chambers this afternoon. I take it you're conducting this interview on a co-spousal basis?'

'If you're both happy with that, then yes,' answered Lydia.   The Greenwoods nodded assent,

Nick read them their rights, and Lydia began.

'Mr Greenwood, we've already got a recorded statement from you confirming your details, so moving on to Mrs Greenwood – please could you give us your full name and occupation?'

'Joan Maureen Greenwood. Artist and sculptor.'

Lydia raised an eyebrow and asked,

'So *Miranda* is your working name, I understand?'

'Yes, that's right. It's a little jazzier than *Joan*, don't you agree?'

'Oh, I don't know … sounds OK to me,' said Lydia, privately wondering why "Maureen" hadn't been an option. 'Anyway, I understand you work from here?'

'Yes. I have my own studio – I can show you if you like – and it's very convenient while the children are still at school of course.'

'On the evening in question, three weeks ago today, you told my colleague here, DI Fairman, that your husband, Anthony Greenwood was home all evening. Can you elaborate, please?' Lydia noticed Anthony shifting slightly closer to his wife. Interesting.

'Well, I was painting as usual in my studio and Tone was here keeping an eye on Hugo and Saskia – our children – until the bedtime routine which we tend to do together.'

'So I take it being eight and six, they don't go to bed too late. What about later on in the evening?' asked Lydia.

'I returned to the studio, and Tone … I guess watched some TV here in the lounge or played around on his iPhone or something.'

'Or on his PC?' put in Lydia.

'No … we have a "no computers at home" policy', you see.'

'OK. Do you know for sure that's what he was doing? How do you know he didn't go out?'

'Because he would have told me, Detective,' replied Miranda, a little sharply, thought Lydia.

'Thank you. Now, moving on to the Tuesday morning, when Ms Radford was murdered. What time did you leave home, Mr Greenwood – Anthony?' Lydia switched her questioning towards the barrister whose whiter-than-white smile was still nowhere to be seen, she noted.

'About six o'clock. It's only ten or so stops from Hampstead to Charing Cross, and then only a few minutes—'

'Isn't that rather early?' broke in Lydia. 'I know you were at Weymouth House just after eight, as I spoke to you myself, but firstly, why did it take you so long to get in that day if you left home at six a.m. for what is a thirty-five minute journey at most, and secondly, why were you even in so early – I understand from Ms Hardy that you normally get in around nine or nine thirty?'

'Yes, well I decided to get in a little earlier than usual to do some urgent work on a case I'm dealing with and which I had to present in court later that week. Plus I felt like having a full English at a good old breakfast café before going into the office.'

'So can you vouch for your husband leaving at around six then, Mrs Greenwood?'

'Yes, I remember that day; he does usually leave later but he did tell me he had to get ahead with some work.' Miranda seemed more in control now.

Lydia nodded at Nick, who then continued with their pre-agreed line of questioning, giving Lydia a chance to sit back and observe the body language between the seemingly very different husband and wife.

'Did you know Belinda Radford, Mrs Greenwood?' Nick enquired

'Not really, poor soul. Only met her the once at her New Year's do – seemed pleasant enough. And what Anthony's told me about her, of course.'

Lydia felt the tension in the air; nothing she could put her finger on, however. Go on, Nick, she thought, dig deeper.

'So what do you know about Ms Radford – by proxy, as it were?' he asked.

Miranda glanced at her husband before replying,

'Oh, good at her job, so I understand, though a bit of a newbie. Anthony had to step in on numerous occasions to sort out her mistakes – that's what you told me, right, darling?'

'Er, yes. Rookie errors and all that,' muttered Anthony, staring out of the window and in fact looking anywhere except at his wife, mused Lydia.

'You spent quite a lot of time helping her out, didn't you, Tone? Very kind, my husband is.'

There it was, Lydia was sure of it. A barely discernible seam of malice hidden deep beneath the plump, motherly exterior of Miranda Greenwood. She wondered whether Nick had picked up on it as well.

'Have you ever been to Weymouth House, Mrs Greenwood?' continued Nick.

'Only a few times, usually if I happen to be passing by. Tone's only been there for just under a year ... oh, there was a works dinner at Christmas, and we all met in the chambers for pre-drinks. But that's about it, I think.'

'So you don't know the other staff well?'

'Not really, Detective. Sir William best probably, as he works in the same office as my husband; there was the tenant who left – John, I think his name was – and Sharon, the clerk.'

'Did you ever meet the cleaner, Sam White?'

'Not at the chambers. Just at Belinda's party ... you don't like him very much, do you, Tone?' said Miranda, turning her striking green eyes towards her husband.

'Not really,' admitted Anthony. 'I always get the impression he thinks I'm a stuck-up prat!'

Hmm, thought Lydia, who interjected,

'Thank you Mr and Mrs Greenwood. DI Fairman, you can stop the recording now. Would it be possible for us to see your studio since you so kindly offered, please?'

'Of course, my pleasure; do follow me,' replied Miranda, standing up surprisingly quickly, given her plumpness, mused Lydia.

The studio, located towards the back of the house, was crammed with canvases of all sizes; some on easels and several propped up against the walls. A study in scarlet was the phrase that came to Lydia's mind, on taking in the overriding colour of red – body parts, veins and blood – that dominated Miranda's artwork.

Noticing the startled expressions on the detectives' faces, Miranda began,

'Sorry … it's a bit of a shock when you see it all for the first time!'

Anthony cleared his throat, and went on,

'Yes, all rather *bloody*! But my wife is so talented, don't you think?'

'Certainly an intriguing form of expression,' said Lydia as diplomatically as she could, watching as Miranda nonchalantly picked up a paint brush and dabbed a few streaks of vermillion oil paint onto the large canvas that took centre place in the studio; obviously a work in progress of a torso, marbled with muscle and body organs.

'Where do you get your inspiration from, Mrs Greenwood?' asked Nick.

'Oh, as I said I'm just building on what I learnt at art school – or should I say, going in more deeply? I look at other artists who've done similar works …' Miranda indicated a wall of art books, '… and more recently, I've even been buying joints of meat from the local butcher, to study the breakdown of sinews and arteries et cetera in more detail. I get quite involved in it all. Call me crazy!'

You don't say, thought Lydia, who continued,

'This room is set quite well back from the rest of the house, isn't it?'

'Yes – it's my haven; lovely and quiet – I can really focus—'

'So you wouldn't necessarily have heard if your husband had slipped out late on the Monday evening then?'

'Detective, I know what you're implying,' interrupted Anthony. 'But as my wife told you, if I was going out, I would have told her. Now, if there's anything else?'

'No, that's all for now. Thank you both; we'll be on our way,' said Lydia. 'Will we be seeing you at the funeral tomorrow?'

'Yes, we'll both be there,' replied Anthony, taking his wife's hand in his.

After the detectives had left, he turned to Miranda,

'I think that went OK. At least we didn't actually lie … we just omitted to mention that you were with me when I went into town that morning.'

'Let's hope that Detective Carlisle doesn't sniff that out – she may look tiny, but I suspect she's a Rottweiler, Tone! Shall we have an early lunch? I've got some delicious smoked salmon and rocket salad. And I dare say we could run to a glass of white!'

Lydia waited until they were through the electric gates and driving along the leafy avenue.

'Nick, café on the left. Stop.'

Parking the car in a convenient slot outside the Italian bistro, Nick obeyed and they both entered the café, rather than sit under its striped awning on the pavement. They ordered coffees, and their drinks arrived promptly.

'Come on then, Boss. Spit it out,' said Nick. 'Not your cappuccino obviously!'

'Miranda definitely knows – or knew – about Anthony and Belinda. Did you pick up on that?'

'Not really—'

'It was nothing she actually said, Nick. Perfectly innocuous. It was the *way* she said it: "*poor soul*" and "*seemed pleasant enough*", my foot. The sarcasm was just dripping off her. And the way they looked at each other. Or rather, didn't!'

'I thought she glanced at him a couple of times?' put in Nick.

'Yes, but he refused to meet her eye, although to be fair, he didn't meet my eye either. He knew exactly what she was playing at ... she's got him on a string, I reckon.'

'Now you mention it, it was interesting that she brought up how Anthony used to help Belinda out ...'

'Exactly. "*Very kind, my husband is*" spoke volumes, I thought. She knew what was going on and was very subtly letting Anthony know she knew,' continued Lydia. 'Making him squirm better than I could have!'

'So the green-eyed dragon and all that ... oh, and are you thinking, as I am, that rather than Anthony killing Belinda to stop her from exposing their dalliance, Miranda might have murdered Belinda out of jealousy?'

'Both motives are possible. Anthony might have been worried that Belinda would've spilled the beans, upset the status quo, costly divorce and so on, but equally, Miranda might have wanted to get rid of Belinda whom she saw as a threat perhaps, being a little younger, fresher and a lot slimmer.'

'Miaow. She also has a lot to lose ... that house, the money ...,' responded Nick.

'Exactly. She may act the bohemian artist-cum-mother hen, but I bet she wouldn't let anything get in the way of her comfortable lifestyle and what's rightfully hers. She's a dark horse and no one's fool. I would hazard a guess she's also covering for him; there's no way she would have heard him leaving the house from her studio, I reckon. And I bet he did ... just like I bet Anthony knows she's holding that over him. And as for that art!'

'Agreed, it was very *red*, shall we say. A fascination with blood and body parts doesn't stand her in very good stead, does it?'

'No, it doesn't. By the way, I noticed that she's right-handed – when she picked up that paintbrush. Get Sergeant Glover to add her to the list of suspects, will you?'

'Will do, Boss. Hey, any chance of another latte? They do them well here in Hampstead, don't you think?'

Back at the Yard, Lydia sent a summary of the interview to CI Cordell, although she did not include her private contemplations on the husband-wife interplay that she had observed being acted out between the Greenwoods. Clearly Miranda was the one who ruled the roost at home, while Anthony expressed his need for control and admiration at work – hence the calculated bravado and magnetism he exuded, in particular towards females. Fascinating stuff, she mused, thinking back to the module on Familial Power Dynamics she'd studied at uni. Lydia then spent some time putting Belinda's ten diaries covering age eighteen to twenty-eight in order, ready for perusal after the funeral. Ah yes, the funeral. That was going to be very interesting indeed.

Chapter 20

Moratorium (an agreement not to take action)

Lydia had decided on a trim, black trouser suit with her most comfortable black leather ankle boots with lowish heels; she anticipated it being a long day ahead. It was seven forty-five a.m. and Nick would be to pick her up from her Battersea flat any minute now. She was grateful for his offer to drive again, leaving her free to text, message and email during the three or four hours it would take to get to Bournemouth. Her mobile pinged, indicating that Nick was outside, and she hurried out.

'Morning, Nick.' Lydia noted approvingly that her colleague had made the effort to put on a dark blue suit and tie.

'Hi Boss. I'm hoping we'll get through the London traffic fairly quickly – after all we're going in the opposite direction of the rush hour – and should make it in good time.'

'Hopefully there'll be time for a quick coffee stop; you'll need a break from the driving – I'm really grateful again, by the way.'

'No prob, Boss. Once we get onto the M3, there are a couple of service stations,' said Nick, indicating his satnav. 'We'll make a stop at one of them.'

One and a half hours later, they pulled into Fleet service station, both gagging for caffeine.

'God, I needed that,' said Nick, after knocking back half of his Americano in one gulp. 'I'm looking forward to seeing some of the New Forest ... but I guess we won't have time.'

'Maybe on the way back, Nick. I can't believe it's only been two weeks since I was down this way visiting the Radfords, though they're further south and more Hampshire heartlands.'

'My parents used to bring us down here when we were small ... usually Southbourne or Boscombe.'

'Sounds like you had a good childhood, Nick! Kent ... Dorset – with the family.'

'Yeah, my father loved to take us camping or caravanning, and we used to love roughing it too.'

'Lucky you. We never got family holidays; my dad was always too busy in the RAF. A day out on a beach was as far as it went,' sighed Lydia. 'Anyway, it's going to be rather interesting to see who shows up at the funeral on Belinda's home turf, isn't it?'

'Absolutely. I dare say it will be the high and mighty of Weymouth House Chambers alongside the Radford family, of course.' answered Nick.

'Probably Belinda's nurse friends ... don't know about Tom Lovell, though.'

'If he does come, he won't be wearing black, I bet!' chuckled Nick. 'Being the anti-establishment type he is.'

'Indeed. What I am 99.9% sure of is that the murderer will be there.'

'Why, Boss? Do you think the perp is one of the people known to Belinda? As opposed to, say, a random burglar or a gangland hitman as we've been led to believe by certain suspects?'

'That, and also because I think the killer is the kind to gloat over their *fait accompli*, and arrogant enough to think they've got away with murder.' replied Lydia. 'Not on my watch though.'

'So, what's the plan today?'

'Eavesdrop and observe everyone carefully – their interactions and facial expressions especially – and make lots of mental notes, given that we can't really be seen to be tapping away into our tablets! I'll be doing the same of course, and afterwards we can compare notes on any nuances we pick up on.'

'Sure thing. Though I'm not as good as you at the nuance thing; I didn't latch on to the Greenwoods so very quickly, did I? I'll try to do better today, Boss!'

Just over an hour later, and they were at Bournemouth Crematorium.

'My dad used to call this the dead centre of town!' said Nick.

'Ha ha. We're half an hour early ... let's park up so that we've got a good view of everyone coming in,' said Lydia.

From their vantage point – at the front of a tiered, gravelled car park overlooking the crematorium buildings – Lydia and Nick could see the three roads that wound through the grounds and then converged in front of the chapel, as well as the smaller roads that led to the three car parks, including the one they were in.

A smart navy blue Mazda convertible was approaching from the left, then entered the adjacent car park.

'Ah – that's Martha Bigbury and Skye Warriner,' said Lydia. 'Looking as chic as ever in their little black dresses.'

'Well, you girls have got to glam up for a funeral, haven't you?' replied Nick. 'Er … just joking, Boss. They look sad, though.'

'Yes, they do,' said Lydia, noting the disconsolate way the young nurses linked arms and made their way slowly towards the chapel. 'Who's this now?' she went on, as a large SUV entered their own car park and pulled up beside them.

'Hello, Sam, hello Joanna,' she called out, while winding down her window.

'Morning, Detectives,' replied Sam White. His wife nodded politely.

'Good journey down?' asked Nick.

'No problem at all. Sad business this, isn't it?' Sam went on, 'I'd better have a fag before we go in though. Calm my nerves and that.'

Lydia and Nick turned back to their view of the vehicles arriving; there were quite a few now. The Greenwoods' silver Mercedes breezed in; of course it's a Mercedes, thought Lydia. A white range rover with The Heathers livery centre logo on its side crunched its way across the gravel to an adjacent car park, and Lydia and Nick watched as their occupants trudged towards the crematorium.

'I think they might be some of the employees of the Radford estate,' remarked Lydia. 'I recognise the old boy at the back – a horse trainer, he is. Lo and behold – Tom Lovell's actually made an appearance.'

They watched as Tom, who was wearing red trousers with a green jacket, parked his Skoda in the right-hand car park, glanced around suspiciously and then followed the other mourners. A few more cars rolled in containing whom Lydia supposed to be Belinda's old friends and acquaintances, possibly some of those mentioned in her childhood diaries.

'I wonder who else could be coming could be apart from the family?' pondered Nick. 'Oh look who's just showed up – Sir William and Sharon, last but not least.'

William parked his dark green Jaguar somewhat haphazardly, and he and Sharon, who looked rather dishevelled, hurried over to the assembled group of quietly chatting people waiting outside the chapel.

'Hmm. Interesting that they came down together,' remarked Lydia, privately wondering if William and Sharon had had a bit of a romp in the car on the way down. In Sharon's dreams, probably.

'Maybe Sharon doesn't drive,' said Nick. Or maybe … it's a *nuance*, Boss?'

'Just what I was thinking,' Lydia replied, smiling inwardly.

Finally, four limousines arrived bearing Belinda's coffin, the immediate family and the extended members of the Radford family, and Lydia and Nick made their way over to join the group. The pallbearers solemnly hoisted the coffin, bedecked with a stunning display of pink and white roses, and moved forward slowly into the now-open door of the chapel.

Belinda's parents followed; the devastation on Felicity Radford's face was terrible to see, thought Lydia. What a good thing Gordon was so composed, never letting go of her hand. Julian, accompanied by a sorrowful-looking Precious, managed to look suitably grave as well. Lydia wondered how the introductions between Precious and Julian's parents had gone … oh to be a fly on the wall! Making a mental note to ask Gordon about it later, Lydia indicated to Nick to hang back and let everyone else in ahead of them, before taking their seats quietly at the back as the poignant service began.

'I counted thirty-five people in the chapel including us,' said Lydia. 'Quite a good turnout, actually.'

'Nice humanist service, I thought,' replied Nick, as he re-set the satnav to take them to the Durley Chine Hall Hotel, where the wake was being held. 'Good combination of Belinda's favourite music, and brave of her father to read out the tribute himself.'

'Yes. I was very impressed that Julian recited the Stop all the Clocks poem by heart; maybe I've misjudged him …'

'No, I doubt it, Boss. He was probably just showing off to Precious! Poor thing, she looked on the verge of tears throughout the service.'

'As were Martha and Skye. And Felicity, of course. The saddest thing I ever saw was those poor parents laying flowers on the coffin and saying goodbye to their child. It shouldn't be like that, should it?'

'Indeed not. On a cheerier note, just look at the sea – doesn't it look amazing?'

Lydia gazed out at the sparkling blue of Bournemouth bay as they drove westwards through the town and past the pier approach plaza. A peppering of pleasure boats and windsurfers bobbing on the waves completed the idyllic scene.

'Did you know that Bournemouth bay was originally an enclosed valley, millions of years ago?' asked Nick. The Needles of the Isle of Wight that you can see on the left used to be linked to the Old Harry Rocks over there on the right, forming a basin. There were dinosaurs roaming around and everything!'

'I'm guessing your dad told you that on one of your holidays,' replied Lydia, thinking that the white chalk formations looked like a row of broken teeth.

'Indeed he did. Ah, here we are; good, there's a parking spot.'

The hotel was positioned on a cliff top to the west of the town centre, and Lydia and Nick took a few moments to again savour the stunning panorama of the south coast.

'What a beautiful day; it's so clear. Warm, too.' said Nick.

'Yes, pity we're here on such sad business. But maybe if there's time afterwards, we could find somewhere for a drink – after all, we'll have to compare notes. Come on, Nick, the others are arriving; we'd better go in.'

Inside, groups of people stood in huddles, clutching platefuls of finger food and cups of tea or glasses of wine. Lydia and Nick helped themselves to a few nibbles and coffee, then found seats in a bay window where they could watch everyone. Felicity Radford, wearing a grey linen dress that looked creased and crumpled, sat red-eyed and hunched up on the far side of the room, her hand held by a similar-looking woman – her sister, Lydia guessed. Gordon seemed more able to suppress his grief, judging by the way he had dressed himself suavely in a pristine dark morning suit, calmly shook hands with his daughter's friends and colleagues, and nodded sombrely at their words of condolence. Catching sight of the detectives, he made his way over to them.

'Thank you so much for coming, DI Carlisle. And—?'

'DI Fairman,' responded Nick. 'My deepest sympathies. Neither of us knew Belinda, of course, but we're so sorry for your loss.' Lydia flinched inwardly at the trite-sounding cliché.

'Are you any closer to catching the monster who took our daughter away from us?' asked Gordon, his voice barely concealing his anger and grief.

'We're following up leads, Gordon. And we *will* catch her murderer,' answered Lydia.

'Christ, I hope so. It's killing my wife. I know it won't bring Belinda back, but Felicity might find some comfort in knowing the brute's behind bars. It's been three weeks now and—'

'Father,' broke in a familiar voice. 'Precious isn't feeling well.'

Once again, Lydia was struck by how similar Gordon and Julian were. Like his father, Julian wore a slim-fitting black morning suit; his, however, complemented Precious's dark grey and bottle green silk wraparound dress which showed off her slender physique. I wonder where she shops, thought Lydia irreverently.

'Ermm … sorry, Gordon,' said Precious, her voice almost at a whisper. 'It's all so tragic … I should be able to cope better seeing as I'm a doctor, but this has really got to me. I suffer from bad headaches, you see. It's been lovely to meet you and Felicity though, despite the circumstances …' Catching sight of Lydia and Nick, she attempted to nod politely to them and leaned in further to Julian who had a proprietorial arm around her.

'I think I might have to take her back to London,' continued Julian. 'It's all a bit much for her.'

'Of course, I quite understand, dear,' answered Gordon kindly, patting Precious's hand. 'Julian, do go, and make sure she gets some rest. Drive safely … and say goodbye to your mother, won't you?'

Julian and Precious turned away, and made their way slowly over to Felicity. Lydia wasn't at all surprised that Julian hadn't bothered to acknowledge herself or Nick, considering the dressing-down she had given him two weeks earlier at Spitalfields.

Turning back to Gordon, she enquired,

'So how did meeting Julian's girlfriend for the first time go?'

'Oh, fine, Detective. We were a little taken aback of course due to Precious being Nigerian, but she seems a lovely girl … and Julian's a lucky man.' replied Gordon.

So no need for Julian to have been so worried then, thought Lydia. However, he might not have been quite as confident about inheriting his share of the estate while Belinda was still alive. She echoed Gordon's words,

'Yes, very lucky.'

'Detectives, excuse me. I'd better mingle a little,' said Gordon turning away.

A hint of mothballs preceded Sharon Hardy as she advanced on Lydia and Nick, closely followed by Sir William. Her dress has definitely been hauled out of that old wardrobe, mused Lydia, thinking back to the tall, dark piece of furniture that dominated Sharon's bedroom in Nunhead.

'Hello, Detectives! Such a sad day, isn't it? The poor family. I nearly didn't get here, did I, Sir William?' gushed Sharon, glancing affectionately at the QC. 'He was at my house on time – very kindly offered to drive me down here – but poor Ruskin was sick! I had to clear it up; couldn't leave him alone in the house all day with that pong, could I? It must have been something he ate during his morning walk. I got up really early to take him out and he ran off, and—'

'Who's looking after Weymouth House today?' broke in Lydia. 'Seeing as you're all here?'

'We've closed for the day,' answered Sir William. 'As a sign of respect to the family.' Sir William's smart grey suit looked as if it was bursting at the seams; not surprising, thought Lydia, eying the plate he was clutching, piled high with sandwiches and canapés.

'How's the investigation coming along?' he continued. 'Any leads?'

'We're getting there,' replied Lydia.

'I sincerely hope so, Detective. Not good publicity ... the press has got wind of Weymouth House being involved, you know. And poor young Belinda, of course. I don't have children myself, but I feel for her parents and —'

'Me too!' Sharon interrupted, then continued in a whisper that was far too loud. 'Her mother looks terrible! Such a shame. At least she's got her husband to look out for her and run the estate ... all those horses! That must be a job and a half! Give me a dog any day. Even if they do puke up from time to time! Scone, Sir William?'

Sir William nodded and the pair toddled off to the buffet table.

'I think she's what's known as a "feeder",' said Nick under his breath. Lydia suppressed a laugh and replied in a low voice,

'You don't say! Excuse me, Nick. I'm just going to "feed" myself again. I must say these are lovely canapés. Keep watching and listening.'

Lydia made her way through the guests, stopping to greet Martha and Skye, who, red-eyed from weeping, were deep in conversation with Tom Lovell, and another couple.

'Nice of you to make it to the funeral, Mr Lovell. Seeing as you usually have your hands so full.' remarked Lydia.

Tom glared at her and answered,

'I was fond of Belinda, you know. Even if it wasn't going anywhere.'

'We've been catching up a bit,' said Martha in a conciliatory tone. 'This is Fiona and Paul Edwards, by the way,' she went on, gesturing at two guests standing in the group. 'We were all students in the same hall of residence together.'

'Yes,' chimed in Skye. 'We haven't seen each other for a while. We're thinking of having a small gathering of our own in memory of poor Belinda. Get a few of our mates together up in London.'

'Nice idea,' said Lydia, moving on towards the table of delicacies which were fairly depleted by now. She passed the Whites and the Greenwoods making small talk; at least, the wives were. Miranda was resplendent in a richly embellished purple kaftan tunic dress while Joanna had dressed in a more understated, yet smart dark grey trouser suit. Of course, they all met at Belinda's New Year's Eve party, remembered Lydia. Helping herself to another cup of coffee and the last remaining sandwich, she turned and came face to face with old Jim, the horse trainer from The Heathers.

'Hello, Mr ... erm ... sorry, I don't know your name,' said Lydia. 'I'm DI Carlisle.'

'Thorpe. Jim. Have we met?' came the gruff response.

'Not exactly. I saw you at the Radford estate a couple of weeks ago training a horse,' replied Lydia. 'Are you here on your own?'

Jim glowered before reluctantly replying,

'Yep. Just work mates with me. No family any more. Only me.'

'Sorry to hear that,' said Lydia. 'What happened to them?'

'Wife died on me, and my daughter ran off. Eloped. Silly cow.'

Jim signalled the end of the conversation by grunting and turning away.

'He hasn't got what you might call social graces! We try to keep a bit of an eye on him,' came a cheery voice. 'I'm Tracey Snow and this is Bryan. We both work at The Heathers.'

Lydia locked eyes with a pleasant looking woman, probably in her mid to late thirties.

'Ah, the cleaner and the gardener, I believe?' she answered. 'Belinda mentioned you in some of her childhood diaries.'

'Bless her,' said Bryan. 'We did start out like that! We're the estate managers now – and married with children of our own.'

'Do you remember Belinda as a child?' asked Lydia.

'Of course. She was a real sweetie,' replied Tracey. 'We're absolutely gutted about what's happened. We all are.'

Before Lydia could respond, a younger woman interrupted.

'Tracey! Bryan! Long time no see!'

'Oh … it's Annie, isn't it? And … Helena? I remember when you used to come and play with Belinda; help groom the ponies and so on?' replied Tracey.

'Yes, that's right. It's so tragic. Poor Belinda. I haven't ... hadn't ... seen her for years – since school actually – but we kept in touch,' said Helena.

'I saw her at a reunion about five years ago,' continued Annie. 'I don't think you were there, Helena.'

At that moment, two more women of about the same age as Annie and Helena joined the group. Judging by their excited greetings, these were more old school friends, deduced Lydia, who picked up their names as being Rachel and Sarah. Noting the conspiratorial glance between Annie and Helena, and guessing that a trip down a rose-tinted memory lane was about to ensue, at least as far as the new arrivals, and the Snows were concerned, Lydia gently interrupted.

'Mr and Mrs Snow, would you mind if I came to talk to you further about Belinda? Monday next week, around lunchtime if that's convenient?'

'Of course,' said Bryan. 'Anything to help. We live at Anemone Cottage – on The Heathers estate.'

After exchanging mobile phone numbers with the Snows, Lydia made her way back to Nick through the groups of Belinda's chattering colleagues, friends and relatives.

'Time to go, Boss?' asked Nick hopefully.

'Definitely. Let's give our condolences to Felicity, and make our escape ... we need to compare notes.'

Chapter 21

De Facto (in fact or in reality)

The Sky Bar of the Bournemouth Hilton certainly lived up to its claim of dramatic views from the highest bar in the South West. Lydia and Nick gazed at the spectacular panorama, unable to tear their eyes away from the magnificent vista stretching from the town roofs and lush greenery of the Victorian seaside town to the distant horizon of the stunningly blue ocean.

'Pity we can't have a cocktail, Boss! I like the sound of the "Sunset Boulevard" …'

'I think the budget can stretch to us having the *mocktail* version, if you like? I think we need one after today.'

'Great, thanks!' Nick replied, only a little sarcastically, considered Lydia. Opening her iPad, she went on,

'So I think we should put together a preliminary report of our immediate impressions of today. OK, who was there and was there anything that stood out?'

'Right. The immediate family were there, of course – Felicity and Gordon Radford, and Julian Radford with Precious Temishe, arrived at the crem in the first limo, followed by two more six-seater limousines for the relatives. I reckon one had Felicity's sister's family in it – that was the woman who was comforting Felicity at the wake – looked quite like her, I thought. I found out while you were raiding the canapés that her name is Niki.'

'Well sleuthed! How did you manage that?'

'Her husband came and chatted to me for a couple of minutes. Said his name was Michael Hurley and that he was there with his wife – Niki – their two twenty-something sons, and Niki and Felicity's elderly mum, Avril.'

'Right. And the other limo?'

'Gordon's sister and her husband and three kids – two girls and a boy also all in their twenties – plus a singleton brother of Gordon called Graham. All found out from said Michael Hurley – very nice chap, by the way.'

'Brilliant, Nick. We observed several more cars arriving for the funeral … obviously, I know the Weymouth House lot were there: Sir William, Sharon Hardy – minus Ruskin, ha ha –, Anthony and Miranda Greenwood, and the Whites,' said Lydia, tapping the names into her tablet. 'Then there was Martha Bigbury and Skye Warriner, who introduced me at the wake to Fiona and Paul Edwards from Belinda's uni days, and of course the ever so charming Tom Lovell.'

'When it comes to employees from The Heathers, there was the couple in the white range rover— '

'Tracey and Bryan Snow, estate managers. I spoke to them,' continued Lydia. 'And they brought Jim Thorpe, the horse trainer with them. He's a crotchety old so and so. Oh, and I met some of Belinda's old schoolfriends; Annie and Helena, plus Sarah and Rachel. Could you find out their surnames, please? I'm going back to The Heathers on Monday to talk to the estate managers, Tracey and Bryan Snow; it would be nice to be able to name-drop a few of these people from Belinda's past into the conversation.'

'Yes, Boss, no problem.'

'Thanks. Did you notice anything that struck you as strange or a bit off about anyone during the service?'

Nick took a sip of his "signature" cocktail, rose petal liqueur, peach bitters and alcohol-free gin alternative, and thought back.

'Not really. They just all sat there in silence, looking down at the programme of service. And some cried during the music. Why, did you spot something, Boss?

'No. The only thing was that they seemed to keep to their family or friendship groups ... the old schoolfriends together, the uni mates together, the Weymouth House lot together, and so on. Talking of the programme of service, I've brought it with me to have a closer look.'

Lydia placed the glossy colour programme on the table, taking care not to spill her "virgin" cocktail, appropriately named "Lawless", all over it. It wouldn't do to show CI Geoff Cordell a piece of case documentation spattered with agave nectar, orange blossom water and bourbon substitute.

'The Radfords must've raided their photo albums for these pictures of Belinda as a child, a teenager, and so on. Nice touch to put the staff of The Heathers in the background of her on a pony. Belinda must've been about eight then ... I think she must have won at a gymkhana – she's got a red rosette. They were obviously proud of her! I recognise Tracey, the cleaner, as she was then; must have been about eighteen. And I like the way guests are encouraged to donate to the Burley Home for Retired Horses and Ponies, instead of buying flowers.'

'And they really took her taste in music into account,' went on Nick. 'Jazz, classical and even a bit of punk rock. Respect.'

'About the wake – was everyone who was at the crematorium at the hotel as well, did you notice, Nick?'

'Yes. I counted thirty-three people, plus us. Nobody sloped off.'

'Hmm. Except for Julian and Precious; they made their excuses and left fairly early on of course,' said Lydia pensively. 'Did you pick up anything with regard to any intercommunications or body language apropos any of the attendees at all, Nick?'

'Loads! All those nuances, Boss. Joking aside, as you said earlier re. the crem, the various groups mostly clustered together bar the odd mingler, like yourself! And Sir William and Sharon broke away from the herd – all the better to gorge themselves on sandwiches and cake, no doubt! Belinda's cousins – five of them – didn't socialise much and knocked back as much free booze as they could. The girls made sure Granny Avril was kept topped up with tea …or maybe it was sherry!'

Lydia noted it all down in her ipad and asked,

'We haven't got the cousins' names, have we? Never mind. I don't think they're really pertinent to the case. Yet. OK, what else?'

'Felicity and Gordon Radford's in-laws also kept pretty much themselves to themselves, I thought, except for Gordon who played mine host rather well. Felicity was in pieces and didn't talk to anyone much except her sister.'

'Unsurprising. I thought Gordon's brother, Graham, was quite convivial. I noticed him talking to the nurses,' said Lydia. 'Gregarious, I'd say.'

'Or likes a pretty girl,' said Nick. Lydia rolled her eyes, and went on,

'The old schoolfriends were interesting. I definitely picked up some tension between the two sets of women; Annie and Helena, and Sarah and Rachel … now I think about it, I'm fairly sure Belinda mentioned some sort of schoolgirl tiff concerning them in one of her old diaries. I'll dig a bit more when I go back to the New Forest to speak to the Snows. They might have been more congenial and opened up more, but I had the impression they felt they had to look out for the old boy, Jim Thorpe.'

'Didn't you say he was a bit grouchy, Boss?'

'Indeed. Probably not helped by the amount of gin and tonic he downed. He practically hogged the drinks table.'

'Ha! I noticed that the "real housewives of Weymouth House" got on like a house on fire,' continued Nick, 'while their husbands stood there glowering at each other.'

'Ah, definitely a nuance, Nick! Remember Sam White can't stand Anthony Greenwood; "jerk" was the word, I believe. And he's not that keen on

Sharon either since she caught him smoking weed and grassed him up to us, excuse the pun.'

'Oh yes. The only one Sam seems to like from the chambers was Belinda. And Tabs, of course,' Nick smirked.

'Going back to the wake, as you said, Sir William and Sharon separated themselves off from the Weymouth House group and came over to us,' said Lydia. 'I was quite surprised really; it would have been a good opportunity for Sharon to regale everyone with tales of Ruskin the dog, in her inimitable style.'

'Quite! Apart from chatting to us, she virtually hid behind Sir William the whole time, turned her nose up at the young women who said hello to her ...'

'... and glared at old Jim when he dared to look at her,' continued Lydia.

'She probably disapproved of the younger females' dress sense; in all likeliness, she considered the nurses' dresses too short and Tom Lovell's outfit too garish for a funeral,' said Nick.

'Talking of him, I'm not surprised he didn't mingle. Miserable git. Just said nothing the whole time as far as I could make out, clinging close to Martha and Skye, and the Edwards couple. In fact, maybe I should follow up on them as well,' added Lydia, typing yet more notes into her iPad. 'Anything else of note, Nick?'

'There was one thing I overheard on my way back from the gents ... before they joined Sam and Joanna, I passed the Greenwoods having a little private chat – they were saying something about *things being so much simpler* for them *now that she's gone.* It may have been nothing or—'

'Or maybe, gold dust, Nick! I wonder ...' said Lydia thoughtfully.

'So, all things considered, Boss, have we learnt anything today?'

'Loads. Especially from a psychological perspective .The funeral and wake were a scene from a play with all our main players ... imagine it as a theatre in the round. Belinda is centre stage and around her are concentric circles where all the audience sit,' said Lydia, taking a pen from her bag. 'Look, I'll show you.'

Grabbing a paper serviette, she drew what looked like a dartboard.

'There's Belinda in the middle, and going around her are three circles, getting bigger as they move away. The first circle – is her inner circle. This could contain, say, her parents, her brother, best mates like Martha and Skye, lovers ...'

'I get it,' said Nick. 'The second circle is her not-so-close people; colleagues, friends and acquaintances.'

'Exactly. And the third circle contains those on the fringes of her life, like Sam's and Anthony's wives, estate workers and old schoolfriends. But – the people in the three circles are flexible. They can move from the outer to inner circle or vice versa, depending on what's going on in Belinda's life.'

Pondering the analogy, Nick added,

'In a real theatre in the round, there would be aisles running between the audience leading to the stage, or on a dartboard, which your sketch also reminds me of, there are arrows that pass through the circles from the outside edge to the bull's eye. These would be?'

'The shortcuts for anyone from any circle to get to Belinda who's at the centre … ie. on the stage or bull's eye,' answered Lydia. 'Quickly and incisively, they can cut straight through to the target, never mind if they sometimes sit in the outer circle. They can move back and forth in the blink of an eye.'

'I like the metaphor, Boss, but how does it help us?'

'It's to remind us that everything is interlinked; nothing must be overlooked. Every single person who was here today is connected to Belinda or to each other in some way or another and I'm absolutely convinced the murderer was there, playing their part as an *innocent* bystander.'

'The cast was assembled. Hey, I'm getting into this imagery stuff, Boss! Or should I call you Miss Marple?'

'Ha! OK, I've got it all down; I'll email it over to you, and you can add anything I've forgotten. Then we'll knock it into shape for Geoff.'

'Will do. So … are we getting warmer, Boss? Are we going to catch this perp?'

'Oh yes. We're going to nail them alright,' said Lydia, sounding more confident than she felt.

Finishing up their drinks, Lydia and Nick began the long drive back to London; they took a slight detour through part of the New Forest, so that Nick could gain an impression of the part of the world the rather affluent Radford family came from, and to show off her knowledge of forest flora and fauna to him, in particular, heather and polecats.

It was eight o'clock by the time Lydia returned home. Nick had dropped her off in Battersea, nodded to Neal Wyton, the police officer who was sitting in his car outside Lydia's flat, and promised to meet her at nine o'clock the following morning for a more formal debriefing. Lydia couldn't wait to lock the front door behind her and get into a hot bath; she wanted to wash the sadder aspects of the day away … the coffin at the crematorium; the grieving parents; the weeping friends. Luxuriating in the scented water, she reflected on her own personal "theatre" or "dartboard". Her inner circle was woefully underpopulated; it contained possibly four people – Marie and Nick, and her parents. After she solved the case, she resolved to catch up with friends she had neglected recently. After she solved the case …

Bloody 'bright- eyes' Lydia flaming DI Carlisle. She's got it coming, that's for sure. Completely spoilt my enjoyment of poor dear departed Belinda's funeral – God bless her soul – not! Sitting there at the back with that other sidekick cop staring at us all from behind … made my hackles rise, it did. What a shame they don't burn the body in front of you at a cremation any more. I'd have enjoyed that, wouldn't I? Would have reminded me of when Father used to light an open fire in the big old kitchen and then cook all the piggy-wigs' trotters and innards; 'barbecue à la carte' he called it.

*Eat up, he'd say: we must not squander; we must not
waste. I felt a bit sick when it was Porky-Worky's turn
to be grilled, to be honest. How could I eat my best
friend? But Father would beat me up to high heaven if
I as much as gagged at my food, like that time after he
boiled Henny-Penny ... he downed a whole bottle of
Polish voddy and left me black and blue he did. Ah
well. What's done is done. Talking of trotters, that
reminds me of damn Belinda tottering around in her
'tart's trotters' – court shoes, they call them I believe –
like a prize mare at a horse of the year show. Wanting
everyone to look at her, didn't she? Specially the men.
Not content with just the one feller, was she? Had to
lead other people's husbands on too, didn't she? Why
she couldn't just settle down with someone, have a few
brats and leave the career path shit to a bloke, I do not
know. Never satisfied, probably. Like always wanting
to be 'svelte' and getting me to do the same; 'just
trying to help' she'd say! Who cares? I got my fill at
that bleeding wake, though. Stuffed my face with all
those posh 'delicacies' – just to stop myself laughing
watching that detective vixen lurking around all over
the place. Pity the party couldn't have gone on longer
really, though I didn't really want to socialise with all
the old bods from the estate and that. I had to crack up
at those nurse fillies, picking at their food and
watching their figures! Who cares? Men like a bit of
fat to hold on to. Anyway, Belinda's ashes now. Good
riddance to bad rubbish, I say.*

Chapter 22

Sine Die (indefinitely)

Sir William Bond let himself into Weymouth House Chambers the next morning; much earlier than usual, as he intended to catch up on some of the cases that had been neglected of late. Closing the office the day before on the day of Belinda's funeral had put him behind even further. He was so early that not even the cleaner had arrived yet. He huffed and puffed his way up to the second floor, considering once again that he must go on a diet, opened the office window blind and switched on his computer. The room was quiet; the brooding law books in their shelves glared at him accusingly for neglecting them for so long – although it had only been a day. On a whim, he crossed over to Anthony Greenwood's desk to see what he was working on. Ah, yes, the Faith case he'd asked Anthony to have a look at. Sir William picked up the fat document folder clearly marked with their names, and as he did so, a piece of lavender-coloured notepaper became dislodged and floated to the ground, trailing a slight floral scent behind it. Bending with some difficulty, he retrieved the letter and went cold as he scanned its contents. He felt rather than heard someone behind him—

'Morning, Sir William!' Sharon's breezy tones broke the silence. 'You're in early, I must say! Especially as we got back so late from Bournemouth yesterday! Would you like a coffee and a bun? And I took the liberty of buying a couple of newspapers to see what they're saying about—'

'Oh, Sharon! Thank goodness you're here. Get DI Carlisle on the phone, would you please?'

An hour later, Lydia and Nick sat staring at the piece of paper that Nick maintained was mauve rather than lavender in hue. Lydia read the printed missive aloud:

'Dear Ant-Honey,

I love you so much ... and I know you love me too. I can tell by the way we were and by the way you looked at my body. And still do look at me, it's been quite difficult feeling your angel eyes on me at work, and re-living what we did together. The secrecy is killing me! Sir William and Sharon just think you're being obliging to a poor, young female barrister ... little do they know how obliging you really are!

I know you don't want Miranda to find out, but don't you think it would be better in the long run if she did know, to be honest? She can start over, meet someone else – you can pay her off – there's plenty of money to go round, I reckon. It's never going to be the same between you and her again anyway, now that we've crossed that lovely sexy steamy line! We can sort something out so that you can see your children, and then, who knows – maybe we can have one or two of our own. Start our own little family.

Tell you what I'll tell her and save you the bother and a scene. Yes, I'll invite Miranda for lunch the next time you're out of the chambers, like at court or something, and I'll explain everything to her. Then you can arrange a quickie divorce and in six months, we'll have our own little love nest. Just you and me, my darling Honey-Ant, my Ant-Honey, for ever and ever. We'll be so happy, I just know it.

Love you always, your Linda-Bee, your Bee-Linda. XXXXXXXXXX'

'So, it looks as though our suspicions about Anthony Greenwood may have been spot on, Boss,' said Nick. 'Belinda was going to let the cat out of the bag and tell his wife about their carrying-on. He got in a panic and topped Belinda to stop her.'

'Hmm. I can see the motive as you say, especially if Belinda read more into it than there actually was. And if she was feeling sore about that rotten Tom Lovell, she might have grasped at the prospect of a future with Anthony. Dreamt of a perfect togetherhood with him and her. But – Nick, how come this letter wasn't found on the day of the murder; exactly three weeks and one day ago? When forensics and we were all over the chambers?'

'I can only imagine that the document folder containing the Faith files where Sir William found the letter wasn't on the premises at the time. Maybe he took it home with him to work on?' answered Nick.

'Who, William? Potentially, I suppose,' mused Lydia. 'And then of course we know that Anthony helped out with the Faith case when Belinda died. He could have slipped the letter into the folder to hide it from his wife, meaning to dispose of it, and then forgotten it was there.'

'In the aftermath of his slitting poor Belinda's throat!' said Nick triumphantly. 'Case solved, Boss.'

'Not so fast, Nick. It may look like prime evidence, but we've got to get Anthony in to hear his side of the story. Plus could you send the letter to forensics for examination? Pity it's not handwritten – that would have made it all the more interesting.'

'I've never seen this letter before in my life!' declared Anthony Greenwood indignantly. Gone was the seductive smile and gone was the 'come-to-bed' look in his blue eyes, mused Lydia, as she considered the somewhat unkempt-looking lawyer sitting opposite her in the interview room at New Scotland Yard. A colour copy of the letter – which Nick was still insisting was mauve – as well as the thick document folder labelled "Amanda and Steven Faith" lay on the table between them; it had taken a speedy warrant to procure it.

He had been apprehended by Sergeant Clive Davis who then drove him in a squad car directly from Hampstead to the station; he'd hardly had time to fashion a proper Windsor knot in his tie and his hair needed a comb-through were the first thoughts that passed through Lydia's mind. Nick had once again read Anthony his rights and turned on the tape recorder. Clive Davis stood silently behind the barrister.

'Once more. This letter was found on your desk at the chambers, in this folder, this morning at seven o'clock by Sir William. Are you saying your superior is lying?' asked Lydia.

'No! I'm not saying that … I'm just saying – again, Detective – that … I've never seen this letter before.'

'The folder is in your charge, though?'

'Yes! I've been assisting with the Faiths' case.'

'Will you admit that some of the contents of this letter are true?'

'No ... erm... well, yes. I did have a kind of fling with Belinda. But just the once, as I told you last time.'

'And did Belinda want to continue with the affair?' continued Lydia.

'I don't know. Er ... probably. Possibly. We had a good relationship – a *working* relationship, that is – which went a bit far, I suppose. But Belinda never gave me any cause to think she wanted more out of it. She knew I was married. Am married.'

'So how do you account for this letter?'

'Goodness knows. Maybe she had second thoughts ... but as I've said several times now, I've **NEVER SEEN THIS LETTER BEFORE!**' Anthony's raised voice showed just how agitated he was becoming and Lydia decided to take a different tack.

'You acknowledge that you were indeed working on these documents pertaining to the Faiths?'

Anthony nodded sullenly, and Lydia went on,

'I'll take that as a "yes" for the record. How long have you been "assisting" on the Faith case?'

'Since just after Belinda ... died. Sir William was quite stressed out, as you can imagine, and asked me to check the intentional tort angle seeing as it's a speciality of mine.' Anthony seemed to calm down a little once he was on steady ground. Lydia smirked inwardly at the memory of Anthony's proud admission of how exactly he had explained intentional tort to a pliant Belinda, and continued,

'When did Sir William actually *physically* hand over this folder to you?'

Anthony considered for a few seconds, and replied,

'A week after Belinda's body was found, I think. Yes, exactly a week. You remember I was *here* on the Wednesday, Detective? Sir William had to go down to Whitstable the day before to take care of his sister – I believe you interviewed him there – and when he came back on Wednesday, he asked if he could pass over the Faith folder for me to have a look at.'

'So did he give you the folder there and then in chambers?'

'No … I met him for an early dinner in Covent Garden and then we went to his flat there and he gave it to me then.'

'Thank you, Mr Greenwood. That will be all for now; we'll be in touch.' Lydia finished the interview formally and directed Clive to drive Anthony to Weymouth House. She also gave instructions for the Faith folder to be returned to chambers as well.

'Boss! Why did you let him go?' exclaimed Nick, once they were on their own.

'Steady on, Nick. I'm in charge, remember?' shot back Lydia acerbically. She went on,

'Despite Anthony being a two-timing cheat, I can't help believing him … at least where this is concerned. There's something off about that letter and the whole Faith-folder thing. Let's see Sir William again – at his Covent Garden flat this time.'

'OK, Boss. I'm on it.'

Nick had been able to arrange for he and Lydia to meet Sir William that very afternoon, at his top floor flat just off Bow Street, a stone's throw from The Royal Opera House. Just before entering the building that William had buzzed them into, Lydia glanced round at the bustling hub of Covent Garden.

'Nice for some, eh, Nick? I'd love to live here with all the market stands and bistros just waiting for me to spend my money!'

'Indeed. You wouldn't get much change out of one and a half million for a one-bedroom apartment here, that's for sure.'

They pushed open the door to the vestibule and entered a lift that transported them smoothly and swiftly to the fifth floor; William was waiting outside when the lift door opened and led them to his flat.

'Welcome to Cliftonville Apartments, Detectives.'

'Wow!' exclaimed Nick on stepping through the front door. 'This is some apartment.' He walked over to the floor-to-ceiling picture windows and gazed out over the Victorian rooftops to the backdrop of London spires in the distance.

'Well, I like to call it my pied-à-terre!' said William in his usual clipped tones. 'As you know, my main residence is in Whitstable but I can only get down there at weekends usually. This is ideal for work … only a few minutes away. I try to walk to Temple most days – trying to lose weight, you know – but sometimes I give in and get a taxi into chambers.'

'This must have cost a pretty penny, Sir William?' put in Lydia, glancing round at the sumptuous interior, replete with marble and Maplewood trim.

'Just William. Well, we – Jennifer and I – inherited a fair amount once our parents had passed on and we'd sold the old farm. There was enough to buy the house in Whitstable, which you've seen, and pay for a full-time carer for Jennifer. Plus I could purchase Weymouth House as well as this little place.'

Lydia considered that "little place" was underegging it a little. The apartment, in striking contrast to the sixties' property in Whitstable, with its grandfather clock and antique furniture, was modern and airy. It had at least two bedrooms as far as she could make out and a sleek top-spec kitchen area opening onto a generous seating area. William continued,

'I acquired it off-plan, when they converted the old fruit and flower exchange into loft conversion-style apartments. Plus, I love theatre and opera, and it's in the ideal location for all that. I don't conduct much business here as a rule.'

'How is Jennifer, by the way?' enquired Lydia politely.

'As well as can be expected, thank you. Olive's a godsend, of course. Now, Detectives, what can I get you, coffee, tea?'

'Nothing, thank you,' answered Lydia. 'We need to get on now; we've got a few questions.'

'Ah, yes. Poor young Anthony's quite ruffled, I gather. Though not half as shocked as I was when I found that letter this morning.'

Once Nick had set up the recording system and read William his rights, Lydia began.

'Please could you tell us why you were so taken aback on reading the letter you found this morning in your office?'

'Well, I had no idea about Anthony and Belinda … he's a married man, and she has, or had, a boyfriend, I believe. I met him at her New Year's Eve party.'

'Such liaisons are not against the law, William, as I'm sure you are aware. Indeed they're relatively commonplace these days.'

'Absolutely, Detective. I know that, especially in my line of work. But the way that young Belinda described how she was intending to let Mrs Greenwood know about the affair with her husband did startle me somewhat … all rather close to home! And to be honest, I will admit the green-eyed monster reared its ugly head somewhat … as I think I mentioned, I did get carried away a little that evening at Belinda's party … such a fetching, pretty girl—' William's voice cracked slightly, and he went on,

'Very touching funeral, wasn't it? Her poor parents; so terrible for them. I don't think I could have got through it all without dear Sharon at my side …'

'Hmm. Going back to the "green-eyed monster", William. Did you seriously think you would have had a chance with Belinda?'

'No, not really. Once she had given me the cold shoulder, as it were, I stood back and that was that … although I have to admit that I did put a rose on her desk on Valentine's Day … just to cheer her up as she'd been looking a bit down. I expect she thought it was from Anthony – it's a little galling that my junior partner succeeded where I had failed!'

'Thank you, William,' said Lydia. 'We appreciate your honesty on that front. Now, as for the letter itself … as opposed to its contents, tell us again when and where exactly you found it.'

'I got into chambers very early this morning – before seven in fact – intending to get ahead with some of my workload. Closing yesterday meant I was quite behind. I was first one in to our office and I wandered over to Anthony's desk … there was the Faith folder, and as I picked it up, the letter must have become dislodged and fell out from between the papers. I couldn't help but read it as it was such a distinctive lavenderish colour, and anyway at first I thought it might have something to do with the Faiths which as you know is my case.'

'Ah yes, the Faiths. You'd asked Anthony's input on their case, hadn't you?'

'Yes, that's right. After Belinda's death, it was all quite fraught at chambers and being inundated with work, I requested Anthony's help … he would, of course, take a share of the fee which we negotiated.'

'Aren't Amanda and Steven Faith rather special clients though? Wouldn't you have wanted to see their case through yourself?'

If William felt surprise at Lydia knowing about how special the Faiths were, he did a good job of hiding it, she thought. He answered,

'Yes, but Anthony specialises in tort and I wanted him to check the finer details before the case got to court. The Faiths were fine about it, by the way.'

'Understood. Did you pass over the actual folder to Anthony?'

'One evening after work. We had an early supper at an Italian restaurant and then I invited him back here for a snifter. I gave him the documents then,'

'Is that usual? You've just said you don't do much business here. Why would you keep such important document folders at home … away from the office? And are you even allowed to take them home?' enquired Lydia.

'Well, er, sometimes I do. Not strictly kosher, I know, and usually If I have to work late on evenings before going to court, for instance. Or if it's a complicated case like the Faiths'. But that's the exception rather than the rule.'

'OK. And when you handed Anthony the folder, there was no letter from Belinda in there?'

William stared at the detectives with an expression of astonishment, which Lydia couldn't tell was real or feigned.

'No! Of course not. How could it have got in there if the folder had been at my flat and therefore out of the office for ages?'

'Well, that would have been my next question, William. How indeed? Belinda was already dead by the time you passed the folder to Anthony, and yet the letter turned up this morning in the Faith folder according to your statement.'

'So how did it get there and who put it there, Detective?'

'Again you've second-guessed me, William! That's exactly what we've been wondering: who put that letter in the folder, when, and why?'

'Um … the cleaner maybe? Or – surely you don't think that I—'

William looked genuinely indignant, considered Lydia, and instructed Nick to stop recording.

'We'll leave it at that for now, William. Let you get back to work. Oh, just one more thing. Would it be possible for us to have a copy of the Faith file?'

'Of course. I'll ask Sharon to organise the copying of all the documents and to courier it over to you.'

'Thank you. And we appreciate your time.'

Once back at New Scotland Yard, Lydia and Nick took a quick break in the staff canteen.

'So, Boss, don't you think it's a bit strange that William wanted to offload the Faith file onto Anthony Greenwood so suddenly? Given that Amanda and Steven Faith are old friends and he'd been dealing with that slightly dodgy tort issue thing for them since last year? I wonder if he was trying to distance himself from the rather unethical side of it all – he might have guessed that we'd find out about Belinda getting wind of the fishy nature of the case.'

'And perhaps he'd found Belinda's letter amongst Anthony's other paperwork – and himself planted it in the Faith file to incriminate Anthony for whatever reason,' said Lydia.

Nick continued,

'Yes … and/or to deflect attention away from himself?'

'Maybe. But it's the lavender letter itself that's bothering me, Nick. There's more than a whiff of perfume about it. I smell a rat.'

Chapter 23

Proviso (a qualifying clause)

By the end of the afternoon, Lydia felt that time had got away from her yet again. Her boss, CI Geoff Cordell, had asked for another team meeting to be convened early next morning to review the case; the preparation for this had taken Lydia right up to six in the evening. Despite this, she was itching to read on in Belinda's recent blogs – this year's entries that had been sent over to her by forensics officer, Beth Monkton – and decided to stay on at work for another hour or two. She turned her computer chair so that she could overlook the Thames which shimmered in the glow of the reddish-gold sunset. After a quick re-scan of Belinda's January entry which covered the New Year's Eve party, Lydia was keen to find out what had ensued in February this year.

15th February

Happy belated Valentine's Day, my dear Blog-Diary! Quite a lot has happened since I last wrote – which was a whole six weeks ago! So here we are; Belinda's Blog Number Two. So, Tom dumped me ... again. Or did I dump him? A bit of both, imho. I thought it was going well between us, especially the next morning after my New Year's Eve do and I couldn't help but mention the whole body-clock thing. I should have known he'd run a mile – he always does.

'You know I'm not the settling kind, Belinda,' he said. 'Why can't we just carry on as we are? It's fine!'

Yes, for him it is, but not for me. I'm not far off 30! Anyway, he wasn't going to budge. Saw him once or twice after that but a few weeks in, and I decided to cut him loose once and for all as it was obvious he wasn't going to commit. Draw a line under it. I called him into chambers for a coffee (Sir W. and Anthony were at court) and told him it was over. He was a bit peeved but we agreed to stay friends. The girls took me out for a drink to comfort me; they said the usual things like,

'He doesn't deserve you!' and 'There's plenty more fish in the sea', but I was rather down tbh. I wished I was going with them to Vietnam and Cambodia, but I just couldn't take the time off ... it's bad enough keeping Sir W. and his attentions at bay without risking my job by aggravating him as well!

Yes, Sir W. Now, there's a thing! After the New Year's Eve kissing gaffe, I'd have thought he got the hint especially as Tom was there ...it's not that Sir W. has actually tried to nuzzle – for want of a better word! – me again, it's just the way he looks at me sometimes, and actually did at the interview, now that I think about it! A lingering gaze I think they call it, and occasionally he puts his hand on my shoulder or my knee ...though I suppose it could be interpreted as completely innocent, like a friendly uncle sort of thing. But would he do that to Anthony? Somehow I don't think so! And yesterday, a single rose appeared on my desk; I bet it came from Sir W. I quickly put it into my briefcase before Sharon could see it. I don't dare tell her about Sir W.'s attentions – you know, I think she'd actually be jealous! She adores him, I'm sure. I

265

remember the way she clung to his side at the party – I think they'd make a good couple actually, but Sir W. probably considers her well beneath his class imho. Talking of bigots, I haven't seen or heard from dear brother Julian in a while. Not since New Year's Eve in fact. He needn't worry I'll tell Mother and Father about Precious; at least not for the time being.

*Now, on to the real news. Me and Anthony, would you believe! You're the only one I can tell, dearest Diary. Last night, we did the deed – here in my very own flat, in my very own bed. I had a feeling he liked me, I mean **really** liked me, from the start – it was just the way he would look at me with those eyes ...and judging by all the extra help he's been giving me at work. He's very knowledgeable about particular areas of law that I don't know much about, and occasionally we've discussed cases further over a drink at Legal Eagles when things get a bit intense in chambers. Anyway, yesterday, we happened to be leaving the office at the same time.*

'Taking Miranda out for Valentine's tonight?' I asked him.

'Oh no, we've stopped doing all that. What with the kids and so on. How about you? Seeing your young man, are you?'

I must have looked a bit downcast, because he then suggested having a light supper together at The Limestone as it's on the way home for both of us. I did get a bit tearful tbh, and Anthony was very concerned and sympathetic. So much so that he offered to walk me home ... the whole fifty metres to the flat; it was a really cold, frosty evening and we fooled around a bit, sliding around on icy puddles and so on, and, well, one thing led to another and he continued to "comfort" me between the sheets. Wow! How very accomplished Anthony is ... I'm still thinking about it today. He must really miss the whole romantic side of things in his marriage. Oh God, I do feel awful about Miranda. I never thought I'd be the type of woman to do that to another woman – steal their husband. I won't be able to look her in the eye next time she comes into chambers. Still, I doubt whether it will ever happen again tbh; Anthony made it abundantly clear that he had to get home, see to the children and so on. A family man. He made it very obvious it was a one-night stand and that I had to keep quiet about it. I said I'd see him in court, which was quite witty even if I do say so myself!

Well, whatever happens, it's cheered me up after the whole Tom thing. Good for my ego and all that, and God knows I need a boost on that front, my dear Diary!

Lydia stopped reading, made a few notes on her pad and gazed contemplatively out of the window at the river which no longer glowed in rays of the setting sun; instead, the smooth surface of the Thames mirrored the thousands of twinkling coloured lights that were reflected from the high-rise buildings of London.

'Belinda,' she murmured aloud. 'You may have written this blog, but you sure as hell did not write the lavender letter.'

In what seemed like the blink of an eye, Lydia was once more at New Scotland Yard; it felt to her as if she'd never been away. She was first one into the conference room at just before nine o'clock and was helping herself to a coffee, when Nick arrived.

'Morning, Boss! You're in early.'

'I know,' answered Lydia, pulling a wry face. 'I can't believe I left the office last night, got home, had supper, went to bed, got up and am here again in just over twelve hours.'

'Don't overdo it, Boss. Have you had any new thoughts on Belinda's love letter to Anthony?'

'That's just it, Nick. I don't think she wrote that letter at all—'

At that moment, CI Geoff Cordell and his PA, Ruth Simons, entered the room, closely followed by Sergeants Clive Davis and Terry Glover; they all made their way over to the beverage station to stock up on caffeine and cookies for the meeting that was about to start. 'Morning all,' began Geoff, as Ruth circulated minutes of the previous meeting and set up the laptop and projector. 'Forensics and the scene-of-crime photographer aren't here this time, as this meeting was such short notice, and they couldn't make it. Thanks to the four of you for being here. As you know, it's now just over three weeks since Belinda Radford was killed, and the press are starting to intensify their hounding of us i.e. the way in which we're attempting to solve this murder and apprehend the perpetrator. Massive sympathy for the parents and so on. Ruth, could you bring up what the papers are saying, please?'

'Yes, Sir,' said Ruth, flashing up image after image of sensational headlines, ranging from:

Police no further in solving barrister's murder. They haven't got a clue say devastated parents.

And:

Tax payers' money going down the drain in slaughtered lawyer case – shame on the Met!

To:

Belinda's killer still at large! Lawyers beware!

Lydia groaned inwardly before adding,

'How about: "Keep your noses out of it and let us do our job!"'

'Yes indeed, Lydia,' said Geoff. 'OK, please could you update us all as to what's been happening regarding this case since our meeting last week?'

'Of course. Thank you all from me, too, for being here this morning. Let me just summarise a few findings that I've already mentioned to Geoff since the last meeting but which you might not all be aware of,' began Lydia, nodding towards Ruth who began to take notes. 'And bring you up to date on the action plan we all agreed on last week.' Lydia took a quick swig of her coffee and went on,

'Firstly, let's look at some of the suspects. Nick and I went to visit Amanda and Steven Faith at their car dealership in Bromley; that would have been Action Point Four from our last meeting as you can see from the minutes. We've concluded that while there might be an indirect link pertaining to their intentional tort case that Sir William Bond, Belinda and latterly,

Anthony Greenwood have been working on, the gangland connection has nothing to do with anything, so we're dropping that lead. Next, the discovery of the knife.' Lydia noticed Sergeants Davis and Glover showing renewed interest; she continued,

'As we all know, the murder weapon was found by Sharon Hardy in Ben James' sleeping bag. I think we've all read the forensics report on the knife which is alleged to be the one used to cut Belinda's throat.' Lydia signalled to Ruth to project the report up onto the screen, and continued, 'It's also fairly certain that the knife originated from Weymouth House Chambers itself – thank you, Sergeant Glover for that intel.' Lydia noted that Terry Glover looked pleased at the acknowledgement. He's not going to like the next bit, though, she thought.

'We've interviewed Ben James again and have come to the conclusion that he's no longer a suspect,' Lydia continued, inwardly grimacing at Terry Glover's disappointed expression. 'I feel certain the knife was planted in his sleeping bag in an attempt to incriminate him. However, the idea of Ben or any other casual vagrant or opportunistic felon committing this crime is now discarded— Yes, what is it, Sergeant Glover?'

'Guv! Those tossers down on the South Bank – they're capable of anything, isn't that right, Clive?' Clive duly nodded, and Terry went on,

'What about the "clangy" knife Ben heard and the idea that he took it down to cardboard city to show his cronies or to keep for himself? We were going to follow that up again—'

'Forget it, Sergeant. Leave the poor souls alone. It's all supposition and it's putting us off the scent. The perpetrator is closer to home,' replied Lydia. 'Norman Combe, chief forensics officer, mentioned that the killer probably knew their way round the chambers, and I'm inclined to agree with him. Hence I'm excluding Ben James and all the other rough sleepers from the investigation. So please update your very good table of suspect height and left or right handedness – Ruth, would you mind putting the original one up on the screen. Delete Ben but … add in Tom Lovell and Miranda Greenwood.'

Terry Glover nodded assent, and Nick piped up,

'That's Action Point One from last week by the way – Sergeant Glover's findings on heights and left/right handedness. Good job, Sergeant, by the way.' Good one, Nick, thought Lydia. Terry Glover duly appeased once more.

'Indeed,' went on Lydia. 'And Action Point Two has also been concluded in that we can more or less deduce, although not confirm, who the mystery fingerprints in Belinda's bedroom as well as identical ones at the chambers belong to – the aforementioned Tom Lovell, Belinda's on-off boyfriend, and now definitely on the suspect list. And a real piece of work. Don't minute that last comment, Ruth!'

'Lydia,' interjected Geoff. 'Why can we only deduce rather than confirm that they are Tom's fingerprints?'

'Because the uncooperative prick wouldn't give us his prints. Don't minute that either, Ruth.'

'So how have we deduced they are his?' asked Geoff.

'Primarily through Belinda's blog in which she states taking Tom "*a special cup of New Year's Day tea*" after the party at her flat the evening before. There are several eye-witness reports of him having been there.'

'OK, do continue, please.'

'Right … just one more thing about the knife; as we know from the initial forensics report, it had been wiped clean and the fingerprinting I requested to be carried out on the cupboard from where it had been taken has shown it as merely being covered in prints from the chambers staff. However, that doesn't mean that the killer is necessarily one of them!' said Lydia. 'Moving on, since the last meeting, Nick and I have visited Sharon Hardy at home in Nunhead, and the Greenwoods in Hampstead for questioning and alibi checking. The latter visit has thrown Miranda Greenwood into the spotlight; one theory we have is that she might have become aware of Anthony's infidelity, felt threatened by it, and went on to murder Belinda out of rage and/or jealousy.'

'Miranda Greenwood is also rather fond of blood and gore, judging by her artwork,' interjected Nick. 'Looks as though she knows her way round a knife. That's why she's on the suspect list as well now … plus I overheard a snippet of conversation between her and her husband at the funeral about "*things being so much simpler* for them *now that she's gone*". Rather suspicious, we think.'

'Absolutely,' said Lydia, continuing, 'I also arranged for Sergeants Davis and Glover to interview any potential witnesses that might have seen Sharon Hardy walking her dog in Nunhead Cemetery on the morning in question. I received your report this morning, Sergeants, but only glanced at it briefly. Please could you elaborate for us?'

'Well, Terry and I took it in turns to do the early "shift"!' began Clive. 'I was there on Friday from six to seven a.m. – the time that forensics have estimated as Belinda's time of death – and on Monday evening from seven to eight.'

'And I did Tuesday morning and last night,' put in Terry. 'We both talked to several dog walkers who all seemed to know Sharon Hardy – and Ruskin – quite well, and confirmed that they often see her in the cemetery, and sometimes stop and have a chat.'

'But although they all verified the morning and evening times of the walks, none of them could specifically recall that particular Tuesday morning, I'm afraid. Nothing stood out for them on that day.'

'Thank you, Sergeants. Good effort and well done for the "graveyard" shifts!' put in Geoff. 'Lydia – what about the nurses and the doctor from Guy's?'

'Ah yes, Martha Bigbury and Skye Warriner; Belinda's friends and confidantes, and who also know Tom Lovell. They're definitely not suspects; they weren't even in the country when Belinda was killed – but they still might be able to give us some valuable information on Tom Lovell. As for Precious Temishe ... my instinct says she's not involved, but as she's backing up Julian, she's still in the picture for now. Julian stays as a main suspect for the time being.'

'Anything else on Sam White?' asked Geoff.

'Not at the moment, Sir,' replied Lydia. 'But we're continuing to keep an eye on the Whites. Sir William Bond is rather interesting. He conducts business not only at Weymouth House, but also works at his house in Whitstable and from time to time at his place here in London –a little irregular if you ask me, though he claims it's legit. He's come across a piece of seemingly incriminating evidence in the form of a letter among some papers – to do with the Faiths no less – but I'll report to you on that later, once I hear back from forensics, if I may.' Geoff nodded, and Lydia continued,

'Action Point Three was in connection with Belinda's diaries and blogs. I now have access to all twenty of them; there are ten physical diaries covering the time from when she was eight years old to the age of eighteen, and ten for age eighteen to twenty-eight, all handwritten. Then I have the printouts of the blogs – courtesy of Beth Monkton from forensics – written by Belinda this year. So far, I've finished going through the first ten diaries – the age eight to eighteen ones, and this year's January and February blogs. They're all extremely detailed,' Lydia said slightly defensively in case any of her colleagues thought she hadn't been assiduous and speedy enough in reading the diaries. 'And it takes ages to comb through them.'

'So anything of interest in them, Lydia?' asked Geoff.

'Well, the early years throw a lot of light on Belinda's surroundings and growing up on the New Forest estate. In fact, we met quite a few of her old friends and relatives at the funeral this week. On that note, Nick and I are just finalising our report of Belinda's funeral and wake – the preliminary report just needs condensing – and we'll send it through as soon as possible.'

'Thank you,' said Geoff. 'What about the recent January and February blogs?'

'The January entry first alerted me to the existence of Tom Lovell, and the February entry is all about the end of the relationship between Tom and Belinda plus the one-night stand she describes with Anthony Greenwood on Valentine's Day ...'

'Right, I see,' said Geoff. 'So we've got quite a lot to be going on with. To summarise, it seems that our suspect pool now consists of nine people: Julian Radford, Amanda and Steven Faith, Sir William Bond, Sharon Hardy, Anthony Greenwood, Miranda Greenwood, Sam White and Tom Lovell. All had opportunity to murder Belinda as they all had access in one way or another to the law building. My suggestion is that you, Lydia, and Sergeants Davis and Glover, meet with the nurses and Precious Temishe again and try to pump them for more info on Tom Lovell and Julian Radford. Nick – please delve into the intentional tort angle itself. Is that OK, Lydia?'

'Yes, Sir. And I'll get on with the rest of the diaries – the age eighteen to twenty-eight ones – and the March and April blogs of this year. Plus ... I'm off back down to the New Forest – probably Monday – to interview some of Belinda's past friends and family.'

'Sure. Lydia – I'm still keeping a car outside your flat as no doubt you've noticed. I'm not taking any chances ....'

'Thank you, Sir. I haven't received any more threatening emails, though.

'Can't be too careful. Keep your doors locked. Meeting adjourned everyone. Ruth, please send out the minutes as soon as you can.'

Chapter 24

Ex Gratia (something done as a favour)

'So, Boss, you were about to tell me more about the mauve love letter?' asked Nick, once they had left the conference room and were ensconced in Lydia's office with a supply of sandwiches, crisps and more coffee.

'Lavender. Well, I know it purports to be from Belinda to Anthony and its contents are probably generally accurate in so far as they had a fling ... but we know all that anyway. Remember that Anthony already admitted two weeks ago to the one-night stand with Belinda? And now I've read the February blog entry where she describes the event, I'm fairly sure it happened pretty much as he told us.'

Nick nodded thoughtfully, and Lydia continued,

'It's the differences in the style of writing that bug me, not to mention the emotions that come through. Firstly, all the schmaltzy stuff in the letter such as "Ant-Honey", "angel eyes"..."

'... "love nest", "Linda-Bee" – yes, I see where you're coming from, Boss.'

'Belinda's diaries and blogs are just not like that. She's less sentimental; in fact, the most sugary thing she writes is that her favourite colour is pink – and that was when she was eight! I know I haven't read the last ten years' worth of entries yet, but I doubt very much whether she's changed that much. Another thing; as Beth from forensics pointed out, Belinda's style of writing is very specific—'

'I remember her telling us that, Boss. Perfect punctuation and so on,'

'Yes! Take "*And still do look at me, it's been quite difficult*". I'm pretty sure Belinda would have used a semi-colon after "*me*", Nick. Her writing is much better than that.'

'And she's been to law school. She would be quite careful about stray commas, I dare say,' replied Nick.

'Exactly. Also, although she uses some abbreviations in her writing like "tbh" and "Sir W." the words are written out in full in the letter: "to be honest" and "Sir William".

'Good point,' said Nick. 'So what about the emotions you just mentioned?'

'Well, in the blog, Belinda seems to accept that it was a one-night-stand. And she feels guilty about Miranda—'

'And in the letter she appears to have second thoughts about a future with Anthony and threatens to tell his wife. Yes – that's definitely very different,' said Nick. 'So unless her feelings escalated in the weeks following the fling, it could well be that Belinda is not the author of the letter, as you say.'

'Thank you for hearing me out, Nick. Right, if she didn't write the letter, who did and why?'

'Probably someone who wanted to frame Anthony? His wife?'

'Maybe, but it could be anyone who knew about the carrying-on and has a grudge against Anthony, or just plain doesn't like him. Sam the cleaner, for instance, as Sir William so helpfully suggested?' wondered Lydia. 'Or, as we've already discussed, Sir William himself.'

'Yes, or Tom Lovell, out of jealousy? Plus there's Julian – he might have suspected something about the relationship, and we told Sharon Hardy ourselves!'

'I don't know how Tom or Julian could have had access to the Faith file in order to slip the letter into it, though,' said Lydia.

'Where there's a will, there's a way!'

'Hmm, well, whatever … I do think it's plain that whoever wrote and planted the letter knew or hoped it would end up in our hands. I'm inclined to think it's a red herring.'

'Or a mauve-cum-lavender one, Boss!'

'Ha ha,' said Lydia. 'Anyway, I'll put it all in the report for Geoff. Now, let's have a lunch break and enjoy our delightful canteen sandwiches, and then write up the final report on the funeral.

'So a summary of the main points would be roughly,' began Nick, clearing his throat, 'as follows:'

- *Thirty-three guests consisting of family, friends and colleagues of the deceased, Belinda Radford, and employees from The Heathers estate attended both the funeral service at Bournemouth Crematorium and the wake held at the Durley Chine Hall Hotel, also in Bournemouth. All guests arrived by car, either singly or in pairs/groups.*
- *Attendees (in no particular order):*

Family: *Felicity and Gordon Radford (= parents); Julian Radford (= brother); Nicola [= known as "Niki"] and Michael Hurley plus two sons (= Felicity's sister and family); Gordon's sister, her husband (= now known to be Caroline and Martin Gray), their two daughters and one son; Graham Radford (= Gordon's brother); Avril Doorley (= Felicity and Niki's mother).*

Friends: *Precious Temishe (= partner of Julian Radford); Martha Bigbury (= university friend); Skye Warriner (= university friend); Tom Lovell (= university friend and ex-on-off boyfriend); Fiona and Paul Edwards (= university friends); Angela [= known as "Annie"] Downes (= schoolfriend); Helena Bletsoe (= schoolfriend); Rachel Collings (= schoolfriend); Sarah Ryden (= schoolfriend).*

Colleagues: *Samuel [= known as "Sam"] White (= cleaner at Weymouth House Chambers); Joanna White (= wife of Samuel White); Anthony Greenwood (= barrister at Weymouth House Chambers); Miranda Greenwood (= wife of Anthony Greenwood); Sir William Bond (= QC/Senior Tenant at Weymouth House Chambers); Sharon Hardy (= clerk to the barristers at Weymouth House Chambers).*

Employees from The Heathers: *Jim Thorpe [= "James"?] (= horse trainer); Tracey and Bryan Snow (= estate managers).*

'I found out the surnames of the old schoolfriends as you can see; but I haven't bothered with Belinda's cousins' names as we agreed. Still OK with that, Boss?'

'Yes, that's fine, Nick. Go on.'

- *Overt sorrow was displayed by Felicity Radford, Precious Temishe, Martha Bigbury and Skye Warriner; Gordon Radford remained composed but anger and impatience beneath the calm exterior were evident.*

- *Shortly after arrival at the wake, Julian Radford and Precious Temishe left, due to the latter's suffering from a headache or migraine. The remaining guests tended to stay in family, friend or colleague groups; mingling was not observed to any great extent. Sir William Bond and Sharon Hardy isolated themselves from their colleagues, mainly monopolising the buffet table—*

'Strike that last part, Nick,' interrupted Lydia. 'Not relevant.'

'I was just joking, Boss!' said Nick with a smirk. He continued reading,

- *Tensions were palpable between Anthony Greenwood and Samuel White, and among the two sets of female schoolfriends.*

- *Segment of conversation overheard between Anthony and Miranda Greenwood along the lines of "things being so much simpler" for them "now that she's gone".*

- *Attachment: Programme of Service (scan).*

'That's it. Anything else to be included?'

281

'No, that's all fine. I'll email it over to Geoff,' replied Lydia. At that moment, a new email pinged its way into her in-box. 'Ah, here's the updated table from Sergeant Glover. Crikey, that was quick!' she added.

Suspects in alphabetical order (updated)	Right-handed	Left-handed	Height
Sir William Bond	Yes		5 ft. 9
Amanda Faith		Yes	5 ft. 7
Steven Faith	Yes		5 ft. 8
Anthony Greenwood	Yes		5 ft. 10
Joan ("Miranda") Greenwood	Yes		5 ft. 9
Sharon Hardy		Yes	5 ft. 4
Thomas ("Tom") Lovell	Yes		5 ft. 8
Julian Radford		Yes	6 ft.
Samuel ("Sam") White	Yes		5 ft. 9
NB: Victim			
Belinda Radford	*Yes*		*5 ft. 10.5*

'OK. Let's get moving on eliminating some of these suspects; we need to reduce the list as much as possible now,' said Lydia. 'For instance, despite the tort business, I'm not really convinced that the Faiths killed Belinda or had a hand in her death.'

'Agreed. There are no real gangland connections and Amanda and Steven Faith are just too blasé about the case to have any real concerns as to how ethical or otherwise Sir William is dealing with it. Plus Sergeant Glover just submitted a report of his questioning of the Faiths' employees; they all state categorically that Amanda and Steven were both at the showroom from seven a.m. onwards on the morning of the murder.' replied Nick. 'However, as you heard, Geoff wants me to look again into the intentional tort proceedings – could be an indirect motive ... I think that's my job for tomorrow.'

'Yep, fine. Let me know how you get on. Could you also arrange for Sergeants Davis and Glover and myself to meet with Martha Bigbury and Skye Warriner, and Precious Temishe, tomorrow morning at Guy's? Precious on her own, but the nurses together, if possible. They're not suspects, but I need to dig a bit more into Julian Radford and Tom Lovell.'

Lydia was pleased to be getting out of the office, even though she was merely changing one corporate setting for another. There were, however, few similarities between New Scotland Yard and Guy's Hospital in terms of architecture, she mused. Lydia, Terry and Clive had been given a quiet third-floor meeting room with an outside terrace overlooking several similar brutalist-looking concrete tower blocks which were in stark contrast to the more modern neo-classical and elegant police headquarters. They had been offered tea and biscuits, and the sergeants were busy tucking in. Lydia hoped that Clive would be able to focus on the job and not on the lovely Precious Temishe ... or indeed on the lovely Martha and Skye.

'Thank you,' said Lydia to the pleasant and helpful member of staff who had brought their beverages. 'Please could you inform Dr Precious Temishe that we are ready to see her now? She is expecting us.'

A few minutes later, Precious arrived, complete with an unbuttoned white coat revealing a silk mulberry-coloured blouse underneath, and a stethoscope round her neck; very much the professional young doctor, mused Lydia. She began,

'Good morning, Precious. This is just an informal meeting to follow up on a few points from your first statement; Sergeant Davis here will be taking notes. Are you feeling better? I was sorry not to have talked longer at Belinda's funeral.'

'Thank you, Detective. Yes, quite a lot better thank you. I've been having quite a lot of headaches and the occasional migraine lately – the death of Belinda, meeting Julian's parents finally, the funeral ...' Precious's voice trembled slightly, and Lydia broke in,

'Not to mention the stress of being a trainee doctor, I expect.' Precious nodded, and Lydia continued,

'How did the meeting with Mr and Mrs Radford go?' Lydia was keen to hear Precious's side of the story; after all, Gordon had told her that it had all gone swimmingly.

'To be honest, it was fine. We'd gone down to the New Forest the evening before and stayed at The Heathers. Gordon and Felicity couldn't have been kinder considering it was the first time they'd ever met me, and in the terrible circumstances of course. Felicity was very fragile of course. I don't know why Julian's been so cagey about me meeting them.'

Lydia knew very well the cause of Julian's reticence in introducing his African girlfriend to his parents; Julian had been keen to ensure his share of the estate would be bequeathed to him, and was afraid that his dating a black woman would have stood in the way. Money or love? That was the question that had been bothering Julian. She continued,

'I'd like to go over the statement you gave us about the night before, and the morning of, Belinda's murder.'

Precious nodded, and Lydia continued,

'We've had confirmation from Netflix that "Orange is the New Black" was indeed streamed to Julian's account on the Monday evening. You claim that you both watched it after having had supper and that you then went home at around eleven that night. Can you tell us again what time you got home and if anyone can verify this?'

'Yes, I arrived back at my flat in Crystal Palace at quarter to twelve; Julian messaged me to make sure I'd got home OK.'

'Thank you. Did he message you just the once?' enquired Lydia.

'No … we carried on "chatting" for about half an hour. Pretty silly really considering we both had early starts the next morning, I guess.'

'You mention in your statement that you can only assume Julian went straight back home after seeing you off that night and that he left Blackheath early the next morning to go to work. Is that right?'

'Yes, that's correct … on the basis of the messages that he sent. We texted back and forth early on the Tuesday morning for at least an hour or so.'

Lydia perked up at that and continued,

'What time did you two communicate that morning, Precious?'

'From about six o'clock till about seven, when he told me he was leaving Blackheath to go into Spitalfields.'

A whole hour, thought Lydia. Must be love.

'Precious, I take it your and Julian's phones have location trackers on them?'

'Yes, Detective.'

If Julian's location tracker showed him as being in Blackheath *and* chatting to Precious between six and seven in the morning – Belinda's estimated time of death – then there was no way he could have killed her and he would be exonerated as a suspect. Bravo, Precious, thought Lydia. You've most probably provided slimy Julian with a cast-iron alibi.

'OK, we'll be looking into the tracking records. That'll be all, Precious. Thank you so much for your time.'

After Precious had left the meeting room, Lydia turned to Clive.

'I trust you noted everything of importance, Sergeant.'

'Yes, Guv. Shall I get onto the mobile phone company?'

'Yes, immediately. And also send an email to DI Fairman telling him about it. Sergeant Glover, please could you ask for nurses Martha Bigbury and Skye Warriner?'

A few minutes later, and Martha and Skye entered the room. Even in nurses' scrubs they managed to look glamorous, mused Lydia.

'Morning. Nice to see you both; it's just an informal get-together as I've got a few questions for you.' Lydia began. 'My sergeant will be taking notes.'

'Hello, Detective,' said Martha. 'Sorry we couldn't talk more at the funeral. It was so very upsetting … plus we got into a discussion with our other uni friends, Fiona and Paul.'

'No problem,' replied Lydia. 'By the way, I think it's great that you're all going to have a memorial get-together for her.'

'Thank you,' said Skye. 'We're thinking of inviting Precious as well; we met her at the funeral and bumped into her just now. She seems such a compassionate person—'

'What about Tom Lovell?' broke in Lydia. 'Is he compassionate as well?'

Martha and Skye exchanged glances.

'Well … not in a conventional sense,' answered Martha. 'He appears to be all confident but I think he really did care for Belinda in a way.'

Confident my hat, thought Lydia. Cocky twat more like. She continued,

'How so? I have the impression that he used her when he felt like it and gave her the cold shoulder when she finally gave him to understand that she wanted more out of it given the whole biological clock side of things. No?'

'To be fair to Tom, he never pretended to be anything other than an easy hook-up,' said Skye. 'What you see is what you get with him.'

'You mean curmudgeonly and rude?' said Lydia, before she could stop herself.

The nurses exchanged fleeting looks with each other and to their credit responded rather diplomatically, mused Lydia.

'We've known him a long time, Detective,' answered Martha. 'He can be a bit short-tempered, but he is a loyal friend.'

'Yes,' continued Skye. 'We didn't like what he did to Belinda, but we're kind of caught in the middle …'

'Do you think he's capable of murder?' asked Lydia.

'No!' Both nurses cried out in unison. 'Is he a suspect then?' demanded Martha.

Lydia chose not to answer and changed the subject.

'How's the litigation going, by the way? You mentioned that Anthony Greenwood is handling your case now?'

'We're meeting with him next week actually,' replied Skye. 'Hopefully we can move forward with it then.'

'Well, I wish you the best of luck with that. I'm sure Mr Greenwood is more than capable. Anyway, I'd better let you get back to work ... and I'm very grateful to you for giving up your time to talk to me today.'

After Martha and Skye had left the meeting room, Lydia turned to Clive.

'Did you get all that, Sergeant?'

'You mean about Tom Lovell being a lovable prat, Guv? Yep!'

'Ha ha. OK, could you send me a brief report by email of today's interviews, and ask DI Fairman to arrange for me and him to visit Mr Lovell at the college he works at. Sergeant Glover – could you get the car and take us back to the Yard. We'll have police sandwiches for lunch rather than hospital ones ... not that there's a lot of difference.'

Chapter 25

De Minimis Non Curat Lex (the law will not take account of trifling matters)

Goldsmiths College looked rather regal at first glance, considered Lydia, as she and Nick walked up the hill leading from the station. Situated on top of a hill in the heart of New Cross, with its royal coat of arms sparkling in the sunlight, the handsome red brick and white building lorded it over the surrounding terraced houses and dusty streetside shop fronts. Signing in at the porters' lodge, she and Nick were directed to the large student coffee bar in the heart of the college where they had agreed to meet Tom Lovell.

'This takes me back, Boss,' said Nick, taking a sip of his cappuccino. 'Though I was at a different college. Queen Mary.'

'What did you study, Nick?'

'Accounting ... don't look so surprised – I'm quite good at maths I'll have you know! I didn't carry on with it after graduating though – that's when I joined the Met. What about you?'

'I read Psychology at uni ... Sussex ... and then went into the police force. Trained as a detective and here I am! Do you think your degree has helped you in your career?'

'In a way, yes. It taught me to be quite logical ... working through things step by step in detail. But I didn't fancy working on company taxes and spreadsheets for ever and wanted to be more hands-on,

so the police seemed a good choice. What about you –
psychological insights and all that, Boss?'

'Definitely. The *Psychopathy v. Sociopathy*
module I studied has been especially useful in our line
of work! I do love to delve into how the mind works
… I discuss it quite a lot with my friend, Marie, who is
actually a psychologist—'

'Afternoon, Detectives. To what do I owe the
pleasure?' broke in Tom Lovell, his voice on the
caustic sounding side as usual, thought Lydia, noting
his red jeans and Sons of Anarchy hoodie.

'Mr Lovell. Thank you for agreeing to meet
with us at such short notice.' began Lydia.

'Hmm. Well, I've got a short break now before
I have to give my lecture on Soviet rule in the twentieth
century. So, what do you want? Couldn't you have
asked me at the funeral?'

'That wouldn't have been very seemly, would
it?' replied Lydia, inwardly seething at the insensitivity
of the man. 'Given that people were, you know,
mourning?' Without waiting for an answer, she went
on, 'I know that you have declined to offer us your
fingerprints which may or may not match those found
at Belinda's flat and in her office. You're not under
arrest … yet. However, you do need to give us the
name of anyone who can vouch for your whereabouts
on the evening before, and the morning of, the murder.'

'I told you to—'

'Mr Lovell,' interrupted Nick. 'Stop this now.
We are not going to waste precious police resources,
which includes our time incidentally, interviewing all
the female students in this college who might or might

not have been sleeping with you at the very moment Belinda Radford was brutally killed. Tell us who it was now, or we will have no choice but to arrest you for wasting time in a murder investigation.'

Glowering, Tom got up as if to leave.

'Sit down, Mr Lovell,' commanded Lydia. 'As I mentioned before, Belinda mentions you in her blog entries. We know all about how you went to the chambers and turned down Belinda's ultimatum to make a proper commitment to her.'

'She invited me over there to talk it over and we agreed to stay friends.' growled Tom, his anger barely hidden.

'Yes, but weren't you just a tiny bit peeved that Belinda wouldn't play along anymore? Maybe jealous about her thing for Anthony Greenwood?'

Tom did look genuinely surprised at that nugget, mused Lydia, who continued.

'Perhaps you wanted to keep her for yourself all along and later in a fit of anger, you decided to return to the chambers and—'

'OK. Stop,' said Tom. 'I only ever went to Weymouth House the once back in January when we broke up as I've just told you. I admit it was a little irksome that Belinda wouldn't be available in the way that I would have liked, but I really couldn't have cared less who she went with after we broke up, so if she wanted to sleep with that barrister, then fine by me.'

'Thank you,' said Lydia, who went on,

'So you maintain that was the only time you went to Belinda's office?'

'Yes, Detective. I was nowhere near there when Belinda was murdered, and I have an alibi for the morning as well as for the evening before. I was at home the whole time in my flat in Wickham Road just near here with my "friend" Gillian Keyte and you can ask her all the questions you like, Detectives.'

'Thank you. So is Ms Keyte a student here at Goldsmiths?' asked Lydia.

'Yes. Over eighteen and not in any of my classes. And she's not in college today.' came the testy reply.

'OK, Mr Lovell. Give Detective Fairman here her details and we'll follow it up. If she can corroborate your story then we won't need to place you under arrest. Or take your fingerprints.'

After Tom had stomped moodily off, Lydia turned to Nick.

'Such a charmer, isn't he? Get onto this Gillian. God knows why females are attracted to such a jerk. Belinda wanted to marry him and Martha and Skye think he's got a heart of gold. I just don't get it!'

'I think it's to do with authority figures, Boss. He's an anarchic, bolshie prick who doesn't like the police and doesn't like being told what to do by us.'

'Yes,' agreed Lydia. 'He's probably terrified of his fingerprints, DNA and so on getting into "the system" so that he can be controlled by the state. Sort of George Orwell. Anyway, let's have another coffee before we go?'

'Oh, very "mind police", Boss! And yes, I was just thinking I need another shot of caffeine and maybe one of those big cookies. I'll get them.'

While Nick went to fetch the drinks, Lydia's phone beeped to inform her that an email had arrived from Sergeant Davis with the report from the morning's meetings with the nurses and Precious Temishe. He'd also noted that the mobile phone company servicing Julian Radford's phone had agreed to scrutinise his call record for the morning of Belinda's murder and that they would come back with their findings as quickly as possible. She quickly fired off a message to Geoff to update him on the facts as they knew them so far and requested permission to take home the box of Belinda's handwritten diaries from ages eighteen to twenty-eight for the weekend. Maybe they would offer some insight into why perfectly normal, sensible women would be attracted to the likes of Tom Lovell or Julian Radford.

After a Saturday morning brunch at her local diner in Battersea, Lydia settled down in her home office to tackle the ten remaining diaries. They were not quite as tatty as Belinda's early girlhood ones and the covers and inner pages featured far fewer hand-drawn decorations and symbols. Lydia noted how Belinda still retained a predilection for lists as well as for both abbreviations and verbatim conversations though, as in:
Wednesday, 6th October
Dearest Diary,
Well, here I am at last – at uni in London! The first two weeks have been such a blur that I haven't had

time to write tbh. These are the events that I've been to:
Freshers' Fair to sign up for a few clubs and societies*
Student Union Voting Day
Intercollegiate Hall of Residence Social Evening
University of London First Years' Ball
*Joined the "Eco-Army", "Help for Battered Women Group" and "Horses for Courses" – promoting riding for the disabled.
The Hall of Residence Social Evening was really great. I've met loads of people from other colleges, not just from UCL. My new besties are Martha and Skye who are studying to become nurses, and Fiona, who's reading Geography – they're all at King's College. Of the boys, there's Paul (at LSE and hugely into investments and wants to go into hedge funding!) and Tom who's also at UCL ... ooh, I like Tom! Long dark hair, a wacky clothes sense and kind of ... mysterious. The first words he said to me are;
'Evening, country lady. I do love the natural look – a Tess to my Alec D'Urberville?'
Well! I think it was a compliment, but imho, I probably need to work on my make-up.
'You need lessons!' That's what Skye and Martha said and they're going to give me a makeover as I'm going out with Tom on Saturday night to see a band play at the Barbican. Who knows where that may lead to?

Lydia had the feeling that she knew very well where that was going to lead to.

Indeed, Tom and Belinda were an on-off item for several years, right up until the end of their respective undergraduate years:

Sunday, 11th May
Dear Diary,
Where has all the time gone? Here I am at the end of my final year at UCL – finals start on Monday week, and all being well, I'll be able to start my Bar Professional training in September. Have been offered a conditional (= as long as I get at least a 2:1!) work-based place at a law firm in Holborn. Still generally my neck of the woods – I consider Bloomsbury to be my home from home! I'm determined to keep in touch with everyone; Martha and Skye will be based at King's College Hospital at Denmark Hill; Fiona and Paul, who've become a "thing", are moving in together in Greenwich; and Tom ... well, what can I say? It's been on-off throughout uni, really.

'We could move in together, too, couldn't we?' I asked him last night. He hesitated a bit too long really and then not so subtly changed the subject. Then off he went to cram for his Politics Paper Two. I don't feel like pushing it with him though, after all I'm not that desperate for a man tbh, and I want to do well in my career and show all those male chauvinist lawyers out there that a woman can be as successful as them. After my exams, I'm going to stay for a few weeks at The Heathers, get some fresh air, ride some horses and spend some time with Mother and Father. Without Julian there, hopefully! The amount of times he's bothered to come and see me I could count on the fingers of one hand, even though he's moved up to

London now as well. Money, money, money – that's all he cares about imho. Banking will be the perfect career for my dear baby brother.
Bye for now, dear Diary. Must do some swotting.

Good, thought Lydia. So Belinda wasn't as devastated as all that about Tom's elusiveness; at least not back when she was twenty-one and on the cusp of her sparkling career in law. The diaries then contained much tedious legal-speak as Belinda got her teeth into her barrister training at Curtis Hall Legal Services in Holborn:

Monday, 13th March
Dearest Diary,
So glad I've got today off, even though I'm very much enjoying being at Curtis Hall. I've got an assessment coming up at the end of the week; these are the topics I've got to make sure I know 100%:

Advocacy
Civil Litigation & Dispute Resolution
Criminal Litigation
Professional Ethics

I love Professional Ethics! This very weekend down at The Heathers, Father and I got into a good debate about whether a lawyer should defend a clearly guilty party.

'How could you be in any way sympathetic to, say, a child molester, Belinda?'

'It's not about being sympathetic, Father! It's about getting them the best possible outcome according to the law.'

'Hmm, well, bring back the death penalty, I say.'

Not for the first time, Lydia reflected on how similar she and Belinda were – they both had backward-thinking fathers, which did not stop them, young strong females, however, from pushing on and trying to become a force for good. She read on:

It was a great weekend overall though. The main reason for going down was to attend my old school reunion in Lymington on Saturday – five years since we all left Talbot Forest! There was a tour of the premises (the new music centre is amazing) and then a "scrumptious"– as they say – tea including mini raspberry doughnuts; what we used to call "white rats" (= iced buns); and even Chelsea slices. It really took me back tbh. Some of the old staff were there, such as Miss Vernon – still exactly the same – and it was wonderful to see Annie again. Pity Helena couldn't make it, but Sarah and Rachel came (= all our teenage acrimony on hold ...), and it was interesting the way we all reverted back to type – going around in a gang and giggling!

On Sunday, Father and I walked down to the stables; it was gratifying the way everyone greeted me so warmly – except for grouchy old Jim of course! I think Bryan and Tracey are together now, which is lovely; stable hand Pam has long since moved on – pity, really, she was good to me back in the day. As ever, it was sad to see Mother so emotional when I left last night; I do worry about how fragile she's become imho. Pity darling Julian isn't a bit more supportive.

Before Lydia could read the final year or so of diaries, she was roused by the sound of something being pushed through her letter box. Another flyer probably she thought, and headed to the kitchen to make a cup of tea. On the way back to her desk, she picked up the envelope lying on the mat; on opening it, she was shocked to see it was another hate letter. Rather than it being sent by email, this one had been printed out and hand-delivered:

Dear "Ms" Detective Carlisle,

Yes, I know where you live so watch your back. I thought I told you to keep your sticky beak out of Belinda's life – and death, ha ha. I saw you at the funeral fucking staring at everyone with those big blue eyes but you haven't got a clue, have you? Just like they're saying in the papers. So much for being the best woman detective in London! Why don't you just leave it to the superior sex to deal with? But you can't, can you? Mind you, those idiot police mutts you hang around with aren't much better ... useless in fact. Well, as I learnt from my dear old Father, give your quarry a bit of a leash and then when they're least expecting it, lunge in for the kill. That's what's going to happen to you if you dare cross my patch one more time, you twiggy cunt. I'm watching you.

With very best wishes from your greatest fan.

PS: A copy of this letter is going to all the dailies!

Lydia immediately phoned Geoff who swore most colourfully when he realised that the note must have been delivered between shifts of the police watch stationed outside Lydia's flat. The deliverer must have watched and waited for their opportunity; more crucial and worrying however, was the fact that the murderer had found out where Lydia lived.

Chapter 26

Per Stirpes (property divided equally between the offspring)

'You're not going down to the New Forest alone, Lydia, and that's final,' said Geoff Cordell first thing on Monday morning.

'OK, Sir, I'll take Nick with me – he'll be pleased to have another day out of the office,' replied Lydia. 'And I'm not scared, just for the record. It's only a poison pen letter, not a poison dart!'

'Hmm. But the perpetrator knows your home address so I'm doubling up on security ... two officers outside your flat at any time whether you're there or not, and they're to send hourly updates as to any suspicious activity. Get the letter and envelope to forensics to see what they can find.'

'Nothing, I expect,' said Lydia. 'This is a very crafty killer – if they can find out where I live and get past a squad car parked outside, they're certainly not going to be stupid enough to leave incriminating evidence on an envelope! It worries me more that the perp is escalating ... I mean, look at the language. It's definitely worse than the poison email I got.'

'My point exactly,' said Geoff. 'You've got to watch your back, Lydia.'

I will, Sir.'

Geoff continued,

'Plus the murderer has made good on their promise to send a copy of the letter to the press –

they're having a field day!' Picking up one of the several papers lying on his desk, he read aloud:

The killer of Belinda Radford, 28, of Weymouth House Chambers, has gone public with their opinion of our tardy police force in solving the promising young barrister's murder. A letter (reproduced in full below) was hand-delivered by an unknown – and unseen – person to investigating officer, DI Lydia Carlisle, at her home in Battersea, as well as circulated to media syndicates. In colourful terms, the murderer makes clear the Met is still scrabbling around in the dark in their hunt for justice and explicitly taunts Carlisle. While this newspaper does not condone this kind of threatening behaviour, it is clear that the police need to up the ante before more violence takes place.

'That's just one of many … and is one of the more restrained articles,' said Geoff.

'Sir, I refuse to be intimidated by the perp or put off by their ploys to discredit us … erm … me' responded Lydia grimly. 'I'm not giving up; in fact it makes me even more determined to catch the lowlife – who in America I guess would be called a motherfu—'

'Just so, Lydia. Now off you go and drive safely.'

An hour later, and Lydia and Nick were on their way.

'Thanks for driving, Boss,' said Nick. 'I wouldn't have minded, though.'

'Well, you drove last week down to Bournemouth, so it's only fair. It's also taking my mind off that poison pen letter, not to mention the press response. Honestly, we're doing our best, aren't we?'

'Yes, but you know how the media like to have a moan about the establishment … and it sells newspapers!' Nick tactfully changed the subject, remarking, 'So this is your third trip down south in as many weeks, isn't it?'

'Hmm … indeed. Could you phone ahead to The Snows to confirm we'll be with them at around one o'clock, and then call the Radfords and let them know as a courtesy that we're on our way. We'll go straight to the Snows and then call in on Gordon and Felicity afterwards. Also, while we're not making this a formal interview, could you take notes on your tablet today? Please.' Said Lydia, wondering if she'd ever get any better at giving orders more agreeably.

'On it, Boss. But only if we can stop at that nice service station at Fleet for a coffee …!'

'Wow, it's fantastic,' exclaimed Nick gazing around the estate that stretched as far as the eye could see. 'Lucky, lucky people to live here!'

'I know – it's amazing, isn't it,' answered Lydia. 'Right, let's park here next to the stables and ask someone to point us in the direction of Anemone Cottage.'

However, as they pulled up at the black and gold sign proclaiming The Heathers Livery and Equestrian Centre and stepped out of their car, they were approached by Bryan Snow himself.

'Morning, Detectives. Lovely day for a visit to the New Forest, isn't it? I'll take you straight to the cottage; Tracey's waiting there. If you're lucky, you might get some of her homemade soup and freshly-baked bread.'

Lydia and Nick followed Bryan as he led them past the paddocks and manèges Lydia recalled from her first visit a few weeks earlier. As before, there were a multitude of ponies grazing, though not quite so many foals.

'Are these all Beaulieus, Bryan?' asked Lydia.

'Most of them, yes. It's our speciality as you probably know … it's nearly auction season now that the fillies and colts are old enough to leave the mares.'

'Are you expecting Julian Radford to put in an appearance this year?' enquired Lydia, trying very hard to appear guileless, and probably failing, she thought.

Bryan cast her a sidelong look and replied,

'Well, young Julian is rather interested in that side of the business … so I expect so. But then he has his new lady so maybe she'll be occupying his time more from now on.'

How diplomatic, considered Lydia privately. As if Julian needs to be so hands-on keeping an eye on the estate's profit margins going forward now that his sister is dead and he'd be getting her share. No more competition, and the parents seem to like Precious, so what is there to worry about any more?

'Hi guys,' called out Bryan to a group of grooms and stable hands, old Jim amongst them, who were sitting on bales of straws and wooden benches eating sandwiches and sipping from water bottles, and clearly relishing the sunshine. 'I've known a lot of these employees for years ever since I started here as a gardener – and we mostly get on well … thank goodness, now that I'm their manager. Right, here we are.'

Anemone Cottage was the epitome of a country cottage, mused Lydia. Thatched roof and a cottage garden brimming with multi-coloured tall lupins and hollyhocks, themselves underplanted with spring perennials such as pale yellow primroses and the ubiquitous heather.

'Great garden,' commented Nick. 'I guess that's all you, Bryan?'

'Yes indeed. I may be an estate manager, but my roots – forgive the pun! – lie in gardening. Flowers at the front and round the back is my vegetable patch. Ah, here's Tracey.'

The detectives were welcomed into the cottage and Lydia was struck by what a quintessential country couple Bryan and Tracey Snow were. Bryan with his neatly cut dark blonde hair, a checked shirt and brown corduroys, and Tracey, her hair tied back in a ponytail, wearing a bottle green blouse and blue jeans. It was she who ushered them into the cosy kitchen complete with range and butler sink, sat them down at the large wooden table, and invited them to help themselves to the vat of steaming vegetable broth and still warm homemade granary bread.

'Wow, this is amazing,' began Lydia. 'Thank you so much.'

'It's the least we can do ... we want Belinda's murderer caught and put behind bars, so if there's any way we can help, we will,' replied Tracey, her voice quavering. 'That poor, poor girl. And the poor, poor parents.'

'Tell us about how you both came to be working for the Radfords ... DI Fairman will be taking i-notes,' said Lydia, laying her own notebook next to her on the table.

'Well,' began Bryan, 'I started here as a teenager after school, doing odd jobs around the estate – a bit of painting, cutting the lawns and so on. Eventually, the work built up as the livery business grew and I was taken on full time as gardener-cum-handyman. Then I progressed to looking after the grounds and stables, and now – twenty years later – I oversee the whole estate operationally. And of course, Tracey and I got together.'

'Yep,' continued Tracey. 'Pretty much the same for me, really. I had a Saturday job up at the house, doing the cleaning and occasionally minding the Radford children. Then Gordon offered me a part-time role meeting and greeting the traders interested in the ponies, as I'm good with people, so he says! So now I manage all the staff on the estate, and any visitors. Bryan and I got married about ten years ago; now we've got twin daughters – Daisy and Rosemary, and a little boy called Rowan ... plant names, obviously!'

'What do you remember of Belinda and Julian as children?' asked Lydia.

'When I first started here, she must have been about eight, and Julian a couple of years younger. When I used to babysit them, Belinda used to like drawing and writing in her diaries a lot ... Julian tended to want to run around more – typical boy, I suppose – and liked getting on his big sister's nerves.'

'Yes,' Bryan picked up the thread. 'Julian was a bit of a nuisance at times. I'll never forget the way he swiped the heads off my dahlias with his wooden sword, laughed, and then ran off. It wasn't something I felt I could tell his parents, seeing as he was the apple of their eye. Good to see he's settled down a bit ...'

'His girlfriend looked very nice,' went on Tracey. 'Pity she felt unwell at the funeral; I would have liked to get to know the woman who's captured Julian's heart at last.'

A short-sighted one, thought Lydia, who nodded and asked,

'Do you think Julian will come back and live at The Heathers one day?'

'No way!' exclaimed Bryan. 'He never liked it here. I wasn't at all surprised when he upped and went off to London as soon as he could. God forbid anything ever happens to the parents ... Julian would just sell up and get his hands on whatever dosh he could get. At least Belinda loved the place; she would never have got rid of it ... '

'Even when she started secondary school, she carried on coming down to the stables to chat to the stable hands, help with the mucking out and so on. Her favourite pony was Posy and Belinda absolutely adored grooming her,' put in Tracey. 'She was a good rider, too. I think she entered a few gymkhanas and it helped with her popularity—'

'How popular was Belinda at school?' enquired Lydia. 'By the way, this soup is absolutely delicious. Your own vegetables, Bryan?'

'Yes, indeed.' answered Bryan, looking pleased at the compliment. 'Potatoes, leek and broccoli … all from last year – frozen obviously! Tracey can tell you more about Belinda's teenage years – she used to confide in you more, didn't she, love?'

'Well, she was quite a bookworm type as well as being into the ponies. I think she found it hard to make friends; but she did invite some of them back here to see the horses and let them have a ride.'

'Would Annie Downes, Helena Bletsoe, Rachel Collings and Sarah Ryden have been among her closest friends?' asked Lydia, consulting her notebook.

'Of course, they were at the funeral too,' said Tracey. 'For a split second there, I wondered how you knew them! Well, Annie and Helena were Belinda's best friends, but they were a twosome really … both lived in the town whereas Belinda was out here at The Heathers. They used to come over and hang out here … all dependent on lifts and so on, though, so not as often as Belinda would have liked, I think.'

'Thank you. What about Rachel and Sarah? It may not be relevant, but I thought I detected a little tension between the schoolfriends at the wake?' enquired Lydia.

'Yes, you're right. If I remember rightly, Belinda started off trying to be friends with Rachel, then Sarah came along and "stole" Rachel away and then *they* became best friends and pushed Belinda away. I know it sounds schoolgirly but it hurts – you know how bitchy girls can be. I definitely recall Belinda when she was about fifteen or so coming down to the stables in floods of tears, saying she had no real friends.'

'So Tracey gave her a hug and said she was one in a million and not to change,' continued Bryan.

'Yes, and I remember we took a flask of tea and sat in one of the meadows and watched the mares and foals,' said Tracey. 'Luckily, Annie and Helena took her under their wing and they and Belinda became a threesome... I think they all kept in touch after she went off to uni in London. But I hadn't seen any of them until the funeral.'

At that point, Nick looked up from his iPad and said,

'This bread is absolutely wonderful, Tracey. Thank you. May I ask about Jim Thorpe – I understand you chaperoned him to Belinda's funeral?'

'Old Jim,' replied Tracey, fondly. 'A bit crabby—'

'More than a bit,' put in Bryan. 'Cantankerous old so and so, more like. He's been here for ever. He even pre-dates us! I believe he owned a homestead with a few animals originally and was taken on by the Radfords on a freelance basis to manage the livestock here.'

'He *is* good with the horses,' continued Tracey, 'and I admit he's crotchety sometimes. But I feel we should look out for him a bit ... he's on his own and occupies Daphne Cottage, down at the far end of the estate. His daughter, Pamela, used to be a stable girl here – same age as me and Bryan – but she's long gone. Ran off with one of the lads from the yard, so

Jim tells us. I don't think he has any contact with her now—'

At that moment, there was a loud knocking on the door, and Bryan strode over to open it. It appeared to be one of the grooms who required his help; one of the mares was foaling and they needed an extra pair of hands.

'Apologies, Detectives, I have to run. It's an older mare and she's late with her foal. Do call if there's anything else I can help with. And nail the prick who took our Belinda, won't you?' And with that, Bryan was gone.

'Tracey, thank you so much for the brilliant lunch. You've got our number if you think of anything pertinent,' said Lydia. 'We're going to look in on Felicity and Gordon now, and then head back to smoky old London, unfortunately.'

Twenty minutes later, the detectives were sitting in the conservatory that Lydia remembered from her first visit. The stunning view of the lawns was made more spectacular by the replacement of the previous gladioli with wonderful wild magenta-hued orchids. The ubiquitous heather held its own, however.

'Thank you, Felicity, but no thank you,' protested Lydia, as the bereaved mother, still visibly distressed with her ashen face and dead eyes, tried to ply them with refreshments. 'Nick and I have just had a marvellous lunch with Tracey and Bryan. We just called in to see how you're getting on before going back to London.'

'Not very well, to be honest,' replied Felicity. 'I'll never get over it … the funeral was so painful … worst day of my life …'

'It's terrible,' agreed Nick. 'But we will find who did this to Belinda.'

At that moment, Gordon Radford entered the conservatory. Shaking hands with Lydia and Nick, he began,

'Thank you for coming to the funeral; it's much appreciated considering you didn't even know our daughter. But I guess that wasn't the only reason you came, was it?'

'Well, to be honest, we wanted to get a picture of Belinda's life, her family and friends …' answered Lydia. 'Off the record, the more I work on this case, the more I feel it was a premeditated murder by someone who knew her. The idea of a rough sleeper or an opportunistic thief killing her just because she got in the way of a couple of oil paintings just doesn't sit well with me.'

Felicity stifled a sob, and in a wavering voice, asked,

'But who would have disliked or hated my darling girl enough to … to … slit her throat as if she were an animal? That's preposterous.'

'I know,' replied Lydia. 'But my hunch tells me I'm right and that the perp is someone who was familiar to Belinda.'

'I do get that you need to get a feel for Belinda's family background, her friends, and so on … but, Detective Carlisle, please just hurry up and gives us closure,' exclaimed Gordon. 'We – my wife and I, and all the family – are suffering so much.'

'I can assure you we're doing our best,' put in Nick. 'I expect Julian is being a real support to you in all this?' Lydia admired Nick's poker face as he said this, and hoped her own expression didn't betray her true feelings towards the oh-so-empathic Julian.

'Humph,' was the sound that Gordon made. Quite understandable, thought Lydia.

'At least he seems to be looking after that girlfriend of his. Let's hope she teaches him some compassion,' he continued.

'Now, now, darling,' said Felicity. 'Julian means well; he told me last night that he really misses his big sister.'

On the way back to London, Lydia asked Nick to read out the notes he had taken that day.

'Hmm … so I think Tracey and Bryan have given us quite a good picture of Belinda's childhood and corroborated quite a lot of what we already knew.'

'How about the friends-but-not-friends, Rachel and Sarah? Why would they have come to her funeral if they disliked her so much back in the day? And could the girlhood "spat" have some kind of bearing on Belinda's murder?'

'Perhaps …girls will be girls, Nick. I'm inclined to think they probably don't even remember what happened fifteen or so years ago. We only know because of what's in Belinda's diary and what Tracey remembers. No, that's barking up the wrong tree, I reckon. Anyway, thanks for coming with me – I do think a few more dots have been joined up today. Oh no, rush-hour traffic … at least it's going the wrong way!'

Chapter 27

Ultra Vires (beyond one's powers)

'I'm sure it's nothing to worry about, Julian,' said Precious sipping her glass of cooled white wine. They were sitting on the first-floor balcony of Julian's house from where there was a stunning view of the evening sunset over Blackheath. From there, they could also see the grand entrance into Greenwich Park and the dome of the old Observatory.

'I don't know why I have to go into the Yard though; that Detective could have just phoned me if it's to do with the phone tracker on the day when Belinda was killed,' grumbled Julian. 'Thank Christ I've got one though ...'

'Exactly,' reasoned Precious. 'They'll be able to see you were nowhere near the law chambers that morning. It's probably just a police procedural thing.'

Julian didn't look so sure but decided not to ruin the evening; it was fairly unusual for he and Precious to enjoy a whole evening and night together, complete with aperitif and dinner – cooked by Precious no less! That was unless she got paged of course.

'Let's raise a glass to your poor dear sister,' said Precious. 'Tomorrow it'll be exactly four weeks to the day since she was murdered ... and the police seem none the wiser as to who did it.'

'Cheers Bel,' muttered Julian. 'Rest in peace.'

The following Tuesday morning found Julian waiting in the interview room at New Scotland Yard. He'd been provided with a plastic cup of watery coffee and was not in the best frame of mind. Twenty minutes later, Lydia, accompanied by Nick entered the room and sat down opposite Julian.

'Morning, Julian,' began Lydia. 'We've got some answers and a few more questions for you in connection with your sister's murder.'

'How long is this going to take? I'm needed at work, you know. I've got to sign off on a very important deal at the bank—'

'I'll cut to the chase. Luckily for you, your mobile communications to Precious Temishe on the morning of the murder have been verified by location tracker services. It looks like you really were where and when you said you were. Blackheath between six and seven a.m. on the Tuesday morning in question.'

Julian smirked and replied,

'Yes … good thing I've got such an insistent girlfriend, isn't it? And that we're so in love, of course—'

'However,' broke in Lydia. 'I'm more interested in the two phone calls you made to Belinda recently. I was under the impression you hadn't seen her since her New Year's Eve party?'

It seemed to Lydia that Julian was genuinely taken aback as he replied,

'What? That *was* the last time I saw my sister.'

'The phone records show that you called Belinda's mobile from Blackheath at eight p.m. on the Wednesday evening the week before Belinda's murder on the following Tuesday morning and that the conversation lasted just over five minutes. Then there was another, shorter call at midday the next day – the Thursday, made from … the mews outside Weymouth House Chambers! I thought you said you'd never been to Belinda's workplace?' At last, she had made the nonchalant brother squirm, thought Lydia.

'Oh … er … yes … but I didn't actually go in!' exclaimed Julian.

'Explain.' put in Nick.

'Well, er, yes I did call Bel – it must have been around the beginning of April … I wanted to meet up with her to talk about Precious and to remind her not to tell Mother and Father about us …'

'Because you were afraid they might write you out of their wills and you would lose your share of The Heathers,' said Lydia. 'Must've been such a worry for you,' she added tartly.

Julian looked a little abashed, but not for long.

'It's a lot of money at stake!'

'Exactly,' answered Lydia dryly. 'So you phoned Belinda to arrange to meet?'

'Yes … we agreed that I'd call her when I got to the mews, she would come down from her office and then we'd go and have a light lunch. So on the day … yes, you're right, it was the Thursday before she died … I arrived outside Weymouth House. I remember seeing – and smelling I might add – that old tramp in the bushes, and then I rang Bel as we'd agreed. But she blew me off! Something urgent had come up at work and she couldn't make it after all. Unlike Bel to cancel and I was quite pissed off, actually.'

'So you're saying you didn't actually enter the building,' asked Lydia, inwardly seething at the cold nature of the man who appeared more angry about not getting his say in to his sister than about her now being dead.

'Never set foot in the place. I just turned round, grabbed a sandwich from a deli and went back to Spitalfields. Waste of a journey.'

'Well, we'll double-check to see if Belinda did in fact get tied up with something that day to stop her leaving chambers. I must say it would have saved us a whole lot of trouble if you'd told us before.'

'It just slipped my mind, Detective. What with supporting the parents down at the estate, Precious, and my job ... talking of which—'

'Yes, you can go back to making big bucks now, Julian – we'll be in touch if we need to talk to you again,' said Lydia.

After Julian had left, Lydia and Nick made their way back up to Lydia's office where there was still some hot coffee left in the machine. Lydia poured them both a cup and opened a packet of chocolate digestives.

'So, is it worth cross-referencing with Ben James as to whether he saw Julian hanging around outside Weymouth House that day, Boss?' asked Nick, before taking a bite of his biscuit.

'No – it'd be a waste of time; his memory isn't the best what with all the booze. His testimony would be worthless. Look how far we *didn't* get with the whole 'clangy knife' business! There might be more mileage going over to the chambers and seeing what happened that was so urgent that Belinda couldn't keep her apparent lunch date with her brother.' answered

Lydia. 'Ooh, I needed this coffee! Julian just gets up my nose—'

'Really?' put in Nick. 'I hadn't noticed, Boss.'

Lydia glanced at him to make sure he was in fact being sarcastic, and continued.

'I'm going to pay Weymouth House an unannounced visit; see what I can find out. I expect the ever-so-helpful Sharon will have it all in the appointment diary. I've got a feeling that Julian was actually telling the truth though about not thinking to mention the cancelled lunch, so what with him being left-handed and being nowhere near the law chambers at the time of the murder itself, I suspect he's off the hook.' Worse luck, mused Lydia privately.

The rhododendron bushes outside Weymouth House were beginning to blossom and Lydia admired their stunning lilac petals. There was no sign of Ben James or his pitiful belongings; perhaps he's moved on, mused Lydia. This time, when she pressed the buzzer, the door was opened almost immediately and Lydia came face to face with a blonde-haired, blue-eyed Germanic type of man, probably in his twenties.

'Hello! I was just going upstairs and I thought I'd let you in. Do you have an appointment?'

'No, I've just dropped by … DI Carlisle,' said Lydia holding out her ID card. 'Lead investigator in the Belinda Radford murder case. And you are?'

'George Dane. I'm the new barrister here; I've taken over from Belinda. So sorry to hear about what happened – terrible business. Do come in—'

'Detective! How lovely to see you again!' broke in an annoyingly familiar voice.

Lydia inwardly groaned but forced a smile at Sharon Hardy who was descending the stairs.

'Good timing! We're just celebrating with some lovely cakes! Up you come, and I'll make you a coffee, or would you prefer tea? I see you've met George?'

All three of them trooped upstairs and entered the top-floor office which looked uncharacteristically light and airy; even the austere rows of books positively basked in the sunlight. George made straight for the sofa to join his colleagues; Lydia was interested to note that Sir William Bond and Anthony Greenwood, who were not sitting at their desks but in the leather armchairs facing a coffee table replete with a selection of cream cakes and buns, looked slightly sheepish when they saw her.

'Morning, Detective Carlisle,' said William, hurriedly swallowing a mouthful of cake. Anthony reluctantly put down his mug; it was hardly surprising that he didn't look particularly pleased to see her, given the grilling she'd given him the week before about the mysterious love letter, considered Lydia.

'Do sit down, Detective!' gushed Sharon, pointing towards the sofa. 'There's plenty of room there next to George. Help yourself to a cake! Now, what shall I get you to drink?'

'Coffee would be fine. Thank you.' answered Lydia as Sharon bustled off. Settling herself next to the young barrister, she asked of no one in particular, 'So what are you all celebrating?'

319

'Ermm, well, it was Sharon's idea to cheer ourselves up somewhat,' replied William. 'George started yesterday and we wanted to give him a little welcome. Plus today is my birthday – Sharon never forgets! – and, well, we thought we'd raise a toast to poor dear Belinda, seeing as it's exactly four weeks ago today that she was so cruelly taken from us … right here in this room. Obviously a toast *without* champagne as it's a working day, but there you are.'

'I see. Well, good of you to remember Belinda this way. Happy Birthday, William. And congratulations, Mr Dane, on the new post,' said Lydia politely.

'Thank you. Do call me George. I'm delighted to be here; actually, I'd applied for the tenancy back in October last year along with Belinda and a few others. In fact, I met her briefly then … she beat me to it but I was shortlisted, and when they contacted me recently to ask me if I was still interested, I was fortunately able to accept – I'd been working on a locum basis and could start here almost immediately. Obviously, I feel bad about stepping into her shoes, but it's such a great opportunity for me.'

'Yes, indeed,' put in William. 'And as I needed to fill the tenancy, Sharon suggested that we look through the former applications again. We're very pleased indeed to have Georgearl, aren't we Anthony?'

'Of course.' responded Anthony. 'Was there anything in particular you came here for today, Detective?'

'Well, actually, yes,' replied Lydia. 'It turns out that Belinda's brother was here the Thursday before she died and we're following up on that lead. It seems that Belinda uncharacteristically cancelled meeting her brother for lunch ... and I'm here to enquire as to why. I seem to recall you telling me that there were some litigation problems that day and that Belinda was quite stressed out?' Lydia decided that now was not the moment to allude to the fact that Anthony had invited Belinda out for a drink that evening; she could already see the red flush creeping up from his collar.

'I've got the diary in my office!' interrupted Sharon, who, bearing Lydia's coffee, had silently re-entered the room. 'I can tell you everything that goes on here!'

Of course you can, thought Lydia, asking politely,

'Shall we go to your office to have a look?'

It seemed to Lydia that William and Anthony hardly bothered to hide their relief when she got up and followed Sharon – still clutching Lydia's cup of coffee – out of the chambers and into Sharon's lair next door.

'Make yourself at home – everyone does!' said Sharon cheerily as she put Lydia's coffee down on her desk and sat down in one fluid movement that belied her bulk. Sharon's office, complete with state-of-the-art coffee and tea machine, was light, tidy and modern, unlike her dark and outmoded home full of tired old furniture in Nunhead. That peculiar musty smell was still discernible even here though, noted Lydia.

'Isn't young George nice?' said Sharon chirpily. 'I'm so glad Sir William took my advice to offer him the tenancy ... I liked him best out of the candidates at the time of course, but Sir William would choose Belinda! He's going to fit in so well, I can tell— '

'Good,' put in Lydia, determined to cut short the garrulous clerk in her tracks. 'So, could you tell me what happened workwise on the Thursday before Belinda was murdered?'

'Of course! It's all in here!' said Sharon, tapping a large black diary in front of her. 'Right … now let me have a look. Ah yes – it was the Georgina Allan and Simon Brough case. They're cousins fighting over their grandmother's will; they're both contesting it because she's left everything to a dog sanctuary – which personally I rather approve of – but the issue is that EACH thinks they should inherit the whole lot while the other gets NOTHING! Apparently, they BOTH feel they were the favourite grandchild; no love lost between them! Families, eh?! The whole thing's very acrimonious. They were both in and out of chambers all that day and poor Belinda had to deal with both of them going like daggers behind each other's backs. She was quite fraught what with having to see both sides of view, as well as trying to put the wheels in motion to challenge the will itself.'

'I see,' said Lydia thoughtfully. 'So she felt she couldn't get away at lunchtime—'

'Exactly! Sir William and Attorney Anthony had their own clients to deal with so they were tied up … otherwise I'm sure they would have stepped in to help – we're a good team, here you know! Belinda did mention to me that her brother was waiting for her outside, but I could see that she was too frazzled to go out for lunch, so I suggested that she put him off and I could warm up some soup for her instead. We've got a microwave down in the ground floor cleaning room … ever so relieved and grateful she was, bless her soul.'

'Well, that seems to answer my question as to why she didn't meet her brother for lunch. Could I take a photo of the diary page in question?' asked Lydia.

'Of course, Detective. Here you are,' replied Sharon, turning the page to face Lydia. At that moment, the office telephone rang, and Sharon picked it up, signalling to Lydia to go ahead and photograph the diary. Lydia listened to the one-sided conversation and noticed how Sharon took notes on a pad – using her left hand. Interesting, thought Lydia. So Terry's findings were correct on that score.

'So, any more news on who killed Belinda?' asked Sharon once she had finished her call. 'That tramp out the front's not there any more … has he been arrested? Or has he been moved on? Hopefully! That horrible pothead Sam White's still coming in so I guess it's not him! What about that boyfriend of hers—?'

'Sorry, I can't divulge anything at the moment, Ms Hardy; the investigation is still ongoing and there's a certain amount of holdback evidence that we can't reveal.'

Sharon looked intrigued at that, but before she could regale Lydia with any more questions or theories, Lydia rose from her seat and bid her farewell.

'Thank you for your help. I'll see myself out.'

As on the day of the murder, exactly four weeks ago to the day, Lydia paused at the top of the stairs and regarded herself in the huge mirror: still tiny and waiflike, but with a few more facial wrinkles, she thought, and once again clad in a close-fitting jumper dress and pixie boots. Reflected, too, was the figure of Sharon Hardy standing in the doorway of her office, hands on substantial hips and wearing a frown as she stared at Lydia from behind.

Chapter 28

Et Seq (and in the following pages)

That evening, Lydia finally settled down to read the last year or so of Belinda's handwritten diary entries; she really had to return the box of diaries to police safekeeping and from there, they would eventually make their way back to her parents. Of particular interest in Lydia's mind was the entries concerning her interview at Weymouth House Chambers and leaving Curtis Hall Legal Services:

Friday, 15ᵗʰ October

Dear Diary,

*I'm so happy!! I've got the tenancy at Weymouth House, starting in December! I wasn't sure at the interview ...I was so nervous and all the other applicants were men. There was one in particular – George, I think he said his name was – who came across as very confident and smartly dressed. Mind you, I was wearing my lucky turquoise suit and had highish court shoes on, so I think I looked the part. Hopefully, that's not the **only** reason I was chosen ... although the Senior Tenant, QC Sir William Bond, did seem to take a gentlemanly shine to me. Very interested in my New Forest background; he grew up on a farm, too, he said. Anthony Greenwood, the other barrister, is definitely easy on the eye ... and talking of eyes, I've never seen such piercing blue ones! He was wearing a wedding ring, so I guess he's taken. The clerk to the barristers, Sharon Hardy, was lovely to me ...she looks older than she probably is – I could give*

*her a few tips about losing some weight and her dress
style. But then, she's the chatty, homely sort which
struck a chord with me tbh ...I wouldn't want to get on
the wrong side of her too quickly!
So Monday I've got to tell Curtis Hall I'm leaving at
the end of November – I wonder if they'll throw me a
leaving do?*

It seemed that Belinda's previous employer did
indeed give her a good send-off; Lydia read on:

Saturday, 17ᵗʰ December

Dearest Diary,

*I can't believe how quickly the last two weeks have
gone by. It seems only a minute ago that I left Curtis
Hall ...how lovely of them to take me out to dinner in
Holborn with the whole team. I haven't had time to
really miss them though – it's been so full on at
Weymouth House. The tenant, John Flint, who's
leaving, has kindly been handing over his cases so I've
had to learn fast. I'm loving it even though being the
only female lawyer in chambers is going to be a
challenge, I reckon. But I WILL prove to them that I
can do anything they can do but better, to paraphrase
that old song!
So much has happened this year; buying the flat,
changing jobs ... not long till Christmas now, and I'm
looking forward to seeing the parents and ghastly
Julian (I suppose); the New Forest always looks
magical in winter especially if there's some snow. I'll
only stay there a few days, because ...guess what? I've
taken up with Tom again! I couldn't resist texting him
with my good news about Weymouth House and he
invited me out for a drink ... and so on and so forth!*

*I'm planning a New Year's Eve party here at the flat
and am going to invite all my new work colleagues, as
well as Skye and Martha, plus Julian (to make up the
numbers!!) with his new girlfriend, whom I'm dying to
meet. And Tom of course!*
*One thing, dear Diary – I'm going digital with you!
Blogging they call it. It will be for your eyes only, of
course.*

Lydia had the feeling that more dots were
beginning to join up in this case; however, there were
still a lot of missing dots and not to mention several
lines that joined up to nothing at all.

Having slept badly and woken with a headache, Lydia
was not in the best of moods at the following
morning's briefing with Geoff Cordell and Nick.
Clutching her strong coffee, she had made straight for
the one chair that was unoccupied and slumped down,
without greeting her colleagues.
'Morning to you, too, Boss,' said Nick.
'What's up?'
'Sorry … morning, Nick and morning, Sir.'
Geoff nodded and Lydia continued, knowing she
sounded peevish and bad-tempered,
'It's this case; it's really getting to me now.
We're four weeks in, and no closer whatsoever to
finding who killed Belinda. The press – needless to
say – and the family are still snapping at our heels and
I can't say I blame them! I had a sleepless night
worrying about it – I know I'm missing something
obvious but … I'm just not getting it.'

'Calm down, Lydia,' said Geoff kindly. 'Don't bank on all the pieces conveniently coming together like at the end of some trashy crime novel! The methodical approach is always best — plus your own special brand of determination, of course. I've still got every confidence in you. But I think we should go through what we know now. Let's start with the letters; any news from forensics?'

Lydia knew that Geoff was trying to smooth her feathers and she was grateful to him for beginning the meeting by reviewing what solid evidence they actually had. She answered less frenziedly,

'Yes, actually I received a report from Norman Combe yesterday. There were no fingerprints on either the poison pen letter, the lavender love letter, or their envelopes; obviously we were expecting the perp to be clever enough to wear gloves, so no great surprise there. More interesting are the findings regarding the ink used. The poison pen letter was printed using an inkjet printer; these are more commonly used at home as the volume of printing done privately is quite low and inkjet printing is quite fiddly and slow. The love letter was printed onto said lavender paper using a laser printer of the sort which tends to be used in offices; laser printing is more expensive, but faster and more efficient, so companies prefer them. I asked Sergeant Davis to phone all our suspects … and surprise, surprise, all of them have access to an office printer. Most have a home inkjet printer, except for, wait for it … the Greenwoods! I guess that might exonerate them from writing the poison pen letter at least.'

'Hmm ... interesting. Anything on the paper used?'

'Yes; just that the paper used in both letters – i.e. including the lavender-coloured paper – is very standard and I'm of the opinion it would take too long to get warrants to go through the homes and workplaces of all the suspects to find out what paper they have, and anyway, the murderer is far too canny to leave incriminating evidence lying around. Do you agree, Sir?'

Geoff nodded, and replied,

'Yes, Lydia. If this case goes on for much longer, we can consider it, but for now, let's put the letters to one side. Nick – did you find out anything more about the intentional tort angle?'

'Yes, Sir,' said Nick, referring to his notes. 'I've read through the copies of the Faith files – the documentation that we asked to have sent over from Weymouth House – and also got the legal department here at Scotland Yard to check them over, as law isn't my strong suit! They've come back with a full report which basically says that the case is above board, that Weymouth House is handling the proceedings correctly and that there's nothing to suggest any malpractice.'

'So do you conclude that any potential motives relating to Belinda Radford's death are not connected to either the Faiths or the way tort law is being interpreted?'

'Correct,' answered Nick. 'We had considered the possibility that as Belinda wasn't very comfortable with the "intentional" aspect of this tort case, she may have been seen as a threat by Amanda and Steven Faith in that she would be an obstacle in them ultimately receiving a lot of money in damages. But the case is so watertight that they really don't need to worry about the outcome and they know that. They have every faith – to use Steven Faith's own joke – in Sir William, who's an old friend of the family, and in Anthony Greenwood who is a specialist in tort law. Whatever we might think of the ethics of it, the Faiths are most likely, as Steven Faith would say, Martin Sheen" … erm, that's "clean", Sir,' added Nick as he noticed Geoff's look of puzzlement.

'Indeed,' put in Lydia. 'There's no evidence that they had anything to do with the murder and their alibis stack up so I really don't think we should waste any more time on them – hence they're off the hook as far as we're concerned. We'd speculated, however, that as Belinda had expressed concerns about the case, it might have been a motive for Sharon Hardy to have *either* wanted to "silence" Belinda in order to protect Sir William who she's obviously got a thing for, *or* felt she had to defend the good name of Weymouth House Chambers, like the dedicated clerk to the barristers she is.'

'But we concluded once again that the whole tort proceedings are so legally within boundaries that it wouldn't have presented a threat in any shape or form to Sir William or to Weymouth House, and Sharon would be well aware of that.' said Nick.

'OK,' said Geoff. 'Are there any other suspects that can be discounted at this point?'

'Well,' replied Lydia. 'As you know, Ben James is off the list. By the way, he seems to have moved on from the mews; I noticed he wasn't there yesterday. Sergeant Davis told me this morning that he's moved in with his mates down at Waterloo – safety in numbers no doubt. Julian Radford – Belinda's brother – has a proven alibi for the time of his sister's murder so he's no longer a person of interest.'

'Thank you,' said Geoff. 'So how did the repeat visit to the New Forest go?'

'Well, the estate managers, Tracey and Bryan Snow, gave us a fabulous lunch!' put in Nick.

'Yes, they did,' agreed Lydia. 'And they filled in quite a few gaps about Belinda and Julian's past – their early life at The Heathers and her old schoolfriends from about fifteen years ago. There'd apparently been a bit of a spat between them and Belinda when they were teenagers, but I don't think it's really pertinent to this case. We also dropped in on the Radford parents who are obviously still in limbo – although the funeral's been and gone, they can't rest until they know who murdered their daughter and why. Hence my sleepless nights!'

'And how are you getting on with the diaries and blogs?'

'I've finally finished going through all Belinda's handwritten diaries from when she was eight to twenty-eight; for the most part everything correlates with what we know about her life up until she started at Weymouth House in December. Her childhood and teenage years, her time at university and her training at Curtis Hall. The people she knew, her colleagues and her ongoing on-off relationship with Tom Lovell. In

January this year, as we know, she changed to using a digital format – a kind of private blog … just as wordy as the handwritten diaries! January was the month Belinda had the New Year's Eve party and things were seemingly going OK with Tom. By February though she had broken up with him and had the one-night stand with Anthony Greenwood on Valentine's night. I've got the last two months to read through which I'll be doing this week.'

'Right, so as I understand it, the remaining suspects are Belinda's colleagues and Thomas Lovell, is that correct?'

'Yes, Sir. And as you know, Miranda Greenwood, Anthony's wife is a person of interest as well.'

'Thank you both,' said Geoff. 'Let me know if anything else of significance comes up. And Lydia – I've still got a car outside your flat.'

Lydia rolled her eyes, and she and Nick made their way back to their respective offices.

Christ I'm so fucking angry I could eat my own feet. Questions, questions, questions … that's all that detective lynx ever does. Why can't she just let sleeping dogs – and bitches, ha ha – lie? I warned her, I did. She's fucking lucky to get any warnings actually … Father had a zero tolerance policy back in the day. A whelp that barked too much? Slashed and slaughtered. A cow that wouldn't be milked? Brained and butchered. A useless cockerel? Garrotted and grilled. He made me watch of course, so that's how I know how to do it. Learnt from the best, didn't I? All

*the while necking a bottle of Scotch between us. That
Belinda cunt didn't have a chance either ... always
trying to 'improve' me, like 'advising' me on what suits
to wear – to show off my physique better! As if she's
some sort of fucking female guru who knows everything
about everything, especially men. Men like a quiet
mousy woman who knows when to keep her gob shut
and just gets on with the real business of breeding.
That's what Father always told me and I think he's
absolutely spot on. Not shagging around like all and
sundry, nicking other women's men – instead of being
satisfied with one good, strict man to keep her in her
place!*

*No more of that, now, though, eh, Belinda dear? Dust
to dust, thank bleeding Christ. But I've really got to
sort out that Carlisle bint. She's getting under my skin
... she's like a dog with a bleeding bone. I can't
believe she got one of her hench-rats to find out
whether we've got access to inkjet or laser printers ...
fucking laugh and a half. I think she'll find I'm better
than that. Plus I know where the bollocking cow lives
so she'd better be on her guard! Nasty, skinny thing.
She's gonna regret ever crossing my path ... she can
try and hide, but I will winkle her out of her hidey-hole,
just like I used to snare those toads before I skinned
them alive back on the farm. I can't fucking wait.*

Chapter 29

Bona Fide (genuine, sincere or in good faith)

Sam White sat bolt upright in bed and switched his bedside lamp on. Glancing at his alarm clock, he saw it was only four a.m. and Joanna was still in a deep sleep, her long dark hair spreading over her pillow. He didn't like to wake her; normally he got up and ready for his early morning cleaning jobs as quietly as possible at around five thirty a.m. so that she could get a couple of hours' extra sleep before starting her day as headteacher at a local primary school. But this couldn't wait.

'Jo!' he whispered. 'Wake up – I've just thought of something.'

'What is it?' came the sleepy reply.

'Something just came into my head about that morning.'

'What morning?'

'When Belinda, you know, the barrister lady, got killed.'

Joanna raised her head at that and looked at her husband questioningly.

'You know that Detective asked me if I noticed anything strange when I was cleaning at Weymouth House and went up to the top floor? From the bottom floor, after I'd picked up all the gear from the cleaning room?'

'Mmm, I think so,' said Joanna sleepily.

'Well, the door to the waiting room was open then, but when I first went in the front door, it was closed—'

'Yes, I remember you telling the police that. But maybe you were mistaken.'

'No, that's not all! It's just come back to me – I smelt something in the air … just as I passed the waiting room … with the open door.'

'What was it?'

'That's just it. I can't remember what exactly, I just know I smelt a whiff of something.'

'I expect it was your wacky baccy, Sam,' Joanna scowled.

'Let's not go into that again, love.' muttered Sam. 'And anyway it wasn't that.'

'Well, was it flowery like perfume? Pine like cologne? Or unwashed body? Talking of which …'

'I just can't recall it … it'll come back to me though I reckon. Should I tell Detective Carlisle?'

'Yes, but not now, Sam. Get a bit more sleep, then shower if you don't mind, and phone her at nine. You've got her number, haven't you?' said Jo, snuggling back down under the duvet.

'OK, Jo,' sighed Sam. 'I suppose now isn't a good time to bring up adopting that moggy I told you about – the one that hangs around the law offices?'

He was met by the sound of light snoring; sighing, he turned over and tried to get back to sleep.

'So, is it significant, do you think, Boss?' asked Nick later that morning, as they sat in Lydia's office with

335

freshly brewed coffee and croissants. 'Has Sam given us a lead, here?'

'Hmm,' replied Lydia thoughtfully. 'It depends if he can actually identify what the fragrance or odour was. I've just come off the phone to my psychologist friend, Marie – she says that smell, our fifth sense, is closely linked to memory, and that it can trigger events from as long ago as early childhood. All very well, but Sam has only had a *memory* of a scent which appears to have been evoked while he was dreaming – even Marie doesn't know if there's been much research into any links between dreams and smells!'

'Interesting stuff, Boss. But at least it gives credence to our theory that on the morning of Belinda's murder, the killer grabbed the knife from the cupboard next to the waiting room, and, having slashed Belinda's throat up on the top floor, might have heard Sam entering the building earlier than usual, waited till he went into the cleaning room, moved quickly downstairs and dashed into the waiting room to hide, leaving the door ajar.'

'And left a whiff of themselves in the air, you mean—'

'Yes, and then when Sam had gone upstairs, the perp then ran into the cleaning room, undid the back door from the inside, let themselves out and legged it, dropping the knife in the alleyway outside between the buildings in their haste to get away—'

'… and then picked the knife up again and took it with them,' finished Lydia. 'Yes, that would account for the waiting room door being closed when Sam came in and crossed the vestibule to go to the cleaning room, and then noticed it being open when he later passed it to go upstairs. And I guess that would also tie in with the fact that Sam swears he locked the back door after he'd gone out for a cigarette, let the cat out and come back inside; yet, Sergeant Glover reports that the back door was unlocked when the police arrived on the scene and searched the building.'

'Exactly, Boss!'

'Well, it certainly might be another piece of the puzzle, Nick, and probably quite likely. Equally, Sam may have been mistaken about both the waiting room door and the back door … and the mystery smell could have been Belinda's perfume. I noticed when we examined her flat, she had a penchant for Dior; there were a few bottles of it in her bathroom. Maybe Sam had false memory syndrome …'

'… caused by his brain and olfactory senses being affected by his dope habit, Boss? I don't think so; I'd say he's pretty much on the ball, but I can look into him, if you like, see if there's anything about rehab or any medical records about memory impairment?'

'Yes, do that, Nick. But I doubt he'd be smoking enough for it to have any real effect. His wife wouldn't put up with that, I reckon.'

'Probably not, but yes – I'll check it out anyway. Plus see if he's had any cautions for possession or dealing. So what's next on the agenda, Boss? Although I have arranged for Gillian Keyte, Tom Lovell's "love interest" to come in a bit later to give a statement as to his whereabouts on the evening before as well as on the morning of the murder,' answered Nick, taking another sip of his coffee.

'Well, this afternoon I've arranged to meet Miranda Greenwood at a café in Hampstead; I'll be taking Sergeant Glover with me seeing as you're going to be looking into Sam White's possible predelictions! If there's time afterwards, we might pop into Belinda's flat at Chalk Farm again, seeing as it's on the same underground route. And I thought that as I've got a little time right now, I'd read the rest of Belinda's blogs for this year; the March and April ones. How about if I read them out? Perhaps you'll pick up on something I might be missing,' said Lydia.

'Sure, go ahead, Boss.'

Lydia pulled up the blog on her computer and started to read.

12th March,

Dear Bloggee!

You'll be pleased to note I haven't left it quite as long this time. I see I'm tending to write a lot in one go rather than several shorter entries like I used to in a real diary. So here we are: Belinda's Blog Number Three. Still reeling (in a good way!) about "Attorney" Anthony and our dangerous liaison; sad to say, there's been nothing more on that front to date ...just a little "naughtiness" now and then ... he gives me those looks that just make my insides somersault and I do try to hold back – after all, I wouldn't like to have Miranda as an enemy; they say red-heads can be fierce – but that's an old wives' tale imho.

I'm really worried about the tort case I'm helping Sir W. with. I know we're supposed to do the best for our clients and I know it's legitimate, but the "intentional" part of it bugs me! It's fairly obvious that Amanda Faith was standing behind that car on purpose ...I actually asked her that, not that she deigned to answer me. Just smirked and batted her eyelashes at Sir W. Apparently their families go back a long way. Of course, she suffered some bumps and bruises (which she had the presence of mind to take photos of!) and I suppose she could've been much more badly injured ...

'The salesman reversing that car should have been more careful,' said Sharon when I moaned to her about it being somewhat unethical. 'He should have looked in his mirror.'

No support there then, surprisingly. Sharon's usually on my side about most things, but I guess when it comes to inferring that her darling Sir W. might be doing something unethical, I hit a brick wall. It was a good excuse to catch Anthony on his own in chambers and pick his brains; as he'd already told me, tort's an area he specialises in. God knows why Sir W. didn't give the case to him in the first place! Oh yes ... it's the family connection thing. And probably the money involved. So, up I went to Anthony, sitting there at his desk.

'Hi there,' I said, very casually. 'What do you know about the Amanda and Steven Faith case? Is it lawful?

'Oh yes, completely,' he replied, gazing at me with those amazing eyes. 'Amanda Faith didn't **actually** *know her action of standing behind the car when it was being reversed would* **actually** *result in her being injured. There's a big file of case histories on the difference between the different kinds of tort –*

negligent, intentional, and so on - in the archive room;
we could go and have a look together if you like?'
Lydia stopped reading at that moment and raised an
eyebrow at Nick.

'No doubt the visit to the archive room resulted
in some *intentional* naughtiness,' she remarked dryly.
She read on:

I'm delighted to be helping Skye and Martha
out with the so-called medical negligence that those
idiot doctors are trying to pin on them. As if my
dearest friends could possibly be blamed for what was
basically not their fault! Thank goodness their
solicitor set all the paperwork in order before they left
for their trip (lucky things!). Of course, I wished them
bon voyage when they came in to see me and we
promised each other that we would definitely do
Machu Picchu together next year! Even though it's my
first litigation to do with medicine, I'm fairly confident
that I'll be able to do them justice in court, and trust
that once it is all sewn up, the hospital will end up
paying the damages to the parents and also all the
legal costs.

'Don't worry, girls,' I said. 'I'm going to do
my absolute best for you ...you've been so good to me
about Tom, and I'm glad to be doing something for you
this time.'

I didn't add that it would be a feather in my cap
and that I'm going to bring it up in my feedback
session with Sir W. that'll be coming up soon ... oh
God, I'm scared about that! I so want to be thought of
in a good light at Weymouth House. Sam says I've got
nothing to worry about, but I guess he's just buttering

me up because I caught him with a spliff ...I'd just popped down to the backyard for a quick smoke (of normal nicotine I might add, dear Diary!) first thing one morning and there was Sam puffing away, not a care in the world! I told him to get rid of it and to never smoke it again at Weymouth House.

'I'm not going to snitch on you, Sam, of course not, but if the clients ever found out, it would definitely damage our reputation. Sir W. would have a heart attack, and Sharon would have a nervous breakdown!'

He was fine about it and promised to refrain in future. I believe him – he's a good guy and is very supportive of me, plus – apart from Sharon when she's being all ivory tower about Sir W. – Sam's the only one I can really confide in at work. He doesn't think much of Anthony tbh but that's probably an alpha male thing.

Anyway, that's all for now; better get on with some prep for tomorrow. Nighty night.

'Pretty much aligns with what we already know, I'd say,' interjected Nick.

'Indeed, but still … nice to hear it from the horse's mouth,' said Lydia. 'Now for the final blog – April—'

Before she could begin reading again, Lydia's phone rang. After listening and answering in the affirmative, she turned to Nick.

'Gillian Keyte – Tom Lovell's potential alibi is here. She's waiting down in the interview room to make a statement. Let's go.'

Gillian Keyte was tall, slim, with dark-blonde, shoulder-length hair. Another example of opposites attracting, thought Lydia privately; Tom Lovell was both shorter and stockier than Gillian and, indeed, Belinda. After instructing Nick to set up the recording system, Lydia read Gillian her rights, and began.

'Ms Keyte – thank you for coming in today. I'm DI Carlisle and this is Assistant DI Fairman who arranged for you to see us in connection with Thomas Lovell, as you are aware.'

Gillian nodded and waited calmly for the questioning to start. Hmm, considered Lydia. Just as unforthcoming as the charming Tom, I bet. Her hunch was confirmed as she began,

'Could you tell us about yourself please, Ms Keyte – date of birth, where you're from, address, what you are studying at Goldsmiths—'

'Here, is this relevant?' came the assertive response, delivered in a broad northern accent. A touch Geordie I reckon, thought Lydia. Feisty lady – takes one to know one, ha!

'Yes, Ms Keyte, it's relevant. We need to know everything there is to know about you if you are to be providing Mr Lovell with a credible alibi. Now, let's start again. Date of birth, where you're from, address and what you are studying at Goldsmiths,' repeated Lydia coolly, missing off the "please" this time.

Bristling, Gillian replied,

'28th January 2000. From near Newcastle. Current address: 52 Hetherington Street, Deptford, SE8 2MK. Anthropology & Media – second year.'

'Thank you. Obviously, we'll check your ID but it's nice to hear it from you in person. Now, how long have you known Mr Lovell?'

'About eighteen months.'

'And how long have you been in a relationship with him?'

'It's hardly a relationship—' Catching sight of Lydia's unrelenting expression, Gillian hastily went on, '... three months.'

Lydia glanced at Nick, guessing he'd also clocked that Gillian had replaced Belinda in Tom's affections ... with maybe a little overlap.

'Is it ethical to be seeing one of your lecturers, Ms Keyte?'

'I'm over eighteen, Detective, and so is Tom. Plus he's not actually one of *my* lecturers. So no need to launch a safeguarding crusade.'

'Thank you – much obliged.' replied Lydia caustically. 'Turning to the Tuesday morning, four weeks and two days ago, when Ms Radford was murdered; Mr Lovell maintains you were with him in his flat at 45 Wickham Road, Lewisham, SE4 7DY. Correct?'

'Yes.'

'What time did you get there and when did you leave?'

'I actually arrived there on the Monday evening before at around eight; Tom cooked me dinner.'

Lydia struggled to hide her surprise. Perhaps the man has his charms after all, she mused.

'And how long did you stay, Ms Keyte?'

'All night and all the next morning through till about twelve. Then we both left at the same time; I had a seminar to go to, and Tom was giving a lecture at college.'

'And during the time you were there, did Mr Lovell go out at all?'

'No, definitely not. I think I would have noticed if he'd gone out, seeing as I was awake most of the time … I was rather gainfully occupied as you might imagine.' said Gillian almost boastfully.

'Thank you. I'll abstain from hearing all the details of your doubtless engrossing activities,' responded Lydia drily. 'However, I'm sure Mr Lovell is quite the catch.'

After reading and signing her statement, Gillian was escorted out of New Scotland Yard. Lydia and Nick looked at each other in mock amazement.

'You should have asked her what he cooked her for dinner!' remarked Nick. 'Steak tartare served with chargrilled asparagus in a saffron jus perhaps? Followed by raspberry pavlova – homemade of course – topped with fresh, triple-whipped cream?'

'Ha ha. Spam and a walnut whip, more like. He probably thinks a bit of retro "cuisine" makes him look quite the debonair man-of-the-world … irresistible to the female sex!'

'Well, it's obviously working, Boss! So, is her story feasible, do you think?'

'Feasible, yes. Whether it's entirely bona fide remains to be seen, though. I'm not letting the charming Mr Lovell off the hook just yet.'

Chapter 30

Pari Passu (equally)

'What the f—?' growled Tom Lovell. He and Gillian were sitting in their favourite greasy spoon in New Cross to recap on the statement she'd given to the police that morning.

'Why the hell do they need to know where you're from?' continued Tom, cramming a large bite of a bacon roll into his mouth.

'Well, they said they needed to be sure I was credible or something. They asked how long we'd been together—'

Tom almost choked and hurriedly washing down his food with a slurp of coffee, asked,

'What did you say?'

'Three months … but I did say that it wasn't an actual relationship *per se.*'

'Isn't it, Gill?'

'No! You'd been seeing Belinda when we first started, erm … "dating" back in January, remember? I've always assumed it's been a kind of open arrangement. On both sides.'

Tom looked slightly mollified, and went on,

'I guess. But I am fond of you, you know, Gill. Sorry – I know I can be a grumpy git at times but it just makes me furious the way the fuzz dig around in one's private life which has no bearing whatsoever on the case.'

'Yes, you can be a cantankerous sod at times, Tom … but I'm fond of you, too. Don't worry; I've given you your alibi. You should be vindicated now.' said Gill, taking a sip of her tea. 'Now let me finish my lunch – I've got a tutorial at one thirty.'

'Thank you, hun. See you tonight?' replied Tom, his voice betraying his profound relief.

On the tube to Hampstead that afternoon accompanied by Sergeant Glover, Lydia mulled over what she knew about Miranda Greenwood and how she might fit into the Belinda Radford case. Tall, large – probably strong enough to overpower a smaller woman; spirited personality, possibly highly strung and given to maliciously controlling her husband, thought Lydia, remembering the way in which Miranda had quite subtly let him know that she knew exactly how *helpful* Anthony had been to Belinda. Large, beautiful home complete with art studio in a leafy suburb of London. All told, a very affluent lifestyle; no need for her to go out to work – she could spend her days dabbling at her canvases, especially now that the children were of school age. She wouldn't want to lose all that and might even fight for it if there was serious competition in the form of a much younger woman homing in on her husband. But did she really fit the clichéd profile of the vengeful, red-haired, green-eyed monster that would resort to murder to protect what was hers?

Arriving first at Dante's, a trendy two-storey bistro in Hampstead village, Lydia and Terry chose a table positioned towards the back of the ground floor so that there would be a lesser chance of being eavesdropped on. They'd arranged to meet Miranda there – without her husband present this time.

'So Sergeant Glover, as always, please don't interrupt while I'm questioning Mrs Greenwood; just take notes. We can discuss any observations afterwards, OK? I'm going to dig around a bit concerning the alibi she gave her husband.'

Terry nodded and took out his iPad.

'Ah, here she is,' continued Lydia, as Miranda Greenwood swept in, eye-catching in what looked like a royal blue coloured kimono embellished in bright red water lilies. Her auburn curls escaped from a silk turquoise headscarf and a waft of jasmine scent preceded her as she looked around, spotted Lydia and Terry and tromped over to their table. Lydia indicated a seat and Miranda lowered her considerable bulk onto the too-small chair.

'Afternoon, Detective Carlisle and—?'

'This is Sergeant Glover. Good afternoon, Mrs Greenwood; thank you for agreeing to meet us today. What would you like to drink?'

'I'll have a mint tea, please.'

Lydia gave the order to the barista and then began.

'How's the blood and guts coming on?' Lydia noticed Terry look up in surprise, and explained,

'Sergeant, Mrs Greenwood specialises in painting bloody body parts!'

Miranda smirked before replying,

'All good, Detective. In fact I sold a canvas last week … to a friend who runs a gallery … I must say I'm rather pleased about that.'

'But you don't really need the money, do you? Your husband, Anthony, must be bringing in a fair amount as a top barrister?'

'You're quite right … but it's good for the ego to be successful in my own small way.' replied Miranda carefully. She was on her guard, felt Lydia, who continued,

'Yes, I expect it must feel good to contribute to such a comfortable lifestyle; beautiful house, kids in private school, exotic holidays … it would be a shame to lose all that, wouldn't it?'

'How would that happen, Detective? If Tone is accused of murdering Belinda Radford and goes to prison, you mean? Don't make me laugh! Why would he kill her? It's not as if she's the first young attractive female he's ever come across in his line of work.'

Lydia considered that her instinct of Miranda being well aware of her husband's peccadillos was probably correct.

'OK. Supposing that Anthony had a thing for Ms Radford, and supposing Ms Radford thought there was more to it than there actually was and threatened to tell you, the wronged wife, might he perhaps have murdered her to silence her? I'm sure he wouldn't have wanted a costly divorce not to mention the loss of his affluent way of life?'

Now Miranda really did laugh.

'You're absolutely right on that. Money comes fairly top of the list in my husband's affections. But

I've always allowed him his little flings – in fact, I can sense when he's going to embark on one almost before he knows himself! As soon as I met Belinda at her New Year's Eve party, I guessed there'd be some hanky-panky between her and Tone; it was the way he looked at her when he thought I was deep in conversation with the cleaner's wife. He can't help himself you see. But he knows when to stop and I know when to reel him back in. There's no way he would have murdered her; and anyway, I vouched for his whereabouts both the evening before the murder and the morning of, remember?'

'Yes, I remember,' said Lydia. 'You said he went in to work earlier than usual that day. But although he left your house at six a.m. and although he *said* he went and had breakfast at a local café, equally, he could have gone straight into chambers and slashed Belinda's throat during the time we have identified as the probable time of death.'

'No! That's absolutely not possible,' exclaimed Miranda. 'You see, I was with him; we went down to the city together that morning and had breakfast together.'

Lydia looked at her coldly.

'And you didn't think to tell us this when we interviewed you before?'

'Ermm … no … we thought it best not to mention it at the time.'

'Why not? Surely it would have made for a stronger alibi for Anthony if you'd admitted then that you'd actually travelled down to Temple together?'

'Yes, you're right, Detective. But well, Tone had a high-profile court case coming up and we decided it would makes things less complicated if we didn't divulge it. The publicity and so on. Sincere apologies.' Lydia thought that Miranda didn't sound remotely sincere let alone apologetic. Fuming inwardly, she continued,

'So why did you go with him that morning and so early? That's not your normal routine, surely?'

'No ... well, because I'd got Tone back on the leash since the Valentine's Day *amour* – which I'd easily figured out ... I can always tell another woman's perfume! – he was bending over backwards to please me. He suggested that we travel down to the city and have a nice big fry-up – like we used to do before the children – then he'd go to work and I'd have his credit card to treat myself to some retail therapy at Selfridges or Harrods or wherever I wanted.'

'Sort of like a guilt "trip"?' put in Lydia.

'Yes, exactly. I've even got the receipts of the items I bought; if you like I can—'

'You know as well as I do that shops don't open till at least nine o'clock. So, you left Hampstead at six a.m. and you arrived at Temple at around six thirty-five, right?'

Miranda was now on the back foot, and Lydia went straight for the jugular without waiting for a response.

'So rather than going to a café for breakfast straightaway ... you could *both* have had time to sneak into the chambers and kill Belinda together? Or maybe Anthony went on ahead to the café while *you* murdered her with his knowledge, and using *his* set of keys to get into Weymouth House?'

'That's preposterous! Why would I want to do that? I've already told you she wasn't a real threat to me – or us!'

'Maybe she was more of a threat to you than you've admitted to us? Convenient for you to get rid of the young woman who was a danger in terms of stealing your husband and bringing down your wonderful life? And convenient for Anthony to keep you happy and no longer at risk of you divorcing him for everything he's got?'

'Detective. I categorically state that neither Anthony nor I, separately or together, had anything to do with the murder. We were nowhere near Weymouth House at around six thirty-five for however long it might have taken to kill Belinda. We had a nice long breakfast together and then went for a walk by the river; it must have been just before eight that he got the call from Sharon to go straight into Weymouth House as something had happened to Belinda. So we parted ways; he went in to chambers – it was only a few minutes away luckily – I had a coffee at a stand in the Victoria Embankment Gardens and then I went up to Knightsbridge. So we can vouch for each other.'

'Do you still have the receipt for the breakfast you had together?' asked Lydia.

'No … Tone paid in cash. But I'm fairly sure they'll remember us … it was a little café on the north side of the Strand called Rise & Shine, or Sun-Up & Run, or something like that—'

'Sun & Go,' put in Terry. 'I know it – I'll check it out, Guv.'

'Thank you, Sergeant Glover. Just one more thing, Mrs Greenwood. Could you explain what was meant by ...' Lydia consulted her notes before continuing, '... *things will be so much simpler now that she's gone'*. We overheard you at the wake.'

For a moment Miranda looked mystified but then explained,

'Not simpler now that Belinda was *gone* as in *dead*! Just simpler that she was *gone* as in *out of our lives* ... no more "helping" her at work – and Tone was mine once more. He promised to be the perfect husband going forward without actually admitting to the affair in so many words. But we both knew what he meant and I was happy again.'

Until the next time some bright young thing catches his eye, thought Lydia, who went on,

'I see,' responded. 'OK, that's all for now. I'm not ruling out a caution for wasting police time by non-disclosure of vital information, by the way.'

Of course. I'll be off now, if I may?' said Miranda, rising and sweeping imperiously out of the coffee shop.

After she'd left, Lydia turned to Terry.

'Well, at least that's cleared up the little matter of the overheard snatch of conversation. Glad she's happy again ... unlike me – I'm rather *unhappy* about the way they've withheld evidence about Anthony's alibi. Ridiculous, and actually, ironic – rather than keep the spotlight off him, it might even damage his illustrious career if I make good on my threat to give him a caution!' Lydia glowered before going on,

'Could you send me a summary of today's conversation today by email? After you've been to the Sun & Go café later of course. It'll be interesting to see if they do recall seeing the Greenwoods there between six and seven a.m.; and if so, that will let them off the hook. But first, we're going to re-visit Belinda's flat at Chalk Farm. Have you got the keys like I asked?'

Terry nodded and Lydia signalled to the café staff for the bill.

Twenty minutes later, they arrived at the flat and Terry unlocked the front door to the block and to Belinda's apartment. On the mat inside lay a pile of letters and flyers which Lydia picked up.

'Looks like nobody's been here in a while,' she remarked. 'I wonder what will happen to the flat.'

'I guess the parents might rent it out eventually,' replied Terry. 'Or sell it.'

'Even more money to go into Julian's inheritance pot.' said Lydia cynically.

As before, Lydia felt reminded of herself as she gazed around the orderly interior of Belinda's apartment; once again, she was struck by the parallels in their lives and their lifestyles. Both were females working hard to get ahead in their respective professional fields, and both inhabited a calm home space in contrast to their fast-paced, high-pressured careers.

'Nothing's been touched,' she remarked. 'It doesn't look as if even the parents have been able to bring themselves to come here.'

Fingerprint dusting powder still peppered the furniture and shelves, and the fusty air was in desperate need of resuscitation.

'Open a couple of windows upstairs and downstairs, would you, Sergeant?'

'Sure, Guv.'

While Terry was occupied in airing the rooms, Lydia retraced her footsteps around the flat, moving through the lounge and kitchen areas and climbing the white metal spiral staircase to the first floor. Again, she stepped into the two bedrooms – the master and the spare – glanced around them and entered the tidy bathroom. She resisted the urge to spray a little of Belinda's Christian Dior perfume onto her wrists, and then descended to the ground floor. The door to the tiny courtyard garden was open, and Terry was sitting outside waiting for her at the small table on which he'd placed an envelope. Lydia sat down on the other chair and sighed.

'So sad being here ... poor Belinda. I don't know how many times I've thought that, Sergeant.'

'Agreed, Guv. Cut off in her prime she was.'

Lydia was still clutching the handful of post she'd picked up from the mat, and went through them.

'Mostly circulars and bills. Newsletters and account statements from the North London Women's Refuge; it looks as though Belinda gave regular donations. Could I leave it with you to arrange to have all her mail to be sent on to the Radford parents in

Lymington? And advise them to arrange a postal re-direction service. Please.'

'Sure. Also, when I was opening the windows I found this on the floor behind the curtain in the spare room; I think Forensics might have missed it.' said Terry indicating the envelope in front of him, his satisfaction at getting one over the specialists rather obvious, thought Lydia.

'Ah, interesting,' she said. 'I was wondering where that photo of the New Year's Eve party I saw on the fridge at Weymouth House came from ... Belinda must have had a set printed out, removed the picture that Tom had taken and took it into work to show her colleagues – hence we didn't click who Tom was at first ... which led to another delay in the investigation of course.'

Lydia and Terry looked through the photos: Belinda herself, with Tom, Julian and Precious, Anthony and Miranda, Sir William, Sharon, Sam and Joanna White. Some in pairs, some in groups, some alone.

'All ten ducks lined up in a row,' she went on. 'Have these copied please, and send the originals to the parents. Please. OK, let's hit the road – after a quick drink at The Limestone.'

They rose, Lydia casting a glance at the hanging baskets that desperately needed watering, re-closed all the windows and exited the forsaken apartment.

The Limestone was indeed very convenient for Belinda; the trendy pub was a few metres away on the next corner. As it was a warm, sunny afternoon, Lydia and Terry sat at one of the wooden tables outside from where they had a perfect view of Belinda's lounge window where they had been standing just five minutes earlier.

'Lime soda for me please,' said Lydia to the barman. 'And whatever the gentleman would like.'

'A slim line cola, thank you,' replied Terry.

After the waiter had moved off, Lydia continued,

'So here we are at the "scene of the crime"; by that I mean the springboard for Belinda and the suave Anthony to take their mutual attraction a little further!'

'Yes,' said Terry. 'Get warmed up with a glass or two of vino, and then a hop, skip and a jump over to her flat! Very convenient.'

'I wonder if Miranda Greenwood is really as unconcerned as she makes out about her husband's dalliances,' remarked Lydia. 'Ah, here are the drinks.'

'I'd bet she's fairly used to his extra-marital hanky-panky, Guv. And who knows what she might be getting up to … the whole day free at home while he's at work?'

'Oh you mean kind of Desperate Housewives of Hampstead, Sergeant?' replied Lydia, raising her fresh and cool drink in an ironic toast.

'Exactly. And fair's fair I'd say! Cheers, Guv.'

'Cheers. To how the other half lives.'

Chapter 31

Actus Reus (an illegal act)

Lydia woke up on Friday morning feeling a sense of excitement which she couldn't quite pinpoint. Things were coming together, she just knew it; and as Marie would most likely have said, Lydia's subconscious mind was buzzing and working away at the conundrum while she slept. She'd had a bizarre dream: descending a spiral staircase leading to her very own ground floor flat; a kitchen knife being projected at a darts board, spinning and catching the light as it flew through the air; her own voice, rasping and straining to be heard; the scent of lavender and the taste of blood.

At New Scotland Yard, having popped her head into Nick's office, she read through all her emails and messages and settled down to read Belinda's final blog entry – the one for April.

5th April
Dear Diary!
*Well, here is Belinda's Blog Number Four – I'm definitely getting the hang of this btw! It's been quite a week. Thursday was such a trying day – the Georgina Allan v. Simon Brough case is a downright war imho. Why they can't be mature about it beats me; but then I guess that's how we as lawyers make our living. The thing is I can see both points of view and they're both right and they're both wrong! It's just so very obvious that they should just share the inheritance fifty-fifty ...that's even if we **can** divert it away from the dog*

sanctuary, which was the grandmother's wish, after all. Anyway, it was so stressful that I had to mug Julian off at lunchtime. I can't believe he came all the way over here from Spitalfields to Temple to see his big sis ... must have been something very important. Knowing my brother like I do, I'd hazard a guess it was something to do with money. Probably wanted to go on again about not telling the parents about Precious in case he loses his inheritance. Ridiculous! At least we're not like the fighting cousins, though, and I like to think he respects my knowledge of the law too much to ever go head to head with me. Mind you, that's the only thing he does respect me for imho.

Sharon was brilliant; made me some soup as I'd hardly had time to catch my breath all morning. 'Here you are, girl,' she said. 'Get this down you! I'll make you some toast to go with it if you like!'

'Thank you so much for waiting on me hand, foot and finger, mother dear!' I said. I think she liked that seeing as she has no children of her own. Sees me as a daughter-figure probably.

Anyway, by the end of the day, I was totally drained and when Anthony suggested a drink after work at Legal Eagles, it was like manna from heaven. He was really helpful ... and no, he didn't "comfort" me like last time! We talked the case through and by the end of Friday (yesterday) I had the clash of the cousins under control. Anthony also talked through Monday's feedback meeting with Sir W., explained what I should expect and tried hard to settle my nerves.

'You've settled in fine,' he said. 'William sings your praises all the time – you'll sail through it. All *you have to do is have at the forefront of your mind* **how** *you've been processing your cases and presenting them in court; it doesn't matter whether you've lost or won them.'*

So that's what I'm doing this weekend – putting my paperwork into order and writing cue cards which I'll obviously have to memorise before Monday.

So it's goodbye from me, my dearest friend.

Pausing, Lydia felt a stab of poignancy at Belinda's final farewell to her diary.

Just before lunchtime, Geoff knocked and entered Lydia's office.

'So, how's it going, Lydia?'

'Sir, I know you're going to remind me that we're four weeks and three days in from the day of Belinda's murder!'

'Well, not in so many words. Just the press hounds breathing down our necks as per usual – and who can blame them?'

'I feel so near and yet so far … but I'm floundering a little to be honest.'

'OK, Lydia. Let's go through everything methodically. May I have a coffee?'

Lydia nodded and Geoff poured out two cups. Sitting in the chairs by the picture window overlooking the river, Geoff began.

'Right. Firstly, primary hard evidence. I'm talking the knife, fingerprints, the lavender letter. No joy there as we know. Next, secondary hard evidence: the poison pen letter and email sent to you. The perp is obviously too devious to be outsmarted on that front. What else?'

'Well,' answered Lydia thoughtfully. 'There's also tertiary – to continue your analogy! – evidence in the form of Belinda's handwritten diaries and digital blogs. As we know, these cover the twenty years of her life from the age of eight until three days before her death. The contents correlate with what we know of Belinda's major life events and her family, friends and colleagues.'

'Many of whom are suspects,' continued Geoff. 'Let's go through the final line-up systematically as well. I know we've discounted the Faith couple and the homeless chap, so ... let's look at family first.'

'That's only really the brother, Julian Radford. As much as I'd like to put him behind bars ...' said Lydia, grimacing, '... I'm afraid he's off the list too, thanks to his girlfriend, Precious Temishe, conveniently letting slip about the exchange of phone messages between them which meant that he was nowhere near the scene of the crime at the crucial time. Confirmed by the telecommunications company.' Lydia mused privately that she'd like to handcuff Julian for being an arrogant jerk ... but that wasn't a crime. Unfortunately. She went on,

'Also, Julian is left-handed, and according to Forensics, the killer is right-handed.'

'Moving on to friends, who've we got there?' asked Geoff.

'The nurses, Martha Bigbury and Skye Warriner, were never really suspects, as they were out of the country at the time of Belinda's murder.

Confirmed by flight records, social media and foreign office intel. Belinda's old schoolfriends – whom we met at the funeral – were never really on the list either, and neither were the estate managers, Tracey and Bryan Snow. There's no evidence at all to suggest that any of these people had the motive or the opportunity to get up to London by seven in the morning, creep into Weymouth House, slip up to the top floor chambers and accost poor Belinda from behind, slitting her throat like a pig being slaughtered.'

'What about the boyfriend?' put in Geoff.

'Ah, yes, the charming Tom Lovell,' replied Lydia, again thinking that there was one who should be incarcerated as a perfect example of dickhood. 'His now-girlfriend, Gillian Keyte, has provided him with a cast-iron alibi in the form of a sworn statement which I'm inclined to believe—'

'So he's off the list. That leaves the colleagues at Weymouth House. What about them?'

'Interestingly, all of them are the same height or shorter than Belinda, who, as we know, was five foot ten and a half. Forensics worked out that the murderer must have been shorter than her. Sam White, the cleaner, discovered the body, and it is quite common for the perp to call in a murder as a kind of double-bluff; however, my impression was that he was too distressed to have made it up. Also, as the time of death is fairly conclusive, between six and seven that morning, I doubt whether he would have had the time, from when his wife confirms dropping him off at six forty-five on Waterloo Bridge to when he phoned the police at one minute past seven. That's only sixteen minutes to wend his way to Weymouth House, unlock the door, sprint up the stairs, take Belinda by surprise and cut her throat, and it doesn't really stack up, even if he's a fitness fanatic. I did ask Nick to look into the drugs angle; he sent me an email this morning to say there's nothing on him – no criminal or rehab history. Just occasional recreational weed use, it seems.'

Geoff nodded thoughtfully.

'Go on, Lydia.'

'Moving up through the hierarchy, we have Sharon Hardy, clerk to the barristers. We have confirmed reports from her co-dogwalkers that she walks Ruskin in Nunhead Cemetery in the evenings at about seven to eight and in the mornings from about six to seven. None of them remember the exact day of the murder though.'

'Does she have a motive for killing Belinda?' asked Geoff.

'A very flimsy one in terms of protecting Sir William's reputation but paper-thin in my opinion. And anyway, I noticed this week when I was at Weymouth House that she's left-handed so it couldn't have been her.'

'So … to the barristers themselves,' put in Geoff.

'Anthony Greenwood, and latterly, we added his wife, Miranda, to the mix, as you know. We thought they could even have been working together. Definitely a motive or three there! Infidelity, jealousy, fear of losing an affluent lifestyle and a comfortable home are the perfect ingredients for a co-called crime of passion.' answered Lydia. 'Unfortunately, though, the opportunity doesn't quite fit. Sergeant Glover reported to me this morning that the staff on duty at the Sun & Go café distinctly remembers the Greenwoods on the day and time in question. They recall serving "quite a large lady" wearing a long orange and yellow dress that stood out, while he looked smart – "just like a lawyer". Which of course he is. So they're off the hook. That leaves Sir William Bond, QC.'

'Ah yes … the top of the pile,' said Geoff.

'He seems to have been too truly fond of Belinda to have wanted to hurt her, but I'm keeping him on the list for now, even though I personally think he's a bit old to be having some kind of teenage crush and then exacting retribution by killing her for declining his advances! Nick informed me earlier that Anastasiya Shcherbyna, Sir William's cleaner, is back in the UK, and has verified his story … I've listened to the interview tape and it all seems bona fide, but Sir William is definitely clever enough to have manipulated the version of events. Cool, calm and collected, he is. '

'Hmm,' put in Geoff. 'OK. Well, I think it's been a worthwhile exercise to go through all this … I know it seems inconsequential at the moment, but there's something there, hidden, which will unlock the mystery.'

'Indeed,' agreed Lydia.

'Remember, too, that this murderer is extremely canny and guileful … they're hiding in plain sight, so please watch your back, Lydia.'

A few hours later, Lydia let herself into her flat in Battersea, having waved politely to police officers Neal Wyton and Bridget Suchard sitting in a squad car just yards from her front door. She felt strangely disconsolate; probably due to the lack of coming-together of all the pieces of Belinda's life and death, nearly five weeks into the investigation. Normally, she would have kicked off her boots and relaxed with a glass of wine; this evening, however, she found herself pacing through the tidy rooms and staring aimlessly out of windows. What was it she was missing?

A notification on her mobile phone roused her out of her reverie, and Lydia saw from the text message that the sender was from Sam White.

'Evening, Detective. Sorry to disturb you after hours, but I've just remembered what that smell was … and Jo said to tell you. Can you call me?'

'Hi Sam,' said Lydia once she'd got through to him. 'What's up?'

'Well, you know I said I got a whiff of something as I passed the downstairs waiting room at Weymouth House the day Belinda was murdered? So today, I was cleaning at my new gig, a theatre down on the South Bank. I'd gone into the wardrobe room with all the old costumes and so on, to vac – and there it was again! That smell. **Mothballs**.'

'Mothballs …' repeated Lydia thoughtfully. 'Thank you, Sam. I've got another call coming in so I've got to go – bye for now.'

Lydia could see that the incoming call was from Tracey Snow.

'Hello, Detective Carlisle,' came Tracey's voice. 'I know it's late but something just came back to me that I think you ought to know. I don't know why I didn't realise at the time—'

'Go on, Tracey.'

'The funeral. Remember Jim Thorpe? The old boy that we hire to train horses? He had a daughter called Pam.'

'I remember Belinda mentioned her in her diaries. She was the stable girl who eloped, right?' replied Lydia.

'Yes! Well, she was there! At the funeral. I didn't recognise her at first and Bryan definitely says he didn't either … twenty years older, different hair colour and a lot stouter … but it was definitely her.'

Lydia felt a stab of excitement as she said goodbye to Tracey and hung up the call. So deep was she in her contemplation and the heady feeling of all pieces of the puzzle finally coming together in her mind, that she did not hear the back door of her flat click softly open. It was only as she turned away from her living room window that she came face to face with whom she now knew to be Belinda's murderer.

Chapter 32

Ex Post Facto (law affecting past and future acts)

'Hello Sharon. Or should I say Pam? Pamela Thorpe, isn't it?'

Quick as a flash, and faster than Lydia could have believed, the clerk to the barristers stepped forward and slid behind Lydia. The cold steel of a knife blade was held steadily against her throat and Lydia froze in shock.

'Don't call me Pam, you scrawny bitch. I had enough of being nicknamed "Spam" by all those skinny cows at school,' growled Sharon. 'As soon as I hit eighteen, I left home and changed my name. Led Father to believe I'd run off with one of those stable boy dolts, and never spoke to him again! I'm actually quite surprised you didn't work it out sooner … you and all your cop mates. Like those twats on so-called "guard" the day I killed Belinda. Ha! Gave them the slip was like taking sweets from a baby.'

Lydia thought that Sharon was actually spot on with her assessment of Sergeants Davis and Glover but didn't dare say anything lest the knife slipped … her nostrils were filled with the stale odour of mothballs and a metallic taste rose into her throat; stress in anticipation of what was to come, no doubt. She thought desperately back to her police self-defence training but knew the hold the bigger woman had over her was nigh on impossible to get out of. Keep her talking, she thought. Fortunately, Sharon kept up her flow of words.

'Just like how easy it was to get past your so-called "guards" in the car out the front there, slip up the side alley to your back yard, prise open your back door – picking locks is one of the many skills Father dear taught me – and help myself to one of your posh set of nice sharp knives I just knew I'd find – duh! Good at being sneaky, I am! Unassuming old lady in oversized mangy coat, woolly hat, sensible sandals, dog on lead … oh yes, Ruskin's here too you know! I've left him out the back, keeping watch, he is, like a good boy! I wore this coat that morning I got rid of Belinda, too. A bit like a disguise … one of the things I've got left of my mother before she died. Big old wardrobe of her clothes – but you know that, don't you? Snooping around upstairs over at my house in Nunhead. I knew what you were up to, of course.'

That accounts for the mothballs, was the thought that went through Lydia's mind. The wardrobe, the coat, the whiff that Sam picked up on. As if reading her thoughts, Sharon went on,

'Nearly got caught by that fucking cleaner though, didn't I? Had it all planned out … in I crept just after six, nice and calm – even hung my coat up! Helped myself to our ever-so-sharp birthday knife I knew was there of course, snuck up the stairs, did the deed, and was just on my way back out when who showed up earlier than usual? Sam bloody White. I just had time to dash into the waiting room and hide behind the door … I thought he might remember the door was closed but the silly tosser was probably in a dope haze and just walked on by. Ha! Just had time to grab my coat, nip out the back, kick that effing cat when it tried to trip me up, and disappear round the corner. Then all I had to do was swan back in at quarter to eight, pretending I'd just arrived and putting on the "poor Belinda" act. I did accidentally drop the knife in the alleyway but hid it in my rather large handbag which none of you lot even bothered to search.'

And then later, having wiped it clean, planted it in Ben James' sleeping bag, realised Lydia. But we knew that was a red herring. She attempted to move very slightly, but Sharon's strong arm pinning her arms to her torso merely tightened.

'Don't you even think about trying to get away. You've got it coming to you – and I did warn you! – just like that Belinda slut. Only she didn't know what hit her … whereas I'm doing you the honour of hearing all the gory details before I finish you off and then just vanish into the night. Hmm – I think I'll send another juicy letter to the papers! I hope you'll thank me, Detective frigging Carlisle, for filling you in on what you and your bloodhounds couldn't see what was before your very noses. I knew my fellow dog walkers down at Nunhead would never remember whether I was walking Ruskin in the cemetery on that particular morning – dozy bunch! Planting the knife on that fucking tramp was just a bit of fun; I didn't actually think you'd fall for that. But nearly got you with that letter apparently from Attorney Anthony, didn't I?'

Lydia fought the urge to shake her head. One slip of Sharon's hand and it would be curtains for her. Now that Sharon seemed to be in telling-all mode, it was probably best to keep still, listen to the psychopath, and figure out a way of escaping from this nightmare.

'Yes. I was quite fond of Attorney Anthony to begin with. One of my "boys", you know. Old Richard Weymouth – such a pussy! –; the lovely Sir William; the dearly departed John Flint and now the delicious George Dane. But Attorney Anthony disappointed me ... cheating on his wife – admittedly a ridiculous heifer – with bloody Belinda. So he had to be punished a little. OK, I know Sir William had a thing for the silly little cow as well, but nothing serious. He's easily kept on the leash, you know. As Father used to say: "keep your females close and your males closer"; bulls are led by cows and rams controlled by ewes. Anyway, there I was, queen bee in the hive with all my drones around me. Weymouth House could never have functioned without me – I know everything about everything. I make it my business, you see. How do you think I found out your address, Ms Smarty-Arse? You really need to tighten up on your procedures over at New Scotland Yard. All it took was a loose-tongued copper!'

Bugger Terry Glover, thought Lydia.

'After I left Father and the farm down in Fordingbridge, I kind of reinvented myself. I wasn't going to let a man beat me ever again. And I mean that literally as well. I moved to London and worked bloody hard ... started from nothing, studied at night and waitressed by day. I'd applied for dozens of jobs before I landed the Weymouth House position – clerk to the barristers! Dream come true, you know. All I'd been good for since Mother died was mucking out stables and clearing up the mess Father made after he'd slaughtered an animal – he was good at the actual killing, but like most men, rubbish at cleaning and tidying. Stood me in good stead at work of course … nothing runs properly without me and nothing gets by me. Knowledge is power, they say. I had those barrister men in the palm of my hand … not to mention eating out of my hand! Muffins and buns and so forth. How I laughed when we "celebrated" Belinda's death with cakes this week! Oh yes, you were there, too, weren't you? Your face was a picture! Not laughing now, though are we? No, don't shake your head. I'll take your silence as acquiescence.'

Despite the rising feeling of panic, Lydia tried to think logically. Could she take Sharon down with a martial art move? She thought back to the taster course in aikido – or was it tai chi? – run by the Met a few years earlier. Dare she try a move? However, there was no sign of Sharon's grip loosening; she was as strong as an ox, and both bigger and taller than Lydia. Belinda would have been taller than Sharon, and she had stood no chance. Sharon rambled on like a babbling brook morphing into a mighty river.

'Yes, everything was running perfectly well. Until bloody fucking Belinda Radford turns up. I recognised her immediately of course … scraggy little runt always hanging around at the stables, hugging me and writing things in her stupid diary like an effing detective. Ha! I'm sure you appreciate the irony, *Detective* Inspector Carlisle. She must have been about eight, swanning around as if she owned the place. Oh, yes, she did own it, didn't she? Along with that brat of a brother of hers. All that land, all that money ... and me just a humble shit raker living in a damp grace and favour cottage once Father lost the farm. Then at eighteen, bloody Belinda goes and throws it all back in the parents' faces and hightails it out of there to become a fucking barrister.'

Lydia could see the contrast in the lives of Belinda and Sharon; the privileged and the downtrodden. The flower and the weed: sustained in the same soil, both growing ... but branching out along wildly different pathways. She could appreciate the sentiment ... but how was that going to help her get out of the stranglehold she found herself in?

'So there I was, proud of what I'd achieved and managing the Weymouth House menagerie very well indeed, thank you. Then Sir William insisted on moving us into the twenty-first century as he put it, and choosing the one and only female candidate for the vacant tenancy last year. And of all the people in the world, it just had to be posh little uppity Belinda, didn't it? Going to be a successful female barrister, was she? Better than all the men ... well, she had another think coming. She may have been a barrister, but no-one gets on the wrong side of me, even if I am just a lowly clerk to the barristers. I was *not* going to have all that princess and the stable girl shit again, even though she didn't recognise me after twenty years, what with me changing my name, my hair and me being ten years older than her anyway. So, as Father always said, slowly, slowly, catchy monkey. Set your trap and bide your time. Then when you've laid your plans, you catch your prey. You'll enjoy the rewards ... the rabbit casserole, the crispy bacon, the calf liver … so much more once you've worked for it. I admit to feeling a bit sick when he cut Porky-Worky's throat and rather sad when he beheaded Henny-Penny– two of the best friends I ever had. But I learnt to stop crying the first time Father clipped me round the earhole. Plus I've never forgotten how he showed me how to push the knife into the neck from behind and cut forward neatly … it worked brilliantly on Belinda, of course.'

And it's going to work brilliantly on me, too, thought Lydia. She strained her ears for any sound of passers-by to whom she could possibly shout out for help, but realised that Sharon would just finish her off before she had even had time to open her mouth to scream. Best to let Sharon keep on spouting and trust that a way out would present itself.

'Dear, precious Belinda. Of course, I became her confidante at work and helped her every step of the way. I had to keep an eye on her just in case she did by some weird coincidence work out who I was … but she never did, silly bint! Too busy thinking about herself and being better than everyone else. But even when she looked me up and down when she thought I wasn't watching and suggested going for a girly shopping trip together – no doubt to choose some "flattering" outfit for me – I kept quiet and didn't lose my rag. When she came up with the shit idea to join a gym together, I just smiled and kept my mouth shut. I fucking hated the way she tried to "advise" me and be so pally with me when we both knew she was anything but my friend! I helped her with bloody intentional tort – silly cow just couldn't get her head round that – gave her comfort food and calmed her down whenever she panicked about anything, like her feedback meeting which of course she did brilliantly in and of course couldn't resist bragging to me about. There were so many, many moments when I wanted to knock her off her fucking pedestal and do her in right there and then. But – the final straw was on the Thursday before I put her out of her misery. She'd been completely unnecessarily stressed out by that case to do with the fighting cousins – you remember, don't you, Detective? I told you all about it when you came snooping around again. So in keeping with my caring nature, I'd made her some soup and toast. Then the fucking cunt said,

'Thank you so much for waiting on me hand, foot and finger, mother dear!'

It just really got to me! In one sentence, she put me in my place … I was the servant, she was the toff … all over again, back at the fucking Heathers, back in the bleeding stables. Not only that, but she obviously saw me as her effing mother! Not her friend, oh no … even though I'm only ten years older than her! Plus I didn't even have the pleasure of a **mother** unlike the honoured "Ms" Radford.'

Sharon's voice rose in pitch and Lydia realised what the trigger had been for Sharon to act as she had: the resentment she had felt on being ousted from her dominion where she was queen bee by the very person she'd imagined looking down on her all those years earlier combined with the two-word put-down of *mother dear*. She wondered how the barristers' clerk had managed to contain her anger for four days before murdering Belinda. This was answered by Sharon's next words,

'But … fools rush in and all that, so I planned it all out meticulously, just like I've been planning to get rid of you as well. Oh, and by the way, you should train your hounds to sniff their way through lies! Yes, I'm left-handed. But I'm also right-handed! Ambidextrous, that's me.'

Ah, thought Lydia, remembering how Sharon had so carefully written with her left hand when she'd been to the chambers earlier in the week. Unbidden, a memory of herself standing on the top floor of Weymouth House and gazing into the large mirror came back to her. Then, as now, Sharon stood behind her … and Lydia felt a spark of hope as she suddenly knew what she had to do to get away with her life. She allowed Sharon to warble on a little more,

'Of course, I knew I was a suspect on your silly little list, but you had no real clue or evidence. Father might have recognised me – even after twenty years – at the funeral, but he was so in his cups that no one would have paid any heed to him. By the way, if you'd been half a good a detective as you think you are, you'd have recognised me in the photo of Belinda on a frigging pony on the funeral programme … eighteen, I was, and I know I look very different now, but still … Those stupid minxes who were at school with Belinda never looked at me back at the stables and they never looked at me at the funeral either. Same with the *poor* parents – nothing all that money and status can do to bring their dear darling daughter back now though, is there? Tracey, who was a cleaner back in the day – she was alright to me actually. Now she—'

Lydia slowly and smoothly lifted her right foot six inches off the floor and with all the force she could muster, slammed the sharp heel of her pixie boot into the arch of Sharon's right foot which, fortunately, had not been quite so well encased in its leather sandal. For a split second, Sharon dropped the hand holding the knife as she bellowed in pain; it was all the time Lydia needed as she broke away from Sharon's grip, bolted through her flat and into her tiny bathroom. She locked herself in just as Sharon barrelled into the door from the outside, roaring and cursing. There was a minuscule window in the bathroom leading to the back yard and Lydia wondered if she could squeeze through it … she just had to try. The sound of Sharon's fists pounding on the door abated and Lydia heard the familiar scraping of her office chair being rolled across the floor, no doubt to be used as a battering ram. Sweeping her lotions and jars off the windowsill, Lydia prised open the window and wormed her way through, head first, thanking God she'd kept supple through her yoga classes. One boot slipped off her foot and she felt her clothes tearing as she landed in a heap on the pebbled yard and came face-to-face with a growling Ruskin. He was the lesser of two evils though as she heard her bathroom door crash open accompanied by Sharon's roar of rage. Lydia scrambled up and stumbled out of the gate leading to the side alley – straight into the arms of Nick Fairman.

Chapter 33

Supra (see above)

'Thank God it's you, Nick.' Lydia thought she was never more happy to see anyone in her life. 'I scrub up well, don't I?' she continued, indicating her dishevelled clothing embellished with several "designer" rips and tears, her outfit completed by just one scuffed boot. Sharon's—'

'We know, Lydia. We've surrounded your flat and Sharon Hardy's not going anywhere ... I doubt she'd fit through your bathroom window like you did, anyway!'

'How did you know to come?'

'Wyton in the squad car outside had the good sense to radio into the station that a lady with a dog had just walked by and then suddenly disappeared. Officer Suchard went out to investigate and caught sight of her slipping up the side alley to your flat. The message was relayed to me; a woman with a dog? Outside your flat? It just rang lots of bells! Geoff got the team down here in minutes and ... I came immediately.'

'I really thought that was the end for me, Nick. I'd literally just figured out she was the murderer when she had a knife up against my throat ...' Lydia hated herself for beginning to tremble and was grateful for Nick's next words,

'Come on, Boss. Let's get you back to the station and checked over. The team here will do the rest and Sharon will be taken into custody. You can tell us everything later. Can you manage to hobble in one boot, DI Carlisle?'

'The boot that saved my life, you mean? Sure.'

'Also, have you got a friend you could stay with this weekend? I don't think it's a good idea for you to return to your flat tonight – plus Forensics will be wanting to go over it.'

'I'm sure my friend Marie will have me … and she'll be dying to analyse poor dear Sharon!'

Nick helped Lydia to a police car and, for the first time in the almost five weeks of the investigation, the weather turned and it began to pour down with rain in a parody of the tears threatening to well up in Lydia's eyes.

After a few hours of debriefing by Geoff Cordell, Lydia was driven to Marie's house in Dulwich. Marie thrust a glass of champagne into Lydia's hands and ushered her through to her bohemian-style lounge with its darkwood Spanish screens, eclectic modern art and tall pillar-like candles.

'I was going to offer you cocoa seeing as it's almost midnight but … thought bubbly would go down better! And congratulations are in order seeing as you've solved the case –which I knew you would of course.'

'Thank you, Marie. It's taken me nigh on five weeks though …'

'Well, you've been dealing with a psychopath – and an accomplished one at that. It was always going to be more complex than your average murderer, Lydia.'

'I feel stupid to have missed the obvious clues: Sharon being ambidextrous; her weird old-fashioned house as opposed to her neat modern office; the animal prints but lack of any family photos at her home; the way her letters and emails were full of animal terminology; how she lorded it over the men at Weymouth House; scowling for no reason we could see at her own father at Belinda's funeral ...'

'What was it that finally struck a chord with you?'

'Mothballs!' Noting Marie's puzzled look, Lydia continued,

'The cleaner had mentioned an unusual smell the morning of the murder and it came back to him what it actually was just a few hours ago. Luckily he had the sense to phone me. I remembered breathing in more than a whiff of mothballs when I opened Sharon's wardrobe at her home in Nunhead—'

'And instead of being transported to Narnia, you put two and two together in the here and now,' interjected Marie. 'Well done.'

'Plus someone from Sharon's past actually did recognise her at the wake and called me ... and yes, it all fell into place just as Sharon was about to end it for me. She must have realised I was on to her.'

Lydia shuddered at the memory of the knife blade being held to her throat.

'It's over now, Lydia, and you'll be on to the next case before you know it. In a way, we can feel sorry for Sharon; she must have had an awful childhood to have turned out the way she did. As we talked about before, the effects of events in our childhood influence our adult selves in mysterious ways. In Sharon's case, I dare say that she'd suffered abuse at the hands of her father ... not necessarily sexual – maybe some physical disciplining. But I'd say most definitely emotional.'

'I think you're right, Marie. Maybe Jim Thorpe wanted a son rather than a daughter, or perhaps he blamed Sharon – or Pam as she was called then – for her mother's death. At any rate, he treated her harshly and probably stopped her from having any friends of her own ... except for the animals she cherished. But then he took those away from her by butchering them and making her eat them for dinner.'

Marie added,

'Yes, and I expect Sharon developed some coping mechanisms – such as trying to please her father by coming across as meek and pliant while seething inside. Inwardly sobbing but outwardly appearing tough and robust.'

Lydia continued,

'According to Belinda's diaries and what Sharon herself told me, as soon as she turned eighteen, she made it out of there, left the New Forest and forged a new life in London. She did fairly well really – to finally land such a cushy job at Weymouth House as clerk to the barristers. And all was fine for years ... she was the matriarchal power behind all the men who worked there. Probably saw them as drones while she was the queen bee, enabling them all to produce honey! I noticed she loved to feed the chaps there sweet buns and cakes ... crikey, I think this champers is getting to me, Marie!'

'Good, you need it. I'm supposing then that Belinda appeared on the scene and upset the applecart. A younger upstart to the throne of Sharon. A rival of sorts to knock her off her perch.'

'Indeed,' said Lydia. 'Belinda was ten years younger, slimmer, better educated and more ambitious than Sharon. Not only that, but by a strange coincidence, Belinda was from her own past which seemed to be catching up with her … it didn't matter than Belinda was only a child back then. I think Sharon managed to keep her conflicting feelings under wraps – for a while at least, and the compulsion to do away with Belinda finally came when she realised that Belinda saw her as a mother figure. But she didn't want to be a mother to a smart woman … only to men, whom she imagined she could control in a way that she couldn't control her own father.'

'It must have been a real strain for Sharon,' went on Marie. 'She was probably paranoid, even if subconsciously, that Belinda might recognise her despite the many years that had passed … it very possibly added to the stress she was under. Plus seeing Belinda must have reminded her of her miserable home life. Then I imagine her thought processes would have escalated as the months went on until she was very close indeed to what provoked her into killing Belinda. Her resentment and stressful feelings, coupled with the brought-back memories of the ill treatment by her father, must have been simmering away in the proverbial pressure cooker until the final trigger – which was as you say, the inference that she read into Belinda's comments about her being "motherly" rather than a successful career woman like Belinda. It was that final trigger that spurred her into action and she just had to do away with the threat to her comfortable place in life.'

'Ironic, because now she really has lost her comfy status and will be enjoying life at Her Majesty's pleasure instead.' Lydia continued, 'She certainly didn't mean to get caught though. She planned Belinda's murder carefully; she planted alibis, she laid false trails ... but she also couldn't resist a little crowing. Tea and cakes to celebrate Belinda's death and there was me believing her at her word that it was to welcome the new barrister to Weymouth House!'

'Lydia, don't beat yourself up too much! I think you were definitely in line to be the next victim anyway. Once she'd killed, and seemingly got away with it with Belinda's death, the trigger points would have arisen more quickly. She saw you as a threat to her position; Belinda threatening her all over again.'

'I nearly *was* the next victim! You're right though and, interestingly, I've often felt an affinity with Belinda seeing as we've both got a patriarchal family background which we're both determined to rise above from. We're also both predisposed to take on the men of the world and be successful in our careers. So, yes, Sharon probably did see me as being of the same ilk as Belinda.'

'And how's this for thought-provoking,' put in Marie thoughtfully, 'Sharon also has a similar background to both you and Belinda as well.'

'Yes indeed. It would make a fascinating thesis for when I do my Master's in Criminal Psychology,

Marie … a three-pronged study into father-daughter dynamics in the modern world,' continued Lydia. 'In the meantime, cheers to my darling girly boot that saved me! And now I know I'd better turn in, Marie. It's three a.m.!'

Two months later, Lydia found herself standing on a podium at the front of a packed conference hall at New Scotland Yard. CI Geoff Cordell stood centre stage, mike in hand, while DI Nick Fairman and Sergeants Davis and Glover were seated behind her.

'Colleagues,' began Geoff. 'As we all know, DI Lydia Carlisle must take the lion's share of the credit for solving the Belinda Radford murder case and putting a dangerous murderer away behind bars for life. Indeed DI Carlisle almost became Sharon Hardy's next victim. In view of our esteemed colleague's persistence in managing the investigation, her ingenuity in managing to escape under desperate circumstances, and preventing other potential fatalities at the hands of this psychopath, I'm delighted to present this year's Police Bravery Award to Detective *Chief* Inspector Carlisle – incidentally, the youngest ever person to be promoted to this rank!'

A huge wave of applause and cheers, and the flashes of cameras accompanied Lydia as she accepted the award. Taking the mike from Geoff, she turned to face the audience and began,

'Thank you so much, CI Cordell, for this honour and, of course, for my promotion. Needless to say, I could not have done it alone and my gratitude towards my colleagues knows no bounds. I, in turn, am proud to announce Nick Fairman's rise from Assistant DI, to full detective inspector, and both Sergeants Terry Glover and Clive Davis to inspectors, in view of the sterling work they all delivered in the hunt for Belinda Radford's killer. Sharon Hardy is indeed a psychopath. However, *every* one of us has psychopathic tendencies lurking deep within us … most of us do not act on them, though. Fortunately for *most* of us, the world does not always conspire to line up life's coincidences which lead to an emotional trigger – the trigger that causes a person to lose their sense of reality and control. I sincerely hope that Sharon Hardy will receive the counselling she deserves while she is in prison and I sincerely trust that the Radford family will be able to come to terms with such a horrific blow to their lives. Thank you once more for your support.'

During the drinks and appetizer session afterwards, Lydia felt her wrist beginning to seize up as she shook hands with what seemed to be the thousandth well-meaning colleague. She was relieved when Nick joined her for a tête-à-tête.

'Well done, Lydia,' he began. 'Nice of you to mention the Radfords – poor old Felicity, mind you.'

'Indeed. Thank God Gordon found her in time before the overdose had time to fully kick in … she's having therapy now and I hear that she and Julian are spending a lot of time together reading all twenty-eight years of Belinda's diaries.'

'Well, Boss – he's got nothing much else to do now that Precious has left him.'

Lydia silently high-fived the feisty young doctor for following her dream and leaving for the United States without Belinda's narcissistic younger brother. She went on,

'Yes, I saw her just before she went. She was at Belinda's memorial service organised by Skye Warriner and Martha Bigbury at King's College Chapel. Quite a few other familiar faces were there too: Tom Lovell and Gillian Keyte, and Fiona and Paul Edwards from her uni days, and they'd also invited the Weymouth House staff. Sir William was truly devastated.' Lydia privately mused that he'd looked rather forlorn without the devoted Sharon at his side, and went on,

'Anthony and Miranda Greenwood showed up, as well as the new chap, George Dane. The Whites were there, too. It was all very sad. I understand there's been a service held down at The Heathers as well … Tracey Snow invited me but I made my excuses.'

'I don't blame you, Boss,' said Nick. 'I understand old Jim Thorpe is quite the local celebrity down there … vile old bugger.'

'One good thing to come out of this is that the Faiths won their tort case and—'
Lydia caught Nick's cynical expression and went on,

'Kudos to them, they donated quite a lot of money to Belinda's favourite charity – the North London Women's Refuge.'

'Hmmm … I bet there's something in it for them though,' said Nick wryly. 'A little mention of Tanleigh Auto Dealers UK, Bromley, in the papers maybe? Talking of which, isn't it amazing the way the press has done a complete volte-face?! My favourite headline is: *"Dogged detective sniffs out barrister slayer – no more pussy-footing around say the Met!'*

Lydia laughed, and Nick continued,

'Anyway, what's next for you, DCI Carlisle?'

'It may surprise you to hear that I'm taking your advice … and getting a dog,' replied Lydia. 'Not Ruskin, before you ask! He's being taken in by one of Sharon's neighbours. No, I prefer a bigger dog – and *after* I've been on a nice long holiday in the sun. Rhodes, no less.'

'And well deserved, Boss. Send us a postcard and don't forget to take a good old-fashioned murder mystery to read on the beach!'

'I won't,' said Lydia. 'It's on my packing list … along with a new pair of pixie boots. You never know when they might come in handy, do you?'

Chapter 34

Epilogue

Pausing at the top of the small flight of stone steps leading up to the glossy black door, Sam White, cleaner, lit up his third cigarette of the morning, turned and surveyed the almost silent mews with its tiny park bordered by rhododendron bushes.

'Déjà vu,' he muttered to himself on hearing Ben James' husky snores. 'And welcome back.'

Catching sight of a not-so-small calico cat making its way towards Weymouth House Chambers in hopes of darting inside for a saucer of milk, he went on,

'Hello, Tabs! Suppose I'll have to call you Mrs Mews now – sounds a bit more dignified!'

Sam eyed her heavily pregnant body.

'I reckon three or four in there ... I think the missus will change her mind about adopting you now. Ha! Come on then, let's get you some breakfast. And then I must get on – let's hope I don't find any dead bodies today ...'

The End

Acknowledgements

For his invaluable help on reading the script in such detail, and providing suggestions and recommendations, I would like to thank my son, Tan Strehler-Weston.

Sterling advice was also kindly given by Amanda Albon, Sarah Armstrong (Open University), Rosalind Belben, Brigitte Collings, Marie-Louise Curtis, Karien Downes, Mike Hurley, Ian Knowles, Lesley Robertson and Heather Weston.

And for much-appreciated encouragement and support, my appreciation goes to Tricia Chapman, Martha Huntley, Maria Vazquez, Skye Strehler-Weston, Mandy Weston, and not forgetting the Whitstable 8 Book Club.

About the Author

Lynn F. Weston

Having completed an MA in Creative Writing at the Open University, this is a debut novel by Lynn F. Weston who has also published a number of English-German language textbooks. An Unlawful Death is the first in the DI Lydia Carlisle thriller series. Lynn lives in Kent with her feline Oriental companion, Dante.

Printed in Great Britain
by Amazon